THE

CERULEAN

THE
CERULEAN

AMY EWING

HARPER TEEN

An Imprint of HarperCollinsPublishers

HarperTeen is an imprint of HarperCollins Publishers.

The Cerulean
Copyright © 2019 by Amy Ewing
All rights reserved. Printed in the United States of America.
No part of this book may be used or reproduced in any manner whatsoever
without written permission except in
the case of brief quotations embodied in critical articles
and reviews. For information address HarperCollins
Children's Books, a division of HarperCollins Publishers,
195 Broadway, New York, NY 10007.
www.epicreads.com

Library of Congress Control Number: 2018959807
ISBN 978-0-06-248998-2 — ISBN 978-0-06-290647-2 (intl ed)

Typography by Anna Christian
18 19 20 21 22 PC/LSCH 10 9 8 7 6 5 4 3 2 1
❖
First Edition

For Molly and Kristen,
my McLellan cousins and sisters in spirit

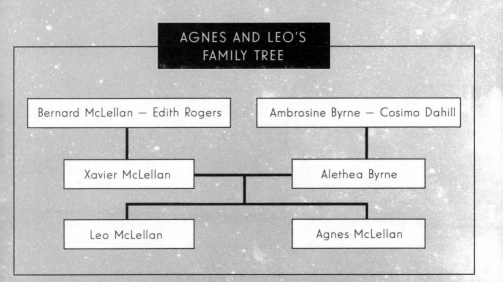

AGNES AND LEO'S FAMILY TREE

Bernard McLellan — Edith Rogers

Ambrosine Byrne — Cosimo Dahill

Xavier McLellan

Alethea Byrne

Leo McLellan

Agnes McLellan

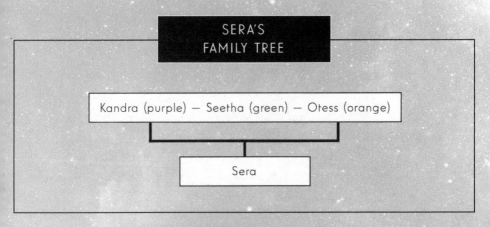

SERA'S FAMILY TREE

Kandra (purple) — Seetha (green) — Otess (orange)

Sera

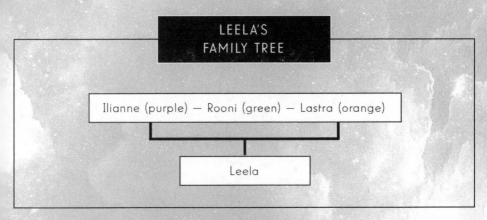

LEELA'S FAMILY TREE

Ilianne (purple) — Rooni (green) — Lastra (orange)

Leela

PART ONE

The City Above the Sky

1

WE ARE THE CERULEAN. OUR BLOOD IS MAGIC.

Sera's mothers had told her this since the day she was born, before she could speak or think or understand what it meant. Every Cerulean child knew there was magic in their blood; it had healing powers, for one, and it could form the most intimate connection of the blood bond.

None of that magic was helping Sera today, though.

The cloudspinners' grove was cold, the only place in the City Above the Sky that wasn't perfectly temperate. Grass crunched under her bare feet as she reached to grab a fistful of clouds from where they clung, delicate as a spider's web, to the black leaves of the nebula tree. The thin strands were slippery and floated up to a higher leaf, out of Sera's reach.

"Drat," she cursed, and a couple of girls closest to her gasped. Koreen shot her a discerning look, then tossed her bright blue hair over one shoulder, spinning her cloud into the most delicate thread, as if to show Sera how it was really done. Sera looked down at her own cloudspun dress, the one her green mother had made for her, and knew she would never be able to spin enough clouds to make one herself.

"Don't try to catch them," Leela said, getting up from her wheel, where she already had a thick spool of spun thread ready to be woven into fabric. "Let them come to you."

"That's easy for you to say," Sera said. "We've been working in the grove for three weeks, and I'm no better at cloudspinning now than I was then."

"We'll be moving on to the stargem mines soon," Leela said. "Perhaps you'll find your calling there."

Leela was Sera's best friend. Her only friend, really. She didn't seem to mind Sera's outbursts or endless questions or the way Sera liked to laugh so big and loud she could scare the birds in the Aviary.

She was looking so hopeful now that Sera couldn't bring herself to say that she didn't think she was meant to hunt for precious jewels in the mines either. She wasn't sure what her purpose in the City was supposed to be. And she was turning eighteen soon, an adult. She feared the High Priestess might simply assign her to the temple to be a novice because she wouldn't know what else to do with her, and Sera couldn't think of anything she'd rather do less. She loved Mother Sun, of course, but she didn't see the need to sing songs about her and clean the temple all day just to prove that.

But it had been a year since her lessons with her green mother had ended and she and the other young Cerulean had begun learning the various trades of the City Above the Sky. She knew her green mother had been hoping she'd take to cloudspinning—it had been her occupation before Sera was born, and she had spun all of Sera's dresses. Her orange mother would love if she became a novice, but Sera had a suspicion that she knew better than to hope for that, based on Sera's consistent tardiness to evening prayers. Her purple mother played the most beautiful music on the miniature harp—she was always asked to play at festivals and celebrations—but Sera had no musical talent whatsoever, and her purple mother had understood this early on and never pressed her. She was too boisterous for the Aviary; she got bored and distracted while overseeing the seresheep in the Meadow; she was too impatient to tend to the bees in the Apiary.

"Perhaps Sera will be the first Cerulean with no true calling at all," Koreen said in a tone that was at once honeysweet and laced with tartness.

Treena and Daina exchanged a glance. Daina had already found her calling, to help care for the orchards, and had received a blessing from the High Priestess. She would begin her work there soon. Sera was fairly certain Treena would be asking for a blessing to work with the midwives any day now.

"Of course she will find a calling," Leela said brusquely.

"She hasn't yet," Daina pointed out.

"Neither have I," Leela shot back.

"Yes but—"

"I would like to tend to the tether," Sera said. She didn't know where the words came from, but once they were out, she knew they were true. The other girls stared at her as though she had just sprouted an extra head.

"The tether?" Elorin gasped.

"No one tends to the tether," Koreen scoffed. "It hasn't *needed* tending in years and years. That was the whole point of attaching our City to that planet down there in the first place."

The City Above the Sky wasn't like the many planets of the universe—it was not a planet at all. It wasn't round like a ball, but flat, a floating oval disk with a temple in its center and two sprawling gardens at either end. A fine membrane of magic protected its outer rim and encased it like an egg, securing its edges so no mindless Cerulean would wander off it and fall into space. Since it had no rain, or snow, or any discernible weather, the City must attach itself to a planet by means of a tether, a tangible, finely wrought chain of magic in links of gold and silver and blue, invisible to the human eye, but perfectly visible to every Cerulean. This tether gave the City life—it drew nutrients up from the planet, minerals and molecules of all kinds, the way grass draws water up from soil. It kept the Great Estuary full and the orchards watered. It kept the air pure and the animals healthy.

Sera's green mother had told her of how dangerous the journey to this planet had been, nearly nine hundred years ago, after the Great Sadness had happened and Cerulean life had changed irrevocably. It had taken so long to find the green-blue-brown orb below, the Estuary had nearly dried up and the moonflower fields had withered and blown away and the seresheep had begun to die.

"How can we be sure the tether is still healthy?" Sera said to Koreen. "My green mother told me that there used to be Cerulean who would look after it and warn the High Priestess when it was time for the City to move again. Our City used to move all the time, didn't it? And now we've been stuck here for almost a millennium."

"Because Mother Sun gave us a great gift," Elorin said piously. Elorin would definitely end up as a novice. "This planet has so many resources to share, we need not move at all."

"But we're *meant* to move, aren't we?" Sera said. "In all the oldest stories, the Cerulean would move from planet to planet, sometimes even twice in one year!"

"I don't know what your green mother has been teaching you," Koreen said. "But mine has never said anything about any Cerulean tending to the tether."

All green mothers were educators, imparting to their daughters the history and stories of the Cerulean people, passed down from generation to generation. The Cerulean had no books or written language, just the symbols on the temple doors, the language of Mother Sun that only the High Priestess could read.

"Maybe that's because you never asked," Sera muttered.

"Not to mention the fact that we are *safe* here," Koreen continued. "What if we go searching for another planet and can't find one? What if we move and there is another Great Sadness? Is that what you want, Sera?"

She felt stung. "Of course not."

The Great Sadness had happened on the last planet the City had been attached to. It was the single worst tragedy in Cerulean history—two hundred Cerulean had been murdered by the humans who lived on the planet, and the City had been forced to move before its time.

Sera would never want that to happen again. She loved her City, she truly did. She just felt a bit . . . bored sometimes. She had become so familiar with the planet beneath them, the shapes of its two countries, Kaolin and Pelago, etched into her brain. She could probably draw them in her sleep—Kaolin was a hulking swath of land shaped like a lopsided star, Pelago a myriad of islands. Besides, she had already gleaned every scrap of information about them that she could from her green mother, who could only tell her what *her* green mother had taught her, and so on and so on. Sera always wondered what stories might have been lost or changed over the generations. For now, she felt there was nothing left to learn. As long as they were attached to this planet, the tether was the only mystery that remained to her. She could see it from the edges of the City, the fine bluish-silvery-gold line cutting through the darkness of space. She wondered what it looked like where it stuck into the underside of the City, if it attached like a spiderweb, or simply thrust out proudly from the City's belly.

Koreen smiled smugly and changed the subject. "Anyway, my orange mother told me something in confidence last night. . . ."

The other girls leaned in, eager to hear what Koreen had to say. Leela rolled her eyes and Sera suppressed a giggle.

"There will be a wedding season soon!"

There were squeals of delight and clapping of hands at this proclamation, and Sera couldn't help joining in—she had not yet lived through a wedding season and had always wanted to see one.

"When?"

"Are you sure?"

"Oh, this is so exciting!"

"The High Priestess mentioned it at her prayer group," Koreen said, pushing her hair back again. Every Cerulean had skin as silvery as moonlight and blue hair and blue eyes that matched the color of their blood, but for some reason it all looked better on Koreen than on Sera. Sera didn't like looking at herself in the one mirror in her house. She felt like her skin was a lie, hiding a secret even Leela didn't know.

"I've been waiting for a wedding season my whole life," Treena said. "Imagine the dresses!"

"Imagine the food," Sera said with a grin that Treena returned.

"How many triads will be married, do you think?" Elorin asked.

"How many do you think will form in advance of the season?" Daina said with a mischievous look.

"Come now," Leela said. "Marriage is sacred. Mother Sun would not allow a triad to marry if they were not truly in love."

Daina shrugged but did not look convinced.

The girls chattered on about who would be marrying

and which in the newly formed triads would be the purple or green or orange mother and what flowers they would use to make garlands for their hair and whether they would finally get their first taste of sweetnectar and feel its heady effects.

As the conversation wore on, Sera turned to her spinning wheel and picked up a clump of unusable thread. "I'm not going to tell Green Mother about this," she said with a sigh. "She'll only be disappointed."

"Your green mother wants you to be happy," Leela said. "She just has more time on her hands now that you are not pelting her with questions from morning until night."

Sera laughed. "I was a difficult pupil, wasn't I?"

"Your green mother is a very patient woman."

Sera dropped the clump of cloud onto the frosty grass. The oldest stories said the nebula trees had come from one of the first planets the City Above the Sky had tethered itself to, long before Sera or her mothers or her mothers' mothers were born, someplace cold and dark and full of mystery. That was another part of the magic of the tether—it could grow little pieces of whatever planet it was connected to in the City Above the Sky, be it a flower or a beetle or a type of stone. "Planetary gifts," the High Priestess called them. There were fish in the Estuary whose scales could light up in all sorts of colors, with long glassy filaments that hung over their eyes—they had come from the last planet, the one that changed everything, where the Great Sadness occurred. Most Cerulean avoided these fish, but Sera thought they were lovely. She liked to sit very still with her hand under the water until they would come and nibble at her fingers.

The gifts from their current planet were rather boring—short, scrubby olive trees and soft white shells from Pelago; gray birds with bright red chests and a bronze-colored metal from Kaolin that could be dug up in the stargem mines.

Leela put a hand on her wrist, and Sera was startled out of her thoughts.

"You will find your purpose in time," she said. "I know it. Besides, you're good at plenty of things, not just at asking more questions in two days than Koreen asks in a year." Sera's lips twitched as Leela ticked things off on her fingers. "You're the fastest runner in the City. You can eat more squash blossoms in one sitting than any twelve Cerulean combined. You climb everything with limbs and many without—I know you still sneak up to the top of the temple."

Sera felt grateful for the millionth time that she had Leela in her life. But the truth was, the only things Sera seemed to be good at besides running and climbing were loving her mothers and being friends with Leela.

She blew on her hands to warm them, thinking she would bathe in the Estuary this evening after dinner. She hoped her green mother would be cooking tonight—now that Leela had mentioned squash blossoms, Sera found herself craving them. Her orange mother loved trying her hand in the kitchen, but she always overcooked everything, and her purple mother would joke that she should content herself with making only salads.

Suddenly, from deep within the City, the clear, rich

boom of the temple bells rang out. All the girls in the grove stopped what they were doing, every face turned toward the sound. It was not time for evening prayers. So why would the bells be ringing?

"Perhaps they are announcing the wedding season today!" Daina exclaimed.

There was a rustling sound and Baarha, one of the adult cloudspinners, appeared in the clearing, flushed and out of breath. "Come, girls, come! Leave the spinning wheels; we must get to the temple."

"What's happening?" Leela asked.

Baarha's eyes were so wide Sera could see whites all around her brilliant blue irises, and they sparkled with fear. "Mother Sun has spoken," she said. "A choosing ceremony is about to begin. The time has come for the City to move."

2

THE BELLS WERE STILL RINGING WHEN SERA, LEELA, AND the other girls ran, panting, over Faesa's Bridge to the island in the middle of the Great Estuary, where the temple stood.

They joined the throng of Cerulean pouring over all three of the bridges that connected the island to the rest of the City, and uncertainty hung like a cloud over the crowds, as black as the leaves of the nebula trees. Sera looked for her mothers but saw no sign of them. Perhaps they were already inside.

"Who do you think will be chosen to break the tether?" Koreen whispered.

"Someone strong, I imagine," Daina whispered back. "Maybe Freeda?"

Freeda ran the orchards and had broad shoulders and muscled arms. But Sera did not think Mother Sun would choose a Cerulean for her physical strength alone.

"No, someone pious," Elorin said. "Perhaps an acolyte."

Sera just hoped it wouldn't be one of her mothers who was chosen. Some traditions may have been lost or forgotten over the hundreds of years attached to this planet, but the ceremony to make the tether and break the tether was not one of them. And what the ceremony required was blood—the sacrifice of a Cerulean.

"Why now, do you think?" Sera said. "What happened to make the City need to move after all these years?"

"Why don't you ask your green mother? She seems to have all the answers," Koreen said.

Sera pressed her lips together. The fact was, her green mother's answers to all of Sera's most important questions were merely guesses. No one remembered if the Cerulean had actually tended to the tether in the past. No one remembered the name of the planet they had left, or how choosing ceremonies had come about; and no one could satisfactorily explain why Cerulean could not visit the planets anymore when it had been so long since the Great Sadness, and this planet was not the same as that one.

Her green mother had taught her as much as she could about Kaolin and Pelago. Sera learned that parents in those countries consisted of one male and one female, and they could have as many children as they wished. Sera didn't like the sound of that, to be honest—she enjoyed being her mothers' only child. Her purple mother would be able to have another daughter only after Sera had left their dwelling to live on her own, and only when a new birthing season was announced. But there were no birthing seasons in Kaolin or Pelago. They could have children any time, in any year. Cerulean birthing seasons lasted anywhere from five to fifteen years—the season Sera had been born in lasted eight. Once the season was over, no children would be born until the next birthing season began, years and years later. Population had to be carefully controlled in the City Above the Sky. It had been eighteen years since the last birthing season.

Sera was curious to see what a male looked like. Cerulean did not need males to procreate; they contained that power within their own bodies. Her purple mother had explained it to Sera when she was twelve, how she carried an egg inside her womb that had split when it was ready and formed Sera. But in Kaolin and Pelago it took one male and one female to make a child, and of course, any information about the planet had unleashed another round of questions, and her green mother did not know nearly enough about the two countries to satisfy Sera's curiosity.

"Other green mothers in times past knew more," she had said. "Especially in the days of old, when we used to visit the planets themselves. But we do not go down onto them anymore."

"Why not?" Sera had asked. It appealed to her greatly, the idea of visiting Kaolin and Pelago. What did the people look like? What sort of clothes might they wear? Were their dwellings made of sunglass like the Cerulean homes? Did they live in the light and love of Mother Sun, too?

"Long ago," her green mother had begun, in the low, smooth voice she used to tell all the best stories, "the Cerulean would travel to a tethered planet to get to know its people and have a better understanding of the wide ways of the universe, in which we are all interconnected."

"How would they get to the planet?" Sera asked eagerly. That sounded like fun, a real adventure, something she would surely like to do.

"I do not know. It is not remembered."

Sera huffed. It was always the most interesting parts of the stories that seemed to be lost in antiquity.

"How would they know its people? Does the whole universe speak the Cerulean language?"

Her green mother had laughed at that. "No, my dear. There are many languages spoken in the universe. But part of the Cerulean magic is that we can understand them all, and learn to speak them in turn. Some were easier to learn than others—I remember my own green mother telling me a wonderful tale of a planet populated by giant birds with colorful plumage and crests of jade and gold. It took quite some time for the Cerulean back then to communicate with these birds, but once they did, they were allowed to fly upon their backs and see the planet as the birds saw it."

Sera could not think of anything more wonderful than flying around a strange new planet on the back of a giant bird.

"I do not know if it is true," her green mother said, as if reading Sera's mind. "It may only have been a story my green mother made up to entertain me."

"But the Cerulean did used to go down to the planets," Sera insisted.

"Yes."

"What if a planet had monsters on it? Or a poisonous atmosphere?"

"The magic in our blood can withstand any atmosphere," her green mother reminded her. "We can breathe in places where colorful birds or monsters cannot."

"But if we haven't gone down onto this planet since we arrived here, how do you know anything about Kaolin and Pelago at all?" she asked.

"The High Priestess has ways of discerning a planet's life, its populations and resources, and occasionally its customs. But those ways are secret, and not to be confided to a lowly green mother. They require a magic more powerful than you or I possess."

Sera felt that if the High Priestess knew how to do this, she should share it with everyone. Wasn't sharing a significant part of Cerulean life?

"She has told us what little she knows of this planet, and that is enough," her green mother said, sensing Sera's irritation. "All she does is to protect us. You spoke of monsters before, but you hit nearer to the mark than you might think. Not all monsters have horns or sharp teeth and claws. On the last planet, the humans who lived there were cruel and selfish. They did not trust the Cerulean who came to visit, and they wished to harness our magic for their own purposes."

Sera gasped. "Can they do that?"

Her green mother held up a glowing finger. "Our magic lives in our blood, but it can be removed, yes. Or consumed, as in the case of the sleeping sickness."

The sleeping sickness was the only disease that could kill a Cerulean—it fed on their magic, and Cerulean could not survive without the magic in their blood. But there hadn't been a case of the sleeping sickness in the City since before Sera was born. She stared at her hands, fascinated. What did her magic look like outside her body, outside her blood?

"So if we were to go down onto the planet, the humans would try to steal our blood?" Sera asked.

"They might. We do not know for certain. But is it not best to be safe, rather than suffer another tragedy like the Great Sadness?"

Sera wasn't sure about that. Of course, she did not want any Cerulean to die, but she also felt there was so much they did not know, and how could they be sure the humans on this planet were like the humans on the previous one? She found herself spending lots of time in the Day Gardens, perched in the old willow that bent over the end of the Estuary where it spilled out into space, watching the planet below and wondering what lives were being lived on it and how they might differ from her own.

No one else seemed to care as much about the planet, so Sera had buried those thoughts deep in the place where she kept all her secrets and questions and longings she could never share.

But now, finally, at long last, one of those questions was to be answered. A choosing ceremony! What would it be like? And then a journey through space to a new planet.

Maybe, after so many years of safety, the Cerulean would be allowed to visit it as they once had. Maybe Sera would find her purpose with a new planet.

Her heart felt as though it was about to beat its way out of her chest as she and Leela walked up the stairs to the temple, its great golden doors flung wide and covered in the mysterious markings of Mother Sun. Once inside, Sera caught sight of her orange mother.

"Sera, come!" she called.

Leela squeezed her hand. "I'll see you after," she said.

Sera nodded and made her way through the crowd. The orange ribbon around her mother's neck glowed against her silver skin as she bent to smooth Sera's hair and adjust her dress. Mother Sun had created the Cerulean by taking a token from each of her three Moon Daughters—a tear from devout Dendra, a strand of hair from wise Faesa, and the sound of gentle Aila's laughter. Each daughter was represented by a color—orange, green, and purple—and each color was given to a Cerulean woman when she married to indicate her role in the family. Orange mothers taught prayer and devotion, green mothers were in charge of education, and purple mothers were nurturers, and also birth mothers, blessed to produce life.

They fell in love in threes, seeking in some sense to reunite the tokens, or so her purple mother had said. Sera knew her mother did not mean it literally—the Moon Daughters were sisters, after all, and not wives. But she knew when she saw her mothers together, in the quiet moments after dinner when they thought Sera was preparing for bed, or in the soft looks they gave each other while working in the garden, that not one would be complete without the other two.

As Sera and her orange mother made their way to their family spot, Sera could not help but be slightly disappointed at the normalcy around her. The temple looked the same as it always did, its wide circular room laid out with cushions like at evening prayers, its vaulted ceiling covered with illustrations of the sun and moons and stars. The only difference was that usually everyone wore hooded prayer robes to the temple, made of soft seresheep wool and dyed pale blue, but since the ceremony had been called so abruptly, no one had had time to change. It was strange to see everyday clothes inside the temple.

Sera's family spot was on the right side near the alcove that housed the Altar of the Lost: a huge, mounted sun made of intertwining threads of sungold and moonsilver. Tiny, dark blue stargems in the shape of tears adorned its gleaming surface, one for each Cerulean who had died in the Great Sadness.

"Are you excited?" her purple mother asked as she took her seat on a cushion.

"You will get to see another planet, at long last," her green mother said with a knowing look.

"Who do you think will be chosen?" Sera asked. She felt a twinge of guilt—it did not seem right to be so eager when the ceremony would sentence a Cerulean to death, however honorable and worthy that death might be. But she also could not help herself.

"Hush, that is not for us to decide," her orange mother said.

Sera craned her neck, looking for Leela—her family

was seated not far from Sera's. Her best friend gave her an excited wave.

As soon as the temple was full, the High Priestess appeared, crossing the chancel to stand behind the pulpit. The novices filed in along the temple walls, and the three acolytes stood behind the High Priestess with solemn expressions.

The High Priestess was the tallest Cerulean in the City, and she held herself with an otherworldly grace. She wore cloudspun robes of brilliant blue that matched her hair, and on her head was a circlet of sungold, a precious moonstone set in its center. Moonstone was exceedingly rare; Sera's green mother told her it had once possessed its own sort of magic, though she could not say exactly what. The only moonstone remaining in the City were the three statues in the Moon Gardens, the obelisk by the birthing houses, and the High Priestess's circlet.

And the stone that Leela had found, but that was a secret that only Sera knew.

The High Priestess was beautiful, the fresh flush of youth still evident in her silver cheeks, though she was ancient. Mother Sun would decide when her work was over and the time came for her to pass on.

The High Priestess placed a bowl on the pulpit, one Sera had never seen before. There were various bowls used for different things, ceremonies and celebrations and such, always filling with the light of Mother Sun in hues that varied from pale yellow to darkest green. But this bowl looked old and crumbling. It was not as stately or impressive as others Sera had seen. She could just make out indecipherable markings scratched around its outer edges, reminiscent of those on the temple doors.

"Welcome, my children," the High Priestess said, raising her hands above her. "May Mother Sun favor us with her light and love. This we pray."

"This we pray," the congregation echoed back.

"The time has come at last," she continued. "Mother Sun has spoken. We are ready to leave this planet behind, to search the recesses of the universe for a new home. Are you ready, my children? Are you prepared to make this sacrifice?"

"We are," the Cerulean chorused back.

The High Priestess placed her palms gently on either side of the bowl. Sera feared for a moment that any pressure might crack it into pieces, but the bowl was sturdier than it appeared.

"Who among us is strong enough to break the tether? Who here is pure of heart and valiant in her faith? Tell us, Mother! Give us the chosen one."

The novices began to hum, a prayer song Sera had never heard before, so she imagined it must be special for this particular ceremony. She wondered how the novices had learned it so quickly or if it was one of those songs they had been taught and then forgotten, and had to brush up on as the bells rang out. She swayed on her cushion along with her mothers and the rest of the Cerulean as the High Priestess closed her eyes and bent her head over the bowl. From within its depths, a rich golden light began to shine. Softly at first, then brighter and brighter, until it was painful to look at and Sera's green mother had to shield her gaze from its radiance. Sera thought she heard strange whispers in foreign tongues coming from the light.

The humming of the novices grew louder. Many of the orange mothers in the congregation began to pray fervently, swaying faster and faster. Some purple mothers were openly weeping. Sera's orange mother had her eyes closed, transfixed in the swath of light. Sera's ears began to ring, the sound growing in pitch until she thought she could bear it no longer. She wanted to look away, but she couldn't seem to move a muscle, not even to blink. Just as she thought she must do something, that she could not bear to keep looking at the sacred bowl or her eyeballs would surely burn in their sockets, the markings *moved*. And though she could not explain how or why, Sera understood them.

They read: *Heal them.*

Then the ringing stopped and the light vanished. The markings were once more illegible and Sera rubbed her eyes, her heart pounding, unable to comprehend what she had just seen. The High Priestess was bent and out of breath, her hands clutching the side of the podium for support. Her three acolytes looked at each other nervously, but as one moved forward to help, the High Priestess straightened.

"Mother Sun has spoken," she said, her voice dull and fatigued. Her eyes scanned the crowd once, twice, then finally came to rest.

"Sera Lighthaven," she called, and the ripple of heads turning was like a wind running through the temple. Sera was vaguely aware of a gasp from her orange mother and a soft whimper from her purple mother. She was mostly conscious of her blood boiling under the surface of her skin, a frightening heat filling her from head to toe, and a prickling sensation in the corners of her eyes.

"Sera Lighthaven." The High Priestess called her name again, and her orange mother whispered, "Stand up, darling."

Sera's legs trembled as she rose to her feet. She could feel every pair of eyes on her, like little points of light stabbing her skin. She wanted to look for Leela but found she could not tear her gaze away from the High Priestess's face. Her heart, which had been thunderous in her chest a moment ago, now felt profoundly silent.

"You have been chosen by Mother Sun," the High Priestess said. "It is you who will break the tether." She held her arms out to the congregation. "Praise her! Praise the chosen one!"

And everyone in the temple bowed low, pressing their foreheads to the ground. Even the novices. Even the *acolytes*.

Sera had always longed to know what else the magic in her blood might be capable of, besides healing and blood bonding. She always thought there must be more to it, especially once her green mother had told her of how the evil humans on the planet tried to steal it. But she had never truly believed a choosing ceremony would happen in her lifetime and so had never considered the dangerous side to her blood.

"In three days' time, Sera Lighthaven will make the greatest leap of faith a Cerulean can make," the High Priestess announced. "She will throw herself from the dais in the Night Gardens and spill her blood to break the tether. She will be honored and cherished by us all as we travel to our new home!"

Hearing her say the details out loud, Sera felt numb. Her brain refused to believe the information, as if the High Priestess were talking about someone else.

We are the Cerulean. Our blood is magic.

The words held a new and terrible meaning for her now.

Her blood meant death.

3

ALL EYES WERE ON SERA AS SHE LEFT THE TEMPLE WITH her mothers.

The High Priestess had declared an evening of silence and meditation, so everyone was sent to their dwellings to pray and prepare themselves for the days to come.

Sera was eager to get away from the crowds. She hadn't even tried to find Leela in the mass of Cerulean that surrounded her, praising her or gazing at her with awe, as if she had become something worthy of wonder over the course of thirty minutes. She didn't like it. She was still the same Sera she had been this morning in the cloudspinners' grove.

"It is an honor," her orange mother said once they were

out of hearing of the others. Her throat sounded tight as she spoke.

"It is a necessity," her green mother said quietly.

Her purple mother said nothing.

For once, there weren't a thousand questions buzzing around in Sera's head. There was only one and it thudded over and over, louder than the beating of her heart.

Why?

Why her? The details she knew of the ceremonies in the past were scant, but she'd always thought an adult Cerulean was chosen. And it wasn't just her age—she wasn't as devout as Elorin, nor as beautiful as Koreen. She wasn't as pleasant as Daina or as patient as Leela. The High Priestess had even called her a nuisance once, when she discovered Sera climbing the temple's spire. Why would Mother Sun choose such a mediocre, bothersome Cerulean to help the City?

"Are you hungry, Sera?" her green mother asked when they arrived home. "I could fry you some squash blossoms."

But the hunger she had felt earlier in the day had vanished, and her green mother's suggestion seemed like a cruel joke.

"Or we could pray together," her orange mother suggested.

Her purple mother simply held out a hand, her index finger glowing bright blue as her magic swirled under her skin. All Sera had to do was call on her own magic and touch her glowing finger to her mother's. Her purple mother would read her heart and she would not have to explain herself.

But Sera did not feel like blood bonding right now.

She turned and ran to her bedroom, wishing, for the first time, that there was a door she could shut. The only doors in the City were on the temple and in the birthing houses.

She heard her orange mother's footsteps approach and threw herself onto her bed, facing the glassy wall.

"Otess," her purple mother called. "Leave her."

There was a pause, and then the footsteps receded. Sera felt shame wash over her, hot and stinging. She loved her mothers more than anything. She hated the thought that she was hurting them.

But she didn't call her orange mother back.

Sera stayed there, staring at the star mobile hanging above her, as evening slipped into night. She heard her mothers preparing for bed, sheets rustling, pillows being fluffed, and murmured conversations. She heard her name mentioned several times, but they did not come to see her and she was grateful for it. Usually there was laughter as the house readied for sleep, and the gentle sounds of kissing, but not tonight. Sera wondered if they were feeling as confused and heartbroken as she was.

She could not understand it. It did not make sense for Mother Sun to choose her. Because there were other things, deeper things that made her different, not just her loud laugh or her endless questions. Hidden inside her was the secret she could never let anyone know—that she was incapable of love. Oh, she loved her mothers and Leela, but that was not the only sort of love she desired. She had listened wistfully a year ago when Leela talked of her first kiss, describing how her heart had felt about to burst right out of her chest, the heady pleasure of the feel of someone's lips, of someone's hands on her skin. And Sera had giggled and laughed and hidden her ache, knowing that she would never feel that way about any of the girls in the City.

She knew it instinctively, the way she knew how to run and climb and breathe. It wasn't like the novices, who chose to forgo marriage in order to serve Mother Sun. And it wasn't like the Cerulean who preferred to live solitary lives, like Freeda—they still engaged in physical pleasure from time to time; they simply chose not to be in a triad. Sera did not choose this.

And worse, she had learned to lie about it. Even during the blood bond. This secret she kept tucked away so deep, not even her purple mother had ever heard it in her heart. And lying was wrong.

The house was too cramped, too stifling, too quiet. Sera slipped out of bed, climbed out the window, and began to run.

She raced along the banks of the Great Estuary, reveling in the feel of the wind in her hair, the mud between her toes, dodging branches of oak and spruce, the golden leaves of polaris trees brushing against her hair, the soothing murmur of the water keeping her company until she came to the island where the temple sat, a giant glass cone pointing up to the stars, its spire glinting in their twinkling light.

Aila's Bridge was bleached bone white in the moonlight. Sera's feet whispered over the wooden planks, and she kept clear of the temple doors as if they had eyes of their own. The doors made her think of the bowl, the way the markings had suddenly made sense to her. *Heal them*, they'd said. Yes, she would heal them. She would heal her beloved City by removing herself from it.

She vaulted over the hedge surrounding the back of the temple and made her way through the Moon Gardens to where a jutting adornment hung over the door that led to the novices' chambers. She hauled herself up onto the glass shingles. Her fingers and toes were sure, her muscles bunching and releasing as she climbed up, up, up, until she was perched by the golden tip. It was peaceful here. She felt as if she was leaving everything behind, the City, her mothers, the dark fate that awaited her. Up here, there was nothing but the stars.

She wished she could spread her arms and take flight, like the laurel doves that lived in the Aviary. Maybe if she could fly, she wouldn't be so afraid of falling.

"Sera!" Leela's whisper bounced across the glass shingles like a skipping stone. Sera could just make out her best friend standing on the ground below, waving up at her.

Leela was a bit of a scaredy-cat. Sera was impressed that she'd snuck out of her bed at all.

"What are you doing here?" Sera called back quietly.

"Come down," Leela hissed.

Sera gave the stars one last glance and slid down the spire, dropping the last ten feet onto the ground to Leela's muffled shriek.

"You look as though you haven't watched me do that a million times."

"Shhhh." Leela held out her finger, which glowed bright blue. "We don't want to wake the novices."

Sera pressed her lips together and nodded. While the temple was technically open to all Cerulean whenever they wished to use it—as were most things in the City Above the Sky—it wouldn't do to have the chosen one caught out of bed, on a night of prayer and meditation, climbing on it.

The chosen one. The words set Sera's stomach in knots.

She held out her own finger, already glowing, toward Leela.

The blood bond was one of the most sacred aspects of Cerulean magic. It was deeply personal and intimate. Sera had only ever bonded with her mothers and Leela. It was not to be taken lightly, the reading of another's heart.

Their fingers touched. Sera felt the familiar rush of heat as Leela's magic entered her, and the exhilarating sense of power as her own magic danced into Leela's veins until it twined and curled around her friend's heart. Sera could feel Leela's heartbeat inside her, a second pulse in perfect rhythm with her own.

Frightened, Sera's heart said.

Cerulean were not meant to be frightened. They were meant to be calm and loving. They were meant to value Mother Sun and their community over all else. They were meant to be better people than Sera was. All of this she poured, unspoken, into Leela.

Frightened, Leela's heart answered, and Sera read her friend's confusion and was surprised to find anger in Leela's heart as well. Both of their fears mixed together and Sera felt a burst of relief, not because she wanted Leela to be scared, but because, for one moment, at least she didn't feel so alone.

* * *

"Sera," her purple mother called. "There is someone here to see you."

Sera rubbed her eyes. Pale morning light filled her room—she had watched it turn from gray to gold as the sun rose, unable to sleep, the comfort of the night's blood bond with Leela fading away, leaving her own fear to grow and gnaw at her.

"Sera." Her purple mother stood in the doorway.

"I do not wish to see anyone," Sera said, keeping her gaze on her star mobile. Why was it so hard to look at her mother?

"It is the High Priestess," her mother said.

Sera sat up so fast her head spun. "Here?" she asked. "At our dwelling?"

The High Priestess had never visited a Cerulean dwelling before, as far as Sera knew.

"Your orange mother is making her tea," her purple mother said, with a halfhearted attempt at a conspiratorial smile.

Yesterday it would have been fun to see her orange mother in a tizzy over such an honored visitor. Yesterday she would have laughed with her purple mother, and perhaps added a jest of her own.

Her knees felt wooden as she got out of bed. Her purple mother helped her into a fresh cloudspun dress and they walked down the hall to the sitting room, just as her orange mother was serving tea. The scent of lemongrass and sage filled the air.

"There you are!" she exclaimed. "Look who has come to visit you."

Seeing the High Priestess sitting on the sofa was bizarre—it was like seeing a seresheep in prayer robes or watching a laurel dove fly backward. It didn't make sense. Her radiance made everything in the room seem a little plainer, from the upholstery to the teacups to the framed pressed flowers that hung on the walls.

"The chosen one," she said in her honeyed voice, standing and holding out her arms. Sera wasn't sure what the gesture meant, but her orange mother jerked her head and so she took a few wobbly steps forward. The High Priestess placed her hands on Sera's shoulders—she could feel the heat of them through her dress. She had never been touched by the High Priestess before.

"Will you come for a walk with me?" she asked. "We have much to discuss."

The thought of being alone with the High Priestess was stranger than having her in the sitting room. But Sera nodded anyway, wondering if she was even controlling her actions anymore or if her body was simply moving on its own through pure instinct. She followed the High Priestess out the door, catching a glimpse of her green mother in the kitchen as they left—she was bent over the table with a sewing needle in her hand.

The air was scented with sunlight and grass, a smell that declared a new day's beginning. It was more pungent today, sharper and clearer, as if reminding Sera of how few mornings she had left. They skirted around her orange mother's garden, a plump red tomato hanging ripe and ready to be picked on one of the stalks. Sera had never truly considered how perfect tomatoes were, their rich color, their earthy scent, their juicy flesh. How could such a simple thing suddenly seem so precious?

Then she saw several pairs of curious eyes watching from the dwelling next door and her mood soured.

"I imagine you have many questions for me," the High Priestess said, turning away from the cluster of dwellings and heading down a lesser-used, hedge-lined path that led to the edge of the City.

"Why me?" Sera blurted out, once the last dwelling had disappeared from view and they were well and truly alone. "Why did Mother Sun choose me?"

"Because she found you worthy," the High Priestess replied. "I know it may seem frightening and strange now, but you were chosen for a reason. You may not see it in yourself, but she sees all. She knows you, Sera Lighthaven, and she loves you." She smiled and took one of Sera's hands— Sera could not help but notice again how hot her skin was. "Do not fear. You will not feel any pain."

Sera hadn't actually considered the pain. She had been occupied enough with the fall. A new dread crept into her stomach.

"You are sure there isn't . . . Perhaps Mother Sun . . . made a mistake," Sera said hesitantly.

The High Priestess released her and took a step back. "Mother Sun does not make mistakes." There was an edge to her voice that made Sera feel ashamed for even suggesting it. Koreen probably wouldn't have questioned Mother

Sun's will, or Treena, or Daina. Why couldn't Sera be like everybody else?

The High Priestess sighed. "It has been so long since a ceremony, I have forgotten some of my patience. I apologize. You are not the first to question your worthiness as chosen one."

"I-I'm not?" she stammered.

The High Priestess leaned down so that her face was level with Sera's, her blue hair partly obscuring her expression. "A Cerulean was chosen to *create* this tether, too. I would have thought you would have remembered that, what with your avid interest in the past."

Sera felt uneasy, as if the High Priestess knew more about her than she realized.

"Your green mother could not answer all your questions," the High Priestess said. "Sometimes she came to me for answers, and I told her what I could. But much has been lost. And some things are not worthy of remembrance."

A day ago, Sera would have been amazed at the thought of her green mother approaching the High Priestess and asking for information on Sera's behalf. But now only one thing was on her mind.

"Who was she?" she pressed, leaning forward like she could peer into the High Priestess's memory. "The one who fell the last time. The Cerulean who created this tether."

There had been so many, Sera thought with a start. Not just the Cerulean who had made the tether they were using now, but the one who had broken the tether after the Great Sadness, and the one who had created that tether before it was broken. . . . They had seemed only stories yesterday, but today they all felt overwhelmingly *real* to Sera, Cerulean who had lived and loved and died for their City.

For a moment, the High Priestess's eyes darkened, the blue of her irises hardening and crystallizing like stargems. Sera thought she felt a chill emanating from the willowy figure before her, but then it was gone, and the High Priestess's face was as it had been.

"Her name was Wyllin," she said, straightening and looking away.

Wyllin. Sera turned the name over in her mind. It was comforting to think of another in her position, someone with a name and a life, someone who also might have taken this walk and asked these questions, even if they were nine hundred years apart.

"Was she young, like me?"

"She was. She was twenty-one when she was chosen. She was one of my acolytes." The High Priestess's mouth pressed into a thin line. "I was still a very new High Priestess then. The wounds of the Great Sadness were fresh in this City. The journey here had been a long and hard one. Many times I felt hope slip away. Wyllin was the one who first saw this planet. I remember thinking, 'Mother Sun, she has saved us.' I did not know how true those words would be. And then she was chosen."

An acolyte seemed a much more appropriate choice than a Cerulean who was barely of age, with no special qualities to speak of.

"She thought herself unworthy as well," the High Priestess continued. "We all doubt ourselves at times, doubt our power, our worth. I have shepherded this City through one of its greatest tragedies, and I often wonder if I have made missteps along the way."

"You do?" Sera asked, shocked.

"I do," the High Priestess said kindly. "At heart I am just another Cerulean, like all others in the City. But I trust in Mother Sun above all else. When I am frightened, she gives me comfort. When I am lost, she lights my way. She led us here, gave us this planet, kept us safe for so long. But the Cerulean are not meant to stay in one place forever."

The hedges surrounding them, covered in thick, glossy leaves, had grown taller as they walked. Suddenly, the High Priestess stopped and raised a hand—one side of the hedge fell away, vanishing to reveal a breathtaking view of the planet below. Sera reached out a hand to touch the invisible barrier that kept her from falling off right this very moment. It was firm yet slightly pliant, like clear gelatin. Below, the many islands of Pelago looked like misshapen insects, crawling on a blue surface.

"You cannot imagine the joy when we first sighted this world," the High Priestess said. "After so many dark days, so much loss . . . this was our salvation. I confess I will be sad to leave it."

"Why now?" Sera asked. "After all these years . . . what happened to make the City move again?"

"We have taken enough from this planet. It cannot sustain us anymore." Her face creased with worry and for a moment she looked old—Sera could sense the ancientness, the many lives that the High Priestess had lived. "Our City needs a new planet to keep us strong. I have faith that Mother Sun will lead us to a better home."

"I wish I got to see it," Sera confessed. The High Priestess lifted her chin with one strong finger.

"I know you do," she said. "It is all you have ever wanted, isn't it? But you will be safe in Mother Sun's everlasting embrace. You will be loved for eternity."

The only embrace Sera wanted was from her own mothers, but she felt it would be impertinent to say that out loud.

"Things will be different for you over the coming days," the High Priestess continued. "That cannot be helped. But you will be free to live those days however you please. You no longer have to attend evening prayers if you do not wish to. You need not trouble yourself with apprenticeships, nor will you have to help with preparations that will be made for the move, harvesting and canning and such. You can stay in your dwelling all day if you wish, or live like a fish in the Great Estuary. You may even"—she gave Sera a knowing wink—"climb the temple spire and nest up there like a bird. The daily patterns of Cerulean life will not apply to you until the afternoon of the ceremony."

Sera swallowed. "So I have today and tomorrow and then . . ."

The High Priestess nodded. "The following day will be the ceremony. At the hour of the light. In the Night Gardens. There will be a feast each evening in your honor. Those you will have to attend." Her face twisted as if she were in pain. "I am terribly sorry. I am not explaining this correctly. There was a time when . . ." She shook her head. "I am sorry."

Sera never thought she would be in a position where the High Priestess would be apologizing to *her*.

"It's all right," she said, even though it wasn't, not really. The High Priestess wasn't the one who would have to throw herself off the edge of the City in three days' time.

The High Priestess stared into Sera's eyes in a way that was nearly as intimate as blood bonding. Sera's stomach squirmed, but she found she could not look away. The moment seemed to stretch for so long, Sera lost track of seconds or minutes or hours.

"You will save us, Sera Lighthaven. Your blood will keep this City strong and vibrant and alive." The command in the High Priestess's voice was chilling. It made the hairs on the back of Sera's neck stand on end. She opened her mouth and found she could not speak. When the High Priestess finally broke their gaze, Sera felt trembly and out of breath, as if she had just sprinted the length of the Estuary.

"I will leave you now. You need time alone, I think."

And Sera did. She was already tired of the weight hanging from her neck, the responsibility and dread all mixed together. She turned to look through the hedge again, staring down at the planet she had felt so tired of just the day before. She realized how much she would miss it. The lopsided star that was Kaolin was just visible through a cover of thinning clouds, the three points close together on its lower left side almost like a hand waving to her, saying goodbye. So strange that she could feel such a sadness for a place she had never seen, a place that did not even know she or her City or her people existed.

When she turned back, the High Priestess had vanished.

4

SERA DID NOT RETURN TO HER HOUSE FOR SEVERAL hours.

She heard the bells calling out midday prayers for the orange mothers and novices. She felt the ache of hunger creep into her stomach and paid it no mind. She simply sat on the ground at the break in the hedge and stared at the planet below, at the silver-blue-gold tether that she would break, and at the space between where her City ended and the planet began. She could not guess how far it was, how long she would fall before all her blood was gone and she left this world, to live in Mother Sun's endless embrace.

She did not return home until the hour of the lamb.

Her orange and purple mothers were in the kitchen

when she stepped through the front doorway. Their voices sounded tense and strained, though Sera could not make out what they were saying. Or maybe she just didn't want to hear.

"Sera?" they called at the same time, as if unsure it was her. Sera realized there might have been many visitors today, not just the High Priestess. Who else had come to call, hoping to see the chosen one? She was glad she had stayed by the hedge.

"It's me," she said as they came rushing into the sitting room.

"We were so—" her orange mother began, but her purple mother cut her off.

"We are so happy to see you," she said.

Sera realized then, with a sharp twist of guilt, that she was being horribly selfish. Her mothers were losing a child. Leela was losing a friend. Would she hide herself away from the ones who mattered most, when she had so little time left to spend with them?

"I'm sorry if I worried you," she said. "I only . . ."

She didn't know how to finish her sentence without sounding awful.

"You needed some time on your own," her purple mother said.

"Of course you did," her orange mother agreed, but Sera could see the panic behind her eyes and wondered with a start if maybe her mothers had thought she was never coming home.

"Did the High Priestess not tell you where I was?" she asked.

Her orange mother looked startled. "We have not seen her since she left with you."

Sera's eyes widened. "You did not go to prayers?"

Her orange mother never missed prayers. Never, not even when she broke an ankle chasing a stray peahen in the Aviary and it took a full day before her blood had healed it.

"She would not leave this house until you returned," her purple mother said.

"We would not have you come home to a house without all of us in it," her orange mother said.

"You didn't fear Mother Sun would be angry with you?" Sera asked.

Her orange mother strode up and looked her daughter in the eye with such ferocity of love, Sera felt her breath stop in her chest.

"She is a *mother*, first and foremost," her orange mother said. "She understands."

Sera blinked. She could feel the tears building, but she was not ready to give in to them yet. "Where is Green Mother?" she asked. Her other two mothers exchanged a look.

"She is sewing you a new robe," her purple mother said. "For the feast tonight."

"Leela said she would come by, if you wanted to go to the Great Estuary to bathe first," her orange mother said.

Sera did not want to go out in the City and be stared at like some spectacle, but she had not bathed yesterday and she would be embarrassed to show up dirty to a feast being held in her honor. So she nodded.

"I am going to change into simpler clothes," she said,

and then headed to her bedroom without waiting for a response. She chose an old prayer robe that was plain and unadorned, nearly worn through at the elbows. She hung up her cloudspun dress, then collapsed onto her bed and stared at the mobile.

"I am a Cerulean," she said aloud. "My blood is magic."

The mobile spun slowly and offered her no comfort.

"Sera?" Her purple mother hovered in the doorway. Sera didn't say *come in*, but she didn't tell her to leave either. Why was it so difficult to talk to her mothers now, especially when she should want to be closer to them?

Her purple mother curled around her on the bed, resting Sera's head in the crook of her shoulder. Sera could feel the lavender ribbon around her neck brushing softly against her own forehead, and she breathed in her purple mother's honeysuckle scent.

"Your orange mother made that for you the day you were born," her purple mother said, with a gesture to the floating stars. "Did we ever tell you that story?"

"Green Mother said that you all went to one of the birthing houses where it was very peaceful, and then a few hours later I was born and you took me home." Sera repeated the story dully. Her birth held no interest to her anymore.

Her purple mother laughed, stirring up wisps of Sera's hair. "Seetha likes to keep things short and sweet, that is certain."

"It wasn't like that?"

"Well, we did go to the birthing house, but we were there for more than just a few hours and it was anything but peaceful. Childbirth is quite a bloody business. Your green mother had to leave the room for a few moments."

"Was Green Mother afraid?"

"Yes. She was afraid for me. She did not want to see me in pain."

Sera sat up straight. "I hurt you?"

Her purple mother put a hand on Sera's cheek. "Oh, my darling, it was a pain I would suffer again in a heartbeat. I have you because of it. And when the midwife placed you in my arms, so tiny and warm, I thought I had never seen anything so beautiful."

Sera threw herself into her purple mother's embrace, the tears she'd managed to hold at bay tumbling over her lids and spilling down her cheeks, jagged sobs ripping through her chest.

Her mother held her and said nothing, and when at last the tears were spent, she raised a glowing fingertip.

I do not want this, Sera's heart confessed in agony. She could feel her purple mother's pain swirling around her own, an older, stronger grief, with wisps and curls of feelings she didn't quite comprehend. For the first time, her purple mother's heart had no words for Sera to read. Just pain.

"Sera!" Leela's voice rang out cheerfully, and Sera could tell she was trying hard to sound like her normal, upbeat self. "Come, if you stink half as much as I do you must be dying for a bath!"

Her purple mother's laugh was cut through with sorrow. "She is a good friend," she said. Then she kissed Sera's forehead, got up, and walked toward the doorway. Pausing and turning back, she added, "You will be loved long after the ceremony, Sera. Remember that. As long as the stars burn in the sky, I will love you."

The Great Estuary was full of Cerulean bathing before the feast, naked and laughing, splashing about or eyeing each other with curiosity and desire.

When Sera arrived with Leela in tow, the laughter and shouting vanished as quickly as if she had clapped a hand over all their mouths.

"Don't pay them any mind," Leela said as they stripped off their robes and waded in up to their waists.

Everyone stared, even the adults. Some bowed to her, others murmured, "Praise her" or "The chosen one." Plenna, Jaycin, and Heena were closest to them—they were a few years older than Sera and had been a triad for many months now.

She remembered what Koreen had said yesterday in the cloudspinners' grove, that the wedding season was coming. The three girls would be getting married soon. And Sera was going to miss it.

"Good afternoon, Plenna," Leela said with a wave. Plenna's mothers lived in the dwelling next to Leela's. She wished Leela didn't have to be so friendly to everyone, and then instantly hated herself for thinking it. It was not Leela's fault that Sera had been chosen, and they would all be staring at her anyway.

The girl gave a start and nodded at Leela, her eyes flitting back to Sera.

"Good afternoon, chosen one," she said.

Sera tried to laugh, but it sounded as forced as it felt.

"Come now, I am still only Sera."

Plenna did not seem to know what to say to that. Jaycin slipped her arm around Plenna's waist and nodded a bit more genially.

"Good afternoon," she said, but Sera didn't fail to notice that she hadn't used her name either.

She wanted to dissolve, disappear. She wanted everything to go back to the way it had been, when she was just an odd, curious girl, nothing more. The eyes on her were like needles pricking her skin. So she took a deep breath and dove into the Estuary, kicking with her strong legs, propelling herself through the water. Under here, there was no sound. The sun trout did not care if she was the chosen one. The silence pressed blissfully against her eardrums, the water rippling over her bare skin.

She swam and swam, surfacing just once for air before she reached the opposite shore.

She sat on the muddy bank, keeping only her head above the water, watching as the playing and laughing and joking resumed now that she'd left. A pall had been lifted. She watched as Plenna washed Heena's back, then leaned forward to kiss her shoulder. Heena smiled and closed her eyes. Jaycin took advantage of the moment and splashed them both. Heena shrieked and laughed, and she and Jaycin fell kissing into the water while Plenna shook her head and pretended to be exasperated.

All she wanted, and all she would never have. The agony of losing her world expanded inside Sera's chest.

A blue-haired head popped up beside her and she let out a shriek of fright.

"I may not be as fast a swimmer," Leela said, settling herself to sit in the mud beside Sera, "but I can hold my breath longer than you."

"That's true," Sera said. Then she nudged Leela with her shoulder. "You are also much better at convincing Freeda to sneak us an extra plum or two from the orchards."

Leela grinned. "Because I am so sweet, no one can resist me."

Sera giggled and it felt good. It felt real. She hoped Leela knew how much she needed her; how much her friendship meant, on this day especially, when everything was so scary and strange.

"But," Leela continued, "you are better at making Acolyte Imima's head spin with all your questions about the Moon Daughters."

"That's *enough*, Sera!" the two girls said together in their best impressions of Acolyte Imima's whiny, nasal voice, before collapsing into laughter. Sera let her head sink under the water, and when she came back up, her brief moment of good humor vanished.

"I wish they would not treat me like I am a stranger," she said, staring across the bank.

Leela gripped her hand. "You are a Cerulean. You are not a stranger."

Sera wanted to smile, but her mouth couldn't seem to remember the shape. "I am different and this proves it. I wonder if it makes them all feel better, somehow, or relieved. I wonder if they will even miss me when I am gone."

The word *gone* hung between them, swaying back and forth heavily like a pendulum.

Leela put both her hands on Sera's shoulders, her blue eyes darkening. "I know that we are meant to trust Mother Sun and the High Priestess. I know this ceremony is necessary. I know it is best for our people. But . . ." She glanced left to right, then held out her finger.

I hate it. Leela's heart spoke the word with force, with fire behind it, and Sera gasped and pulled her hand away.

Hate was worse than being frightened or angry. Hate was not an acceptable word or feeling in the City Above the Sky. The Cerulean did not hate.

"I hate that they are taking you away from me," Leela whispered, as if she could sense that Sera needed to hear the word aloud. "I hate that you were chosen. I hate that I will be left alone, to live the rest of my life without you." A tear fell from Leela's eye and landed with a tiny *plink* in the water. "I hate that I cannot do anything to help."

Sera felt as though someone with very big hands was clamping them around her throat. She looked at Leela's warm, open, loving face and held out her glowing finger.

Their magic shone together, and Sera poured all the love she had for her friend into the connection. Every memory, every moment. She gave Leela her heart, all of it, every last shred.

Love, love, love.

There was only one thing she held back, the thing she always did. Even in this bleak time, Sera would not relinquish it.

She felt Leela's love fill her up, their hearts beating in unison. They stayed like that, the Estuary breaking in tiny waves against their bodies, until at last Leela looked up and her eyes were dry.

"Let's go see the dress your green mother is preparing," she said. "I'm sure it will be beautiful."

Sera nodded and swallowed her fear. She glanced across the water to where their clothes lay out on the bank with so many others.

"I would prefer to take the long way back, if you don't mind," Leela said, standing and wringing the water out of her hair. "We will dry off as we walk."

Sera knew she was only saying that to help her—that she had sensed Sera's reluctance to return to the opposite shore, even if it meant leaving her robe behind. Surely her mothers would not mind. She would not need robes soon anyway.

Leela helped her to her feet. "We will have to stop at my dwelling first," she said with a sly grin. "And don't worry, I have told my mothers that under no circumstances are they to call you the chosen one or any other such thing."

"Thank you," Sera said. "It's just awful, isn't it? Everyone gaping at me and saying 'praise her.'"

"I wonder if Koreen will suddenly act as if you are best friends now that you are so popular."

"I wouldn't call it popular."

"I bet you could get her to do anything you want," Leela said wistfully, tugging on a lock of her hair.

"Trying to get the chosen one to abuse her power already?" Sera teased.

"Oh, it would be fun. Imagine the pranks you could

pull. I bet Freeda would give you as many plums as you wanted now if you asked."

They arrived at Leela's house, and she lent Sera a robe but made her wait in the sitting room while she changed in her room. Leela's mothers were kind to her as they always were, no trace that there was anything different about today, and Sera was grateful for it.

When they returned to Sera's dwelling, they found that Sera's green mother had truly outdone herself.

The cloudspun dress fell in ripples to the floor, the fabric so light and glittering Sera wondered if she had spun the thread and woven the fabric this very day. It was adorned with new rose blossoms and baby's breath. On her head, her green mother placed a wreath of bright purple forget-me-nots. When Sera saw herself in the looking glass, she had to admit the overall effect was very becoming. She had never truly liked her reflection. Leela clapped her hands and cried, "Oh, Sera, you are a vision!"

Her orange mother knelt before her and tied three strings of stargems—one purple, one green, one orange— around Sera's left wrist.

"Oh, Mother," Sera gasped with delight, holding them up. The tiny little lights that shone within each gemstone seemed to wink at her.

"We had them specially made," her orange mother said, her voice trembling. "For your birthday this year."

Sera was too overcome to speak.

"I have a gift for you too," Leela said. "But I . . . I would like to give it to you privately."

"Of course," her purple mother said. "We will wait for

you girls in the sitting room."

Once they were alone, Leela dropped a fine gold chain into Sera's palm, and Sera understood why Leela had not let her into her room earlier, and why she had asked Sera's mothers to leave.

"Leela, no!" she cried. The moonstone pendant glowed in her hand—Leela had found the stone nearly a year ago when she and Sera had been digging in the banks of the Great Estuary for skipping stones. They'd kept it a secret, hoping it would reveal some of its magic to them, which it never had, much to their disappointment. And then Leela had set it in a classic Cerulean design, the many-pointed star, when she was practicing her hand at jewelry making. She had never worn it, though, as far as Sera knew, and the girls had an unspoken rule that they would not tell anyone of the moonstone's existence.

"I could not possibly accept this," Sera said.

"You must. For me."

"But moonstone is so rare. It should stay in the City, shouldn't it?"

"No one knew we had it anyway, so it will not be missed. It's yours now," Leela said, taking the chain and fastening it around Sera's neck. "There is nothing more precious to me than your friendship. I would not have you leave without taking a token of me with you."

Her voice cracked on the word *leave*. The chain was quite long, and Sera tucked the star under her dress so it nestled against her breastbone, keeping it hidden but close to her heart.

We are the Cerulean. Our blood is magic.

Sera clung to that thought. She was a Cerulean. She loved her City and it did not matter that she was terrified. She would not allow it to matter. All she had ever wanted was adventure, wasn't it? She should think of this as a journey, something that no other Cerulean had done in nearly a thousand years. She gathered up her courage and wrapped it in careful layers around her heart.

Maybe if she pretended hard enough, she would not feel afraid at all.

She and Leela left the bedroom together and headed into the sitting room, where her mothers were waiting.

"I am ready," she said.

5

THE DAY GARDENS WERE AT THE VERY WESTERN EDGE OF the City Above the Sky, filled with the brightest flowers, purple hydrangeas and yellow tulips, red-gold fireflowers and pale pink ladyslips, and Sera's favorite, minstrel flowers— they had iridescent petals in a rainbow of colors, and when they opened and closed, it sounded like singing.

Her reception here could not have been more different than it was at the Estuary. Everyone wanted to talk to her now. Everyone wanted to kiss her hand or the hem of her dress. Perhaps because this feast was for her, because she was meant to be ogled, the Cerulean did not find her presence so uncomfortable. The moonstone was warm against her skin, hidden under her dress, and she felt like she was carrying Leela's heart as well as her own.

Koreen came rushing up to her as she entered the Day Gardens, followed by Treena and Daina.

"Oh, Sera," she gushed. "I'm so happy for you. Mother Sun has graced you! How does it feel?"

That seemed to be the question everyone wanted an answer to, but no one wanted the answer Sera had to give. "I am honored, thank you," she said, because it was easier than explaining the truth.

"I thought I was going to faint when the High Priestess called your name!" Daina exclaimed. "It was so very exciting, wasn't it?"

"It's the most exciting thing that's happened in years, that's what my green mother said," Treena added. "She never thought she'd live to see the City move again."

"Oh, Sera!" Atana hurried over and kissed her on the cheek. Sera had always suspected Atana found her annoying, but it seemed no one remembered how they used to feel about her, just how they decided to feel about her now. "You must be so honored. What did it feel like, when your name was called?"

"Hot," Sera answered truthfully.

Atana could not seem to decide whether she thought Sera was joking. "Oh. Yes. Well, you look lovely. Did your green mother make this dress?" Sera nodded. "I will have to see if she can give me some tips. Did you girls hear there is to be a wedding season soon?"

Sera couldn't believe how quickly things had turned from her impending sacrifice to dresses and weddings. Her head hurt and she wanted to hide someplace quiet where no one could see her.

Koreen was smiling at Sera with a look she had never been on the receiving end of before. "We could go for a walk by the Aviary later if you'd like," she said, twirling a lock of hair around her finger.

Sera was stunned. Was Koreen *flirting* with her? She couldn't remember anyone flirting with her, ever. She had tried flirting herself once or twice, with dismal results. The girls were never interested. And neither was Sera.

She looked at Koreen's smooth silver skin and big azure eyes, her breasts curving under her dress, her silky blue hair swept over one shoulder. And she tried. She tried so hard to find something arousing about her.

But inside she was empty.

Sera didn't realize she hadn't given a response until Leela cleared her throat.

"Oh," she said with a start. "I . . . I can't. I'm sorry."

Then she turned and wove her way through the crowd, trying not to make eye contact lest someone ask her again how she felt about being chosen.

Leela had a hand over her mouth to stifle her laughter. "You just said no to Koreen. Koreen!" She shook her head. "I bet that was a new experience for her. See, I told you she would be after you now that you are—"

"The chosen one," a green mother said, coming up and kissing Sera's hand. "May I ask—"

"The chosen one is thirsty," Leela interrupted, in a most un-Leela-like fashion. "Please get her a refreshment."

The green mother ducked her head, the jade ribbon around her neck creasing. "Yes, at once."

Leela pulled Sera behind a large rhododendron bursting with magenta blossoms. "This is better," she said. "A little quiet. Just for a second or two."

Sera wrapped her arms around Leela. They did not need to blood bond in this moment to read each other's hearts.

"It's awful," Leela said. "Everyone pulling and tugging and wanting a piece of you. And only yesterday they—" She stopped talking abruptly.

Sera sighed. "I know. Yesterday they all thought me a nuisance. And today . . . well, I will be out of their hair soon enough." Her attempt at bravado sounded weak in her own ears. Leela wasn't fooled.

"You are everything a Cerulean should be," she said.

But Leela didn't know. Not really.

It was then that the minstrel flowers began to sing, joyful yet ethereal, heralding the beginning of the celebration.

"Come," she said, taking Leela's hand. "Time to stop hiding."

There had been little time for planning, and so gossamer blankets were laid out, each piled with platters of food and pitchers of clear water and sweetnectar. There was a table set up under a dainty elm for the High Priestess and Sera and her mothers. Sera sat on a stool beside the High Priestess and wished she were home eating dinner in her kitchen. Leela and her family sat close by, and Leela kept making silly faces at Sera whenever their eyes met, until Leela's green mother noticed and whispered in her ear to make Leela stop.

The acolytes served those seated at the table, and Sera could tell her mothers were just as uncomfortable in this situation as she was. Her orange mother kept half rising from her seat every time one passed, until her green mother put a hand on her thigh and murmured, "Otess, stop."

"I don't like being served by an acolyte," she whispered back. "It isn't right. *I* should be serving *them*."

"We all serve in the City Above the Sky," the High Priestess said, and Sera's mothers started. "Do not let it upset you. My acolytes are honored to attend to the family of the chosen one."

Acolyte Endaria nodded as she refilled her orange mother's glass. "Indeed, we are. You have given us a great gift."

"And what is that?" her purple mother asked. Sera was surprised by her terseness. She had never heard her purple mother speak in such a tone.

Acolyte Endaria smiled. "Why, you have given us the chosen one." She set down the pitcher and took both of Sera's purple mother's hands in her own. "The City thanks you."

"I did not birth Sera for the City to take her away, thank you very much," her purple mother said, pulling her hands back.

"Kandra," her orange mother said, shocked.

Acolyte Endaria looked to the High Priestess, who waved her away. "It's all right, Endaria. Gather the novices. The time of adoration is nearly at hand."

Sera didn't like the sound of that.

"I cannot pretend to understand the pain you all must be feeling," the High Priestess said to Sera's mothers. "And

I cannot prevent the suffering you will feel at Sera's loss. But know that you are helping to keep all these families together." She swept out a hand at the Cerulean sitting on blankets, laughing and eating and teasing one another, casting furtive glances at the table. "There is great worth in that."

Her purple mother muttered something Sera could not hear, and her green mother was sitting ramrod straight on her stool.

"Of course there is," her orange mother said, but she was looking down at her plate.

Sera felt miserable. It was one thing to be frightened herself, but to watch her mothers being told they should be honored and thanked was unbearable. She picked morosely at her salad of melon and pomegranate seeds and wondered when the feast would end and she could go home. She wanted her orange mother to make lavender tea like she always did after dinner, and her purple mother would take out her harp and play for them while Sera and her green mother washed and dried the dishes.

The High Priestess stood and silence fell. "My children," she said in a ringing tone. "It is nearly time for the adoration of our chosen one. Think about what you will say, how you will honor her. For she is the light that Mother Sun has chosen for us." She turned to Sera and held out a hand. "Come," she said.

Sera stood but didn't take the proffered hand. She did not need the High Priestess to lead her like a little child. If she was old enough to die for her City, she was old enough to walk on her own.

The High Priestess hesitated only a second. Without another word, she turned and walked off down a path between two hydrangeas. Fireflies lit their way as they wound deeper into the Day Gardens. Sera had to duck to avoid a low-hanging bough of ivy, and then they came upon a clearing at the edge of the City, where the Great Estuary spilled over. The planet below was dark, as if it too was having a moment of adoration for Sera.

"The Day Gardens represent life and new beginnings," the High Priestess said. "As the Night Gardens represent death and endings. Your journey begins here, in the farthest spot from death. Tomorrow the celebration will be in the temple, halfway between life and death. And then the next day . . ."

"The Night Gardens," Sera said.

"I know this is hard for you," the High Priestess said. "But it will only be hard for a short while. By allowing the City to thank you, to spend time with you, to know you and appreciate you . . . it will be better for everyone. I hope you can see that."

Sera thought it might have meant more if anyone in the City besides Leela had tried to know her *before* she was chosen. She could hear voices, the acolytes leading the way, the whispers of excitement from the Cerulean following them down the path. How many families would leave this celebration feeling uplifted? How many would stay up late into the night, whispering excitedly about the new chapter their City was about to embark on?

How many would feel even a shred of pity for her, or her mothers?

Sera had to decide who she was going to be, in this moment, at the end of her days. Would she be selfish and tell them all how she really felt? Or would she smile and thank them and give them hope?

What did Wyllin do? she wanted to ask. She imagined the Cerulean woman standing here, in this very spot, beside this very High Priestess, waiting to be adored. Did she stand tall and proud, or did she lash out in fear? Sera felt an overwhelming sense of connection to the stranger who died so many years ago. The tether Wyllin created, Sera would break.

We are the Cerulean, she thought determinedly. *Our blood is magic.*

Acolyte Klymthe's face peered around the edge of a rosebush. The High Priestess looked down at Sera, as if waiting for her permission.

"Let them come," Sera said.

6

THE SECOND EVENING OF CELEBRATION WAS MUCH LIKE the first, only in the temple this time. And before she knew it, it was the morning of the ceremony, and Sera awoke with a knot in her stomach and shards of fear lodged in her heart.

She could hear the novices singing, welcoming the start of a new day. In dwellings across the City, Cerulean were waking up and preparing for a great change. Sera could imagine the excitement, the nervousness, the giddy anticipation. And she found she couldn't begrudge her people their joy. If she hadn't been chosen herself, how much sympathy would she have spared for the one selected to bear this mantle?

At least there would be no more celebrations in her

honor—she'd had quite enough of those. The one in the temple had been as exhausting as the one in the Day Gardens. She'd done her best to be strong, to be kind, to listen to her people as they thanked her or praised her. Some had been so effusive, an acolyte would have to step in and lead them away. Others had cried, confessing their fears of leaving this planet behind and heading into the unknown of space. Sera had found that she didn't need to say anything, that a simple nod or a touch on the shoulder was sufficient. Which was good, because she did not know what to say.

Sera got out of bed, her skin tight on her bones. There was a dry spot on her tongue that wouldn't go away. When she brushed out her hair, her scalp prickled.

She slipped into her dressing gown and padded down the hall to the kitchen, following the smell of garlic and tomato.

The sound of voices made her stop just before the arched doorway.

". . . another child," her green mother was saying.

"That isn't the point and you know it, Seetha," her purple mother said.

"I know." Her green mother sounded contrite. There was a pause, and when she spoke again her voice was quiet and laced with pain. "I don't know what else to say. I don't have any answers. This is an agony I have never felt before."

There was a silence—Sera assumed they were blood bonding—then her purple mother muttered something angrily. Sera caught the word *curious* before silence fell again, followed by the unmistakable sound of kissing.

"I know, Kandra," her green mother said again, softly. "I know."

Sera didn't wish to hear anymore.

"Good morning, Mothers," she said before walking into the kitchen, giving her mothers enough time to jump apart and pretend they were merely preparing breakfast. There were tiny goldfinch eggs boiling in a pot on the stove, next to a pan of tomatoes and hyacinth leaves simmering in garlic.

"Good morning, Sera," her green mother said, pushing the thick discs of tomato around in the pan.

"Good morning, darling," her purple mother said, coming over to kiss the top of her head.

"Is Orange Mother at prayers?" she asked, taking a seat at the table by the window. There was a little window box with a small herb garden, and Sera tried to memorize the scents of basil and thyme, as if she could take them with her. Her purple mother poured Sera a cup of thistle tea, then poured one for herself and sat at the table with her.

"Your orange mother has been up since dawn sewing a robe for you," she said. "For the ceremony."

On any other day, there would have been a joke about thimbles or a reminiscence of the last time Sera's orange mother had tried to sew her a prayer robe and it was six inches too short. But today was not just any day. The memory of that too-short robe stuck in Sera's throat like a pebble. She took a sip of tea, but its warmth did nothing to soothe her or ease the tightness in her chest. When her green mother set a plate of eggs and tomato in front of her, all Sera could do was pick at it with her fingers.

"Sera, you really should ea—" her green mother began, but was silenced by one look from her purple mother.

They sat around the table pretending to eat but mostly sipping tea and watching the clock on the wall. It was past the hour of the serpent. The ceremony would take place at the next hour, the hour of the light.

"I am sorry, Green Mother," Sera said, staring at her plate. The guilt hit her with sudden force, that perhaps if she had been a better daughter, this would not have happened. "You were such a good teacher to me and I . . . I was not . . . I didn't . . ."

"My sweet girl." Her green mother was on her knees, cupping Sera's face in her hands. "You were a joy to educate. All the other green mothers wondered how I was able to handle your questions—and you had so many! And do you know what I told them?"

Sera shook her head, her throat too swollen to speak.

"I said, 'Each question she asks is a gift to me.' Some green mothers think only of the wisdom they are meant to impart to their daughter, of our ways and our history. But you showed me that true wisdom is in learning from each other. You taught me so much, my child."

"You are not disappointed in me?" Sera asked, and she knew this was the question she was burning to have answered. She needed to know, before the end, that she had not let her mothers down.

"Oh, Sera," her green mother said, and then her arms

were around Sera, and her purple mother's too. "No," she whispered.

"You are our greatest love," her purple mother said, and her voice broke. "You have changed us with your infectious joy and your expansive heart and your beautiful mind." She clasped Sera's hands in her own. "Remember what I said to you."

"As long as the stars burn in the sky, you will love me," Sera whispered. She breathed her mothers in, honeysuckle and peppermint, and tried to lock their scents away with the basil. *Please, Mother Sun,* she prayed, *let me take a piece of them with me, no matter how small.*

"Sera," her orange mother called. "Can you come in here, please?"

Sera's body felt unnaturally heavy as she made her way to her mothers' bedroom. The bed was a giant circle with lots of fluffy pillows and gossamer blankets. A long, oval looking glass stood off to one side. Her orange mother seemed tired—there was a redness in her eyes and her face had a pinched look.

She held out the silky material with both hands. "I hope you are not disappointed."

Sera turned away to put the robe on, keeping Leela's necklace hidden beneath it so the moonstone could rest against her heart. She wasn't sure why she hadn't told her mothers about the necklace, except that it felt like the right thing to keep it private, to keep it just between her and her best friend.

The robe was cloudspun, not made of seresheep wool

like her other prayer robes, and it left her arms completely bare, the hood embroidered clumsily with golden thread. It was belted with finely woven moonsilver, and the hem was adorned with green and orange and purple thread that zigged and zagged in an erratic fashion.

"The High Priestess said it was tradition for her to make the robe for the chosen one," her orange mother said, eyes downcast. "She would have done a better job. But I . . . I asked if I might . . ." She swallowed and pressed her lips together.

Sera had never loved a prayer robe more. "It's perfect," she said, wrapping her arms around her orange mother's waist. "I wouldn't want to wear anything else."

"You have been our sun, Sera Lighthaven," her orange mother said, her eyes glittering with tears. Sera had never seen her orange mother cry. "You have been the light in our world." Her voice cracked and she began to say something else, then stopped herself. "Are you ready to go to the Night Gardens?"

Sera had never felt less ready for anything.

"Yes, Mother," she whispered.

The Night Gardens were on the eastern point of the City Above the Sky.

As the Cerulean began to gather for the ceremony, the streets filled with women in white robes. Today, no one had spoken to Sera. No one spoke at all. She caught a glimpse of Leela in the crowd. Her friend gave her a tight smile that Sera found herself unable to return, as if the smallest movement would be too much for her muscles to bear.

Sera's heart was beating so fast she wondered if it had been stolen during the night and replaced with a humming-bird's wings.

The Night Gardens were resplendent as the hour of the light drew near. The colors were darker here than the bright hues of the Day Gardens, scarlet dahlias and somber pur-ple lilacs, scattered nebula trees with their black leaves and silver bark, pure white lilies and gray roses, all intermixed with tiny, floating will-o-wisps. The Cerulean followed the shore of the Great Estuary, which narrowed as it neared the edge of the City, before falling off its end in a waterfall. At this edge was a raised glass dais that jutted out beyond the waterfall into the void of space. Sera's stomach swooped. Many of the Cerulean were already kneeling. Sera and her mothers picked their way through the crowd to where the High Priestess stood.

"The chosen one," the High Priestess said as they ap-proached, spreading her arms wide. Sera wished she would just call her by her name; her *own* name, the name her mothers had given her. The High Priestess looked into her eyes again, in the same way she had that day by the hedge. Sera felt exposed, like a raw nerve.

"There is much power in you," the High Priestess said. "Mother Sun could not have chosen a worthier candidate." She lowered her voice and, to Sera's shock, knelt before her. "I know you are frightened. But Mother Sun chose you for a reason. This is your destiny. This is who you were *meant* to be."

Then she stood and turned to Sera's mothers. "For devotion," she said, kissing her orange mother on the cheek.

"For wisdom," she said, kissing her green mother. "And for love," she finished, planting the lightest of kisses on her purple mother's forehead.

Sera's legs were trembling like a newborn seresheep as she climbed the steps of the dais behind the High Priestess.

"Today is a momentous day!" the High Priestess cried. "The beginning of a new chapter for our beloved City, at long last. This ceremony will free us from the bonds to this planet as Mother Sun will guide us to our new home. All praise her everlasting light!"

"Praise her!" the crowd cried back. Sera searched for Leela and found her off to the right, near a cluster of silvery white moonflowers. She touched the place where the star hung beneath her dress and Leela nodded, tears falling thick and fast down her cheeks.

As the High Priestess continued, Sera wondered why she herself wasn't crying. Perhaps because right now, this moment did not seem real to her. She felt as though she were inside another's skin, as if she were watching this ceremony happen but was not a part of it.

The High Priestess anointed Sera's wrists and temples with dots of lilac perfume. Then she drew an ancient iron knife from her belt. Sera tried to consider how Wyllin had felt in this moment, when the knife was drawn. But Wyllin held no comfort now. She was long dead, and Sera was very much alive and afraid.

The echoing wail of a horn filled the air; sad, like a dying star, like the emptiness of space. Tears were falling freely down the faces of all three of her mothers as the High Priestess's knife bit into Sera's skin, just below the elbow, releasing brilliant blue blood.

Pain. Sera had never truly felt it before. Her skin burned where it had been cut. The pain seemed to sharpen everything around her. Suddenly her fear was everywhere. It was climbing her rib cage, it was crushing her shoulders, it was choking her, strangling her. She could not do this.

The cut did not heal itself instantly, as all other cuts had throughout her life. The knife was imbued with a magic to keep her blood flowing. Sera felt nauseous as she watched the blood trickle down her arm. Her tongue felt swollen, making it hard to breathe. Her head swam, and when the High Priestess spoke again, she sounded very far away.

"For our City," she said, making the same mark on the other elbow. "May Mother Sun embrace you and cherish you for all time."

Then she waved a hand and Sera could sense the barrier part behind her, letting in a gust of air colder than anything she had ever felt in her life, a cold that gnawed at her skin and ate right through to her bones.

The Night Gardens were silent. Sera knew what she had to do, but she didn't know how to do it. Her hummingbird heart was throwing itself against her chest as though trying to fly away. Everyone was watching her. It felt like an eternity passed before she could even form the intent to move her legs to step out onto the jutting glass.

Beyond the barrier, the cold enveloped her and everything felt impossibly still. How strange that only a few steps could make such an overwhelming difference. The trickle of blood was hot as it made a slow path down her arms. She gazed up at the stars for the last time and prayed for strength. She could not look back, not even for one last glimpse of her mothers or Leela. If she looked back, she would never look away again.

Sera opened her arms wide, squeezed her eyes shut, and fell from the balcony, so that her blood could help her people.

PART TWO

Old Port City, Kaolin

7

LEO

Leo was sick of Old Port City.

No, not sick. Bored. Bored to *death*.

No, even death would be less boring.

The air was thick with heat and humidity, so thick you could put it in a bowl and serve it up as soup. Sweat soup. Kaolin's finest delicacy.

Maybe there was a place far to the north, in the Crag Mountains, where it was breezy and cool and some goatherd was enjoying a glass of lemonade and savoring the smell of goat crap. Though if what the papers were saying was true, it wasn't cool anywhere in Kaolin at the moment. The heat wave was setting records, with reports of droughts in the

Knottle Plains and wildfires raging in the forests around Lake Looten.

Leo could hear the clip-clop of horses' hooves mixed with the puttering of car engines as they passed by on the street outside. The curtains in the library were closed. The curtains in the entire house were closed. It was supposed to keep out the heat, but all it did was make the air more stifling. Leo's thick black curls were plastered to his forehead, and his shirt stuck to his chest in places. Even lounging on his favorite leather sofa was uncomfortable, the material sucking at his exposed skin. So instead he was sprawled across an overstuffed armchair, tossing a squash ball against the floor so that it bounced off the wall and back into his hand.

Thud, thump, smack. Thud, thump, smack.

He should be in his family's summerhouse in the south, near Pearl Beach, having parties with his friends, swimming in the cool waters of the Adronic Ocean, and convincing the local girls to show him what was under their skirts. Not stuck in the brownstone on Creekwater Row, dying of heat and bored to tears. When his father announced that they would not be vacationing this summer, he had hoped it was because at long last, Xavier McLellan was going to bestow upon his only son the one thing Leo had wanted since he was a child—a place in the family business. But the days had stretched into weeks. August was nearly over, and Xavier showed no signs of including Leo in anything, business decisions or otherwise. Perhaps Leo should have expressed a desire to go to college, like Robert and his other friends. But he'd always thought—or maybe assumed—that Xavier was simply waiting until he was old enough, and now that Leo was eighteen, shouldn't he be learning the ins and outs of the McLellan empire?

The ball ricocheted off a piece of molding and bounced out of Leo's reach. It rolled under the couch, and he was too hot to get up and look for it. There was an open book on the table beside him—*A Complete History of the Wars of the Islands*, by Edward G. Bates. Leo skimmed a few pages. It was all politics, the trade deals that fell through and prices on imported goods from Pelago being jacked up as demand spiked—there had been droughts in Kaolin back then too, like there were now, and famine in the south, where overfishing had depleted the food supply from the Gulf of Windsor. Pelago had never suffered from the weather like Kaolin did; their waters were always plentiful, their soil always fruitful. Threats had been tossed back and forth between the president of Kaolin and the Triumvirate of Pelago until the inevitable breaking point, when Kaolin sent its fleet to attack the Pelagan armada. But it was the Pelagans who had won in the end.

Agnes had probably left the book out. It seemed like the boring sort of thing his sister would enjoy reading. And she was far more interested in the Pelagan side of their family than he was—too interested, if you asked him. It was almost as if she didn't notice that their father, in addition to his famous freak shows, ran a chain of the most successful anti-Talman theaters in the country, producing plays that railed against the goddesses of Pelago. Xavier McLellan had only married their Pelagan mother for her money, and since she had died in childbirth, Leo felt that he was barely Pelagan at all. Even though, according to their Pelagan chauffeur, Eneas, he was her "spitting image," with his fair skin and turquoise eyes. Well, Leo didn't want to be her spitting image. The only comfort he got out of it was how much it clearly rankled Agnes, who looked like a female version of their father—brown skin, chestnut hair, eyes the color of cinnamon. For twins, they didn't seem to have anything in common, from appearance to sensibility.

"Studying in the summer, are we?"

Leo jumped at the sound of his sister's voice. She leaned in the doorway, a half-eaten apple in hand, her hair pulled up in a messy knot on the crown of her head. Leo closed the book with a dull thud.

"*The Wars of the Islands*, huh?" he said. "Better not let Father catch you reading about a Pelagan victory over Kaolin."

Agnes shrugged and tried to look nonchalant, but Leo knew better. If there was one thing he and his sister had in common, it was a healthy fear of their father.

"It's his book," she said. "It's not like I bought it."

"What are you doing here anyway?" Leo grumbled. "Don't you have a frog to dissect or something?"

"It was a rat," Agnes said, taking a bite of apple. "And I've already finished."

"Ugh."

Agnes loved science. Although upper-class women weren't allowed professions in Kaolin, their father indulged her privately, something Leo envied and also never quite understood. It was so out of character for him. He'd even built her a little lab out of the walk-in closet in her bedroom. Leo found it macabre—who would want to sleep with frog corpses and snakes suspended in formaldehyde next door?

"For a big strong man, you're awfully squeamish."

"For a delicate lady, you're awfully disgusting." He gave her a cursory once-over. "I assume Father isn't home yet." Leo could imagine the fallout from Xavier seeing Agnes walking about the house in her lab attire.

She was wearing an old shirt of Eneas's—he was always spoiling her, giving her whatever she wanted—and a pair of pants that had once belonged to Leo. By the time he realized she'd stolen them, they were covered in all sorts of disgusting stains.

"No, so I don't have to wear a stupid dress until dinner," she said. "Which reminds me—Eneas said it's to be quite the affair tonight. That Pelagan man Father has been working with all year has finally arrived in Old Port. He's coming to dinner, and I think Father has invited some single Kaolin society women to entice him."

Leo smirked. His father was such a clever man. After living in Pelago his whole life, this man was sure to be pleased with the way proper Kaolin women behaved around men.

A thought occurred to him. This was his chance! He would impress the Pelagan and show Father that he was capable of handling international affairs. He knew nothing about this new project (his father was incredibly secretive), but he would do some light research on his other shows— the one with the two-headed man and the bearded ladies in Pearl Beach was doing quite well, he seemed to remember, and *The Great Picando* had just closed at his father's renowned theater, the Maribelle, in Central Square. Leo had seen it several times—he liked that it had women actors in it, unlike some of the plays in Old Port that cast young men to play women. But it was quite stuffy as far as the writing went. Your basic save-the-Kaolin-woman-from-the-evil-sins-of-polytheism. The Great Picando had been played by James Roth, a rising star in the theater scene. Leo had asked his father to introduce him, but he must have forgotten. Which was understandable—his father was a very busy man.

This was Leo's moment to prove he was important. He was a McLellan.

Agnes groaned. "Whatever thought is behind that smug look on your face, keep it to yourself. I don't want to know. Dinner's at eight. You better look sharp."

"I always do," he said, and it was true. No one knew how to put an outfit together better than Leo did. All his friends said so. "Do let me know if you need any assistance with your wardrobe. I'm sure you must have something from the current century in there somewhere."

Agnes smiled at him sweetly. "Thank you, dear brother, but I'd rather take fashion advice from the dissected rat."

Then she turned on her heel and slammed the door behind her.

By seven forty-five, Leo was dressed and ready and had even had Janderson, his manservant, get him some figures on the business to look over.

It seemed that the anti-Talman plays were doing very well in the rural areas around the Knottle Plains and on the coast of the Gulf of Windsor. The Points, the three peninsulas that jutted out from Kaolin's southwestern edge, seemed to prefer Xavier's more outrageous theater, dancing bears and men with flippers instead of feet. Old Port enjoyed a healthy mix of the two. Leo was surprised to find that *The Great Picando* hadn't done quite as well as he'd imagined—ticket sales had declined over the course of the run.

He studied his reflection in the large, gilt-framed mirror over his vanity and had to admit, he looked rather dashing.

The blue-green tie matched his eyes perfectly, setting off the crisp ivory shirt, and his beige linen waistcoat and slacks completed the outfit. Leo didn't usually play up his eyes but thought perhaps it would help with another Pelagan in the room. The only thing missing was a beard. It was some genetic quirk of his mother's, he was sure, but Leo could not grow a beard, and it caused him everlasting shame. A few sparse whiskers would sprout on his upper lip but nothing more. A Kaolin man's beard was his pride—Xavier McLellan's was practically a work of art.

Leo turned away from his reflection and held out his wrists so Janderson could do his cuff links.

"No, not tonight," he said, when the man reached for his favorites, light blue encircled with diamonds. "Bring the Solit triangles."

He was impressed that Janderson had chosen the blue, as they were what Leo would have wanted to wear otherwise. He didn't say anything, though—he'd never once heard his father praise a maid or a servant. Not even Swansea, the old butler who had been around since the dawn of time, received a kind word. His father was meticulous and he maintained respect at all cost. Leo would follow his example.

Xavier would like that he wore the Solit cuff links. The symbol, a triangle with its apex crossed by a crescent to represent the light the One True God shed on the people of Kaolin, shone as golden as the sun and was impossible to miss. Leo felt it declared: *I am righteous. I belong.*

"How do I look?" he asked Janderson.

"Very good, sir," the young man replied. "Your father will be pleased."

Leo thought perhaps he should give some sort of order before he left. Xavier was always giving orders as he left a room. "Do clean up that mess before I'm back," he said, waving a hand in the direction of the papers scattered across his desk. He left without waiting for a response.

Agnes was already in the parlor when Leo arrived.

True to form, she was wearing some hideously ancient thing; a dull-colored, high-collared dress with ruffles poking out of the sleeves. And it was maroon. In August! Leo honestly had no idea how they were related.

Agnes was standing between two attractive women in their early twenties, a glass of champagne clutched in one hand and an unhappy expression on her face. Leo didn't recognize one of the women, but the other was Elizabeth Conway, his best friend Robert's sister. The Conways had built most of the railroads in Kaolin and had acquired a massive fortune over the years. Leo thought it highly unlikely that Elizabeth would be interested in marrying a Pelagan, though maybe his father had invited her as a show of strength, to prove to this man that he had important friends.

To be honest, Leo was surprised Elizabeth was still eligible. She was far too attractive and far too rich.

Agnes caught sight of him and gave him a grimace that he thought might have been intended as a smile. His sister hated social gatherings. And for good reason: she was terribly awkward. Elizabeth turned and her face lit up.

"Leo!" she exclaimed. "Why, don't you look handsome." She glided over to kiss him on the cheek. Her jasmine scent clung to him when she pulled away. Her dress was pale pink with capped sleeves and a pretty bow on one shoulder. It fell to the floor in tiers of taffeta, and the color offset her dark brown skin. The front part of her thick black hair was pinned in elaborate curls, the back hanging loose around her shoulders in heavy spirals. "You must meet my friend Marianne. She's visiting all the way from Lady's Point."

"How do you do?" Leo said politely, taking Marianne's hand and kissing it.

She was not quite as pretty as Elizabeth, but still a good deal more fashionable than Agnes. Her dress was dark blue chiffon with golden roses set at intervals on the skirt, draping the fabric in pleasing curves, and her bodice was encrusted with tiny sapphires. Her corset was laced quite snugly, her breasts pushing up out of the square neckline. West coast girls weren't quite as modest as east coast ones. Leo's pants suddenly felt quite tight.

"A pleasure to meet you, Mr. McLellan," she said.

"Please, call me Leo."

"I was just asking Agnes about this new project your father has been working on, but she doesn't seem to know a thing about it!" Elizabeth exclaimed. "Perhaps you could shed some light on the matter."

"Well, you know Father," he said. "He keeps his cards close to his chest." His eyes strayed to Marianne's cleavage, and he had to remind himself that she was not here for him.

Girls never seemed to be here for him. Not the highest society ones, anyway. The daughters of local merchants or the waitresses at the clubs were another matter, but Leo would never actually marry one of them.

"Leo doesn't know anything," Agnes said, speaking for the first time and, as usual, embarrassing everyone. Thankfully, the doorbell rang. Swansea was there in an instant, opening it and bowing low.

"Good evening, sir. May I take your hat?"

"You may indeed, my good man!" The voice was cheerful and more boisterous than Leo had expected for an associate of his father's. The Pelagan stepped inside and passed his hat and cane off to the butler.

He wore a suit, thank god, not the tight pants and billowing silk shirts that the upper-class Pelagan men were known for. His eyes were lined in kohl, though, another embarrassing Pelagan male fashion, and his hair was a mass of bright red curls, with a single seashell, a creamy white miniature conch, pinned on the left side. Leo was pleased he wasn't wearing one of the ridiculous headdresses that most elite Pelagans (both men and women) favored. Agnes was obsessed with Pelagan fashion, and he could see her eyeing the conch shell with interest.

"Good evening!" he said to the room at large. "What a delightful house!"

Everything he said seemed to end in an exclamation

point, and Leo couldn't tell whether the man was being sincere.

"I am Ezra Kiernan," he said with a flourishing bow that had Marianne and Elizabeth giggling behind their hands. "And where might I find Mr. Xavier McLellan?"

"You may find him here." The voice that spoke was deep and grave, imbued with unmistakable power.

And with that, Xavier McLellan stepped into the room.

8

AGNES

Agnes *hated* formal dinners.

She hated social events of any sort, especially when her father and brother were involved. If she could have her dinner sent up to her lab and eat among the frogs and rabbits and rats, she'd do it gladly. They were better company than most of the men in Old Port City, and smarter too.

She would have given anything to have been born in Pelago. She hated Old Port, with its stuffy ways and rules. She hated the starched dresses and tight corsets, the way she was expected to be silent and pretty when she wasn't good at being either, the fact that every second brought her closer to the one thing she hated most about being a woman in Kaolin: soon she would have to marry.

As if in response to that thought, her eyes flicked to Marianne's cleavage. Agnes had tried not to stare when the girl had been introduced, but she couldn't stop herself from imagining tracing a finger over the lush curve of skin, how warm and soft it would feel. . . .

But her father was in the room now, and she pushed the image away quickly. Those thoughts were dangerous. Lethal. Not even Xavier's money or fame or reputation would be able to save her if it came out that she was *that* sort of girl. Knowing her father, he would probably be the one leading the charge against her.

"Ah, my dear Xavier, we meet at last," Mr. Kiernan said exuberantly, making another big bow. "After so many months of correspondence, it is a pleasure to be face-to-face."

It was hard to tell what Xavier thought of this flamboyant Pelagan man—though Agnes had some guesses—because her father was an expert at hiding his emotions. She had learned to read him a bit after eighteen years of study, but not enough to say that she understood him. Their main commonality seemed to be looks. Sometimes she studied her hair before bed, searching for any hint of her mother's red in it. She'd even put a few strands under her microscope once, but no, it was brown brown brown.

Her father smiled and held out his hand. "I do hope your trip wasn't too taxing."

"Not at all," Mr. Kiernan said, grasping Xavier's hand in both of his. "But it is a relief to have such a long journey at last be at an end."

"I'm certain it is." There was a surety in her father's

tone that made Agnes feel like she was missing something. "May I offer you a refreshment?"

As if summoned by magic, Swansea appeared with a tray of champagne for the men, as the women had already been served. Agnes gripped her flute, thinking it might be the only thing to help her through this night. Then she could go back to her lab and be herself, and wait, without much hope, for a letter that could change her life.

Agnes had a secret: she had applied to the University of Ithilia's Academy of Sciences, Pelago's most prestigious school. With Eneas's help, she had procured an application, filled it out meticulously, and sent it off to be considered. It was the bravest thing she'd ever done, but she had mailed it two months ago and received no word yet. Eneas had set up a box at the post office in Olive Town, the Pelagan district of Old Port, so no letter would arrive at the house—Agnes would be in more trouble than she cared to consider if her father found out. But the truth was, she probably hadn't been accepted. And even if she was, how was she supposed to get there, or find the money to pay for tuition? It was nearly impossible for a woman to do anything without a man's consent in Kaolin. She would need her father's permission to take out money from the bank, or book a ticket on a ship.

But she couldn't relinquish her dreams, not yet, not when she had at least a modicum of freedom left to her. Once she was married, even that small flame of hope would be extinguished.

"Now let me present to you my son, Leo," Xavier said.

Leo's smile was so ingratiating, Agnes thought she might vomit.

"It is a pleasure to meet you, sir," he said.

"Oh my," Mr. Kiernan gasped. "You look exactly like her."

This observation never ceased to rankle Agnes *or* Leo, though for different reasons, but tonight he smiled and said, "Yes, sir, so I've been told."

He must be up to something, to take the comment so easily—and he was wearing a tie that matched his eyes, a feature he never played up. But Agnes had no interest in her brother's schemes at the moment.

"You knew my mother?" she asked Kiernan.

He cleared his throat. "Not personally, no."

"But you know what she looked like?"

Kiernan seemed to regret the path this conversation was going down, and Agnes knew she was walking a fine line, but she could not stop herself.

"Everyone in Pelago knows the Byrne family. Their features are striking," he said, gesturing to Leo as if to prove his point.

"Do you know my grandmother?" As soon as the words were out, Agnes knew she had gone too far.

The look Xavier gave her would have withered even the strongest of trees. Agnes felt herself shrink, and her face grew hot. Their mother's family, the Byrne family, was off-limits. No one was allowed to bring them up. Not even Eneas would talk about them, and he had worked for them his whole life before moving here from Pelago with her mother.

Agnes had sent letters to her grandmother, Ambrosine Byrne, every year, hoping for a response and never receiving one. To be honest, Agnes was not convinced the letters had actually been mailed at all. She had trusted Swansea to post them when she was younger, which had been foolish, and then, when she got older, went directly to the post office herself. But she suspected her father had a man in his pocket there. Eneas had flat-out refused when she'd asked him for help. She got the sense he was frightened of her grandmother, though he never said anything about her except that she was a "formidable and impressive woman."

"We do not discuss the Byrne family in this house," Xavier said, and Mr. Kiernan seemed all too eager to change the subject.

"You must be the daughter? Agnes, is that correct?"

"She is," Xavier said.

Agnes made an awkward curtsy—she had never learned to do it right—and cursed herself internally. She should have asked Mr. Kiernan in private, where he might have been more forthcoming.

"And may I present Miss Elizabeth Conway of Old Port and her companion Miss Marianne Ellis, from Lady's Point," Xavier said. "Miss Ellis is visiting for the month."

Marianne was eyeing Mr. Kiernan with great interest. Agnes didn't see anything particularly attractive about the man, though she wasn't the best judge. She liked the kohl around his eyes, though. And the seashell in his hair.

Brief pleasantries were exchanged, champagne was toasted, and then Swansea announced that dinner was served.

"Nice tie," Agnes muttered to her brother as she took her seat beside him. "Are you trying to be Pelagan now?"

Xavier and Mr. Kiernan sat at the ends of the large mahogany table. Elizabeth and Marianne were across from the twins.

"Nice dress," Leo shot back under his breath. "Are you trying to be an eighty-year-old widow?"

A cold vegetable soup was served first, and Mr. Kiernan happily commented on just about everything in the room.

"Delicious! I adore zucchini."

"What magnificent candlesticks!"

"My dear Xavier, this is an absolutely beautiful spoon."

"Aren't these napkins a delight!"

Agnes wondered how he didn't pass out at the table from expending so much positive energy.

"How do you find Old Port City, Mr. Kiernan?" Elizabeth asked, taking a dainty spoonful of soup. Elizabeth Conway was one of those girls Agnes wanted to hate but could never quite bring herself to. She was wealthy and beautiful and popular, but she had always been kind to Agnes. Most of the daughters of Old Port society found Agnes strange and unpleasant, something she often encouraged, since she didn't particularly enjoy their company. But still, it was nice not to be treated like an absolute freak all the time.

She wondered for a brief moment if her father knew Elizabeth was kind to Agnes, if that was why he'd invited her in the first place.

"It is a joy to see," Kiernan replied. "The cars! The buildings! So much industry. And of course, the theater scene is unparalleled." He winked at Xavier.

"Do tell us about this secret project, won't you, Mr. McLellan?" Elizabeth pleaded.

"Yes, do!" Marianne chimed in.

"Why, whatever are you girls talking about?" Xavier said with feigned surprise.

"I have it on good authority that you have been up to something this whole summer since *Picando* closed," Elizabeth said.

"James Roth has been running his mouth to impress the ladies again, it would seem."

Elizabeth gave a sly grin. "Why, Mr. McLellan, I haven't the faintest idea what you mean."

Her father chuckled as Swansea and two footmen came in to clear their bowls and bring in the next dish. He dabbed at his mouth to ensure there was no trace of soup in his beard.

Xavier had a fantastic beard. Many Kaolin men wore theirs long and artfully braided or bushy and pruned into various shapes, but not Xavier. His was sleek and close-cropped but with the most magnificent patterns carved along his cheekbones and under his jawline, swirls and points crafted with the utmost precision. There were two large dips that rose to a point at the center of his lower lip, and he stroked that spot often, usually when buying time to come up with a response or when savoring a particular moment before speaking. This was certainly the latter instance.

"Swansea." Xavier spoke no louder than his usual tone,

but there was a clear undercurrent of command.

"Yes, sir?"

"Bring the portfolio in from my study."

"Right away, sir."

Once he was gone, Xavier leaned forward, pressing his hands together so that his fingertips formed a steeple. "Allow me to ask you ladies a question," he said with a mischievous smile. It was unnerving how charming he could be when he wished. "Have you enjoyed the McLellan productions you've seen?"

"Oh yes," Marianne gushed. "I saw *The Wayward Woman of Weltshire Street* last month, and it was to die for. And *The Lizard and the Frog* has been running in Lady's Point for quite some time now. That man with the flippers who plays the frog is just marvelous!"

Agnes clenched her jaw. That man was named Jeremy. He'd worked in one of Xavier's freak shows in Old Port until the audiences had gotten bored and Xavier moved the production to the west coast. He was shy, and kind, and he used to tell Agnes the funniest jokes when she was younger, before she understood that her father didn't want her talking to "the grotesques," as some of the staff had called them.

"So it would disappoint you to hear that I am currently working on my final show before leaving the theater scene for good?"

Elizabeth gasped, and Marianne cried, "No!" but Xavier's children simply stared at him, dumbfounded. His *final* show? Agnes took some comfort in the fact that this appeared to be news to Leo, too.

"But . . . *The Great Picando* made over fifty thousand krogers in its first week," Leo said, as if he'd just memorized the list of facts and figures.

"Fifty thousand is nothing to boast about, Leo," Xavier said, the hint of a chill in his voice. "*Picando* did not have the run I expected it to. There are far too many anti-Talman plays glutting the theaters of Old Port. No, it is time for a change in direction."

Swansea glided in at that moment and handed Xavier a leather portfolio.

"I saw the old advertisements for this *Picando* at the Seaport when I arrived," Kiernan said. "I am sorry to have missed it."

Agnes wondered how a Pelagan would feel about a play that essentially called his entire religion heretical and amoral. And she was further confused when the main course was served, a classic Pelagan dish from the main island of Cairan—grilled tuna over a bed of sharp greens, drizzled with garlic and olive oil. Agnes couldn't remember the last time they'd eaten fish in this house—her father preferred red meat.

Kiernan looked delighted by the food and picked up his fork before adding, "Though perhaps I should finish my conversion to Solitism first."

"You're converting?" Agnes asked, surprised. Not that there weren't Pelagan converts in Kaolin, but they were rare.

"Indeed I am," Kiernan said. "It seemed only fitting to adopt the religion of my new home."

"Well done to you, sir," Leo said, raising his glass of champagne and taking a long drink.

"How wonderful," Elizabeth added.

"Do you plan to live here long?" Agnes asked.

"For the rest of my life, as long as that may be."

"So you'll never return to Pelago?"

"No," he said to her firmly. "I will not."

"And in the meantime, we will be making great strides together," Xavier interrupted. Kiernan cast him a nervous glance. "Do not fear, Ezra, I will not reveal all our secrets tonight." He ran his fingers down the length of the portfolio and studied the two girls sitting opposite Agnes. "Now, if I share this with you, will you ladies promise to keep it a secret?"

Marianne and Elizabeth nodded so eagerly, Agnes knew they would be bursting at the seams to tell anyone and everyone they could as soon as they left the brownstone.

And suddenly she realized why her father had invited these two girls, girls who were high-society gossips and moved in all the right circles.

He *wanted* them to blab. It was genius, really—free advertising from the perfect sources. Kaolin might be a more conservative country than Pelago, but it didn't matter where you lived: beautiful women sold tickets. Add into the mix that this would be the final McLellan production . . . well, Old Port would go nuts over that news alone. And it would probably spike ticket sales for Xavier's other shows in cities across Kaolin.

Agnes felt the heat of embarrassment on the back of her neck. Of course her father hadn't wanted Elizabeth here because she was kind to Agnes. What a stupid thing to think. The only nice thing her father had ever done for his daughter was build her the lab in her walk-in closet. That should be enough.

Somehow it wasn't, though.

Then Xavier opened the portfolio and held up a photograph, and Agnes forgot about gossiping rich girls, forgot about the fact that her father always, *always* let her down, because she was staring at something that couldn't be real.

"It's . . ." Elizabeth was frowning.

"A tree," Leo finished, looking just as confused.

Kiernan grew serious for the first time since dinner had started. "It is not just any tree, my young friends. It—"

"It has a *face*," Agnes said. How could they not see it? The photo was in black and white, the tree small and willowy with pale bark and dark leaves. And about halfway down the trunk were three eyes that formed a triangle and a slash of a mouth underneath.

"Well spotted, Miss McLellan! What sharp powers of observation you have," Kiernan said, impressed. Xavier's face was unreadable; Leo took another drink, looking disgruntled.

"Why, what *is* it?" Elizabeth asked.

"It is called an Arboreal," Xavier explained.

"They are an old myth in my country," Kiernan said. "Though clearly a myth no longer. Your father and I worked diligently to discover this fellow's location, and my associates brought him over from Pelago two months ago."

"What does it do?" Marianne asked.

Xavier smiled and shook his head. "Now that I will not reveal. Not yet." He put down the photo of the Arboreal and picked up another. This photograph was dark and murky—Agnes could only make out two bulging orbs that looked like . . .

"Eyes!" Marianne shrieked. "Those are eyes, aren't they?"

"They are indeed," said Kiernan. Leo was looking more and more unhappy, and he drained the last of his champagne. Agnes assumed he was disappointed the conversation was not revolving around him. "This is a mertag, a sea creature that travels the currents around the Pelagan islands. We caught this one just off the coast of—"

"He was a slippery little bugger," Xavier said, interrupting. "Very hard to catch."

"And I assume you won't tell us what he does either?" Elizabeth asked.

Xavier winked. "Smart girl."

Leo shifted in his seat as a footman came over to refill his glass, and Agnes wondered if he was thinking what she was—these photographs should have been shown at a private family dinner. It felt as if Marianne and Elizabeth were stealing her and Leo's lines.

"And these creatures will feature in the new show?"

"They will," Xavier confirmed. "They will do that and more." He gave Kiernan a significant look. "But we are still searching. We have heard of sprites that live in the grasses of the Knottle Plains. There will be an expedition shortly to see if they can be found."

Agnes was surprised to see the color drain from Kiernan's face, and his hand curled tightly around his glass.

"What do they look like?" Marianne asked.

"Now, now," Kiernan said before Xavier could respond.

"We don't want to reveal too much."

A look passed between them that Agnes did not understand. But then her father's face relaxed.

"Too true, my friend, too true. Ladies, suffice it to say that this show will be unlike anything seen in Kaolin *or* Pelago before. And it will be for one night only—one night of magic and mystery that I promise you will not want to miss."

"Father," Leo burst out, the champagne giving his voice a passionate ring. "I wish to go on this mission. I will help find these sprites and bring them back to you, I swear it. Give me this opportunity and I promise I will not let you down."

Xavier McLellan's impressive eyebrows rose about an inch up his forehead. Agnes felt that Leo's fate was balanced precariously as if on the edge of a knife. He whined about wanting to take over the business all the time, but offering to actively search for some creatures in the Knottle Plains was new for him. Agnes couldn't decide whether she was annoyed or impressed.

Everyone at the table was watching Xavier and Leo— even Marianne seemed to understand that something important was happening.

"Very well," Xavier finally said, giving his son a curt nod and holding out his glass for Swansea to refill. Then he smirked. "Perhaps you've got more of me than your mother in you after all."

It was like a punch in Agnes's gut. She was far better suited than Leo to join this expedition to the Knottle Plains. She had knowledge of medicine, anatomy, science. She could study the plant life, or search for footprints, or . . . anything. She was smart and capable, more than her stupid brother with his sycophantic smile.

Elizabeth and Marianne seemed to think Leo's outburst quite bold, and they gushed excitedly about the upcoming production while Kiernan and Xavier indulged them with smiles. And Agnes kept silent, staring at the cut of tuna on her plate and fuming.

9

LEO

Dinner hadn't gone quite the way he'd hoped, Leo had to admit.

He sat in an armchair in the drawing room, sipping an espresso and straining to hear any conversation that might make it through the door of his father's study. Xavier and Kiernan had been holed up in there for nearly an hour now, since dinner ended and Marianne and Elizabeth had said their good nights. Agnes had long gone off to bed, but Leo stayed up, hoping to catch a private moment with his father.

He couldn't believe Xavier had decided to stop financing new productions without telling his family first. And what were all those creatures about, that mertag and the tree? Why was the show only for one night, and why hadn't

Xavier explained this "new direction," whatever it was? Leo had been caught completely off guard. And he hadn't been able to sneak in a sliver of the business knowledge he'd acquired in the afternoon. The two girls had captured most of his father's attention, and Kiernan's too. Leo didn't understand why his father had gotten so involved with the man. Obviously he had been useful in finding those weird Pelagan creatures, but why bring him to Kaolin?

Leo would just have to find these sprites himself and prove to his father that he was worthy of being included, too.

Perhaps you've got more of me than your mother in you after all.

The words made Leo feel proud and itchy at the same time. He watched the pendulum on the grandfather clock swing back and forth and wondered how much longer the two men would be.

I'll show him, he thought. *I'm his son. A McLellan, through and through.*

There was no trace of their mother in this house, no picture or token, nothing except Eneas. Eneas, who never stopped telling Leo how much he looked like her, no matter how many times Leo asked him not to.

Xavier had never loved their mother, and Leo's face must have been a daily reminder of the fact that he had been forced to go against everything he believed in, to marry a heretic, because he needed the money. But he didn't need Pelagan money anymore.

Or maybe he did. Leo remembered the declining figures he'd seen for *The Great Picando*, and how his father had said the play's run had been cut short. Maybe the business was in trouble. Was that why he was branching out into something new? Sure, there had been more theater companies popping up lately, as Xavier had noted, but none of them had the prestige and panache of the McLellan empire. Or was Leo just too biased to see the competition?

He put his espresso down and began to pace the room. Tomorrow he would be on his way to the Knottle Plains. He hadn't realized how unsure he'd been that Xavier would even let him go on this expedition until he was halfway through asking. The humiliation of his father's refusal would have been severe. Elizabeth would have told her brother, and Robert would have tried to make Leo feel better in all the ways that actually made everything worse. Robert was a great friend, but he was a fool sometimes. He assumed all fathers were proud of their sons. He assumed everyone had mothers who loved them and sisters who weren't complete and utter embarrassments.

Leo couldn't do much about the mother or the sister, but he could damn sure make his father proud. And starting tomorrow, that was exactly what he was planning to do.

The study door opened and the sound of voices made Leo jump.

". . . not likely to be able to produce any again," Kiernan was saying.

"That is not what you told me when we had it shipped here," Xavier replied sharply. "You said that tree could make hundreds of them."

"I told you we were entering uncharted territory. Factors are different here—climate, soil, water quality . . ."

"I am not interested in a geology lesson."

"I'm merely saying we should have kept the sprites in Pelago if you are so sure they can find the island."

"I am aware of what we *should* have done," Xavier said, and his words were threaded with warning. "But you yourself said it would be far too dangerous to leave anything behind that could be traced back to you."

"To *us*," Kiernan said.

Leo had no idea what was going on. He'd thought the sprites were from Kaolin. And what was this island Kiernan was talking about? Pelago had hundreds of islands, but the way Kiernan said it, Leo did not think he meant Thaetus or Cairin or any of the major ones.

Something about the tone of this conversation made Leo hesitate to reveal himself. He had been hoping the men would let him in on whatever it was they were planning, now that he was part of the expedition and all. But he did not want to interrupt his father during an argument. In fact, he was pretty sure his father would be livid if he knew Leo was overhearing this. He wondered if he had time to make it upstairs when the voices came closer, the men walking down the hall toward the front door.

"It is as I said before: if you truly wanted to understand these creatures, you should have come to Pelago yourself."

"I will never set foot in that goddamned country again for as long as I live and you know it, Ezra. Don't act the fool, it doesn't suit you."

Leo was less stunned by the vulgarity and more by this revelation. As far as he was aware, Xavier had never been to Pelago in the first place. So how could he set foot in it *again*?

"We do not have limitless resources, Xavier."

"Don't we?" There was a cold silence. "Do not forget, Ezra. I know who you are and I know what you've done. I can protect you here. Do not test me, though, or you will be back on a ship to Pelago in the morning. And that bitch will not be as forgiving as I am."

"Yes, yes, I know." The Pelagan sounded frightened. "You should not have told them the sprites lived in the Knottle Plains," he said after a moment.

"That's where they would go, you said. Grasslands."

"Yes, but that isn't where they are from!"

"I honestly don't see how it makes a difference."

"Credit should be given where credit is due. The creatures are Pelagan."

"Don't tell me you have developed a sudden *pride* in your heritage?" Xavier sneered, and Leo felt there was an insult in the words that he did not quite understand. "Besides, the creatures are dead, if what you have told me about them is correct."

"Then why search for them at all?"

Leo pressed himself against a bookshelf, his heart pounding.

"Because I do not give up until I have exhausted all options," Xavier replied. "If there is the slightest chance of reclaiming them, we have to try. Unless you have another idea, or a magic compass or map that will tell us where the island is."

Kiernan muttered something too low for Leo to hear. But when Xavier laughed, it felt like an ice cube had slipped into Leo's stomach—it was a laugh that held all the darkness of a threat and not a shred of good humor.

"Did you think I was joking when I told you not to mention that name, Ezra? Did you think I was putting on a show for the sake of my children? You're lucky I got you out of Pelago when I did. Ambrosine Byrne could snuff out this operation before you can say 'mertag.' I'll not dangle my family as bait."

That didn't make sense at all—Xavier had had no contact with the Byrne family, much less Leo's own grandmother, since his mother had died. But he was talking about her as if he knew her.

Kiernan's reply was muffled, but Leo caught the words, "could be useful, is all."

"I'm fully aware of what he looks like, thank you very much. But it would be Agnes she'd want, and I will never let that happen," Xavier said with a tone that declared the matter finished. "Forget the sprites. Branson will find them or he won't, and that will be the end of it. What we really need is another Arboreal, a bigger one, a stronger one. The droughts and heat waves are getting worse. The timing is ripe for the show to get on the road, so to speak."

"We are trying but—"

"Try harder. They're *your* sacred trees. Shouldn't they be easy to find?"

"Not all naifa trees are Arboreals, Xavier. And we *cannot* go back to Culinnon."

Leo knew from his father's plays that naifa trees were sacred in Talmanism, and they only grew in Pelago. He had no idea what Culinnon was—another island, perhaps? Leo found himself wishing he had just gone up to bed when his sister had.

"Besides," Kiernan continued, "many Pelagans will not accept the job we are offering, no matter what price."

"Use my men then. They aren't squeamish about some goddamn trees."

"You really are the coldhearted bastard they say, aren't you?"

"Yes," Xavier said. "I am."

Leo kept stone-still as he heard the front door open.

"The island, Ezra. That's all that matters."

Kiernan sighed. "Xavier," he said, "you are quite, quite sure this was not just some story she told you? To impress or—"

"It was not a story. It is real." His father's voice was brittle as new frost. "And she never sought to impress me."

The silence that followed lasted so long, Leo wondered if they had simply parted ways without saying good night.

"We will speak again tomorrow," Kiernan said, and Leo jumped. Once the Pelagan was gone, his father called for Swansea.

"Yes, sir?"

"Have that man followed," Xavier said. "I want to know his every movement. Get Roth on it. He knows enough seedy characters and he damn well owes me."

Roth? Leo thought. *James Roth?*

"I take it you don't trust this Pelagan then, sir?" Swansea said.

"I don't trust anyone, Swansea." There was a pause. "Why are the lights in the drawing room on?"

"I'm not sure, sir. I was in the kitchen, I thought Janderson—"

Leo was intimately familiar with the sound of someone being silenced by his father. Quick as a flash, he sank into the nearest armchair and closed his eyes, his head lolling to one side to feign sleep. He heard footsteps approach and tried to keep his breathing steady. If his father knew he had been listening in on private conversations . . .

"Leo."

He opened his eyes and rubbed them for effect.

"Oh, sorry, Father. I must have dozed off."

"Mm." Xavier frowned. "Get to bed. You have a big day ahead of you."

"Yes, of course." Leo got up and stretched. "Good night."

But Xavier was already walking toward his study. Swansea disappeared after him and Leo was left alone, his heart pounding, wondering what exactly his father was up to.

10

AGNES

AGNES SAT IN HER LAB, A CANDLE BURNING DOWN ALMOST
to the nub as she scribbled in her journal, trying to put down
on paper as much as she could remember about the Arboreal and the mertag and her guesses as to what her father
was planning to do with them.

There was no place in Old Port where Agnes felt more
comfortable than in her lab. She had painted the walls a
light green, but they were spattered with specks of blood,
smeared guts, scorch marks, and various scratchings from
when her notepad had been too far away. She didn't have
as much equipment as she'd like—just a lone microscope, a
Bunsen burner, a few beakers in various shapes and sizes,

some graduated cylinders, and a set of scalpels. She had bottles of chemicals too: hydrochloric acid, ethanol, xylene, paraffin . . . she'd been working up the courage to see if her father would allow her some potassium hydroxide.

She put the pencil down and cracked her knuckles. This one-night-only endeavor looked to be the splashiest of Xavier's productions, as well as his last. She didn't care a whit for her father's plays, and she would be happy to see less anti-Talman shows being performed in Old Port. Agnes was not particularly religious, but it seemed to her that everyone in the world was required to ascribe to *something*, and as far as she could tell, science didn't count. Talmanism didn't seem as oppressive as Solitism; certainly not where women were concerned. But something about this new project left her with a cold feeling of dread that she couldn't quite put her finger on—as if her father was moving past simple propaganda and on to something more dark and dangerous.

The candle sputtered and went out, dousing the lab in darkness. Agnes stood and stretched, then left her lab, locked it, and hid the key in its usual spot in an old jewelry box. She peered out her bedroom window; Creekwater Row was dimly lit with gas lamps and lined with brownstones as large and handsome as the one she lived in. All were silent and dark. The night air was thick with humidity.

Just as she was turning back, she heard a noise, like a hoot owl. It hooted twice, paused, then hooted again. Agnes went still.

"Eneas?" she called softly. The chauffeur stepped out from behind the motorcar, covered for the night in the driveway, and waved up at her. There was an envelope in his hand. Her knees turned to jelly. She pointed down toward the kitchen door and Eneas nodded and disappeared.

Agnes wanted to take the stairs two at a time, but she couldn't risk waking anyone up, especially not Leo or her father. She froze when she saw the light was still on in his study, the door closed. Ever so cautiously, she crept to the kitchen, skirted the long table that dominated the room, copper pots and pans hanging from the ceiling, and eased the service door open. Eneas was bouncing on the balls of his feet, a wide grin spread across his face. Agnes put a finger to her lips and pointed in the direction of her father's study. He nodded and handed her the envelope. She took it with trembling hands. The postmark was from Pelago.

She stared at her name, *Miss Agnes McLellan* written out in perfect curling script. And the return address: University of Ithilia. Academy of Sciences. The envelope was thick and cream-colored and made a satisfying rip as she opened it. The paper that fell out shook in her trembling grasp, and she read it in the faint light from the kitchen.

> *Dear Miss McLellan,*
>
> *Thank you for your application to the University of Ithilia's Academy of Sciences. I am pleased to inform you that your application has been accepted and you have successfully passed the first round of admissions. We invite you to submit a secondary essay for consideration, followed by an interview with the academy Masters, before the decision to officially*

offer you a place at the university is made. Please
return your essay to us by the twelfth of September.
Interviews will be scheduled the first week of October.
We look forward to hearing from you.
    All the best,
    Magdalena Lokis
    Dean of Admissions
    University of Ithilia

"I passed," she said breathlessly. She looked up at Eneas, her eyes brimming with tears. "I passed the first round of admissions!"

A bird screeched and took flight from a nearby dog-wood, and Eneas wrapped her up in a tight hug.

"Your mother would be so proud," he whispered. "Now get upstairs before your father sees you!"

Agnes nodded and whirled around, not daring to breathe until she was back in her room. She collapsed onto her bed and read the letter several times before it really began to sink in that she had been *accepted*. Well, there were still a few more hoops to jump through, but that was better than no hoops at all. The essay shouldn't be a problem, but her heart sank at the thought of an in-person interview. How was she ever going to get to Pelago by the first week in October?

There was a second sheet of paper containing instructions for the essay. It was only one sentence, which read, *Please describe in detail the bravest thing you have ever done in the name of science.*

The first thing that came to mind was the day she had asked her father to build the lab for her, but that didn't seem very brave if you didn't know Xavier McLellan. And it wasn't any sort of scientific discovery but more of a personal triumph. All her experiments felt silly and childish, not anything she would classify as brave.

She sat on the edge of her bed and chewed at her thumbnail. She had to stand out. She had to think of something impressive, something unique. . . .

It hit her in a flash. The sprites. What could be bolder than sneaking onto an expedition in the name of science? And for a magical creature, no less? She could discover a new species. That should get their attention. She could steal one away back to her lab to study it.

She'd have to be careful. If she was caught . . . well, she didn't want to dwell on that thought. But Agnes knew in her heart that this was the thing that would set her apart. She clutched the letter and felt her world turning, shifting, moving closer to what she so desperately wanted it to be.

She slid off the bed and slipped her hand under the mattress, feeling around for the slit she'd cut into its underside, her fingers digging into it until they touched the sharp edge of her most sacred and illicit possession.

Ever since she could remember, Agnes had wondered why there were no pictures of their mother in the house. Until one day, when she was eleven and playing at being the great Pelagan explorer Cadhla Hope, she discovered a whole box of them in the attic. There were letters, and pictures, and even a ring. But Swansea had found her—she'd only just slipped the photograph into a pocket she'd sewn on her skirt before she was yanked away and sent to her room.

When she'd snuck back to the attic the next night, the box was gone.

She pulled the picture out, leaning back against her bed. She didn't know where it had been taken—somewhere in Kaolin, she assumed, but the countryside, not Old Port.

Her mother, Alethea Byrne, was standing with a bicycle in front of a small stone cottage with an arched door. The roof was thatched, and there was ivy growing up one side. She wore a thick sweater, pantaloons, and high-laced boots, one foot put up jauntily on a bike pedal, one hand on her hip. Her face was alight with joy. The camera had caught her mid-laugh, and the wind was playing with her curls—red, Agnes knew, though they were dark gray in the photo. She looked vibrant and happy and carefree. She looked alive.

On the back of the photograph, written in a looping scrawl, were the words:

Taken by X, March 12. Runcible Cottage, the Edge of the World.

Agnes traced her mother's handwriting with a finger. She had tried to copy the style to no avail. *Taken by X, March 12.* Her father had taken this photograph. Of his wife laughing. With a bicycle. Wearing *pants*.

She flipped it over and stared at her mother's face. "I've been accepted to the Academy of Sciences," she said. "Well, almost accepted—I passed the first round of admissions. Eneas said you would be proud. Would you, Mother? Would you be happy for me?"

Her mother laughed and laughed but never answered.

Finally, Agnes shook herself and returned the photograph to its hiding spot. She tucked the letter inside a book on her nightstand. Then she got into bed, her brain whirring, planning and plotting for what tomorrow would bring.

11

LEO

LEO WAS EVEN HOTTER IN THE BACK SEAT OF THIS CRAPPY
car than he'd been in the library in Old Port.

If the temperature rose any higher, his skin would melt
off. He could already feel it on his hands and face, a creeping red that itched and burned when he scratched it.

There were no windows on the car, and only a canvas
roof, so sometimes the sun would scorch him for hours and
other times he'd be blissfully in the shade. His driving gog-
gles were coated in dust. In fact, everything seemed to be
covered in a fine layer of dirt—his brand-new boots, his
shirt, his hair. Even his mouth felt grainy.

They had left at the crack of dawn and hadn't stopped
driving since. The man at the helm of this expedition was

a burly beast named Branson, and he had three men under him, all dour fellows. One had a constant lump in his lower lip where he kept his chewing tobacco. Leo's back seat companion was a consummate nose picker. Leo didn't know anything about the man driving the supply truck behind them.

"How much farther?" he asked. He'd been asking the same question every hour for the past five hours. He couldn't help himself. Why hadn't they taken the railroad? It had a café car and large, comfortable seats, and there were plenty of stops in the Knottle Plains. And Leo always rode first class—one of the perks of being best friends with the future head of Conway Rail. But the more they had driven, the more he realized that they weren't going to Alacomb or Oakbend or any of the cities in the more rural areas. They were driving right into the heart of the plains themselves, where there was nothing but grass and sky and more grass and more sky. But not nice, thick, green grass, like the fairways at the Old Port Country Club. This grass was tough and yellow, like straw. They'd passed streams and ponds that had all dried up, or had a trickle of sludge running through them at most. Many of the farmhouses looked abandoned. It was quite a depressing sight.

Branson grunted from the driving seat. That was the only answer Leo had gotten since the last time he'd asked.

Agnes would probably love it if she were here. She'd find a million weird insects to put in jars and dissect once she got home. Leo's stomach turned just thinking about what might be lurking in the high grasses.

Several beads of sweat trickled down his lower back,

pooling unpleasantly under his backside. He was aching for a shower. As it turned out, the Knottle Plains were boring. Maybe this was why his father hadn't gone on the actual expeditions himself. He delegated it to ruffians like Branson. Did that make Leo a ruffian in his father's eyes? No. He refused to believe that.

Perhaps you've got more of me than your mother in you after all.

Leo couldn't shake the conversation he'd overheard between his father and Kiernan. The Pelagan man seemed to think the sprites were dead. If that was true, then why even bother with this search in the first place? And what did he want another Arboreal for? And what was that island he kept mentioning? There were too many questions, and Leo didn't know if he'd ever get any answers.

What felt like hours later, just as the sun was beginning to kiss the horizon and the sky lit up in searing pinks and fiery oranges that might have been pleasant to look at if Leo's ass didn't hurt so much, Branson turned off the car engine. "All right, boys," he said. "Everybody out."

The relief Leo felt at standing upright was indescribable. He moaned with pleasure as his muscles unwound, raising his arms above his head and giving his back a good long stretch. Branson opened up a map and spread it out on the hood. Chewing Tobacco and Nose Picker gathered around him. Leo took a swig of lukewarm water from his canteen, wishing he could call on Swansea to bring him an iced tea.

The man in the supply truck came out to join them. He was a thin, nervous-looking fellow with a twitchy mustache. He lit a cigarette and glanced back at the truck as if he were frightened it might drive away on its own.

"Here," Branson said, shoving a small, crumpled piece of paper into Nose Picker's hand. "This is what them sprites look like. They light up at sunset, so this is the best time to find them."

"Don't much like looking for these bastard Pelagan creatures," Nose Picker complained as he studied the drawing. "They shouldn't even be in our country anyway."

"They're gonna make the boss money and that makes us money," Branson said. "So shut your mouth and do your job."

Nose Picker handed the paper to Leo. He stared at a crude drawing of a tiny creature who looked like . . . a blade of grass. Grass with tiny arms and legs and some kind of weird crown on its head. Leo looked up at the endless prairie stretching out in all directions.

This was going to be impossible. He didn't know the first thing about how to find a sprite. He hadn't known sprites were things to find until about twenty-four hours ago.

"Someone must stay and look after the car," he said. "Right? And these sprites may be close by. Why don't I, uh, search this area? And I will keep an eye on our belongings as well. Does that sound amenable to you gentlemen?"

Chewing Tobacco spit a long stream of disgusting reddish brown at his feet and Branson smirked.

"Good idea," he said. Leo had the feeling he was being mocked. "We'll see you back here around calamity's hour."

Leo had no idea what calamity's hour was, but he couldn't very well let these men know that.

"Excellent," he said. "Calamity's hour. And best of luck to you lads. We better get looking while there's still some light."

"Too true," Branson said. "We'll just grab a few things and be on our way."

Leo spent just enough time kicking at tufts of grass and making a big show of looking for sprites until Branson and his crew faded to small dark specks in the distance. Then he threw himself down in the shadow of the car and promptly fell asleep.

He awoke in darkness, sudden and alert, aware of some figure creeping around nearby.

"Who's there?" he called, his speech slightly slurred. His tongue was clumsy in his dry mouth. Blades of grass were poking at him through his pants.

The figure froze, and then a familiar voice muttered, "Crap."

"Agnes?" Leo gasped. He was feeling completely out of sorts. The expedition, the sprites, it was all coming back to him in a rush.

"Where is Branson?" he demanded. The car and truck were still here, but there was no sign of the men. "They said calamity's . . ." His stomach gave a loud growl. "Where— what are *you* doing here?"

"I hid in the supply truck and bribed the driver," Agnes said unapologetically. Her hair was tucked up under a newsboy cap, and she wore boys' clothes. "Calamity's hour is midnight, by the way. It's long past."

"You aren't supposed to be here," Leo said, scrambling

to his feet. "Father is going to kill you for this."

"He won't if you don't tell him I was here."

He smirked. "Nice try. I don't tell him and he finds out anyway and then I'm dead, too. Don't worry, I'm sure he'll just marry you off to some low-class Old Port boy and wash his hands of you."

He knew that would touch a nerve—she seemed to deflate, turning away from him and gazing up at the sky. "There are so many stars here. It's beautiful."

Leo had no interest in stars or their numbers at the moment. But Agnes kept staring at them as she murmured, "I had to try."

"Try what?" he asked. "Try melting in the back of a truck for an entire day?"

She glared at him. "You wouldn't understand." She put her hands on her hips and surveyed the area around them. "I don't think the sprites are here. And even if they are, the plains are too big. But I honestly thought I would find one." She snorted, like she was disgusted with herself.

"Kiernan thinks they're all dead," Leo said.

"What? When did he say that?"

"Last night. I heard him say it to Father."

"Then why—" She stopped herself and shook her head, as if she'd answered her own question before finishing it.

Leo's stomach gave another growl. "Have you eaten?"

"They took the food," Agnes said dully.

"What? Why didn't you stop them?" The thought of no dinner was a terrifying one.

"Why didn't *you*?" she retorted. "You were supposed to go with them. And then I could have explored the plains on my own and no one would have been the wiser. But no, you have to be the sulky spoiled rich boy they think you are."

"But they're coming back, right?" Leo couldn't even muster up irritation at his sister right now in the face of going without dinner.

Agnes shrugged. "I doubt it. I bet that was why they took everything with them. To teach the boss's son a lesson. I wouldn't be surprised if Father told them to." She sighed and Leo shuddered. That truth hit a bit too close to home.

"But . . . but . . . what are we supposed to do, sleep out here? With no bed? And no meal?" He sat back down again and cradled his head in his hands. "This was a mistake," he mumbled. "I'm not . . . maybe you're right. Maybe this was what he wanted all along."

The pain was there, like it always was, waiting just offstage. *Not good enough,* it said to him. *Worthless. No matter what you do, no matter how hard you try, you'll never win his respect.* Leo tried to focus on the quiet, and the sharp scent of the grass, but the fact was he would have to go home at some point and face his father empty-handed. After a moment, he heard Agnes sit beside him.

"Here," she said. "I have a bag of peanuts we can share."

Leo accepted the peanuts gratefully. They were good, crunchy and salty, and gone far too soon. Agnes didn't seem to mind the lack of food, which made Leo's irritation spike again. Instead, she lay back and started naming the constellations.

And she wonders why she has no friends, he thought.

"The Fire Starter. The Lady of Justice. The Winged Horse. Aetheus's Harem—"

"That's not Aetheus's Harem," Leo said.

"Yes, it is," Agnes insisted.

"No, it isn't." Aetheus's Harem was the only constellation Leo knew because he had once seen a picture of the actual harem in a book when he was nine, and the women were all topless. The constellation was much less exciting than the picture, but still. It wasn't something he was ever going to forget.

"Leo, I think I know better than you."

"There are too many stars," he said. "Look, it's supposed to be that one, that one, that one. . . ." Leo pointed each of them out in turn. "But that star, that big bluish one, that's not part of the harem."

Agnes was silent for a moment, which Leo took to mean he was right.

"What *is* that star?" she said.

"I don't know, but it proves that that is *not*—"

"Oh, get over yourself for one second. Look. It's . . . it's getting bigger."

"Agnes, I really don't . . ." But his voice trailed off as he gazed at the bluish ball of light. She was right. It *was* getting bigger. And it was moving. When he first saw it, it was near the right side of the harem, but now it was definitely closer to the middle.

"Maybe it's a shooting star?" he said.

"Shooting stars leave a trail as they enter the atmosphere."

"Well, I don't know, what's your suggestion?"

Agnes didn't get a chance to answer because the star flared up, streaking across the sky. Leo was about to rub it in her face that he was right, it *was* a shooting star, when suddenly, something crashed into the ground nearby. The car was lifted up in the air before thudding down again, and Leo found himself toppling over onto his sister. A wave of dirt slammed into his face, making him cough and choke.

"What . . ." Agnes spluttered, pushing Leo up off her. "What was that?"

"I don't know," he said, a sudden determination setting in. "But we're going to find out."

PART THREE

The Knottle Plains

and

Old Port City, Kaolin

12

SERA

Sera was flying.

She'd felt frightened for only the first few seconds, when the City Above the Sky swirled in her vision as she tumbled through space. Its underside was a beauty—sloping sheets of sunglass that ended in long stalactites, hanging suspended like icicles with the tether nestled in among them.

So that's what it looks like, she thought.

Her fall followed the line of the tether, and it was even more beautiful up close, an iridescent, shimmering chain of gold and silver and blue links. Sometimes it sparkled like dewdrops in the moonlight. Other times, it glowed like a Cerulean's finger before a blood bond.

Slowly, the City grew smaller and fainter. Then it

disappeared. And she was flying among the stars.

Of course, she wasn't anywhere near close enough to touch one of them, but she sensed their presence as if they welcomed her to share their sky. Sometimes flying felt weightless. Other times, it felt like not moving at all. Sera marveled at how her lungs expanded and contracted, even as the air was so thin it didn't feel like air, really, and how her body had acclimated to the strange, new, cold environment. It was just like her green mother had said: her magic allowed her to withstand all sorts of conditions. But this was not how Sera would have chosen to experience the unique phenomenon of her people.

The planet came closer so gradually, she didn't realize it at first. The familiar shapes of Kaolin and Pelago did not seem to get any larger.

Until flying turned to falling.

All the peacefulness evaporated. Falling was terror. Falling was upside down and inside out. She hit the planet's atmosphere and her skin began to sizzle.

This is it, she thought. *My blood will spill, the tether will break, and Mother Sun will take me.*

In the atmosphere, the tether was fire. It was red and orange, a flickering candlelight. The blood oozing from her elbows began to flow faster, boiling on her skin, little blue bubbles popping. Sera felt herself weaken. The bracelets on her wrist were like tiny balls of flame, but the moonstone necklace was a cool circle against her chest. The heat grew more intense, and just when she was sure this must be it, the end of it all, everything stopped.

What's happening? she thought. Her body hung suspended in a pearly mist. The heat lessened. Her blood stopped flowing out of the cuts on her arms. The mist was soothing on her skin, like a balm. The High Priestess had not told her about this part. Was there something else she was meant to do? Surely dying should be enough. Perhaps the High Priestess had made this mist to help her, to calm her mind, but if anything it was making Sera more frightened. The tether was just outside its pearly border, and she felt this must be the moment she was meant to break it. She reached toward it, steeling herself, waiting to see if it would be hot or cold, if it would dissolve at her touch or snap clean in two. . . .

And somewhere in a place she did not want to give voice to, she wondered if it would hurt *very* much to die.

But just as she was about to touch it, the mist shifted—it swirled and spun, wrapping tight around her like a cocoon, and she was wrenched back, as if by a giant elastic, and then catapulted forward so fast that tears filled her eyes and everything became a white-gray-blue blur. She couldn't breathe. Deep down inside, she knew something was wrong. This was not what was supposed to be happening.

She hit a solid surface and dirt filled her throat and ears and eyes and nose. Her lungs ached to breathe, and when at last the dirt was all coughed up, she drank the air in heaving gulps. The mist, whatever it was, had vanished. She lay back, reveling in the feel of her chest moving up and down, of her limbs on something solid. The cuts on her elbows had been seared shut.

I'm alive, she thought.

Then she rolled over and threw up what little was in her stomach. Wiping her mouth with the back of her hand, Sera took stock of her surroundings. She was in a large, deep, earthen hole. The dirt was dry and crumbly, not like the thick, rich soil in the gardens of the City Above the Sky. Her robe was torn and filthy, but to her great delight, the three bracelets and Leela's star necklace were still intact.

"I'm alive!" she cried, letting out a wild laugh. She hadn't died. She was still here, still breathing. She gripped the pendant in one hand and raised her head.

Her heart dropped.

Through the opening of the hole, she could see the sky. It was black, like the sky she knew, but so far away. And the stars were mere pinpricks, tiny things no bigger than the stargems on her wrist. The loss of her home, her people, everything she knew, rose up with shocking force. Where among those stars were the Cerulean? They might have already detached from this planet, floating through space until they found a new home.

Sera gasped. She hadn't died, which meant she hadn't broken the tether, which meant . . . was the City Above the Sky still up there?

She stood and found that her body felt different—her arms and legs didn't have the lightness she was used to. Breathing wasn't as uncomfortable as it had been when she was falling, but it wasn't quite like breathing in the City either. The air around her was hot and sticky but the dirt was bone-dry.

What was that mist, and where had it gone? Why hadn't

she broken the tether like she was supposed to? Why could she not even get dying right?

"Oh, Mother Sun," Sera said, collapsing back to the ground and pressing her palms against her eyes. "I failed."

There were so many shades of awfulness, Sera did not know how to process them all. She had not wanted to die, but she had been meant to die, and now here she was, alive and alone, with no idea where she was or what to do. The only home she had ever known was miles and miles away. She felt sick at the thought of letting her City down. Surely they would have noticed the tether hadn't broken. Sera wished she could be back in her bed with the star mobile and her purple mother's embrace. She would gladly fall again—she'd get it right this time, if she could just have another chance—if it meant one more moment with her mothers and Leela.

She didn't know how long she sat, giving in to the overwhelming despair, before she heard voices approaching. Hopelessness melted away in the face of a new fear. There was no place to hide. What should she do?

"The wind blew the dirt *this* way," she heard a girl's voice say. "See, it left a trail." Another voice responded, but it was too low for Sera to hear. She waited, still as a statue.

When the heads popped up over the lip of the hole, Sera couldn't make out their features in the dark. They were black outlines against the sky. She shifted slightly, trying to see them better.

"There!" the girl said. "Something moved."

Sera cursed herself internally.

"Where? I can't see anything. Give me the flashlight."

The second girl had a deep voice, like Koreen's orange mother, who was very old. Except this girl didn't sound old at all.

Then another star lit up. This one was much brighter and closer than the others, right at the edge of the crater. It cast a thin cone of light over the sloping dirt until it reached Sera's feet. She quickly backed away from it.

The girls above stopped bickering.

"Did you see that?"

"There's something *down there*," the low-voiced girl said.

Sera didn't much like being called some*thing*.

"Of course there's something down there," the normal-sounding girl said. "Those looked like feet." Then, in a louder voice that was entirely unnecessary, she said, "We come in peace!"

That made Sera feel a bit better. She decided to risk speaking—maybe these girls could help her. She certainly had no idea where she was.

"Me too!" she called back. Something about her voice sounded wrong.

"Do you think it's a wounded animal?" the low voice said.

"What sort of animal sounds like that?" the girl replied.

"I'm not an animal," Sera said indignantly, without thinking. "I am a Cerulean!"

"I think it's getting angry," the low voice said.

"Shhh," the girl hissed, and then the cone of light swung up right into Sera's eyes.

"There it is!" the low voice shouted, as Sera scuttled

away from the strange starbeam. "It's moving, get it, get it!"

"Shut *up*, Leo," the other girl said. "You're scaring it."

Sera *was* scared. She didn't like that low-voiced girl, or the strange star, or the fact that she felt and sounded different. Maybe the girl had been lying when she said they came in peace. People on planets lied all the time, her green mother had said. Telling the truth wasn't important to them like it was to the Cerulean. That was how the Great Sadness had happened, lies and deceit, humans trying to steal Cerulean magic.

Sera's heart plummeted. Would these girls try to take her magic away? Oh, why had she spoken up at all in the first place? Why had she not run when she had the chance?

Well. She wasn't the best climber in the City Above the Sky for nothing. She grasped the crumbling earth, finding balance on the balls of her feet, judged the angle of the slope, and raced up it. The dirt disintegrated beneath her, but she was always one step ahead, until she shot upward and landed silently on solid ground.

It was lighter up here than in the hole. The moon was bright and easy to see by. The other two girls still seemed disoriented. They were peering over the lip of the crater, the starbeam swinging this way and that.

"I think it crawled out," the girl said.

"Ah!" the low voice cried. "Something touched me."

"Leo, that was me."

"Oh."

Sera didn't know what to do. All around her was empty space. No trees, no dwellings, no temples. Just . . . nothing. For a second, she was frozen with indecision.

Suddenly, there was a snapping sound, and Sera was hit in the face and fell to the ground. Whatever the thing was that hit her had surrounded her whole body, and the more she struggled with it, the tighter it held her. It almost felt like the twine her green mother used to tie tomato stalks to stakes, but it was thicker and rougher.

The starbeam drew closer and Sera shrank from it. She shouldn't have hesitated. She should have just started running.

"What are you doing?" the girl demanded.

Sera thought the girl was talking to her until the low-voiced girl replied, and the triumph in her voice sent a chill up Sera's spine.

"I caught it. It's *mine*. And I'm taking it back to Father."

13

AGNES

THE LOOKS ON BRANSON'S AND HIS CREW'S FACES WHEN they finally returned the next day to find Leo, Agnes, and the silver girl with blue hair had been priceless.

But then the whole situation devolved into a lot of chest thumping and arguing over who would present the "prize" to Father. Branson insisted that since they'd used *his* net launcher, he was partly responsible. Leo laughed and said he'd let Branson have 10 percent of the credit, since that was how much he'd contributed. It was nearly mid-afternoon by the time they were packed up and ready to head back to Old Port.

The girl was only an inch or two taller than Agnes, and slender—Leo carried her easily to the back of the truck.

Though it was cramped, Agnes stayed with her, refusing Branson's offer of sitting in the front car. She couldn't imagine how frightening this all must be for the poor thing.

"I'm sorry," she said over and over on their way back to the city.

The girl's skin was iridescent silver, more beautiful than any chain or watch fob or brooch, and her hair was a rich, vibrant blue that matched her eyes exactly. Cerulean blue, if Agnes wanted to be specific. Otherwise, she looked quite like any Kaolin girl. She wore a necklace with a pendant shaped like a star, but it wasn't the way Agnes would have drawn a star, with five even points—it was made of points in all shapes and sizes, some long and delicate, others short and stubby. In its center was a beautiful stone, similar to an opal but richer in color and vibrancy. Three jeweled bracelets hung from her right wrist, and her dress, torn and filthy but made of an impossibly soft material, had a detail around the hem, poorly sewn in a zigzag fashion in the same colors—purple, green, and orange.

The girl spoke in an unfamiliar language, her voice high and musical, but even though they couldn't understand each other, Agnes decided to talk to her all the same. It felt like the decent thing to do.

"You're in Kaolin," she said. "It's a pretty big country, and quite hot at the moment, as you may have noticed. I don't know what the weather is like where you're from, but here every year seems to get hotter and hotter." She bit her lip and cringed.

The weather, Agnes? she thought bitterly. *You have a*

potentially new species of human sitting in front of you and you're talking about the weather?

But the girl didn't seem to care. She kept pushing at the net.

"I'm sorry," Agnes said for the millionth time. "I would take that off you, but I'm in quite enough trouble as it is." *Or I will be, once I get home.* "My father is sort of . . . well, he's a difficult man, to put it mildly. He'll probably lock me in my room for a month after this. I just can't seem to act like the daughter he wants me to be. I don't fit in Old Port society and I don't want to." She knotted her fingers together. "I only snuck onto this expedition so I could catch a sprite and write an essay and be accepted to the University of Ithilia. And now I'll never get there. I'll be stuck in Old Port for the rest of my life, forced to put on a face and act like all the other girls when I'm just *not.* Life isn't fair sometimes, you know?"

Agnes assumed she'd been rambling to herself until the girl nodded with a sympathetic look on her face.

"Can—can you *understand* me?" she gasped.

Another nod.

"But . . . how do you know Kaolish?" The girl thought for a moment, then shrugged and pointed to the crook of her elbow, which was covered in dirt. Agnes didn't know what that meant. She was still wrapping her head around the fact that the girl could understand every word she was saying. This was truly incredible. Agnes felt herself on the brink of something not even the great Cadhla Hope had ever experienced.

"Are you from Pelago?" she asked, wondering if maybe this girl was like the Arboreal or the mertag, before realizing she probably had no idea what Pelago was. But the girl shook her head and Agnes was once again surprised. "You know Pelago?"

The girl nodded. Then she started speaking very fast, her musical gibberish forming what must have been a string of questions, each one growing more insistent than the last.

"I wish I could help," Agnes said. "But I don't know what you're saying. I've never heard anything like your language before."

The girl leaned back, gazed at the roof of the truck, and made a sad, five-note wail.

"I don't understand," Agnes said with a sigh. The girl sighed too, and they lapsed into silence. Agnes felt her wonder turn to worry. Whoever she was, wherever she was from, this girl was intelligent and sensitive and extraordinary. She would surely be snapped up by Xavier McLellan and held along with his other creatures. Agnes found herself growing protective. The poor thing didn't deserve the life her father would force her into. She probably just wanted to get back to whatever place she came from.

"I think it would be best if you don't let anyone else know you can understand Kaolish," she said. She felt certain her father would use it somehow. The girl stared at her warily for a few seconds, then nodded.

They had left the plains too late to make it back to Old Port that day, so they stayed the night at an inn. When it became clear they were going to leave the girl in the truck overnight, Agnes refused to take a room and insisted on staying in the truck as well. Her reasoning was twofold. In the inn, she'd have to act like a proper lady and force smiles and all that awful stuff. But really, she didn't trust Branson's crew. The leering looks they had given the girl had turned Agnes's stomach, and she wasn't going to let them put their dirty hands on her. She'd already stolen a small dagger from the supply truck, and she kept it tucked in her belt.

"At least let her out of the net so she can get some sleep," Agnes said to Branson.

He laughed. "What, so she can run off in the night? I know you women are tenderhearted, but this is business. She's got to be worth more than the tree and the little fish-man combined." He leaned in close, and she could smell his foul breath as he gripped her shoulders. "If you even think about cutting her out of that net, you'll have more than a slap on the wrist from your father to worry about."

Agnes's throat closed up, but she couldn't afford to show him fear. "Get your hands off me."

Branson snorted and released her. "Just remember what I said," he warned before following the others into the inn.

It was a fine establishment, with a large common room and wide, open windows. The night was windy, and carried the voices inside out to where she sat at the edge of the truck, keeping a watchful eye on the door. Leo was clearly drinking too much whiskey, because he got insufferably loud. She thought back to the moment last night when he'd let all his stupid bravado fade, when he admitted that perhaps their father had sent him on this mission to fail. That

was the Leo she wanted to share a bag of peanuts with. This
Leo she wanted to punch in the face.

"She's out in the truck." Leo's boasting was getting
louder. "Caught her myself."

Was he a complete and utter idiot? Didn't he know the
danger he was putting the girl in? Another burst of raucous laughter came from the inn, and Agnes took the dagger
from her belt. Damn the consequences, she wasn't about to
let the girl be hurt—she would cut her free regardless of
any threats. But just then, the inn door opened and two of
Branson's men came swaggering out.

"We're to stay out here for the night," one said. "Make
sure nothing happens."

Agnes subtly slipped the dagger back into her belt, cursing herself for her hesitation. The two men threw themselves
on the ground at the edge of the open truck door, and Agnes
retreated back inside to perch on a crate beside the girl, who
was looking back and forth between Agnes and the men
with alarm.

"Sorry," she said. "Those guys are real jerks." The girl
looked confused. "Not nice people," she tried to explain.
The girl's eyes narrowed, and she made a sound halfway
between a growl and a purr.

Agnes had to laugh. "Wherever you come from, it's got
to be better than here," she said.

The girl shrugged modestly.

"I'm Agnes, by the way," she said, suddenly conscious
that she hadn't introduced herself. The girl gave a short but
beautiful wailing word that Agnes took to be her own name.

"I wish I could understand *your* language," she sighed.

The back of the truck was crammed with boxes and equipment, but there was a small square of floor exposed, covered in a layer of sand and dust and dirt from the long ride. The girl poked her fingers through the net and began drawing shapes in it. It was mostly squiggly lines, triangles or circles with slashes through them, and other strange markings Agnes didn't recognize. When she ran out of space, she erased the symbols with a brush of her fingers. She tried again and a word appeared. A word with letters Agnes could read.

Sera.

"You can *write*?" she cried. The girl was staring at the letters, looking as shocked as Agnes was. "Sera—is that your name?"

She nodded eagerly. A strong gust of wind blew into the back of the truck, clearing the dirt and dust from the rudimentary chalkboard and making both of them cough.

"Well . . ." Agnes wasn't quite sure what to say. "It's nice to meet you, Sera. I mean, not *nice* given our present circumstances but . . . I'm glad to know your name."

Sera said something back, and Agnes felt the girl shared her sentiments.

What a crazy turn of events. She had come all this way looking for sprites and ended up finding something even more unique.

The idea struck her like a thunderclap. She didn't need the sprites to write the essay. She was sitting here communicating with a creature from . . . another world, as far as

Agnes could guess. Surely that would count as a brave step in the name of science! She would need a token, though, something to prove that Sera was real. She couldn't very well bring her over to Pelago and show her to the Masters. A fingernail clipping, perhaps, or . . .

"Sera," Agnes said hesitantly, because she wasn't a thief like her father or brother. She wasn't going to take anything from this girl without her consent. "This may seem an odd request, but . . . might I have a strand of your hair? To study in my lab. I'm a scientist, you see, and I would like to know more about you, where you come from, that sort of thing. Would that be all right with you?"

Sera bent to scratch out more letters, but the dirt was gone. She made a plaintive wail and even though they did not speak the same language, Agnes understood her all the same.

"You just want to go back home, don't you?" she said. Sera nodded, tears filling her eyes. "Well, I will help you as best I can. That much I promise."

And she would if she could—she would try at least, even though she hadn't the faintest idea of how to go about doing it. But she felt like she'd already let this girl down once.

Sera studied Agnes's face for a long moment, as if deciding whether she could trust her.

"I won't let anyone know I have it," Agnes said, for she felt she needed to prove her sincerity.

Sera reached up and plucked a thin blue strand from her head. She looked at it for a moment, as if it was meaningful to her in some way Agnes couldn't begin to guess, before poking it through the net. Agnes took a glass jar from her pocket, one she had brought to keep a sprite in, unscrewed the top, and carefully placed the hair inside.

Then she fingered the dagger again, her eyes darting back and forth between the men outside and the net, considering her options.

14

LEO

LEO HAD OVERSLEPT, MAKING THEM LATE LEAVING THE inn. Then when they'd finally reached the city, a trolley had derailed, causing a mess of backed-up traffic in the financial district.

Leo's stomach was twisting itself in knots. He shouldn't have gotten so drunk last night. He should have volunteered to stay outside and guard the truck. What would his father think if he heard about his behavior? He'd been feeling on top of the world after capturing the weird silver girl. She was so much more impressive than a tiny sprite. Leo wondered if even Kiernan knew something like her existed, or if he had actually discovered a brand-new species all by himself.

Well, Agnes had helped. He wondered what she was thinking, back there in the truck, knowing that soon she'd have to face their father. And this was a serious infraction, even for her. As much as he hated to admit it, though, it was pretty impressive—Agnes might be embarrassing at social events, but Leo couldn't imagine someone like Elizabeth Conway daring to brave the Knottle Plains in a supply truck.

"Are we taking her to the theater with the others?" Chewing Tobacco asked.

Branson shook his head. "Gotta show her to the boss first. See what he has to say about her."

The sun was just beginning its descent toward the horizon as they reached the southeastern edge of Jevet's Park and left the traffic behind at last, weaving through the quieter streets of Upper Glen. Leo had developed quite a headache by the time they reached the brownstone on Creekwater Row.

He stepped out of the car, straightened his shirt, and ran a hand through his curls, hoping he looked somewhat presentable. Eneas was washing the dark green motorcar in the driveway.

"Back already, young master Leo?" he called with a wave.

Leo kept his eyes on the front door as he walked up the steps.

Father, you'll never guess what I found in the plains!

If you'll just come out to the truck, Father, I've got something I think you'll like. . . .

We couldn't find the sprites, but—

Before he had a chance to decide just how to break the

news, the door was flung open and his father was looming over him.

"It's not sprites," Leo said, the words tumbling out clumsily. "But we found something else."

"What is it?" he asked.

"You'd best see her for yourself, sir," Branson said. Leo hadn't realized he had followed him up the steps.

Xavier's eyes narrowed at the word *her*. "Very well."

Branson headed toward the truck doors, but Leo beat him there. He'd be damned if he wasn't going to be the one to show his father the girl. He wrenched down the handle and pulled.

"I got her with a net launcher," he said. "And we've kept her tied up. We aren't sure what—"

But his words were cut off as he opened the back of the truck and a silvery-blue streak crashed into him.

"Grab her!" Branson shouted.

More out of instinct than actual skill, Leo's arms reached out and closed around the delicate figure. She felt more human than he'd expected—through the dress he could feel her ribs, her spine, her stomach. Her skin was warm and soft where it touched his, and her hair gave off a fragrance that he couldn't place. She was stronger than she looked, and he tightened his grip on her as she struggled against him, wailing and kicking wildly.

Then there was a smacking sound and her head snapped to one side as her whole body went limp. He hadn't even seen Branson throw the punch. Everything happened so fast.

"No!" Agnes was standing in the truck bed, staring in

horror at the girl's unconscious form. "What did you do?" she screamed at Branson.

Xavier had one hand around Agnes's wrist in an instant, yanking her down from the truck.

"What in god's name were you thinking? You nearly gave Mrs. Phelps a heart attack when she discovered you were gone. What's wrong with you? What the *hell* are you wearing?" He looked up and down the street as if terrified someone might see his only daughter outside in pants. "Get into the house this instant."

Agnes knew better than to argue. She ducked her head and, with a last glance back at the girl, hurried through the gates and up the steps to the brownstone. Leo wasn't sure what to do. The girl's body was folded over his left arm, her hair hiding her face.

"Well, well," Xavier said, walking over. "What do we have here?"

"I found her in the plains, Father. She—"

"Put her back in the truck," Xavier said. Branson bent to grab her feet, and together he and Leo wedged her in among the crates and tools. A bruise was forming on her temple. She seemed . . . young. Vulnerable.

He looked away. "We don't know what she is, Father. I found her in a pit in the middle of the plains."

Xavier was inspecting her, turning her head side to side, examining her palms and her feet, fingering the material of her dress.

"Get her to the theater with the others," he said to Branson. "Keep her locked up. And get Kiernan there first thing tomorrow morning to find out exactly what the hell she is."

He clapped Leo on the shoulder. "Good work, son. At the very least she'll be a stunning addition to the new production. If we can't find other uses for her." He smiled, and Leo felt proud and uneasy at once, which made for a rather confusing combination.

But he shook it off and forced himself to focus on the here and now. His father was *proud* of him. That was what mattered.

"Come," Xavier said, as Branson and the others secured the truck and prepared to leave, "let's have a drink in my study and you can tell me the whole story."

Leo had never in his whole life been invited into Xavier's study, except when he was being punished. But to have a drink and regale his father with the story of his adventure in the plains? It was a dream come true.

"Yes, Father," he said eagerly.

"Just a moment." Xavier turned to the man who drove the supply truck, the one Agnes had bribed. "Did you know she was stowing away on this vehicle?"

The man blanched. "N-no, sir, I swear. Not until we were well away from Old Port, and then—"

"And why did you not return her to this house immediately?"

"Well, I . . ."

"She bribed him, Father," Leo said.

The only sign Xavier gave of his irritation was a slight flaring of his nostrils.

"Do I not pay you enough?" he asked the man.

"Of course you do, sir. I'm sorry, I—"

"Clearly not, if you are willing to take money from my

daughter to line your pockets. Greed is a sin." He stepped forward, and Leo felt as if the temperature had just dropped a few degrees. "You will never work in this city again if I have anything to say about it. And my reach is long. Do you understand me?"

The man was shaking, his face turning the color of porridge. "Y-yes, sir."

"Good. Now get out of my sight."

He jumped like a frightened rabbit and scurried off to the cab of the truck.

"Choose better men next time," Xavier said to Branson. "Or you'll be looking for employment yourself."

Branson wasn't the type to scare so easily, but his nod was terse, his jaw set. "Yes, boss."

"Imbeciles," Xavier muttered as the men drove away. He strode back up to the brownstone, Leo trailing in his wake. Swansea stood by the door, and Leo heard his father say to him, "Get word to Forester Grange immediately. Tell him it's a done deal."

Forester Grange ran a successful carpeting business in Old Port, but his family was not a prestigious one, however much Mr. Grange would like to hope otherwise. You could not simply buy your way into the Old Port elite. Leo wondered if his father was getting new carpets for the Maribelle.

Xavier's study was in the back of the house, an oval-shaped room with large windows that overlooked their garden patio, full of pristine leather couches and impressive-looking old tomes. There was a portrait of Leo's grandfather on one wall, though since he had squandered the McLellan fortune and was the reason for Xavier marrying a Pelagan in the first place, Leo was always curious as to why his father didn't have it removed. A crystal decanter of whiskey sat on his desk, and his father uncapped it and poured two glasses, handing one to Leo.

"To a successful expedition," he said, raising his glass.

"Hear, hear," Leo said. They drank, and Xavier settled himself in his plush leather chair. Leo took one of the hardback ones that faced the desk.

"So," Xavier said, eyeing his son over his drink. "Tell me everything."

And Leo did. He fudged a bit on the part where he'd fallen asleep, saying only that he had decided to search for the sprites near the car when he discovered Agnes. But he described the rest in detail. Xavier asked all sorts of questions about the girl, most of which Leo could not answer, as he knew nothing except what she looked like and that she spoke in a strange, almost musical language.

"And nothing out of the ordinary happened around her?" Xavier asked.

"No, sir. Nothing." He had a feeling there was a correct answer to give, but he didn't know what it was.

The room had darkened over the course of the evening, and Xavier leaned forward to turn on his desk lamp. "You have done well, Leo. Better than I expected."

"Thank you, Father."

"I want you to attend to Kiernan tomorrow as he makes his examination of her."

Leo's chest swelled. He was being included, at long last. He hesitated for a moment and then decided to press his luck.

"Why is this your final show, Father?"

Xavier drained the last of his whiskey and set the glass down on the desk. The movement felt calculated, as if he was deliberating what to say or whether to answer at all. Leo held his breath and waited.

"Do you know what it feels like to have nothing, Leo?" he asked in a voice as lethal as a snake's hiss. "To have everything you hold dear crumble and turn to ashes? No, of course you don't. Because I have ensured that you never will." He turned to the portrait of Leo's grandfather, eyeing it with disdain. "I keep this painting here to remind myself of how close I came to utter ruin because of one man's unforgivable weakness. My father was much loved in Old Port—he was a jovial man, a prolific storyteller, and a big spender. But he was a drunk and a fool. What money he didn't gamble away he spent on whiskey and women of ill repute. And through it all he lied, to me, to my mother . . . he lied with a slick tongue and a smooth grin, and we bought it hook, line, and sinker. Until the day one of the maids found him dead with a pistol in his mouth and a pile of bills at his feet. And just like that, the man I thought I knew, the man I loved and respected, was gone and my world came crashing down."

Leo sat very still. He had never heard the story of his grandfather's death told quite like this. He had never thought of Xavier as a son who loved his father before.

Xavier shifted in his seat, the dim light making his brown eyes look black. "Those were a hard few years. Your grandmother almost did not survive the shame. It was up to me to find a new influx of capital, and when I did, I swore to myself that I would not fail my mother like my father had. I would keep this family's reputation intact by any means necessary." It was a cold way to describe a marriage, but honest, Leo thought. He wondered what life had been like in this house when his mother was alive. Maybe the two of them had simply avoided each other.

"And behind every reputation," Xavier continued, "there must be respect but, more importantly, *money*. The anti-Talman plays have given this family both for many years, but competition has increased and the theater scene has become glutted. If I want to keep the McLellan name relevant, it is time to move on, to adapt in ways my father could not. Innovation, Leo. That is the key to success."

"And that's what those creatures you found in Pelago are about? Innovation?"

A smile of steel curled on his father's lips. "That is exactly what they are. Have you ever wondered why Pelago is so rich in resources? Why Kaolin seems to suffer from heat waves and overfishing and Pelago does not?"

Leo had always thought it had simply been a luck-of-the-draw-type situation—that Pelago happened to be fortunate in ways Kaolin wasn't. He'd never imagined there was a specific reason behind the difference.

"The Arboreal and the mertag are not merely grotesques," Xavier said without waiting for a response. "They have abilities, Leo. Powers you and I have never dreamed of."

"Like . . . magic?" he asked. It sounded awfully far-fetched.

His father chuckled. "I suppose you could call it that. Magic seems too frivolous a word, too fantastical, and these creatures and their skills are very much real."

"What do they do?"

Xavier leaned forward. "They replenish. They can make this country as fruitful as Pelago. Imagine not needing to bow to the demands of the Triumvirate. Not to be dictated or talked down to by those three scheming, godless queens. And we will own this power, Leo. *We* will control it, the McLellans alone, and our name will go down in history as the family that saved Kaolin." There was a fanatical gleam in his eye that made Leo uneasy. "They've been keeping this secret to themselves, all these years, those greedy and grasping Pelagans. She thinks she is untouchable. But she will see. . . ." He trailed off.

She? Leo thought. But he decided not to press that matter—something about it felt dangerous, especially in tandem with the conversation he'd overheard with Kiernan. He wondered if he should stop asking questions altogether, but his father had never confided in him like this, and the need to know more was irresistible.

"So then why perform a play at all?" he asked.

Xavier refilled his own glass. "Advertising," he said. "And money. No reason not to have one last hurrah before I bow out of the theater scene, and no better way to get the word out than to make a big splash about it. It will leave no doubt as to who they belong to, who is responsible for bringing them to Kaolin. Those creatures are *mine*, and no one is going to take them from me."

Something about this version of his father scared Leo more than the version he was used to.

"I have dedicated my whole life to repairing the damage

my father has done, to ensuring that this family lives on with the respect it deserves." There was a haunted look in Xavier's eyes. "Think about what kind of man you wish to be, Leo. Think about the mantle you will wear one day. I would hate to see everything I've worked for, everything I have built, squandered as it once was. I would hate to think my own son capable of such ruin."

Leo swallowed hard and gave a curt nod.

"You have surprised me with the ingenuity you showed in the plains, catching that girl and bringing her back to me. Let us hope she does not disappoint."

There was a knock on the door, and Swansea poked his head in. "I have heard from Mr. Grange. It is done, sir."

"Good." Xavier stood and moved to stare out the back window at the garden. "You are dismissed, Leo. Go send your sister down to me."

It was only after he left that Leo realized he'd forgotten to ask his father about the island he had seemed so intent on finding. But then, perhaps it was for the best—he'd gotten more than he'd ever dreamed, and he didn't want Xavier to think him an eavesdropper.

15

AGNES

AGNES SAT IN THE TUB WHILE HATTIE, THE MAID, scrubbed her back, her mind replaying on a loop the moment when Branson had hit Sera.

She hated herself for just standing by and letting them take her away. But what else could she have done? The truth was, no matter how much she might wish otherwise, she was unable to disobey her father when he was standing right in front of her. Sneaking out was one thing. Ignoring a direct command was quite another.

"So Mrs. Phelps told him I was gone?" she asked. She hadn't taken the housekeeper into account when she'd planned her escape.

"Yes, miss," Hattie said. Then she lowered her voice.

"I've never seen him so angry. He got all quiet. Like he turned to stone."

Agnes shivered. Mrs. Phelps bustled into the room and Hattie fell silent.

"How are you feeling, dearie?" she asked, checking the temperature of the water and wiping her hands on her apron. "More hot water, Hattie."

Hattie curtsied and left. Mrs. Phelps wasn't as forthcoming as the young maid, but Agnes had to know what was happening.

"Where did the truck go?" she asked.

"Never you mind about that." The Solit triangle brooch at her throat gleamed as Mrs. Phelps bent to wet a washcloth and scrubbed down the length of Agnes's right arm before moving to the left. "Let's get this nasty dirt off you."

"I don't mind a little dirt," Agnes grumbled.

Mrs. Phelps sighed. "I know you don't. But your father does."

It was always what her father wanted. She thought about the jar with Sera's hair in it, now hidden safely away in her lab. And the letter from Ithilia, tucked inside a book. She had thought she would feel prouder of herself, but mostly she felt like she hadn't done anything at all. She should have let Sera escape right away. She should have found some way to get to Pelago already, her father's money be damned— she had some jewelry of value she could pawn. Surely there was a Pelagan ship that would take her. They wouldn't care about Kaolin rules, or needing a man's permission. University or not, at least she could be herself there. Leo's words rang in her ears.

Don't worry, I'm sure he'll just marry you off to some low-class Old Port boy and wash his hands of you.

And she knew he would. If Agnes was honest with herself, it was a miracle he hadn't already. Her stomach clenched at the thought of being married to a man, sharing a bed with a man. If her mother had still been alive, Agnes wondered, would she have been able to confide in her about the type of person she truly wished to marry? Pelago wasn't as strict as Kaolin when it came to matters of sexuality. There were two southern islands, Lisbe and Crake, that were almost exclusively homosexual. Agnes used to dream of living on one of them when she was younger and beginning to understand that she was not like the other girls she knew. But even as a child, she recognized the danger in expressing that dream aloud.

"My mother wouldn't have minded," she muttered.

"Oh yes, she would have," Mrs. Phelps said. "I know you like to romanticize her, but I'm sure she would have wanted a clean daughter as much as your father does."

For a heart-stopping second, Agnes thought the woman had read her mind; then she realized Mrs. Phelps was just talking about the dirt again.

"But you didn't even know her," she said. Mrs. Phelps had been hired after her mother died.

"No, I didn't, and I can't say I'm sorry for it. I worked for the Hornes back then. But everyone knew about Xavier McLellan's Pelagan wife. All those parties she used to throw, the way she dressed . . . I don't like to speak ill of the dead, but she was a dangerous woman, your mother. Wild. Unconventional. There were stories flying about that she had used her Talman magic and invoked some goddess or other to trick him into the marriage."

Agnes snorted. "That's ridiculous."

"Well, he started acting strangely after a while, that's for certain. But then she died and he came back to his old self and that was that. Best to keep the past in the past."

"Acting strangely?" Agnes asked, surprised. She'd always been so obsessed with learning about her mother, she'd never given much thought to how her father might have been back then. She'd assumed he was simply the same as he was now. "How?"

"They weren't rightly home much," Mrs. Phelps said as she worked some gardenia shampoo through Agnes's hair. "Traveling all the time. And the parties, with foreign foods and all sorts of people—not proper company, if you catch my drift. She was wild, like I said, and it rubbed off on him for a bit. Wouldn't even deign to have you and your brother born at the hospital in Old Port. No, it was some private facility outside the city, that was the only place that would do for *her*."

"How do you know that?"

"Servants talk, my dear. I may not have worked in this house then, but gossip like that travels fast, especially in this city. The McLellans left Old Port together, and only you children and your father returned." She tilted Agnes's head so she could look into her eyes and smiled. "But that woman gave us you and Leo, and that's all that matters. Ah, Hattie."

The young maid came hurrying in with a bucket of

water, steam rising gently from its surface. She dumped it over Agnes's head, rinsing away the shampoo.

"All right, that should do it," Mrs. Phelps said. "Up you get."

She covered Agnes in a big fluffy towel as she stepped out of the tub. Hattie wrapped another towel around her hair and led her off down the hall to Agnes's room. Leo was lounging in the doorway of his own room, looking as smug as a cat with a fresh kill.

"Father wants to see you," he said.

"Where did they take her?" Agnes demanded.

"Please don't fight," Hattie begged, glancing over the railing to the foyer below.

Leo shrugged. "Ask him yourself. If he'll even tell you. I'm going to be seeing her tomorrow, though. I'll send your regards." Then he sauntered back inside his room and closed the door.

Hattie wanted her to wear one of her nicer dresses, but Agnes did not feel like dressing up to be yelled at. She chose a simple white blouse and gray skirt instead, shoving her damp hair up into a bun. Hattie stuck a few decorative pins in it and laid out a gold necklace with a Solit triangle pendant. Before she left for Xavier's study, Agnes checked the door to her lab to make sure it was locked. Now that Sera's hair was hidden inside, she felt herself becoming paranoid.

Her father stood leaning over an open desk drawer when she knocked. The drawer clicked, locking as he closed it.

"Sit," he said without preamble, gesturing to one of the two hardback chairs facing the desk. Xavier liked to keep his guests uncomfortable in this room. Agnes sat in silence—she knew that no amount of apologizing would help her cause. He would punish her as he saw fit.

Besides, she wasn't sorry, and she wasn't going to lie and say she was. Xavier leaned back and studied her. The grandfather clock ticked loudly, and Agnes tried to focus on its steady beat. She felt as though he was looking inside her, peeling back the layers of her skin, but she wasn't about to give him the satisfaction of seeing how much it unnerved her.

"If only you had been born a boy," he said at last, and the words were a knife to Agnes's heart. She knew, of course. She wasn't stupid enough to think that her gender did not offend him, or that at the very least he wished she would act like a regular girl. Leo commented on it all the time.

But her father had never said it out loud.

"I'm sorry to disappoint you," she said. His stare somehow became even more penetrating.

"No, you aren't." He turned in his chair to look out the window. "I have been far too lenient with you. The lab, your behavior, letting Eneas teach you Pelagan . . ." Agnes's chest seized up. "That ends now. Ebenezer Grange's father has made a very good offer for your hand, and I have accepted on your behalf. You will meet with Ebenezer tomorrow and make it official."

"What?" Agnes yelped. She had always thought that when the time came, at the very least she would be involved in the decision. She knew her father would have the final say, but this was cruel even for him. The Granges were a social-climbing merchant family; Ebenezer was a thin, nervous boy whom Agnes had never given much thought to.

Now, all of a sudden, she was to *marry* him? "Father, don't you think—"

"Do not tell me what to think, Agnes, and be grateful I am not sending you away to a sanatorium for hysterical young ladies." He turned back to face her. "I should never have indulged you, but I thought . . ." He clenched his teeth, and Agnes knew he had been about to mention her mother. She drew on every shred of courage she had left to ask a question that had been brewing for years.

"Couldn't you send me to live with my grandmother? I wouldn't be such an embarrassment in Pelago, and per- haps . . ." But the words died on her lips. Agnes remembered what Hattie had said, that Xavier had turned to stone with anger when he'd discovered she was gone. She saw it hap- pening again now. One hand curled into a fist and his eyes narrowed a fraction. Otherwise he was completely still.

"You think sending you to that godforsaken country to live with your witch of a grandmother will make you *less* of an embarrassment?" His voice was slow, deliberate. "I thought you were the smart one, Agnes."

The knife in her heart twisted.

"Mother would have wanted me to know her," she blurted out.

Xavier slammed his fist down on the table, rattling his fountain pen and making her jump. "You do not know what your mother would have wanted," he snarled. "And you cer- tainly don't know the first thing about Ambrosine Byrne. You think your grandmother is some kindly, gray-haired schoolmarm? Think again, Agnes."

Heat rose in her cheeks, because to be honest, that

was exactly how she'd pictured her.

"Tell me about her then," she said. "If I'm so stupid, enlighten me."

"I did not say you were stupid," Xavier said. "If I had to choose a word, it would be naive. You romanticize Pelago, and your mother, and her family. The Byrnes are not what you think they are—they are selfish and greedy. They are arrogant. You have created a world that doesn't exist. You are living in *this* world and you must abide by its rules."

"I wouldn't have to romanticize Mother or her family if you talked about them," Agnes said. She knew she was pushing her luck, but she couldn't help herself. What did he mean by selfish and arrogant? Maybe he was making up a tale to dampen her desire to know the Byrnes. Eneas had called her grandmother formidable, which made her seem like a woman of stature. Agnes had always pictured her as someone noble and respected.

She was sick of getting only bits and pieces of information. The spectacular unfairness of it all was making her irrational. "Mrs. Phelps said you and Mother used to travel all the time together. That you threw parties here with all sorts of people. She said you were different then."

Xavier's face had become a mask, but Agnes could sense some strong emotion pulsing beneath it, and she immediately regretted bringing the housekeeper into this discussion.

"Mrs. Phelps hasn't the faintest idea what she's talking about," he said coldly. "She was not in my employ during that time."

"If you truly want to shatter my illusions about Pelago," Agnes said, "you'd let me see it for myself."

"No."

"Why not?"

"You know why," Xavier said.

"Because it would look bad for *you*," she grumbled.

"It would."

"But you're working with a Pelagan!"

"A man. And Kiernan has skills and assets that I need. You do not, and sending you to Pelago would be a mistake of epic proportions."

"My mother would have wanted more for me than Ebenezer Grange," Agnes insisted. "And she would have let me have some say in the decision at least!"

"*Enough*. You will do as you are told and there will be no more discussion of your mother."

"Why not? Why can't I know anything about her? What are you so *afraid* of?"

Agnes knew instantly that she had crossed a line. She felt something snap in the air between them.

"Go to your room." Xavier's voice was like iron, his face dark as a beet. A vein throbbed in his neck. "Now. No dinner. Go."

She didn't hesitate. She flew through the doors and up the stairs, past a bewildered Hattie, and nearly plowed into Swansea. She didn't stop until she had collapsed onto her bed.

"So what's the punishment? Miss Elderberry's Finishing School again?" Leo was standing in her doorway, grinning. Agnes felt a stab of relief that her father had not told her brother she was engaged. When one of them was punished, it was a McLellan sibling tradition for the other to gloat.

But this was different. This wasn't time away from her lab or etiquette lessons or finishing school. This was the rest of her life.

"Honestly, I don't know why he keeps sending you there," he continued, oblivious. "Perhaps Larker Asylum would be a better fit. . . ."

"Go away, Leo."

"Agnes . . ." He frowned and took a step into her room. "I'm—"

"What?" she snapped. "You're sorry?" She snorted. "I can't believe you just let Branson hit her like that." She hadn't meant to bring up Sera, but she found it was easier to be angry about that than to think about Ebenezer Grange.

"What was I supposed to do?" Leo said. "It's not like I hit her myself."

"No, you just snapped her up in a net, that's much better."

"If you remember correctly, you *helped* me find her."

"I didn't know she was there!"

"Neither did I!"

They stared each other down, and Leo must have seen something in her expression, because his eyes narrowed.

"What's really going on?"

"Nothing," she said. She could feel the tears welling up, and she tried to blink them away.

"Come on, you're a terrible liar. What, is he padlocking your lab for the rest of the year?"

It pained Agnes to think that although Leo had been the one to suggest it, even he had not thought Xavier would marry her off quite so abruptly.

And just like that, she saw understanding click behind his eyes. The one thing that would make her this upset. The one punishment she would not want to joke about.

"Is it . . . are you en—"

"Don't say it." The tears were coming, she couldn't stop them, and she had never let Leo see her cry before. "Please, just . . . leave me alone."

"Agnes, I . . ." His arms twitched like he wanted to comfort her, and that made everything worse. She wrenched off her shoe and threw it at him, missing his head by inches and hitting the door instead.

"Get OUT!" she screamed. He cursed and vanished.

She got up, slammed the door shut, then went to her bed to retrieve the hidden photograph. Her mother's face was blurred through her tears.

"Why did you have to leave me?" she demanded. "Why couldn't you be here to protect me from him?"

Her mother only laughed. Agnes wiped her nose on her sleeve.

Engaged. It didn't seem real. Tomorrow she would meet with Ebenezer Grange, the man who would be her husband. Her entire body rejected the idea.

She lifted her gaze to the book with the letter inside it and a steely determination set in. She was just as much a Byrne as she was a McLellan, goddamn it. What had Mrs. Phelps called her mother? *Wild. Unconventional.* Well, so was Agnes.

She grabbed the book off the table and headed to her lab. She would write this essay. She would book a ticket to Pelago and leave as soon as possible—Eneas would take her to the Seaport tomorrow without question. She would meet her grandmother and attend the interview with the university Masters and she would live her own damn life the way she wanted to.

She took the jar with Sera's hair out from where she'd shoved it in the very back of her supply cupboard and carefully unscrewed it. She sterilized a set of tweezers, then laid the hair on a slide and put it under the microscope, turning the magnification to 10X. She peered through the scope and saw nothing more than a strand of blue hair. She increased the magnification to 20X, then 50X. The hair was the most perfect color blue she had ever seen—she'd called it cerulean before, but really it was much richer. Like a cloudless summer sky. She was so awestruck by the color that it took her a moment to realize something was missing.

Agnes increased the magnification to 100X and gasped. There were no ridges or overlapping scales on the cuticle to protect the cortex. This strand of hair was entirely smooth. That didn't make sense. That wasn't how hair worked. She took it off the slide and sliced it in half with a scalpel. Pinching it carefully with the tweezers, she held the cross section up under the scope.

The medulla, or the core of the hair, was nearly impossible to see—Agnes had tried when she studied her own hair, with dismal results. But in the center of Sera's strand was a tiny light that pulsed like a star. She sat back and placed the hair on the slide again, rubbing her eyes. Hair was made of dead cells, but Sera's hair seemed to be *alive*. She didn't know what it meant, but she knew it was important. The Masters at the university would never have seen anything like it. She began to scribble in her journal, writing down her observations and thoughts, jotting down notes about how she might test its properties.

She felt a twinge of guilt that the hair had not held any answers that would help Sera return home, wherever that might be. But Agnes had her own prison to worry about. She bit her lip, hating that she could not be more helpful, loathing the idea of leaving the girl in her father's clutches.

She worked until well past midnight, when she finally collapsed, exhausted, into bed and sank at once into a blissfully dreamless sleep.

16

SERA

WHEN SERA CAME TO, SHE FOUND HERSELF INSIDE A large crate with wide slats. There was a chain wrapped all the way around it, and no matter where she kicked or pushed, the wood refused to budge.

"Let me out of here!" she screamed. "Mother Sun, hear me! Help me, please!" She fell back against one of the slats, hot tears filling her eyes. No one answered her. The only sound was her labored breathing. Light was coming from the ground a few yards away, an odd purple-pink glow. Slowly, her eyes adjusted, and she was able to take stock of her surroundings.

She appeared to be on an elevated platform made of dark wood, with thick red curtains hanging on either side of it.

Mossy banks grew up at its edge, dotted with luminescent pink, purple, and orange flowers that provided the light.

At the back of the platform, the wood vanished and a garden had been planted, thick grass and tiny flowers growing among spry saplings. In the center of the garden stood a slender tree, its bark silvery white, with leaves of jade inlaid with blue veins that made them look turquoise. The saplings were not nearly as magnificent in color, plain brown trunks and green leaves.

For some reason, Sera felt the tree seemed sad. Its branches were bent like it carried a heavy load, and there were markings on its trunk that looked like a face frowning. It was not a very big tree—she would be able to reach its topmost branches if she stood beside it on her tiptoes. She wondered what it was doing here, inside . . . whatever this place was. And the moss and flowers too. Why would the people of Kaolin grow moss and trees inside?

And what was *she* doing here? What did they want with her?

She shuddered, recalling the events of the previous evening. The low-voiced girl was actually a *male* named Leo—Sera had realized it when she saw him in the daylight. Males looked sort of like females, except they had no breasts and were taller and hairier and meaner. She touched the spot on her temple where the other male's fist had crashed into her skull. Sera had never been hit in her whole life. It had hurt so much, but the magic in her blood had healed the bruise, leaving her skin smooth and unblemished so that only the memory of the pain remained.

The one person who had shown her kindness was the

girl called Agnes. Sera had been hesitant to offer up her hair, worried that Agnes would try to steal her magic like the humans on the last planet had, but it was only hair, not blood, and Sera had felt she needed *some* kind of help if she was to ever have any hope of getting home.

But Agnes wasn't here now, and Sera didn't know if she'd ever see her again. Her pulse quickened, her mind turning over her options, the slats of the crate closing in on her. The truth was she had no options. She was trapped. Her City was far away. And she couldn't even speak the same language as these people. Her green mother had said the Cerulean could communicate with those on the planet, but Sera couldn't see how. Was there some secret, lost over time, some ritual or practice that would unlock the barrier of communication?

You can write, though, she reminded herself. That had been shocking. She had only meant to trace what she remembered of the symbols on the ancient bowl that had told her *Heal them.* She thought maybe the symbols held some clue as to why the ceremony had failed, why she'd ended up here— and secretly, in her heart of hearts, she hoped maybe they could help lead her home. She should have told the High Priestess about them, but she had been overwhelmed then, and had never considered the possibility of being trapped on Kaolin. So she had poked her fingers through that horrible net and written out in the dirt what she could recall and then, while Agnes was wishing aloud that she could understand Sera's language, she found herself making different sorts of symbols, ones she'd never seen before. Sera did not know how she knew it was her name she was spelling out, but she did, as certainly as she knew the sound of her purple mother's harp or the scent of a moonflower. And Agnes had been able to read it.

Maybe there had been another ceremony already, to make up for her failure. Perhaps a better Cerulean had been chosen, one who was truly worthy, and the City was already drifting through space, leaving Sera stuck on this planet forever. The thought was so unbearable, she began kicking at the crate again. If she could just see the stars . . .

Or the tether! She stopped kicking and sat up. If she could find the tether, she would know her City was still up there. Maybe it even held a clue as to how to get home. The problem was she didn't know where the tether was attached. She was in Kaolin. What if it was in Pelago? Would she be able to see it if it was so far away? And how far away was far away? She had no concept of distance here. She'd only ever seen the planet from high above, where everything looked small and simple. Pelago was to the east of Kaolin, across an expanse of water. And Kaolin itself seemed a very large mass of land. Where on the lopsided star was she being held? How far apart were the two countries?

She went back to kicking the crate, over and over until her feet were sore and her legs gave out. Her stomach ached, despair threatening to swallow her whole.

"Please, Mother Sun," she whispered, tears spilling down her cheeks. "If you can hear me . . . help me, please."

"*It cries.*"

Sera's head whipped up. The voice was raspy and hissing, and there was something off about it, like it was coming from inside her head. A pair of bulging eyes hovered above the edge of the platform. A clawlike hand emerged, then another; then a strange creature wriggled itself over the moss and onto the platform itself. Sera shrieked and scuttled back as far as she could go.

The creature was small, only about three feet long, and pale green. From the waist up it had a torso and two arms and a head that were all humanlike. From the waist down, it had the scaly body of a fish. Its head was perfectly round, with luminous eyes and teeth like razors. Its skull was bare and pocked. Instead of eyebrows, three glowing filaments stuck out over each eye—they dipped and swayed with the creature's movements. The clawed hands had seven webbed fingers.

The filaments were beautiful and delicate—like spun glass, they refracted the light that shone from the flowers. And on the end of each filament was a tiny bulb. Sera could not help but be reminded of the fish in the Great Estuary, the ones that had filaments just like these, fish that no other Cerulean would go near but herself. Except they were fish through and through, without arms or heads.

The creature stared at Sera and Sera stared back. It never blinked. She was fairly certain it didn't have eyelids.

"Did . . . did you say something?" she asked, feeling a bit stupid but unsure of what else to do. Even if it had been the creature who had spoken, it wouldn't understand her.

"*It cries in its box, so sad, so far from home, the sea, the sea.*" Its mouth didn't move, but the filaments lit up in a distinct pattern—red-gold, magenta, blue. Something about the voice made Sera guess the creature was male.

"Is that how you talk?" she asked, crawling forward

and gripping the slats. "With lights?" Suddenly, she noticed her fingertips were glowing, like the blood bond, except this wasn't just one index finger, but each of the three middle fingers on both her hands. She stared at them, aghast. "What is happening?" she said aloud.

Her fingertips lit up in flashes, just like the filaments. Purple, yellow, green, purple again. She recalled the story her green mother had told her of the planet with the giant birds. Could her magic let her communicate with this sea creature?

Sera hesitated, remembering what Agnes had said. *Don't let anyone else know you understand us.* But she felt that applied to humans, and this creature was not human. She held up her hands so he could see them and said, loudly and clearly, "My name is Sera Lighthaven. I am a Cerulean and my blood is magic."

Lights flashed across her fingertips. The creature's entire body reacted, a rainbow erupting over his skin and scales.

"It speaks!" he cried. *"It speaks the colors!"*

The relief that flooded through her at being heard, at being understood . . . it was a joy so sharp it was almost painful.

"Where are we?" she demanded, her fingers lighting up in amber-jade-scarlet. "What is this place? Who are you?"

"Who am I? Why, I am a mertag, proud and cold and true. My name . . . my name is too long for land dwellers and old, very old, yes, bubbles and blowfish, but no one speaks to me here, no one understands. They call me Errol, over and over, Errol Errol Errol. Errol is my name here and as good as any, Sera Lighthaven."

"Errol," she whispered. The mertag seemed to be taking just as much pleasure in being heard as Sera was in being understood, and his lights flashed again and again.

"From the sea I came, yes, the dark cool waters of Pelago, but they took me, they took me from my home, nasty humans with nets and tricking lights, they stole me away and put me in this false sea, this tiny ocean." He turned back and made a derisive sniff in the direction of the moss. Sera figured there must be water on the other side. *"Long now have I been here, too long, too much light, no current to move by."* Errol shuddered and rubbed a webbed hand over his pocked skull.

"What do they want from us?" she asked. "Why are they keeping us here?"

"Who knows why humans do the things they do? They come, they go, they destroy, they take, by seaweed and starfish they care not for the homes of others, only for themselves. More fish they want, always more and more, and flowers too, and all the while Errol is so tired."

Sera wasn't quite sure what he meant by that, but she agreed humans were cruel and selfish. She remembered how intrigued she'd been about life on Kaolin and Pelago, wishing to visit them as the Cerulean had visited planets in days of old. Now she felt ashamed of that curiosity. She should have appreciated her beloved City more when she had the chance.

A thought occurred to her.

"Could you help me get out of this crate, Errol?" she asked.

The mertag cocked his head. *"I can try,"* he said. He

pulled himself across the platform with his arms, his fish tail wriggling behind him. He got to the chain and inspected it. *"I am afraid it is locked, Sera Lighthaven."* He yanked on a heavy iron padlock. Then he bit the chain. *"And too thick for old Errol to bite through. I am sorry."*

"Oh." Sera was unable to suppress her disappointment. She watched the mertag as he began to chew on one of the slats, then spit out splinters in disgust. "If you can leave your pond, then why don't you run away?"

Errol made a croaking sound that Sera decided was a laugh. *"Do not think I have not thought of that, Sera Lighthaven! Mertags are smart, smarter than humans, by fins and feelers. But there is no way out of this place that I can find, walls and walls and more walls and no way through them. You will see soon enough, the lights will come back. And I cannot be out of the water forever, no, not forever, just a little while."* He laughed again. *"But they do not know that, oh no, humans think Errol needs water always. Humans are blind, no brains at all."*

Sera wasn't sure if the humans she met were stupid— Agnes certainly did not seem to be. But at least for now, Sera was not alone. She could speak to someone, even a someone as strange as Errol. She pressed her glowing fingertips together and sent up a prayer of thanks to Mother Sun. Then she held her hands back up so that she could talk to her new friend.

The lights did come back, as Errol had said they would.

Sera did not realize she had fallen asleep until a loud bang woke her up with a start. A series of lights switched on and a cheerful voice called out, "Morning, Boris. Morning, Errol, old boy. Hope you all slept—"

Sera blinked in the bright light and saw a young male standing before her, with a pale face and a mop of sandy hair. He looked just as shocked to see her as she was to see him. She froze, not trusting what he might do to her.

"Hello," he said. "I didn't know there was anyone new coming." He crouched in front of the crate. "Wow. You're quite something. I've gotten too used to Errol, and Boris over there." He nodded to indicate the tree. "You must be hungry."

It took everything in her to keep still, not to nod and beg for food. She was starving, but she would not let this male know she understood him.

He inspected the crate and shook his head in disgust. "Not even a cup of water? Or a bucket to relieve yourself? Typical Branson," he muttered. "I'll be right back," he said to Sera.

Why did he keep talking to her? Did he know she could understand his language? Her heart sank as she wondered if maybe Agnes had told.

Now that the lights were on, she could see the space she was being kept in more clearly. It was larger than a dwelling, with a vaulted ceiling like the temple, except there was some sort of dark cover over it. Three-quarters of the room was taken up with neat little rows of seats covered in red—they stretched all the way to the ceiling, three balconies mounted one on top of the other. There were objects carved into the walls, fruit and flowers painted gold, and a covering on the floor that matched the color of the seats.

The male came back with a bowl, a small bucket, and a saw—Sera scuttled away from its sharp teeth.

"Don't be afraid," he said, putting the bowl and bucket down. "I'm just going to cut one of the slats so I can get these in. I'm not allowed keys, and besides, Mr. McLellan would have my hide if I unlocked that chain." He looked at her with pity in his eyes. "They should have left all this for you last night. I'm sorry about that."

He seemed sincere, but Sera did not believe him. She watched as he cut away a piece of wood, enough to slide the bowl and bucket through.

"Barley and carrot soup. It's cold, but it'll have to do for now."

Sera waited until he and the saw had vanished behind the curtain before crawling over to inspect the food. She knew she should be careful, but at the smell of broth and carrot, her stomach let out a great roar and she found herself halfway through the soup before she knew it.

Once she'd finished, she watched the male water the tree called Boris with a huge watering can and realized that he talked to everything, not just her.

"How's that for a good breakfast, Boris? Your saplings are looking quite nice today. They're bigger than they were yesterday, I'd wager. I'll get you some sun just as soon as I've fed Errol."

Then he left and returned again with a different bucket filled with something that smelled pungent and meaty.

"Time for some grub, Errol," he called as he stood on

the moss's edge and scattered whatever was in the bucket into the water where Errol lived. It made wet, plopping sounds.

Sera was confused by this behavior—he seemed kind, certainly the kindest male she had encountered so far. But he would not let her out, and he was part of whatever operation had brought her here to begin with. How could someone so kind be involved with people so cruel? After he fed Errol, he disappeared again. There was a loud cranking sound, and the cover on the ceiling began to retract. Sera dropped her soup bowl and pressed her face against the top of the crate as, inch by inch, the sky began to appear.

The sky! It was not the sky she knew, but a crisp, robin's-egg blue, not a star in sight. Sunlight shone through the glass panes on the ceiling, a richer yellow than the sunlight she was used to, and landed on the slender tree and its saplings. Sera thought the tree seemed to straighten a bit, its leaves rustling and its branches stretching.

"Bet that feels good, doesn't it?" the male said, coming back and giving the trunk a pat.

Just then, a door at the back of the dwelling opened and a man with a mass of red hair carrying a small black bag bustled in, followed by a very familiar face.

Sera hissed as Leo walked up the aisle between the red-covered seats.

"Good morning, Francis," the red-haired man said cheerily.

"Good morning, Mr. Kiernan," the kind male replied.

"I heard we have a new addition," he said, walking up a

set of steps on the side of the platform.

"Indeed, sir."

"Have you met Leo McLellan? Xavier's son. He and his sister Agnes are responsible for this latest capture."

Sera had not realized Leo and Agnes were related—they looked and acted nothing alike. Francis and Leo gripped each other's hands and moved them up and down.

"Boris is looking happy today," the man named Kiernan said. "That's what we call the Arboreal," he added, explaining to Leo. "And Errol is our mertag. He's quite shy, I'm afraid. Spends most of his time at the bottom of that pond. Now." He clapped his hands together and turned his attention to Sera. "Let's have a look at what you discovered in the plains!"

He crouched by the crate, and when he saw her, the pink flush in his pale cheeks vanished, and his eyes grew so wide Sera thought they might fall out of their sockets.

"My . . . my goodness," he said breathlessly.

"What is it, sir?" Leo asked. "Do you know what she is?"

"I am a Cerulean, you idiot," Sera snapped at him. Leo looked startled at the fierceness of her tone, and Sera felt a grim sense of satisfaction, before she remembered she shouldn't have spoken at all. But the two males did not notice she understood him.

"She doesn't seem to like you much," Kiernan said with a chuckle. "And I do *not* know what she is. She almost looks like . . ." He hesitated, leaning forward to study her more closely, then shook his head. "No, she is nothing I have seen before. But let's find out a bit about her, shall we?"

Sera didn't know what was happening. Kiernan was rifling through the bag, pulling out a long needle with a bulb on the end of it—Sera had a wild thought that he was expecting her to sew something when the needle pierced the skin on her foot and she gave a cry and then everything went dark.

17

AGNES

AGNES WAS MOROSE ALL THROUGH BREAKFAST.

Her father stopped in just as she was finishing her coffee. "Good morning," he said.

"Good morning," she replied stiffly.

"Ready to meet with your fiancé?" He frowned. "I should have had Leo pick you out something to wear."

Agnes didn't see anything wrong with her dress—it was navy blue with red accents and a white ruffle on the neck. Hattie had insisted on pinning a matching navy-and-red hat to the front of her hair. For Agnes, this outfit was positively flamboyant.

"I'm sure Ebenezer won't mind," she said sweetly. "He doesn't have a choice, does he?"

"Sir." Swansea came up behind her father, the day's paper in his hands and an anxious expression on his face.

"What is it?" Xavier asked.

Swansea held out the paper. Agnes couldn't see the headline, but whatever it was had her father out of sorts in a flash. "Get Kiernan back here at once. And Roth. *Now.*" He gripped the paper so hard Agnes thought he would tear it in two. "At last," he said, and his tone was almost reverent.

Without a word of explanation or even a goodbye to his daughter, Xavier strode off to his study, leaving Agnes thoroughly confused.

Eneas popped his head into the dining room. "All set, miss?"

His thick, wavy black hair was spilling out from under his chauffeur's cap, and his usually cheerful expression was tempered with pity. He knew where they were going and why. Agnes nodded and followed him out to the car.

"Have you seen the papers today?" she asked as he opened the door for her.

"I have not, but Olive Town was abuzz with some news about a discovery on one of the Lost Islands. Not sure if I believe it, though," he said, starting up the engine and backing out of the driveway. "No one has seen a Lost Island in . . . well, not in my lifetime, or my mother's, or her mother's. That's why they call them Lost, isn't it?"

"Mmm," Agnes murmured. Eneas was from Thaetus, the southernmost island of Pelago, and he always talked about it lovingly, the olive trees and vineyards, the rolling hills and warm crystal waters, and the big bustling market in the main city of Arbaz.

The Granges lived on the west side of Old Port, in an area called Ellsbury Park, not as posh as Upper Glen but still a nice neighborhood. It took forever to get across town, though—they were stopped for a full ten minutes in Central Square when a hansom cab wheel got stuck in one of the tram rails. Any other day Agnes would be pestering Eneas to teach her a new Pelagan word or phrase, or maybe wheedling some more information out of him about her mother.

But not today.

Whenever Agnes had thought about getting married, usually Susan Bruckner was the first person who came to mind. Susan had been in her class at Miss Elderberry's Finishing School—her family was from Pearl Beach but they had sent Susan to Old Port for one year. She hadn't minded Agnes's eccentricities the way the other girls did; once she'd asked Agnes to help her with her corset, her smooth dark skin glowing against the white lace, her breasts spilling up in a way that set a sweet ache between Agnes's thighs.

She opened the drawstring on her red satin purse and fingered the jewelry inside, her most expensive pieces. It wasn't much, but Agnes hoped it would be enough to buy her a ticket at least to Arbaz. Thaetus was closer than Cairan, the main island where Ithilia was located, and hopefully less pricey a voyage. She had never arranged for her own travel before.

The motorcar stopped and she was brought abruptly back to reality. The Granges' brownstone was only two stories, made of red brick with white trim, a large bay window on the ground floor and a small balcony above the front door. Agnes swallowed and found her mouth had gone completely dry. The car idled for nearly a minute before Eneas said, "I think it's time to go in, my dear."

Her legs felt disconnected from her body as she walked the path to the house, up four steps; then somehow, she was pressing the ivory doorbell. A great booming clang rang from inside. A few moments later, an aging servant with graying hair and a large Solit triangle pinned to his breast answered the door.

"Miss McLellan," he said, bowing. "Young Master Grange is expecting you. Do come in."

She followed the man into the drawing room, her stomach crawling with spiders. The room was decorated in light-colored wood with blue and copper accents. An oil painting of a ship in a storm hung over the mantel. There was a small bar cart with crystal decanters in one corner and a bookshelf with leather-bound volumes in another. The coffee table was set for tea, and there was a bouquet of lilacs and lilies on a side table. The air was muggy, even though the windows were open.

Ebenezer Grange sat on a periwinkle sofa, looking nearly as anxious as Agnes felt. He jumped at the sight of her, shoving something behind a throw pillow and standing.

"Miss McLellan, sir," the butler announced.

"Thank you, Peter," he said. His voice was slightly nasal. He had thick brown hair and a very simple beard, Agnes was pleased to see—she hated all the ornate ways men in Old Port wore their beards, with ribbons or pins or curls or, worst of all, perfume. Ebenezer's olive skin had a sallow quality, and his wire-rimmed glasses slid down the bridge of his nose; he pushed them up and blinked at her. He gave her the overall impression of a very thin owl.

"How do you do, Agnes?" Ebenezer said, stepping forward and offering his hand, before seeming to remember that men and women did not shake hands. He put the offending appendage in his pocket, took it out and wiped it on his trousers, and then put it back in again.

"Very well, thank you," Agnes said stiffly, making her traditional awful curtsy. Her father must have had quite a laugh at this pairing. Two misfits who couldn't do anything right.

"Would you like some tea?"

Agnes thought she might have preferred whatever was in the crystal decanters—she never drank hard alcohol but was willing to make an exception on this day.

"Yes, please, that would be lovely," she said, sitting on the sofa by the lilies and trying to keep as much distance between her and Ebenezer as possible. His hands shook so hard as he poured that he nearly spilled the tea. Agnes almost felt bad for him, but still not as bad as she felt for herself.

She held her saucer and sipped her tea. The silence was oppressive. Ebenezer took a great amount of time adding the correct ratio of milk to sugar in his. She wondered if he was merely nervous or if it was a compulsion.

They sat and sipped and sipped and sat. The only noise was the occasional hum of a car passing or the chirp of a bird.

"Quite the heat wave we're having, isn't it?" Ebenezer said at last, and she groaned internally.

"Yes," she replied. "Even hotter than last year."

They fell into silence again. Agnes had just about had it. She hadn't asked for this arrangement, and she certainly wasn't going to twist herself into knots for Ebenezer Grange.

"At least you don't have to wear a corset," she said. "I feel as though my ribs are trapped in a very sweaty vise."

Her words certainly had an effect—Ebenezer choked on his tea, his cheeks darkening.

"I—I—I—" he stuttered.

"What?" she asked innocently. "You do know what a corset is, don't you?"

"Of course, but . . ." His whole face was coloring. "I've never heard a lady speak of one quite like that in public before."

Agnes swept a hand out at the room around them. "We are alone in your parlor. It isn't exactly the lobby of the Regent."

Ebenezer went to drink more tea and found he had finished it. He put the cup down with a clink. "My father told me of our engagement only last night," he said. "I am feeling quite . . . unprepared."

"So did mine," she replied. "And so am I."

He cleared his throat. "It isn't fair, is it? To have them decide."

"It isn't." She put her teacup down as well. "Look, Ebenezer, I know I'm not the greatest catch for a wife. My father has money and a good name, sure, but I'm not a pretty little Kaolin society girl. I say the wrong things and I wear the wrong clothes and I hate parties and small talk. And to be perfectly honest, if there was any way I could get out of this arrangement, I would."

"So would I," Ebenezer said miserably, and Agnes felt herself warm to him. He looked mortified, however. "I don't mean that you aren't . . . I didn't . . ." He wrung his hands. "I meant no offense."

"None taken," she said. "If we have to endure this dreadful charade, we should at least be honest with each other, shouldn't we?"

His thin lips twitched. "You are not like other girls, Agnes McLellan."

"No," she said. "I'm not." It felt good to say that, at least. She was glad she wasn't being forced on someone like Robert Conway or Bernard Foster-Brown or one of her brother's other awful friends. She would gladly take awkwardness over arrogance.

"Did your father say when the wedding will take place?" he asked.

"No, did yours?"

"No."

"Maybe we have some time then."

Ebenezer snorted. "Not likely, knowing my father. He's ready to get me out of the house so he can focus on Gerald and Louis like he's always wanted to." He made a gasping croak, like he was trying to suck the words back into his mouth. "I'm sorry, I shouldn't have—"

"Ebenezer." Agnes cut him off before he could keep

apologizing. "Nothing you say will offend me. My father wishes I had been born a boy; he even told me so to my face. I am not one to adhere to manners and courtesy, and I know firsthand how cruel fathers can be. Never apologize for telling the truth, at least not to me. It's refreshing, to be honest."

He grinned. "Old Port society can be quite stifling, can't it?"

"You have no idea." She sighed.

"I didn't know your father was aware of my existence, actually," Ebenezer said, taking off his glasses and cleaning them on a napkin.

"He makes it a point to know everything about everyone," she said. "So he can better exploit weakness."

"He seems a terribly frightful man."

"He is." She remembered the vein throbbing in his neck when she'd challenged him the night before. "I'm afraid he will not make a pleasant father-in-law. But then, I don't imagine he will be visiting much."

"Mine won't either," Ebenezer mused. He looked at her fearfully. "There isn't some other young man in Old Port who will be angry with this . . . arrangement? I cannot imagine my family was the only one that made an offer for your hand."

"No, there is no one," Agnes said. "I don't know who else offered. Father would never let me in on such minor decisions like who I marry."

She smiled at him so he knew she was joking, and he relaxed.

"What about you?" she asked, realizing she was being quite selfish. For all she knew, Ebenezer was in love and was now being ripped from his own happiness.

His ears turned pink. "There was one girl, but she, ah, did not share my affections."

"I'm sorry."

He shrugged. "It's all right. I was not surprised, really. I know my family isn't as rich as some, and I'm certainly not as handsome as . . . well, as your brother, for one. Girls seem to like him."

She rolled her eyes. "Don't let him hear you say that. He'll be even more insufferable than he already is."

"I must say, Agnes, I'm quite relieved. You are not at all what I thought you would be like."

"And what was that?"

He cocked his head and thought for a moment. "I imagined something along the lines of an overbearing headmistress."

"The horror," she said, grinning. "I only dress like one."

Ebenezer let out a loud laugh. "You have the sharpest tongue of any girl I have ever met."

"Perhaps," she said. "Or maybe it is just that none of the other girls are brave enough to use theirs."

He looked surprised. "I never thought of it like that."

Of course you haven't.

"Would you like some more tea?" he asked.

"Thank you," she said, picking up her cup and holding it out.

"Have you seen the papers today?" he asked as he poured. "There's a whole to-do over—"

"Do you have a paper?" Agnes interrupted. Why hadn't she thought to ask him before? "My father took ours, and I've only heard bits and pieces from my chauffeur."

"Yes, I was just reading it when you arrived." Ebenezer pulled a folded newspaper out from where he'd stuffed it behind the throw pillow and handed it to her.

ANCIENT RUINS DISCOVERED! the front of the *Old Port Telegraph* screamed. And underneath, in smaller lettering, *Could buried treasure await on this remote Pelagan island?* Agnes put her cup down on the table and gripped the paper with both hands.

Famed Kaolin sea captain Wendell Rivington and his crew were making their way home after a long journey to the very eastern islands of Pelago when a storm blew their ship off course. For five days they steered through the fog-covered waters, uncertainty plaguing them at every turn. On the sixth day the fog lifted, revealing the island of Braxos, one of what the Pelagans call the Lost Islands due to the dense fog that hides them from view.

Captain Rivington and his crew had to use all their skill not to run aground, and as they passed the island they saw the ruins of an ancient fortress, guarded with doors of gleaming metal adorned with strange markings. Gemstones in magnificent colors sparkled underneath the water, leading the men to cast nets down in the hopes of culling them from the seabed. Seaman Harry Withers, an amateur photographer, managed to snap a photograph of the ruins (seen here) before the fog swallowed Braxos up again and the ship was forced to turn away and head for safer waters.

How long have the ruins sat, untouched, on this remote island? What mysteries lie waiting behind those doors? What caused the surrounding waters to be filled with gemstones? And, most importantly, who will be the first to explore this elusive discovery and claim its riches for their own?

"It was all Gerald and Louis could talk about at breakfast," Ebenezer said. "I think Louis has forgotten he cannot swim." He chuckled at his own joke, but Agnes wasn't listening. She was staring at the grainy black-and-white photograph. The ruins were enormous, poised on a cliff jutting out high above the whitecapped waves. They rose to a lofty point with towers curling out from all sides like stone snakes. The doors were clearly visible, shining with a white light.

And perched atop them was a symbol that set Agnes's heart thrumming in her chest.

"Do you have a magnifying glass?" she demanded.

"I think there's one in the secretary," Ebenezer said, taken aback by her intensity. He went to the tall rosewood structure by the door and rifled through one of the lower desk drawers. "Here you go."

The magnifying glass had a polished ebony handle and was well cleaned. She held it up to the photograph.

A star stared back at her, a star with varying points, none of which were the same size or height. A star that looked shockingly similar to the one she'd seen hanging from the neck of a silver girl with blue hair.

It was the star from Sera's necklace.

18

LEO

LEO WATCHED WITH GROWING DISCOMFORT AS KIERNAN dragged the girl's limp form out of the crate.

As thrilling as the conversation with his father had been the previous evening, reality was setting in now. He was being included, at long last, but for what? Leo had wanted to run a theater company. He had dreamed of it his whole life. He'd thought when he volunteered for the expedition that in return he might get to assist the director or have a small role himself. He'd thought he would learn the ins and outs of the theater, what went on backstage during a play, and maybe flirt with the costume mistress. And then eventually he would take over his father's position and choose playwrights and help with casting and do whatever else it was Xavier did to keep the business running. But there wouldn't be a theater company for much longer, and Leo did not know how to feel about these stolen creatures from Pelago or the girl he had captured, or his role in all this.

She was still wearing the same filthy dress. The first thing Kiernan did was remove her bracelets and necklace.

"My, my, my," he said, holding the star-shaped pendant up to the light. "I have never seen a stone like this before, and my aunt was a jeweler. Whoever this girl is, she isn't from Pelago."

Leo could have told him that—unless she had jumped from Pelago to the Knottle Plains, there was no way she was from the islands. He had a feeling that she was somehow related to that shooting star he and Agnes had seen, as crazy as that sounded. Kiernan slipped the jewelry into his medical bag, then took out another needle and syringe.

"What's that for?" he asked.

"For her blood, dear boy." Kiernan sank the needle into the crook of her elbow, and what he drew out amazed them both. The girl's blood was as blue as her hair. He held the vial up and Leo stared in awe—flickers of light ran through it, crackling and vanishing like synapses.

"Whoa," he whispered.

"Indeed," Kiernan said.

"What do you think it means?"

"I have no idea, but I promise you I am going to find out." He tucked the vial away and took out a small pair of scissors, then cut strands of her hair and took clippings of her fingernails and secured them in their own vials. Then he shone a small flashlight into each of her eyes—their color was stunning, like a sapphire but clearer and brighter. Finally Kiernan took out a measuring tape. First he measured the length of her arm, then her leg, then around her neck and her head, then finally her waist, making notations in a notebook.

"Help me lift her," Kiernan said, as he tried to get the measuring tape around. Leo rolled her onto her side—he didn't like moving her unconscious form today any more than he had yesterday. It felt wrong. As he touched her, he saw her eyelids flutter.

"I think she's awake, Mr. Kiernan," he said.

"Nonsense. That anesthetic I gave her will keep her out for a good two hours at least." He made his last notation and snapped the book shut. Something niggled at Leo, something he couldn't place besides the fact that he was sure her eyelids had moved. Her face was peaceful, and Leo noted that her eyelashes were a very dark blue. Her skin was a color any silversmith in Old Port would drool over, her lips were parted slightly, and Leo detected the fragrance of her hair again, an intoxicating scent that he still could not place.

"All right, let's get her back in," Kiernan said.

"In the crate?" he asked.

"Of course in the crate, where else would we put her?"

Leo looked at the box of wood. She was just . . . a girl. It felt wrong to put her back in there. Kiernan had grabbed hold of her legs.

"Come on then," he said impatiently. "We haven't got all—"

He was interrupted by the door to the theater bursting

open, and Leo stared, starstruck, as James Roth ran down the aisle.

"Kiernan! They said I'd find you here. We've got to see Xavier at once." He stopped when he caught sight of the girl. "In the name of the One True God and all his holy missives," he gasped. "Who is that?"

"We aren't entirely sure," Kiernan said, standing and wiping his hands on his trousers before extending one to James to shake. "I've taken some samples, so we should know more by the day's end. What on earth is all this fuss about then?"

Leo couldn't stop staring. James Roth looked just the same as when Leo had seen him in *The Great Picando*, except he was in normal clothes. He had brown skin, thick, dark hair, and piercing green eyes, and he was a bit shorter than Leo had thought—perhaps he seemed taller onstage.

"My god, haven't you seen the papers?" James said. "There's been a development. An island in Pelago has been discovered. We're needed at—oh, hello," he said, just noticing Leo. "Sorry, are you new to the production?"

"Why, this is Xavier's son," Kiernan said, surprised. "Surely you two have met before."

"I haven't had the pleasure," James said, holding out a hand. "James Roth."

"Leo McLellan."

"Leo caught our newest addition here," Kiernan said with a nod to the girl.

"Really?" James looked impressed. "Any idea what she does? Is she like the others?"

Leo assumed he meant the mertag and the Arboreal, but

since he still didn't feel entirely confident of what *they* did, he shrugged and said, "We don't know much yet."

"Well, you're Xavier's son, so I'm sure you'll have it solved and sorted in no time." He gazed down at her, cocking his head. "She's sort of pretty, isn't she? In an odd way. Unique."

Leo hadn't thought much on the subject either way. James glanced at Kiernan.

"All right, come, we've got to get going."

"What does Father want us for?" Leo asked as Kiernan knelt to pack up his bag.

James's eyes filled with pity. "Sorry, old chap, but he didn't ask for you, just Mr. Kiernan."

"Oh," he said, trying to swallow his disappointment. "Right."

He had thought things would be different now, after the talk in Xavier's study. He supposed he should have known better.

"Just about ready," Kiernan said. "We need to get her back into the—"

Suddenly, the girl leaped to her feet in a movement so fluid Leo could not discern the shift from when she was prostrate on the ground to when she was standing.

"Hey!" James cried, stepping back.

Her eyes darted from Kiernan, to Leo, to Francis still hovering off to one side through this whole conversation, to James, then up to the glass ceiling, then back to Kiernan.

"How is this possible?" Kiernan said with astonishment.

The girl looked down at her wrist, then clutched at her

neck in desperation and let out a mournful stream of unintelligible words.

"I think she wants her jewelry back," Leo said.

Her head snapped toward him and she growled.

"She doesn't seem to like you," James noted. "All right then, my lady," he said gently, taking a careful step toward her, hands outstretched like he was talking down a skittish horse. She stepped back. "No one is going to hurt you. I promise. We just want to keep you safe."

Another round of gibberish followed that remark. She was backing up closer and closer to the Arboreal, which, Leo noticed somewhere in a distant part of his mind, was far more beautiful than in the photograph he'd seen, with silvery bark and turquoise leaves. It was also quite small, six feet tall at most. He'd thought a magic tree would be more intimidating.

"Francis, get the dogcatcher," Kiernan said, keeping his focus on the girl. Francis looked torn, staring at her with pity until Kiernan snapped, "Dammit, Francis, now!" and he jumped and scurried offstage. The girl's eyes were wild, desperate to find an exit, as Leo, Kiernan, and James began to encircle her. Leo was closest, on her right side, with James in the center and Kiernan on the left.

Quick as a whip, she darted toward the space between James and Kiernan, knocking over the medical bag and spilling its contents across the stage.

"My vials!" Kiernan cried, as James reached out to grab her. She wrenched free of his grasp and ran in the opposite direction, around behind the Arboreal, as Kiernan bent to collect the spilled items. Leo stepped on something and looked down to see the necklace with the star pendant—without thinking, he picked it up and put it in his pocket. Francis came running back with a long pole with a loop on its end, and Kiernan snatched it from him.

"Get her in a corner," he demanded. Leo could see her through the tree's branches, her face alight with fear. He took a step closer.

"Leo, to your right!" James called, as the girl shot out from behind the Arboreal and made a mad dash for the edge of the stage. Just as Leo reached for her, something rough and solid smacked him across the face, sparks exploding in front of his eyes as the theater and the girl were swallowed up in darkness.

He awoke in his bed.

His head throbbed, and he moaned and touched his cheek. Pain shot through his jaw like fire.

"Swansea!" Janderson's voice was muffled, as if Leo was hearing it through a headful of cotton. "He's awake."

Leo's vision was blurry, and it took a second for the world to focus. His body was stiff, the slightest movement setting off a series of jagged aches. A minute later, his father entered his room, followed by Kiernan and James. Having James Roth in his bedroom was not something Leo had ever anticipated, and he tried to sit up and look nonchalant but instead cried out in pain.

"Be still," Xavier said.

"That was quite a blow to the head you took," James said.

"It was absolutely incredible! I had no idea the Arboreal

could *move*." Kiernan seemed delighted, as if it was a minor detail that Leo's skull had been the price of this discovery.

"Incredible, indeed." There was a feverish look in Xavier's eyes. He turned to James. "And you said it was trying to protect the girl?"

"That's how it looked to me. Just as he reached for her—wham! One of Boris's branches shot out across his face and knocked him to the ground."

"Luckily, she seemed as stunned as we were," Kiernan said. "I was able to catch her, and James and I returned her to the crate."

"Is this something we need to be concerned about?" Xavier asked. "We can't have the Arboreal attacking our buyers."

"Or actors," James added.

"I'm not rightly sure, to be honest," Kiernan said. "I've never known it to happen before. Boris has not moved once, in all the months we've had him. He mostly hums those strange songs that help his saplings grow."

"Francis said he'd never seen anything like it, and he spends the most time with them," James said.

"Such a wondrous turn of events," Kiernan was muttering to himself. "First this girl appears, then those ruins in Braxos, then Boris comes to life."

Leo could see the gears in his father's head working. "Wondrous," he murmured. "Yes. But fortuitous or something more?"

"You think these events are connected?" Kiernan asked.

"I do not believe in coincidence," Xavier replied dryly.

"I told you, Ezra. I *told* you the island existed. We must get to it before anyone else. That is imperative. A Pelagan ship is what we need—it'll be faster and will draw less attention once it reaches Pelagan waters. There are going to be a lot of people, Kaolin and Pelagan alike, who will be tracking Braxos down." His eyes grew distant. "Braxos," he murmured, as if the name was a long-forgotten friend.

But the moment vanished as quickly as it had come, and when he spoke again, his voice was stony.

"Ambrosine will be assembling ships as we speak. We have to act quickly." The name Ambrosine was familiar, but Leo couldn't seem to place it. Everything felt dull and fuzzy, as if this conversation was happening in a dream.

His father turned to James. "You still know people at the Seaport?"

"A fair few, from my old days playing the taverns and such."

"Yes," Xavier drawled. "And such." James's face flushed, and Leo felt he was missing something. "I want to know everything that goes on down there—who is setting sail, and in what ships. I need a sense of the competition. And the rumors, too, no matter how far-fetched. Is that understood?"

James nodded curtly. He looked down at Leo. "Your son should put some ice on that cheek. He's going to have one hell of a bruise."

The word dislodged something in Leo's brain. When he'd been with the girl, stared at her face, noticed the color of her eyelashes . . . there had been no sign of Branson's fist, of the bruise he had seen forming the day before. How was that possible? Surely there should have been some mark left at least.

"No bruise," he mumbled. His jaw ached.

"Not to worry, it will be gone in a couple of weeks," Kiernan said.

"The ladies like a man with some battle scars," James said with a wink. "Just don't tell them it was a tree that hit you."

They weren't understanding at all. "No." Leo pushed himself up on his pillows despite the pain. "The girl. She had no bruise." He looked to his father. "You saw how hard Branson hit her. Her face should have been bruised, but it wasn't. It was . . . like he hadn't hit her at all. You saw her," he said, turning to Kiernan.

"I did," he said. "She was assaulted, you say?"

"She was trying to run," Xavier said. "Something of a pattern, it would seem."

"But the boy is right, she did not have a scratch on her." Kiernan rubbed his chin, muttering to himself, then gasped. "Perhaps her blood."

"Her what?" James asked.

"Her blood—it is blue and . . . and it sparkles."

James snorted.

"See for yourself," Kiernan said indignantly, taking the vial out of his bag and holding it up. It was even more impressive drenched in the sunlight pouring through Leo's windows than it had been in the theater. The light that flickered through its rich blue depths was captivating to watch, like flames of silvery fire. James's doubtful expression turned to one of wonder.

"Perhaps there is something of a healing nature that lives in her blood, an antibody of some kind, or . . ." Kiernan sighed. "But I am just guessing."

"Test it." Xavier's voice had the edge of a man trying very hard not to sound too excited. His eyes were fixed on the vial.

"I beg your pardon?"

He nodded at Leo's face. "If this blood has healing power, test it. On him."

"Sir, I do not think that would be wise. It was merely speculation on my part. We have no idea what—"

"Leo, will you allow Ezra to test his theory on you?" Without waiting for a response, he turned back to Kiernan. "It's only blood, for god's sake. What's the worst it could do?"

Leo was not thrilled with the idea of being a guinea pig for this experiment. He wished he'd kept his mouth shut about the bruise. But he could not disappoint his father.

"It's all right," he said. "I don't mind."

Kiernan hesitated. "I don't know. . . ."

"He said he didn't mind," Xavier said.

Kiernan looked as nervous as Leo felt as he took out the vial, unscrewed the top, and then carefully inserted an eyedropper into the blood. "We do not know if it should be ingested, or if a topical application will suffice."

"Let's try topical first," Leo suggested, before anyone could say otherwise. He did not want to drink blood if he didn't have to. But he knew that if push came to shove, he would do it if his father ordered him to.

Kiernan approached the bed like he was approaching a

wounded animal. He held the dropper over Leo's battered face, took a deep breath, and carefully released three drops of blood.

The effect was instantaneous. Leo could not help the moan of pleasure that escaped his lips as a soothing coolness spread across his face. He could feel the blood seeping into his wound, the bizarre sensation of his skin knitting together, the swelling decreasing until the pain had vanished completely. A crackle of heat ran through his veins, making his scalp prickle, and he heard the sound of a girl's laugh as a familiar scent filled his nostrils—it was the one he had detected in Sera's hair but more potent. Flowers, Leo realized, but also not flowers; the alluring smell of freesia mixed alongside the freshness of basil with an undertone he couldn't place but that made him think of starlight. Then it was gone, and the laugh disappeared, and the heat vanished.

"Holy shit," James muttered, staring at Leo, awestruck.

Kiernan was shaking. Leo sat up, rubbing his face. The aches were gone. He opened and closed his jaw, and it felt like it did on any other day.

"I have never seen anything like this in all my years," Kiernan murmured. "And I have seen a fair many things."

"How do I look?" Leo asked, and James laughed.

"Good as new," he said. "My god. Who *is* this girl?"

Triumph lit up Xavier's eyes, small torches of greed that made Leo wish for a split second that the blood had done nothing and he'd been left to suffer the pain. He could still hear the laugh in his ears; it was carefree and full of joy, and something about it made Leo feel deeply ashamed.

"That," Xavier said, "is not our concern." He took the

vial from Kiernan's hand and held it up to the light. "We are going to need more of this. Much, much more."

They left him to convalesce, even though he didn't really need to. Leo felt that they wanted to talk about all this without him being there, which shouldn't have hurt as much as it did. He swung his legs over the edge of the bed and sat up gingerly, testing out his newly healed head. He walked to his vanity, staring at his face in the mirror. It was exactly the same as it had been this morning.

Incredible, he had to admit. But also confusing and a bit worrying. He felt like he'd unlocked some secret door that wasn't his business and was best kept closed. He straightened and put his hands in his pockets, wondering what he should do now, when he felt something sharp against his palm. He pulled out the star necklace, its stone glowing like moonlight.

He held it up, deliberating. He should hand it over to his father—surely Xavier would be pleased by the show of loyalty. But he remembered how desperately the girl had clutched at her neck, the agonized wail when she discovered it was gone. The stone was cool against his hand, reminding him of the soothing sensation as her blood had healed his wounds.

His father had the girl locked in a crate in his theater. Surely that was enough.

Leo hid the necklace in the back of his sock drawer.

19

AGNES

Eneas drove her to the Seaport after she left the Grange house.

The docks were always bustling with activity, but they were more crowded this afternoon than usual. In addition to the ships unloading various cargo—large crates of produce and heavy sacks filled with spices and olives or ornate trunks stuffed with Pelagan aurums ready to be exchanged for krogers—there were now hastily erected tents promising maps to Braxos, infallible compasses, and manuals for discerning gemstones. Signs were posted in front of most ships, announcing exorbitant prices for berths and schedules of departures. Agnes knew it would only get worse in the coming days, as more and more treasure seekers swelled into Old Port in search of passage to Pelago.

Fishermen sold skewers of grilled cod and scallops while fresh octopus tentacles cooked under their watchful gaze; prostitutes leaned out of the windows of brothels, wearing wisps of clothes and calling down to the sailors below. The wide main walkway was spattered with blood, cigarette butts, fish guts, and other fluids whose origins Agnes did not wish to think about.

She had told Eneas to wait by the car, that she was only going to buy some bracelets that the fishermen's wives sold, but she wasn't sure he believed her. She made certain to pick up a few at the first stall she passed as evidence; she bought him a bag of his favorite candied walnuts as well, hoping that might placate him.

Agnes kept her eye out for the Pelagan flag, green with the silver crest of Pelago emblazoned on it, two horses rearing on either side of an olive tree. But the only flags she saw bore the red stripes and golden sun of Kaolin. Then she noticed two women wearing the traditional lace gowns and ornate shell headdresses of the Pelagan upper class, weaving through the crowds arm in arm. She fell into step behind them, hoping they might be searching for a ship as well.

They spoke in Pelagan, and Agnes's grasp of the language was not strong enough to understand them. But they led her to a ship and her spirits leaped. It was a large but graceful galleon with a horse's head carved into the bow. The captain, a middle-aged Pelagan woman, called out to the ladies on the dock. She strode down the gangplank and welcomed them in their native tongue, kissing their hands and fawning over them. Agnes loitered around, waiting for the women to finish their dealings so she could approach the captain herself. She felt in her pocket for the bag of jewelry and worried that this ship might be too grand for her meager payment. If only she could access her account at the bank herself! She had a trust with enough krogers to buy her passage on this ship, she was sure. But her father would never give her permission to take out so much money.

Suddenly, a sign by the gangplank caught her eye.

PELAGAN PAISIVATIS MONACH

And underneath, in Kaolish, was written:

PELAGAN PASSENGERS ONLY

Agnes's heart sank. This ship wouldn't take her no matter how many krogers she offered. She left the women and wandered down the docks, seeing similar signs on other ships flying the Pelagan flag. She reached the end of the docks and was about to turn around and head back to the car, in shame and defeat, when she saw the schooner. It was unimpressive and ramshackle, a tattered flag hanging from its prow, faded to nearly colorless, but Agnes could make out the shape of a horse and part of a tree.

The ship appeared to be deserted except for a single girl, maybe a year or two older than Agnes herself, sitting on a wooden bollard at the foot of the gangplank, smoking a clove cigarette and whittling away at a chunk of driftwood. Agnes stood for a moment, unsure of what to do, if this girl was even part of the crew of this schooner or if she'd just found a convenient spot to sit and smoke. Finally, she decided she had to try.

"Hello," she said. "I would like to book passage on your ship."

"This is not a passenger ship," the girl said in heavily accented Kaolish without looking up from her whittling. Her skin was freckled and sunburned, her thick auburn hair tied back in a loose braid. Agnes cursed herself for not saying hello in Pelagan.

"*Se parakhair maitorese mi,*" she said, and the girl looked up at the formal Pelagan apology. "It is of great importance that I get to Pelago as soon as possible."

The girl's eyes narrowed. They were a gray as soft as a mourning dove's wing but keen and full of suspicion. Agnes felt this was someone who had seen much over her short lifetime.

"A Kaolin lady who speaks Pelagan?" she said. She took a long drag of her cigarette. "Now that is not something one sees every day."

"My mother taught me."

The girl raised an eyebrow, her face skeptical. "That is a lie."

Agnes flushed. "It was my chauffeur," she admitted.

"And what does the lady's parents think of a servant teaching their daughter such a heretical language?"

This really wasn't the direction Agnes wanted the conversation to be going in, but she felt if she pushed her agenda too hard, the girl might balk.

"My mother was Pelagan," she said. "But she died when I was born. My father . . . doesn't know."

The girl laughed at that, slapping her knee. "Good for you, Kaolin lady. A girl must have some secrets, right?" She winked and Agnes felt herself momentarily exposed, as if this girl could see right to the heart of her.

"Will you give me passage to Pelago then?" she asked. "I can pay."

She held out the bag and the girl took it and peered inside.

"This is not enough to get you to Pearl Beach, much less across the Adronic to the great nation of islands," she said, handing the bag back.

"How much would it take to get to Ithilia?" Agnes asked.

The girl's eyes roved over Agnes's body, taking in her fine dress, gold jewelry, and the little hat perched on her head. Everything about her screamed money, and this girl knew it.

"One thousand krogers," she said.

"One th—have you lost your mind?" Agnes cried. "That's highway robbery!"

The girl shrugged and stubbed her cigarette out on the bollard. "That is my price. Take it or leave it."

Agnes was about to storm away when a thought occurred to her. She glanced at the empty ship and then back at the girl. "You aren't the captain of this vessel, are you?"

The girl's posture shifted slightly. "So?"

Agnes folded her arms across her chest. "I would like to speak to the person in charge, if you please. Perhaps we will be better able to negotiate a deal."

At that, the girl stood. She was taller than Agnes had

expected, and she wore supple leather boots, dark pants, and a black vest over a white shirt, a fang hanging from a leather strap around her neck. The overall effect was quite impressive.

"I am Vada Murchadha," she proclaimed. "Daughter of Violetta, who is captain of the *Maiden's Wail*, and I am charged with its protection until my mother and the crew return from their business outside this filthy city. So as far as this Kaolin lady should be concerned, I *am* the captain and I make the decisions."

If they were going to be throwing around mothers, then two could play at that game. Agnes saw an opportunity and drew herself up, trying to imitate her brother's swaggering arrogance as she said, "I am Agnes McLellan, daughter of Xavier McLellan and Alethea Byrne, and I demand you give me passage on the *Maiden's Wail* so that I may return to my mother's family in Pelago. You have heard of the Byrnes, I assume?"

Vada rolled her eyes. "Of course I have heard of the Byrnes. Who in Pelago has not? But you do not have the look of a Byrne." She spit on the ground at Agnes's feet.

"If you could see my brother, you would believe me," Agnes grumbled. Goddamn Leo and his goddamn face.

Vada looked with exaggerated movements from left to right. "I see no brother," she said.

"He isn't here *now*, but—"

"Then you have no proof. Am I just to take your word?"

Agnes was beginning to feel helpless, and the worst part was that Vada seemed to be enjoying herself.

"Besides," she continued, sitting back on the bollard and

taking up her whittling, "I know how things work here. You need your papa's permission for travel." She looked from side to side again. "I also see no papa."

"I did not think a Pelagan sailor would care a whit for Kaolin rules," Agnes said. "I thought she would respect a woman's right to do as she pleases."

"Ah, but Kaolin women are not women. They are mice."

Agnes bristled. "I'm no mouse. And I don't think my grandmother would appreciate me being treated so rudely." For the first time in her life, she prayed her father was right—that Ambrosine Byrne really was as intimidating as he had made her out to be.

Vada hesitated. Agnes could see her deliberating and held her breath.

"Eight hundred krogers," she said.

"Five," Agnes countered.

"Seven."

"Six."

"Six and fifty."

"Done," Agnes said. Vada held out her hand and she took it. Her palms were calloused, her grip steady and sure, and her smile was a clever one full of salt and schemes. Agnes found her mouth suddenly quite dry.

"You have a deal, Kaolin lady."

"Agnes," she corrected her.

"Agnes," Vada said. Agnes quite liked the sound of her name the way Vada said it. "We leave in eleven days' time."

"What? No, that's far too long!"

Vada pulled another cigarette out of her vest pocket. "It

is not up to the lady when we leave. She is lucky enough to be buying passage."

Agnes knew the truth of this and could not argue. But eleven days felt like a lifetime. She wanted to be on her way *now*.

"And I will be needing the payment up front," Vada added, striking a match on the bottom of her boot and lighting the cigarette.

"I will give you half by the end of the week." She wasn't about to let this girl steal her money and run off to Pelago.

"You will give me all or the agreement is off."

"And how do I know you will hold up your side of the bargain?"

Vada touched the fang around her neck. "Every Pelagan woman gives her daughter an *endexen*, a . . . how you say it, a *token*, at birth. This is mine. It was my grandmother's and hers before her. Verini Murchadha chased a great blue-finned shark deep into the northern waters of Pelago and killed it with a single harpoon thrust. This is one of the beast's fangs. It is more precious to me than anything in the world. I swear on the soul of my great-great-grandmother and the monster she killed, this ship will not leave without the daughter of Alethea Byrne on board." Her voice held such passion as she made this vow that Agnes did not realize her body had inclined toward Vada until the girl grinned and said, "Or we could kiss to seal the deal. It is your choice."

"What? I . . . no, I . . . that vow will do nicely," Agnes stammered, her cheeks burning. She glanced around to make sure no one else had heard the offer.

Vada shrugged. "Suit yourself." She tossed her whittling knife in the air and caught it deftly. "It's a shame. A pretty lady should be kissed well and kissed often. Or at least that is what my aunt says."

Agnes was confused—was Vada flirting with her or mocking her? She'd never been flirted with before, so she couldn't tell. And no one had ever called her pretty. She felt it best to leave while the deal was still in place.

"I shall return by week's end with the money. Will I find you here?"

"At the Wolfshead Tavern," Vada said. "Their ale is passable. Better than the piss most of the places around here serve."

Agnes had never been to any of the Seaport taverns, nor had she ever tasted ale. "I will take your word for it," she said. "Good afternoon, Vada. And . . . thank you. Um, *feados na thaeias dul leatsou.*"

Vada raised one eyebrow. *"Feados na thaeias dul leatsou,"* she replied. It was a typical Pelagan farewell that meant "May the goddesses go with you." "Your chauffeur teaches you well."

Agnes hurried back along the docks, not daring to stop until she saw the green motorcar. She could still feel the rough warmth of Vada's hand on her skin.

"All right then, Miss Agnes?" Eneas said. He was leaning against the hood of the car with the *Old Port Telegraph* in his hands. "Did you find the bracelets you were looking for?"

She'd forgotten all about the bracelets and took them

out to show him, along with the walnuts, which he accepted eagerly and shared with her on the ride home.

They arrived back at the brownstone on Creekwater Row to find the house in utter tumult. Mrs. Phelps was ordering Hattie and Janderson around, Swansea kept bustling from room to room, and there seemed to be a slew of new servants cleaning everything from the carpets to the banisters to the lamps.

"What's going on?" Agnes asked as a flustered Hattie came rushing up to unpin her hat.

"There's to be a party here tomorrow evening," she said. "A private party for some very important people. Your father wants the place spotless. He's ordered food from the finest shops in Old Port, and wine too. He was very particular."

"A private party? For what?" Agnes couldn't remember the last time her father had held a party in his own house.

"I don't rightly know," Hattie said. "But miss, I've got to polish the silver. . . ."

"Of course. I'm going to retire to my room for a bit."

"I'll come to dress you before dinner," Hattie said before scampering off to the dining room.

Leo was standing at the railing, looking down at the hustle and bustle in the foyer below. His face was pensive, his mood almost brooding. Agnes thought that strange— Leo loved social gatherings more than anyone else in the family.

"What's this party for?" she asked him.

He started, as if he hadn't even seen she was there, and

touched his cheek, an odd gesture Agnes didn't understand.

"Her, I think," Leo said, and he sounded distracted. "The silver girl."

"A party for Sera?" Why on earth would her father be throwing his captive a party?

"What did you call her?" he asked, and she pressed her lips together. She hadn't been thinking. Vada's soft gray eyes and sly smile had her all out of sorts.

Leo took a step forward. "Sera?" he said. "Agnes, how do you know her name?"

"Oh, like I'm going to tell you," she said. "You'll just run off to Father, and the two of you will find some way to make that poor girl even more miserable. And I won't help with that."

She expected some sharp retort, but instead her brother seemed to sag. "You don't know anything," he said, turning and trudging back toward his room.

"Leo," she called. "Are you . . . all right?"

His door closed with a click, and Agnes was left with more questions than her mind could answer.

What had her brother so gloomy?

And what was this party about?

But the most pressing of all: How on earth was she going to get six hundred and fifty krogers by the end of the week?

20

SERA

Sera sipped at the cup of water Francis had left her for the night as she waited for Errol to emerge from his pond.

She had been so close! She had gotten free of the crate. Whatever that red-haired male had given her to make her fall asleep, she didn't like it. It had made her limbs slow, her brain fuzzy, until her magic had burned away every last trace of it. She had been shocked when Boris had *moved*, knocking Leo right off his feet.

Well, now he knew what it felt like. Sera could not spare an ounce of pity for him. She only had enough for herself. She had not been able to see the tether through the glass ceiling, but that did not mean it was not there. If only she could get outside. She needed a spire to climb, someplace high where she could see for miles. Until she was certain her City was truly gone, she would not give up hope.

Her thoughts turned to the other male who had come yesterday, the one with the green eyes and dark hair who they called James. His face kept popping up in her mind for some reason. It was extremely irritating, but she could not seem to stop it. She rubbed at her eyes, as if that would make the vision disappear.

"No *nasty humans poking and prodding at Errol today!*" The mertag climbed out of his pond, cackling his strange croaking laugh. He plucked one of the luminescent flowers and popped it into his mouth.

"Oh no, don't!" Sera cried. "Those are our only lights."

"*Don't, she says? Don't?*" Errol squared his small shoulders. "*I am a mertag and I make these flowers. More light she wants? Well, by urchins and eels, more light she will have!*"

He dug his clawed hands into the moss and gritted his teeth. His whole body, from head to tail, began to pulse in stunning colors, like his filaments but on a much larger scale. Purple, then pink, then orange. Purple-pink-orange. Purple-pink-orange. Sera watched with wonder as tiny fronds began to sprout from the moss, blossoming right before her very eyes. Soon it was dotted with glowing flowers, giving off more than enough light to see by.

She could not help herself—she clapped enthusiastically at the display.

"How did you do that? It's beautiful."

Errol looked smug. *"It is all part of being a mertag, Sera Lighthaven. We have sharp brains, yes, but not only brains. There is magic in our scales."* He examined his handiwork. *"Though I confess I have never made so many at once before."*

"There is magic in my blood," Sera said. "But it isn't helping me much now."

"You are speaking to a mertag," he pointed out. *"Humans cannot speak the colors."*

"That's true," she agreed. "But I want to go home, Errol."

"Yes, home." His filaments lit up in mournful greens and grays. *"I am not meant to be here either, Sera Lighthaven. I miss the dark waters, the feel of the cold current over my scales, the familiar colors of my fellow mertags."*

They lapsed into silence. Sera clutched her neck where the pendant had hung, wondering if Leela had thought about her at all, if she missed Sera as desperately as Sera missed her.

The silence was broken by a gentle humming sound.

"What's that?" she gasped, looking around.

"That is Tree," Errol said. *"Tree likes to hum sometimes."*

"They call him Boris," she said.

The corners of Errol's mouth turned down. *"Tree is female."*

"Oh." Sera glanced at the silvery trunk. "How do you know?"

He shrugged. *"It is obvious."*

There was something soothing about the song Boris hummed that reminded her of the moonflower fields at sunrise and of the thick, soft fleece of a seresheep.

"*I know you.*" The voice came out of nowhere, and it seemed to echo in Sera's head the way Errol's did, except this voice, while deep and rich, was distinctly feminine.

"What was that?" she said.

"*What was what?*" Errol looked up at her, his mouth full of flowers.

"*I know you,*" Boris said again, and Sera was sure this time that it was directed at her. The Arboreal's three eyes turned in her direction. They were dark and smooth like pebbles along a riverbank, full of wisdom and sadness. "*Mother,*" she hummed.

Sera was not a mother, and if she had been, she would certainly not be the mother of a tree.

"Who is your mother?" she asked, but Boris did not speak the colors, and Sera did not know how to speak the humming tree language. She splayed her hands wide and stared at them, as if she might be able to see through her skin to the magic inside. Mother Sun, but this was frustrating.

"*I know your face,*" Boris hummed.

"*Tree likes you,*" Errol said.

"She says she knows me," Sera said.

"*But you only just got here.*"

"I know." She felt as if she was on the brink of understanding something very important, but the answers were just out of her reach, like a butterfly flitting from flower to flower, never settling down. She gazed up at the covered glass ceiling and wished she could see the stars. She had always felt guided by them. But now she was untethered and alone.

More humans came the next day, and this time there were females as well as males.

She was determined to be ready. She would not be stabbed with a needle or captured by a hoop. A change was happening inside her—she could feel it even if she did not truly understand it, and there was no green mother to ask. To be honest, she doubted her green mother would be able to tell her anyway. She had to learn for herself now.

The first to arrive after Francis had given her food and more water and changed the bucket she used to relieve herself was an older male with a tremendous amount of hair on his face. He had it tied in two prongs braided with red and gold ribbons. His skin was wrinkled as a walnut, and he wore two pieces of glass connected with wire over his eyes.

"Let me see her, Francis," he said, climbing the steps to the stage and rubbing his hands together. He knelt by the crate and peered inside. Sera hated the way he was staring at her, like she wasn't a person at all.

"In the name of the One True God . . ." he murmured. The green-eyed male James had used the same invocation. Sera didn't know who this One True God was, but she didn't like him. "I heard she tried to run yesterday."

"Yes, sir, but Mr. Kiernan and Mr. Roth caught her." Francis stared down at his feet as if ashamed.

"I hope they have sorted out some way to transport her for this evening."

"I believe Mr. McLellan has hired Pemberton men, sir."

"Ah! A wise decision."

Transport her? This evening? Sera's mood lifted. Maybe they would take her out of the crate again. Another chance to escape was presenting itself so soon.

Others filtered in after that—there was a boisterous male with black hair on his upper lip and chin and a large woman with a heavily painted face who shrieked when she saw Sera and clutched at the male.

"Grayson, what is it?"

"My dear Gwendivere, I haven't the foggiest," the hairy-lipped male replied. "I barely understand any of this." He gestured to Boris and then to the pond. "Old Xavier's gone off his rocker, if you ask me."

The woman named Gwendivere slapped his arm playfully. "You're just mad he won't be casting you in every play he produces anymore."

"Yes, shockingly, I've enjoyed having a steady pay-check," Grayson said. He called out to the man with the beribboned face hair. "What's this one do, Martin? Will she turn all our hair blue or make our skin silver as the moon?"

What a ridiculous thing to say, Sera thought. How on earth would she be able to do either of those things?

"James will find out tonight," the man named Martin replied. "There's to be a little gathering at the McLellan house."

"Xavier is throwing a party?" Grayson asked incredulously.

"Good morning, fellow thespians!" James's voice echoed

throughout the room as he strode up the aisle to the stage, taking the steps two at a time and finishing with an elaborate bow.

"Good morning, James," Gwendivere said in a fluttery voice that made Sera's nose wrinkle.

"Have you all become acquainted with our newest addition?" he asked. "She's remarkable. Gave us quite the scare yesterday, didn't she, Francis?" Francis looked like he'd rather not be included in this conversation.

"But what *is* she?" the woman demanded.

"Don't be frightened, Gwen, she's harmless. And you have no idea what she can do," he added with a wink. That brought Sera up short. What did James know? Or was he lying to impress this woman? Sera wasn't sure what to believe on this planet.

"All right, it's time to get started," Martin said, clapping his hands. "We'll do a full run of the first act today. Francis, move her backstage for now, please. I'm not sure what role Xavier has planned for her yet. Everyone else, places for act one! Places!"

Sera did not know what any of that meant, but the humans sprang into action. Francis slid a large metal hook onto the chain around the crate and dragged it away until she was behind one of the red curtains. Other people were back here too, but they gave her a wide berth and she was fine with that.

The day progressed and all Sera could do was sit in her crate and watch. They appeared to be telling a story of some kind, except that instead of one person telling it, like

Cerulean storytellers, many people acted out the different characters.

The plot seemed to revolve around Gwendivere and James—Gwendivere was an evil woman from Pelago, Sera gathered, who had hidden Errol and Boris away because they had great power and she wanted to keep it all for herself. James played the hero, who was searching for them to bring them back to Kaolin and save its people from famine and death. The hairy-lipped Grayson appeared to be playing a comedic role, something called a *pirate*. The other humans behind the curtains would laugh at his antics and silly faces. Sera didn't find him very funny.

Her eyes were drawn again and again to James. There was something magnetic about him, as he prowled the stage and delivered his lines with passion and gusto. He was captivating to watch, and the more she watched him, the more intrigued she was by him, his build and stature, the muscles in his arms, his shirt open enough to reveal the skin of his chest, which also had hair on it. His hands were broad and sure. And his eyes were the most beautiful color green she had ever seen. Over and over she told herself to stop staring, and over and over her gaze would find its way back to him.

What was this . . . this . . . compulsion? Did James possess a magic of his own, like Errol and Boris? But no, humans did not have magic, her green mother said. And surely she would have seen human magic by now if it existed.

At last, the storytelling was over and suddenly James was kneeling by her crate.

"Almost time to leave, my lady. We're going on a little

trip," he said with a smile that made Sera's mouth water like she was hungry, except she did not feel hungry at all. His face was so close to hers, she could smell his skin—it had a woodsy scent that reminded her of walking through the Forest of Dawn at twilight, but with an undercurrent of something she could only identify as *male*. She had a sudden desire to run her fingers through his hair and see what it felt like.

It hit her then, with the force of her orange mother's cherry cordial. This was not magic. This was *attraction*. She wanted this male, the way she had tried to want Koreen or Treena or any of the other girls her age and failed. The thing she had longed for above all else, the one secret she had kept from those she cared for . . . she had been wrong. This whole time. She was not incapable of love.

She loved males.

All the air left her lungs in a whoosh. How could she have known? She had never seen a male until she had come to this planet. And now she knew and the knowing was painful and confusing.

And yet, there was a strange sense of comfort too, as if a missing puzzle piece had been found and the picture of who she truly was came into perfect clarity. She understood herself in a way she had previously been unable to, and there was relief in that.

"Are you all right?" James asked, his voice thick with concern. Sera blinked and realized there were tears in her eyes. She turned away, embarrassed. "Francis, help her out of there, will you?"

The young male crouched beside her, taking a ring of keys from James's outstretched hand.

"Listen," Francis said softly. "I know you don't know what I'm saying, but . . . I've got to let you out and they're going to take you away now for a little while, and it would be best for you if you didn't try to run. They'll hurt you if you do, I think." As if to prove the point, two shadowy figures, males in dark suits and hats, appeared around the crate. Boris was too far away to help her.

Sera had to be honest with herself. Her two previous escape attempts had not gone particularly well. Maybe she would have a better chance once she got to wherever they were taking her.

Once she was out of the crate, Francis handed James the keys, and James put bracelets on her wrists, but not delicate ones like her stargem bracelets. These were heavy and iron; they kept her hands close together with a strong chain, and they chafed against her skin. She pulled hard to see if she could break them apart, but they were stronger than the slats of the crate.

A shiny black car waited for them outside. Sera caught a glimpse of tall buildings lining a very large street before James opened a door and helped her into the back—the seats were sticky with heat and the windows were darkened so she could not see out. The other men got into the front two seats.

This car moved faster than the one she had been in with Agnes, and the ride was smoother. When it stopped, James opened the door, and she found herself in front of a grand dwelling, multistoried with lots of windows. There were even more men in suits prowling around it, and Sera had the sense they were guarding something.

Me, she realized.

They walked through a garden and her heart ached at the scent of hydrangeas. The sky was a darker blue than she had yet seen it, the sunlight a rich honeyed yellow tinged with orange. She, James, and the two men entered the dwelling through a door that led to a kitchen. Lots of people were bustling around, but they all stopped to stare at her.

"Mr. Roth." An older woman with a golden triangle at her throat and a tiny white cap pinned to her head came hurrying up. "Mr. McLellan has been expecting you. He is in his study and told me to send you there as soon as you arrived. I can take her from here."

"Gladly, Mrs. Phelps. I assume she'll be cleaned up a bit before the evening," James said.

Mrs. Phelps glanced at Sera, the corners of her mouth turning down at the sight of her dirty cloudspun robe. "Yes, Hattie is just filling the tub now. Mr. McLellan has hired private security, so you needn't worry, she won't be going anywhere."

"Yes, ma'am, I know. Pemberton men are the best."

"Mr. McLellan spared no expense. Take those handcuffs off for now. You can put them back on once she's cleaned and ready."

Sera was only half listening. This dwelling was quite tall. Maybe if there was a way to get to the very top of it . . .

James took off the bracelets with a key. Sera shivered when his hands brushed her skin. "I will see you at the party, my lady."

The two men shadowed her as she followed Mrs. Phelps out of the kitchen, and the stares continued as she entered a large area covered in plush carpet and then climbed up a set of stairs with a wooden banister. How many people lived in this dwelling? Most of the women had little white caps, and the men wore the same jacket-and-trouser combination.

Mrs. Phelps opened a door to a windowless room filled with steam. A girl in an apron was pouring a bucket of water into a massive porcelain basin large enough for Sera to lie down in. There was a sink inlaid with a mosaic of roses and a dress hanging up by an oval looking glass similar to the one in her mothers' bedroom. A little dresser sat in one corner with brushes and combs and tubes and powders on its surface.

"Here she is, Hattie," Mrs. Phelps said, and the girl nearly dropped the empty bucket at the sight of her. "I've got to get back to the kitchen. Have her washed, dressed, and ready in one hour sharp."

"Y-yes, Mrs. Phelps," Hattie stammered. Once the older woman had left, the girl reached for Sera's dress.

"Stay away!" Sera cried, backing up against a wall.

Hattie looked confused. "I was only trying . . . you have to disrobe before you bathe."

"My orange mother made me this," Sera said, wrapping her arms around herself. "You will not take it from me."

They'd already taken so much. Her bracelets. Her necklace. Her freedom.

"Please." Hattie could not understand her words, but her actions were clear. "I've got to get you clean and you can't bathe in that thing, it's filthy."

"You will not take my robe!" Sera shouted.

"Hattie?" There was a loud banging on the door.

"Agnes?" Sera gasped. Hattie looked torn.

"Hattie, open this door at once!"

Sera's knees went weak with relief as Hattie opened the door and Agnes strode into the room.

"You shouldn't be here, miss," Hattie was saying, but Sera had already run over and thrown her arms around Agnes, who stiffened, as if surprised at being hugged, but then returned the embrace with feeling.

"It's so good to see you," she whispered in Sera's ear.

"You too," Sera whispered back, not caring that Agnes couldn't understand.

"Leave us, Hattie," Agnes said, releasing her hold on Sera. "I'll get her ready."

"Your father—"

"My father wants her clean and dressed, and I'm more than capable of doing that. Go see if Mrs. Phelps needs any help in the kitchen."

Hattie hesitated, then made a dipping movement with her legs and left. Agnes took a key out of her pocket, closed the door, and locked it.

"Oh, Sera, I've been so worried about you," she said. "How have they been treating you? Where have they been keeping you? They haven't hurt you, have they?"

But Sera had questions of her own. "Did you find anything in my hair that would help me get home? Is there a way to get to the roof of this dwelling? I need to see the sky and find the tether!"

But it was hopeless. They could not understand each

other any more than a starbeetle could understand a sun trout. Now that they were face-to-face once again, Sera was desperate to be able to communicate, to tell Agnes everything, to have someone to confide in, to help her. Talking to Errol simply wasn't the same. Agnes felt more like . . . like Leela.

She looked down at her hands again. Her green mother had told her it had taken the Cerulean quite some time to talk to those giant birds, but they had figured it out. And they were more knowledgeable then—they had visited planets regularly. She'd never been challenged like this before, and maybe the trick was simply in believing it could be done. Her brow furrowed as she concentrated on her heart pumping her blood through her body, sensing the magic within her. A smattering of light crackled across her palms.

"Of course you can't answer me," Agnes was muttering to herself. Then she slapped her forehead. "But you can write! Pen and paper, that's what we need. . . ."

She went over to the small dresser and started rifling through its drawers. But Sera's mind was churning. Agnes was more like Leela . . . like Leela . . . had she given herself the answer? Humans and Cerulean were similar in physicality. They spoke in words, not colors or hums. The difference was their coloring and the magic in Sera's blood. Could she *blood bond* with Agnes? Sera did not know if her magic alone would be enough to let this human girl read her heart, to open some line of communication. It was daunting, not only because Sera had blood bonded with only four others in her whole life, but because Agnes's blood did not contain magic. So would it even work?

"You *will* let me speak to her," she said to her hands in what she hoped was a commanding tone. "You will work as you did in the days before the Great Sadness."

"Are you all right?" Agnes asked, stepping away from the dresser.

Sera called on her magic and her fingertip began to glow.

Agnes gasped. "What is that?"

"Give me your finger," she said, holding her own up and motioning for Agnes to do the same.

The girl was sharp—she held up a finger and said, "This? Is this what you want?"

Sera nodded. The human finger looked so plain next to her own. A seed of doubt began to sprout, and Sera squashed it before it could fully blossom.

I am a Cerulean, she thought fiercely. *My blood is magic. And it will do as I command.*

Then she pressed her glowing fingertip against Agnes's.

21

AGNES

AGNES DID NOT FULLY COMPREHEND WHAT WAS HAPPENING.
She wasn't sure what she expected when Sera held out
her fingertip, glowing with a bluish-silver light. It reminded
her a bit of the medulla she'd seen in Sera's hair, but bigger
and brighter—it pulsed and twinkled like starlight. It was
fascinating and beautiful and more than a little scary.

She hadn't really considered what she was doing until
their fingers touched and Agnes felt a rush of heat enter
her body through the point of contact. It was shocking and
disorienting—she found she had no sense of where she was,
if she was standing or sitting or if she even had legs at all.
She felt like an empty vessel, more spirit than flesh. The heat
that crawled up her arm was a tangible thing, wrapping itself

around veins and bone and muscle, crackling and spitting like a fire. It raced to her elbow, then up into her shoulder, growing stronger in intensity, and Agnes wanted to shout, *Stop!* but she could not find her mouth.

The heat curled around her heart like a fist, squeezing it with every beat. She felt another heartbeat fall in line with hers, a secondary pulse in her chest that was both comforting and unfamiliar, and she thought she said, *Sera?* but she had no mouth so she could not have spoken aloud.

Yes, a new voice replied, and it was everywhere, it was echoing in her ears and wrapping around her knees and beating alongside her two hearts, and all of a sudden Agnes felt herself pulled in a thousand different directions. There was a hard jerk in the place where her stomach used to be; her eyes were squeezed shut but she could not stop the images and feelings that rose up with shocking clarity.

She was seven, snooping in her father's study for some evidence of her mother, when Leo caught her and pulled her hair, telling her she was going to be in trouble.

She was a child in a massive, circular room with moons and stars and a sun painted on its vaulted ceiling. A silver-skinned woman with an orange ribbon tied around her neck was chastising her for asking an impertinent question.

She was sixteen, at Miss Elderberry's, helping Susan Bruckner lace up her corset, her heart bursting with desire.

She was in a bed in a room made of opaque glass. A mobile of glittering stars hung above her, and a young woman with a purple ribbon around her neck was telling her she would love her as long as the stars burned in the sky.

It was her twelfth birthday and she was standing in

front of her father, hoping that maybe *this* year, her Grandmother Byrne had sent a present. He handed her a small box wrapped in pink foil with a yellow bow, and she unwrapped it to find a Solit triangle necklace from Grandmother McLellan. Tears of disappointment pricked her eyes.

She was running along the banks of a large river of crystal-clear water, dodging low-hanging boughs of trees with golden leaves as another girl, silver-skinned but her own age, called out from behind her, "Sera, wait up!"

Sera must have pulled her hand away, because Agnes came back to the present abruptly, falling against the vanity and knocking over a bottle of talcum powder. She gaped at her arms, silvery blue sparks bursting underneath her skin, then fading away, leaving the brown color she had always known. She could still feel them though, faintly, a tingle in her veins.

Sera was watching her finger, the glow dimming until it disappeared completely. Agnes could not think of a single thing to say. She did not know if she would ever be able to speak again. The memories had been so sharp, so precise; some of them she'd nearly forgotten, like Leo catching her in the study. But others were definitely not hers at all—who were the women with the ribbons around their necks, and the girl she had been racing? They had silver skin and blue hair just like Sera. Had Agnes managed to see into Sera's memories too?

"Mother Sun, what was that?"

Agnes's head whipped up at the sound of the *Yes* she had heard in her heart before the memories took her.

"What did you say?" she gasped.

"Can—can you understand me?" Sera choked on the words.

Agnes nodded, her mouth open, her face dazed. "I need to sit down," she croaked, collapsing onto the vanity's bench and putting her head between her knees. This couldn't be real. It couldn't be. It was too much, too bizarre, too impossible.

"My name is Sera Lighthaven," Sera said. Her voice was so much lower and richer than it had been before. "I am a Cerulean. My blood is magic. And you can understand me now!"

She looked ecstatic, but Agnes could not share her mood, not yet.

"What . . . this is . . . it can't be . . . magic, you said? You . . . have magic? In your blood?"

"Yes," Sera said triumphantly, like she had passed some test. She held up her finger and Agnes froze—she was not certain she wanted to experience whatever that was again. But the finger did not glow this time. "We just blood bonded. I think." Sera frowned. "It was not quite like real blood bonding, though—I have never shared memories during a blood bond before. Your brother does not seem to have been any nicer when he was a child than he is now." Agnes let out a bewildered sigh that may have been intended as a laugh. Or a cry. She had not realized Sera had been seeing the memories too, and she wasn't sure she liked that fact now that she knew. "But maybe that is how blood bonding works on planets," Sera mused. "I think I may have given you a little bit of my magic. And we can talk now!" She knelt before Agnes, looking up at her with pleading eyes.

"I need to get someplace where I can *see*, someplace very, very tall. Do you have dwellings like that here, or a temple I could climb? I must find the tether. I must know if the City Above the Sky is still out there."

This was all rather more information than Agnes found herself able to process. Sera seemed to realize this—she sat back and scratched her neck, her face pensive.

"Hmm," she mused. "This is a lot to explain."

"Yes," Agnes agreed. She tried to organize her thoughts, but they remained stubbornly scattered. "Who were those women with the ribbons around their necks?"

Sera's expression grew mournful. "Those are my mothers. Two of them, at least."

"How many do you have?" she asked incredulously.

"Three. Purple, orange, and green. For the three Moon Daughters. But that's not how it works here, right? Here you have a mother and a father."

"Yes, that's right," Agnes said, feeling faint. Three mothers? What were moon daughters?

"My City is tethered to this planet, you see," Sera continued. "And I was chosen to be sacrificed to break the tether so it could move to a new planet, but . . . I didn't do it right and I fell into that hole that you and Leo found me in. So now I need to know if the tether is still there or if another Cerulean has been chosen, and the sacrifice worked, and the City is lost to me forever, traveling through the vast expanse of space to find a new home." Her tone shifted throughout this speech and ended on a melancholy note.

"You were *sacrificed*?" Agnes cried.

"I was chosen," Sera said, "by Mother Sun, to throw

myself from the dais in the Night Gardens."

"And you *did*?" Agnes knew the answer to that, of course, but still . . . she saw this sweet, slender girl in a whole new light.

Sera nodded. "But I was meant to die, to spill my blood and break the tether, and clearly that did not happen." She put her hands on Agnes's knees. "It is such a joy to be able to speak to you. You have no idea how hard it is to not be understood."

Agnes knew that somewhere inside, she was happy about this development too, but she couldn't seem to settle on any one emotion right now.

"And this city . . . it's in the sky?"

"Above the sky," Sera clarified. "In space."

"And this tether, what does it look like?"

"Like a finely wrought chain of magic," she said, as if that should explain it. "In links of blue and silver and gold."

"And it's attached to our planet? This planet? To Kaolin?"

Sera sighed. "I do not know where the tether has buried itself. It could be in Kaolin, but it could be in Pelago. Or it could be in the middle of the ocean. That's why I need to *see*." She looked at the windowless walls around them.

"Well, I can certainly help you look for it," Agnes said.

"No, you can't. It is invisible to human eyes. Only a Cerulean will be able to see it."

Agnes supposed that the papers would have already reported if a chain of magic shooting down from space had been discovered.

"I wish I could see it," she said. "Your city. I want to

understand . . . where you come from, who you are. This is all pretty overwhelming."

Sera went silent and stared at her hands. Agnes realized this was pretty overwhelming for her, too.

"Maybe I can show you."

"That glowing thing again?" Agnes asked with trepidation.

"Yes." Sera's fingertip lit up. "I *think* . . . if I focus on what I want . . ."

She did not sound nearly sure enough of herself for Agnes's liking, and she had no desire to have her memories probed again.

Describe in detail the bravest thing you have ever done in the name of science.

The essay subject popped into her head, and she saw it in a new light. Was she really going to run from this new, albeit frightening, discovery? This was more important than an essay or an interview or even studying at the University of Ithilia at all. This was her chance to help someone, a person who had no one else on the entire planet but her. Was she a mouse, like Vada had said? Was the fear of someone uncovering a few embarrassing moments or the secret of her sexuality going to keep her from exploring an entirely new world?

"I can do it, Agnes," Sera said, her face set. "I can feel it. I . . . I'm stronger on this planet in some ways. I understand myself now, I think, or a little better at least. I can show you. I *will* show you."

It seemed they were both entering uncharted territory.

With grim determination, Agnes pressed her finger once more against Sera's.

The heat was bearable this time, maybe because she was better prepared for it. It raced up her arm, dancing in her veins and closing around her heart. The sense of being an empty vessel was not as unpleasant now that she had some small concept of what was happening, and when her body jerked and her mind was transported to another place, she stared around in wonder and did not question what she was seeing.

She was standing beside Sera on a small island in front of a tall building, shaped like an upside-down cone and made of thick glass with golden doors. It reached up high into the sky, but this sky wasn't blue and dotted with clouds, it was just . . . space. Stars and darkness. A luminescent butterfly flitted past, its wings flashing blues and yellows. There was a hedge surrounding part of the structure in a semicircle. Agnes could see at least two arching white bridges connecting the island to the land across the river, where other structures sat, little domes that must be houses—they were made of glass too. Many had gardens surrounding them.

The temperature was mild, the air fresh and crisp like newly washed sheets. The grass was a vibrant green and it looked so springy Agnes felt she would bounce if she stepped on it.

There were no people.

"This is the City Above the Sky," Sera said, and her connection to the place was palpable.

"Where is everyone?"

"I don't know." She looked at her palms. "I am still figuring out how my magic works, its capabilities. Cerulean do not go down onto planets any longer. I am discovering things that my green mother could not have prepared me for."

"Why don't you go down onto planets? How many planets have you been to?" Agnes found the questions piling up in her mind, and she had to bite her lip to keep from asking them all at once.

"I have only ever known this planet," Sera explained. "We have been tethered here for over nine hundred years."

"You're nine hundred years old?"

She laughed. "No! I am not yet eighteen. But the High Priestess has been alive since the planet before this. She is ancient."

Agnes decided to let that one go for now.

"What is that?" she asked, pointing to the cone. It sharpened into a golden point at the very top.

"That's the temple of Mother Sun. It lies in the center of the City."

"Who's Mother Sun?"

Sera took a moment before responding. "She is everything," she said.

Agnes was not as interested in gods as she was in the logistics of this place. "What is this temple made of?"

"Sunglass," Sera said, as if it were obvious.

Observe, Agnes thought. *Don't disturb.*

The steps of the temple were smooth, the doors engraved in markings, geometric shapes, spirals and slashes and squiggled lines. Some seemed to glow when she looked at them, others to fade. They looked sort of like the symbols Sera had scratched in the dirt of the truck bed.

"I used to climb up there all the time," Sera said, gazing up at the golden spire twinkling overhead. "It made my orange mother furious, but I couldn't help myself. It was the best place to see the stars."

Agnes felt that any spot in this city would be an excellent vantage point for stargazing. The stars around them were big and bright, not like the tiny pinpricks visible from Old Port at night.

"Do you think you could show me what happened to you?" she asked.

Sera closed her eyes and a tear fell onto her cheek.

Agnes suddenly found herself kneeling inside the circular room she'd seen in Sera's memory earlier, with the painted ceiling. Every inch of space was filled with silver-skinned, blue-haired women. There were no men.

Sera was kneeling beside her, surrounded by three women, each with a different color ribbon around their necks. Agnes recognized the purple and orange women. The green one was new. These must be Sera's mothers.

Another woman stood at a podium, leaning over an ancient, crumbling bowl filled with light. There was something regal about her, something that declared power and demanded reverence—Agnes wondered if this was the High Priestess Sera had mentioned, except that she did not look nine hundred years old. The light in the bowl went out. The woman called Sera's name.

The room dissolved, and Agnes found herself in one of the glass houses, standing in front of a mirror beside Sera.

The three mothers were there too. Sera wore the very same robe she was wearing in Kaolin except it was fresh and clean. The clumsy embroidery matched the bracelets on her wrist: purple, green, and orange. The bracelets were gone now, Agnes realized, as was the necklace; her father's men must have taken them. There was so much love in this room, it hurt her chest to contain it.

"You have been our sun, Sera Lighthaven," the woman with the orange ribbon said. She was older than the other two and her eyes glittered with tears. "You have been the light in our world." She looked like she wanted to say something else, then stopped herself. "Are you ready to go to the Night Gardens?"

Sera did not look ready at all. Agnes's pulse quickened.

"Yes, Mother," Sera whispered.

Then Agnes was in the most exquisite garden she had ever seen. Snow-white lilies, dark purple dahlias, and soft gray roses were all mixed together with other flowers Agnes couldn't name, flowers that couldn't actually exist—buds that lit up like glowing sapphires floating through the air, flowers as big as hibiscuses but that shone like the full moon on a cloudless night, trees with silver trunks and leaves as black as pitch. The garden was full of people, like the temple had been. She stood with Sera on a glass dais that jutted out over a waterfall. Beyond her was nothing except the dizzying vastness of space. Beside her was the regal woman from the temple who had called Sera's name.

"Today is a momentous day!" she cried. "The beginning of a new chapter for our beloved City, at long last. This ceremony will free us from the bonds to this planet as

Mother Sun will guide us to our new home. All praise her everlasting light!"

"Praise her!" the crowd cried back.

Agnes watched in horror as the woman took out a knife and cut Sera's arms, just inside her elbows.

She caught sight of a young girl in the crowd that she recognized—it was the girl she had been racing along the banks of the river in Sera's memory. Tears streamed down her cheeks.

She saw the mother with the purple ribbon clutch at her heart, as if trying to keep it inside her chest.

Then Sera turned and threw herself off the dais.

Agnes screamed, her eyes flying open, and she was back in the bathroom on Creekwater Row. Her heart was beating against her rib cage with enough force to make her vision blur. It took several deep breaths before she was able to form a coherent thought.

"You're telling me," she said, panting, "that some-where . . . up there . . . is that place? That . . . city?" It seemed the wrong word for it—it was so much more beautiful and wondrous than any city Agnes had ever seen or heard of.

"I think so," Sera said. "But I do not know."

Agnes was reeling at everything this girl had gone through, the devastating loss she had suffered.

"I'll help you find this tether," she vowed, taking Sera's hands in her own. "I'll help you get home if I can." She was suddenly grateful Vada's ship wasn't leaving right away. She could not abandon Sera, not now. She had never felt so connected to someone, even though they had only just met.

Sera smiled, and there were tears in her eyes. "You are

as kind as Leela, Agnes. And that is the highest compliment I can pay."

"Who is Leela?"

"My best friend."

Agnes knew instinctively that she was talking about the girl she'd seen crying at the sacrifice and found she did not mind the comparison.

A knocking on the door made them both jump.

"Are you nearly done in there?" Hattie's voice seemed too mundane, too normal, breaking the spell that had woven its way into the bathroom.

"Just about!" Agnes called. "Take your robe off and get in the tub, quick," she said to Sera.

"My orange mother made me this robe," Sera said, clutching the dirty fabric.

"And I will make sure no one else touches it," Agnes said. "But we've got to get you clean and dressed or my father will be very angry. And trust me, you do not want to incite his ire."

Sera nodded and slipped off the robe, stepping into the tub.

"It's warm!" she cried with delight.

"Yes, of course it is," Agnes said.

And with that, she dunked Sera's head underwater.

22

LEO

Leo could not recall the last time his father had thrown a party in his own house.

Xavier had insisted the event be black tie. Representatives from Old Port's wealthiest families were in attendance, men with connections and business interests all over Kaolin. Leo saw George Wilkes of Wilkes Dairy fame, Sebastian Horne of Horne Mills, and Wilbur Grandstreet, whose family owned the shipyard that had built much of the Kaolin naval fleet. A delegate from the Ministry of Agriculture was also in attendance, and Xavier was chatting him up when Robert Conway and his father arrived. Leo welcomed them in the foyer.

"Leo," Robert said, clapping him on the back and

shaking his hand, like he was a politician and not Leo's best friend. "Quite the do your father's throwing." A footman stationed by the door handed him a glass of champagne. "Elizabeth told me all about that tree with the face and that odd sea creature. Are they here tonight?"

He looked around eagerly, as if Leo might be hiding Errol behind a potted plant.

"No, he's got a different trick up his sleeve," Leo said. "I think your father will be impressed."

He wanted to sound jaunty and confident, but his words felt hollow. He didn't like talking about Sera as if she were some party trick, especially now that he knew her name. Hattie had told him Agnes was getting her ready. His father had asked him to choose a dress for his sister, and Leo had picked out one for Sera too. He wasn't about to leave anyone in Agnes's hands when it came to dressing for a party, no matter how odd or magical they might be.

He touched his cheek again—he could not seem to stop doing that, as if waiting for the bruise to reappear.

Robert laughed. He had the laugh of someone who'd never had to worry about a thing all his life. The white tuxedo he wore contrasted smartly with his dark skin, and his neatly trimmed black beard was dotted with crystals.

"He must be quite confident, then." Robert up looked past Leo and his eyes widened. "My god."

Leo turned and saw his sister coming down the stairs. The dress he had chosen had been shoved in the back of her closet with a few other fashionable options, ones that must have been gifts, because he could not imagine Agnes choosing them for herself. It was a pale green the color of sea foam, with small puffed sleeves and a scooped neckline. The skirt had layers of tulle underneath, giving it a pleasing bell shape, and the only decoration was around the hem, a floral pattern sewn with copper thread. Hattie had curled her hair and decorated it with copper pins shaped like flowers, tendrils hanging down her back.

"Why, Agnes, you look absolutely stunning," Robert said, coming over to kiss her hand as she reached the last step.

"Thanks," she said, tugging on one of the sleeves as if trying to make it longer. The doorbell rang and Swansea went to open it.

Mr. Grange entered the house and descended on Agnes with a sycophantic smile.

"My dear Agnes, how lovely to see you!" he cried. "I cannot believe it was only yesterday that your engagement to my son was made official. I feel as if you are part of the family already."

Ebenezer Grange stood behind his father, looking like he'd rather be anywhere else.

"Agnes and Ebenezer?" Robert murmured, and Leo could sense his eagerness to spread this fresh gossip. Leo had had a few too many things on his mind to worry about his sister's engagement. Besides, as fun as it had been to hang over Agnes's head all summer, once it became a reality, he lost his taste for the jest. Especially after he'd seen the look on her face when he'd guessed as much, the bleak tears that had filled her eyes. He'd never seen his sister cry before.

"Hello, Ebenezer," she said. "Mr. Grange, it is, um, nice to see you too. Excuse me, I think I need a refreshment."

"I shall accompany you," Ebenezer said, holding out an arm awkwardly. Agnes took it and they left the foyer. Mr. Grange followed them, craning his neck to search for Xavier.

"Do you think they *rented* those tuxedos?" Robert asked with a smirk. "Oh, I heard James Roth is here as well. He's starring in this mysterious, one-night-only production, isn't he?"

"Yes."

"He must be sad Xavier's getting out of the theater business. Your father made him famous."

"Master Leo, there you are!" Kiernan came hurrying up to him. He looked a proper Kaolin gentleman this evening— gone was the kohl around his eyes and the seashell in his hair. His tuxedo fit him well, though the cummerbund was a bit tight around his stomach.

"Mr. Kiernan, may I present Robert Conway, of the Conway Rail family," Leo said. "Robert, this is Ezra Kiernan. Mr. Kiernan has been instrumental in helping my father with this new endeavor."

"How do you do," Robert said politely, shaking his hand. But Leo could read the look in his eyes that said, *So this is the Pelagan.*

"A pleasure, dear boy, an absolute pleasure. My apologies, but I need to steal your friend away. It is nearly time for the demonstration!" Kiernan was close to bouncing up and down with excitement.

Leo thought he was going to be asked to recount his

experience with the Arboreal and Sera's blood. He hadn't been looking forward to sharing that he'd been attacked by a tree.

"What demonstration?" he asked as Kiernan led him away into the drawing room. Xavier stood by the mantel talking to Robert's father, both with drinks in hand. Mr. Grange hovered close by, pretending to be part of the conversation. But Xavier was focused only on Mr. Conway; he'd never invested in any McLellan productions, and Leo knew it was a sore spot for his father.

"Ah, Leo." Xavier waved him over. "I was just telling Hubert that he's going to be exceedingly grateful I invited him here tonight. I'm letting him in on the ground floor of an earth-shattering discovery. Isn't that right?"

"Yes, sir," Leo said, but neither man was really paying attention to him.

"Now, Xavier, you don't want to oversell yourself," Mr. Conway said, wagging a finger.

"Oversell? Why, not at all. Just wait till you see what she can do."

"*She?*" Mr. Conway raised an eyebrow. "What's going on here, McLellan?"

Xavier smiled and put his glass down on the mantel.

"If I could have your attention, please," he called to the room at large, and silence fell. Agnes and Ebenezer were standing off by the windows, and his sister kept glancing toward the stairs. Leo guessed she was worried about Sera. With a start, he realized he was worried too. And not just about her but about everything—this party, this new direction the business was taking, whatever role he would be expected to play in it. The future he had so confidently envisioned for himself only a few days ago was not so clear anymore.

"As many of you know," his father continued, "I have been working in secret for quite some time on a brand-new venture, one that will reshape the McLellan empire. Ezra, if you please."

Swansea came in with an easel and several large boards. Kiernan took one and placed it on display. It was a blown-up photograph of Boris, the one Leo had seen at dinner, only much larger.

"It's just a tree," Sebastian Horne scoffed. "What are you playing at, Xavier?"

"This is no ordinary tree, Sebastian," his father said. "It is called an Arboreal, and it possesses a unique and wondrous power—laugh if you must!" he added, because there were some chuckles among his audience. "But this creature can turn a crumbling farmland into a green oasis. How many of you have ties to the agricultural industry? How many resources have been lost this year, burned in the wildfires, drained to dust by droughts, crops ruined by blight and rot? This tree can change all that. Plant it on your property and I guarantee in one week your soil will be as rich and yielding as if freshly tilled. In two weeks, you'll be ready to plant, and by the third week, I promise you'll have a harvest unlike any you've seen before."

"Impossible," George Wilkes cried.

"I assure you it is not," Xavier said. "And I would appreciate being allowed to finish without any more outbursts."

Wilkes fell silent, and Leo could sense his father's

pleasure grow. There was nothing he enjoyed more than dressing down one of his peers.

He motioned to Kiernan, who replaced the photograph of Boris with one of Errol. Leo had yet to see Errol out of his pond, and the picture was murky, mostly just a set of bulging eyes.

"Up next, we have a mertag. Very hard little creature to photograph. Have you ever thought about why Pelagan waters never seem to run dry, especially when Pelagans dine on fish day and night? And meanwhile the waters around Old Port have become too toxic for sea life, and the Gulf of Windsor is once again in danger of being overfished." He looked at Wilbur Grandstreet. "Wilbur, how many more ships might you sell if the eastern seaboard, from Wenton to Pearl Beach, were suddenly flush with life? If the oyster beds returned, and trout and carp and pike became plentiful once more?"

Mr. Grandstreet looked pleased at being addressed personally. "Why, I can imagine a fair few. But we've been busy with orders since that island was discovered too, Xavier."

"Ah yes. Braxos. I'm glad you mentioned it."

Kiernan replaced the photograph of Errol with the one of the ruins from the *Old Port Telegraph*. Now that it was blown up to a much larger scale, Leo saw a shape on top of the doors to the ruins, and it looked sort of like the star pendant on the necklace hidden away in his sock drawer. But they couldn't possibly be related. Sera had only just gotten here, and those ruins must have been hundreds of years old.

"The island of Braxos has not been seen in our lifetimes," Xavier said. "Until now. Many believe these ruins hold gold or jewels or other riches. The deputy mayor was claiming last night at the Regent that it was filled with beautiful women who could make a man hand over his fortune with a single kiss."

There were some chortles at that.

"But the legends I have heard come from a more reliable source and contain wonders greater than precious stones or women," Xavier continued. "I have been told that the waves lapping at its shores can tell the future. I have heard that within its forests lies the power to speak to those who are dead. And I believe that these ruins' walls contain the answer to a secret every man here would sacrifice anything to claim for his own." He paused for dramatic effect. "The secret to eternal life."

The men looked at each other uncertainly. Leo felt his own face go blank. Who was this source that told his father all these fantastical stories, and more importantly, how could he possibly believe them?

Hubert Conway was the first to speak up.

"Come now, Xavier," he said. "These tales you tell are like fairy stories for children. A magic tree? A fountain of youth? You must think us mad to believe a single word you say."

"I would think you mad if you did *not* harbor some doubts," Xavier said calmly. "Which is why I have an offer of proof to show you, right here this very evening. James!" The sound of footsteps could be heard from upstairs. "You all know James Roth. A marvelous actor and the star of my final production. Well, perhaps the star no longer."

Xavier gestured with a flourish as James led Sera down

the staircase and into the drawing room. Leo had not had much to choose from in Agnes's closet, nor had he considered how Sera might actually look in a formal dress, thinking only of finding the right color so as not to clash with her skin and hair. The gown was quite simple, ivory silk with a pink lace overlay and train. No frills or ruffles, just a golden detail around the bodice and lace sleeves that covered her shoulders. Hattie must have done her hair too, an elegant crown of thick blue curls dotted with pins of pearl and rose quartz.

When he saw her, Leo's stomach flipped like he'd missed a curb while walking down Creekwater Row.

She was frightened, clearly—he could not blame her for that, being stared at by a bunch of men in an unfamiliar home. He told himself he should stop staring too, but he couldn't seem to tear his eyes away from her; she carried herself with an otherworldly grace, and her skin shone like a silver pearl in the light of the lamps. Leo caught sight of Robert ogling her, and his hands clenched into fists. Robert was known among their friends for his conquests, and Leo had the sudden urge to throw himself in front of Sera, to protect her from Robert's possessive gaze.

James held her elbow firmly, her arms clasped behind her back; Leo saw the handcuffs hidden in the folds of her skirt as she came level with him, and it made his stomach churn. Two Pembertons shadowed her every movement, hovering just inside the doorway to the drawing room.

There were gasps and murmurs from the men, and more than a few covetous looks.

"What is she?" Mr. Conway demanded.

"She's marvelous," Mr. Wilkes said.

"I call her Azure," Xavier declared. Agnes's face twisted in distaste at the name. She had her arms folded across her chest, alternately glaring at their father and casting Sera worried glances.

Sera saw his sister and a look passed between them, something Leo didn't understand, but Agnes gave a tiny shake of her head and Sera responded with a nod. Then she caught sight of Leo and her eyes narrowed. She took a small step away from him. Leo was seized with the impulse to shout that he was sorry, that he hadn't known what was going to happen when he caught her with the net launcher, that he'd only been thinking of himself and how he might impress his father. He hadn't thought of her as a person. He hadn't thought about her at all.

"I think it is time for a demonstration," Xavier said. "Ezra, if you will."

Kiernan held up a syringe, showing it off to the crowd like a magician about to perform a trick.

"No, no, please . . ."

The voice caught Leo entirely off guard. It was low and musical and distinctly female. It certainly wasn't Agnes's voice, but the only other girl in the room was Sera. That didn't make sense.

Leo watched, stunned, as Sera spoke again.

"Please don't do this," she begged.

What . . . was . . . happening? How was he able to understand her all of a sudden? Maybe everyone else could hear her too. Perhaps his father and Kiernan had figured out—

"What is that gibberish she's speaking?" Mr. Horne asked.

So Leo was the only one who had understood. He rubbed at his ear.

"She cannot speak our language," Xavier explained. "But she is not here to dazzle us with words."

Leo thought he saw his sister mouth "I'm sorry" to her. Could Agnes understand her too? His mind was spinning, making it hard to focus on anything. Maybe he'd been hit on the head harder than he thought. Maybe his brain had suffered some sort of damage that Sera's blood couldn't cure.

Xavier grabbed him by the wrist and held up Leo's hand.

"You see my son's palm here—unblemished, not a scratch on it. Do you all agree?"

Leo's instinct to yank his hand away was tempered only by eighteen years of absolute obedience to his father. Xavier nodded to Kiernan—James was gripping Sera's elbow so tight that his knuckles were white. She shrieked as Kiernan sank the needle into the crook of her arm.

"No!" she cried, and Leo knew this was no hallucination. "Stop, stop, please! I am a Cerulean and my blood is magic and you cannot take it from me!"

Kiernan held up the blood, part two of this magic trick—its rich blue color was shot through with glimmering facets of light, and there were gasps from the audience. Leo felt a sharp slash across his palm and his father held up a small knife, wet with his son's blood. There was a dull thrumming in Leo's ears, and the edges of the room went fuzzy. Agnes looked like she was going to be sick, and in some faraway part of his brain he thought, *That's strange, I thought she liked dissecting things.*

"Xavier!" Mr. Conway bellowed.

"My son will be fine," he said. "Watch and be amazed, Hubert."

Leo's hand throbbed, the pain setting in like a thin streak of fire. James had to actively hold Sera back as Kiernan approached Leo with the syringe. He removed the needle and carefully administered three drops of blood along the length of the cut.

"No," Sera moaned, and she seemed to weaken as she struggled against James's grip.

It was awful, being able to understand her. All the times he had heard her speak came back to him in a rush—what had she been saying when she clutched for her necklace? What had she cried out when he caught her with that net?

She looked to his sister. "Agnes, help me!"

She knows my sister's name. Agnes's face was chalky, her hands gripping the fabric of her skirt, her shoulders tense. Leo was certain Agnes could understand Sera too. But she was as powerless as he was in this room, in this moment. No one besides the twins paid Sera any mind; all eyes were on Leo's hand. The audience surged forward and the men's faces lit up with shock and amazement as they watched his skin knit itself back together until his palm was once again smooth, not even a scar to show where Xavier had cut him.

"In the name of the One True God . . ."

"How can this be?"

"It is as if he was never cut at all!"

"It's a miracle." Hubert Conway was thunderstruck. "It's an absolute miracle."

"This blood is a gift, bestowed upon my family for a purpose. As are the Arboreal and the mertag," Xavier said. "And I intend to use them. Who here will join me in this venture? Who will invest in the future of Kaolin and the health of its people with me?"

As if Xavier cared a jot for the health of Kaolin or its people, Leo thought grimly. The men were clamoring for his father's attention, eager to outdo each other, waving their checkbooks and shouting to be heard. Leo's hand was grabbed and examined and poked at like he was a magician's assistant and not the future leader of the McLellan enterprise.

Suddenly, Sera let out a scream, and it seemed to him like it had an edge of excitement.

"Can someone stop that god-awful shrieking?" Wilbur Grandstreet muttered.

"Perhaps our Azure is tired," Kiernan said, trying to smooth things over. "She is a lady, after all, and must be fatigued. I shall—"

"The tether!" Sera cried. She was staring at the photograph of the ruins. "Agnes, it's the tether, I can see it, it's coming right out of that stone temple!"

Agnes's mouth fell open, but the next moment the Pembertons had descended on Sera and were dragging her away.

"I have to get to the tether!" Leo heard her shout before her voice was cut off.

Agnes knew something, he could see it in her eyes, the cogs and gears of her brain working furiously. She knew what this tether thing was. Did she know where the girl was from? Did she know how her blood healed him, or why he could suddenly understand her?

Leo wanted answers. Whatever Agnes knew, he wanted to know too. Even if it meant going against his father. Even if it meant losing his place in the business.

As the men continued to pass him around, patting his father on the back and speculating wildly about how else they might use Sera's blood, Leo found his thoughts taking a path they had never ventured down before, new and unfamiliar, but one that felt right.

For the first time in his life, he *wanted* to talk to his sister.

PART FOUR

The City Above the Sky

23

Leela had always known her best friend was brave—far braver than Leela herself could ever be.

But when Sera turned so calmly and stepped out past the barrier of safety, blood streaming down her arms, her body willowy in stillness, Leela was hit with the enormity of what she had been chosen to do.

And then she watched helplessly as Sera spread her arms and fell from the dais. In the span of a heartbeat, she was gone.

Leela could not bring herself to stay, to witness Sera's mothers' agony or hear words of comfort from the High Priestess. She only wanted to be alone with her grief. Her mothers did not try to stop her as she slipped away back home.

Her dwelling felt like a stranger, a different place than it had this morning when Sera was still alive and the world made sense. She sat in her bedroom, as still as one of the statues in the Moon Gardens, until she heard the Cerulean returning to their dwellings, catching bits of conversation as they passed her window. Most were hopeful. Some were excited. A few were somber. Leela could feel Sera becoming less and less of a person with each passing hour. She was a martyr, an idol, a story to be told.

"She was so pious," Leela heard one woman say.

"She was a great asset to our City," another murmured.

"Mother Sun saw much in her."

"She will be praised in everlasting grace once we reach a new planet."

Leela could not stand it. She did not know this person they were speaking of. Sera had been bold and curious and silly. It had been her dream to see a new planet, one she had been teased about or hushed for expressing out loud. And she was the one missing it. It wasn't fair.

That night was the longest of Leela's life. When the gray light of morning crept into her room, she roused herself, sat up, and tied her hair back. She had to know if they were moving yet. She had to learn as much as she could, about space, about everything they passed on the way to the new planet, about the journey ahead. She had to know for Sera.

But when Durea, one of the beekeepers, stopped by the dwelling to deliver the day's honey, Leela could sense instantly that something was wrong.

"We are still attached," Durea said softly to her green mother. "The High Priestess has not been seen since last night."

Her mothers looked worried, but not for the reason Leela did. If the City was not moving, did that mean that Sera had sacrificed herself for nothing?

She accompanied her purple mother to the Aviary to collect eggs, and Ileen, one of the midwives, stopped them on the way.

"The tether has not broken," she said. "I heard the High Priestess has sequestered herself in the temple."

Her purple mother glanced at Leela, then said, "I am sure all will be well. We must trust in the High Priestess and in Mother Sun."

Leela felt an unfamiliar jerk of irritation. Once Ileen had gone, she snapped, "You do not have to say those things for my sake."

Her tone was sharp as nettles, and her purple mother looked hurt. Leela knew she was being unfair, but she could not bring herself to apologize.

By the hour of the dove, the novices were spreading throughout the City.

"Do not fear," they said. "The High Priestess is seeking guidance. All will be well. Stay in your homes. Do not go out. Pray. Pray for our City."

Her orange mother gathered the family in the common room. And they prayed, until almost the hour of the serpent, when Leela felt like she would burst if she had to sit still any longer.

"Orange Mother," she said. "I would like to pray in my

room. Alone. If that is all right," she added. She did not want to hurt another one of her mothers, no matter how raw she felt.

Her orange mother was about to protest when her green mother interjected. "Of course you may," she said. Leela escaped gratefully, hearing a whispered, "Leave her be," from her green mother as she did.

But her room was too small and confining. She rested her arms on her windowsill, remembering the first time Sera had coaxed her out late at night, when they were only ten. The memory was torture. Leela felt the whole City was now designed to torment her daily. Because every place reminded her of Sera. The moonflower fields where they used to play Seek Me If You Dare. The orchards where Leela would wheedle extra pieces of fruit from Freeda, because Freeda would never give Sera extra anything. Every part of the Great Estuary where they had raced or swam or bathed was its own private hurt.

Leela tried to tell herself that Sera would not want her to be sad, but how could she not be? It was as if a piece of her had been torn out and lost forever.

Finally, she couldn't stand it any longer. She had to know for certain that the tether was still there. She needed to see it with her own eyes, even if it meant going against the directive of the novices, of the High Priestess herself.

In one swift movement, she was out the window and running. The banks along this part of the Estuary were close and heavily wooded with golden-leaved polaris trees, so she was able to slip away unseen, avoiding the bridges that led to the island where the temple stood and running to cross at the Western Bridge, by the seresheep meadows. She reached the Day Gardens and found them just the same as they had been only days ago, a riot of blooming color as if nothing were wrong, as if the world hadn't been turned upside down and Sera was still here to listen to the ethereal songs of the minstrel flowers.

She made her way to the very edge of the gardens, to the place where a large willow bent over the Estuary as it spilled into space. Leela climbed up and nestled herself into a crook between two branches. She peered out over the lip of the City, at the blue-green orb below, thin clouds passing over the familiar shapes of Kaolin and Pelago.

And there it was: the tether, looking just the same as it always had. It seemed to wink at her, glowing silver, then blue, then gold, then silver again.

Leela felt anger rise in her heart, a hot fury at this beautiful chain of magic. It was one thing to have lost her friend. It was wholly another to have lost her with no purpose to it, no reason. She felt powerless as the tether twinkled at her innocently, mocking her loss.

And then hope pierced through her, lighting up her soul like a sunburst.

The tether had not broken. Perhaps Sera was still alive.

"Sera!" she cried. The leaves on the willow rustled and the tether kept winking. "SERA!" she screamed, sure that if she called out loudly enough, her friend would hear her.

She shouted until she was hoarse and the sunburst of hope had burned itself into ashes. Sera was not out there. She was dead.

It was the first time Leela had thought the word. *Dead*.

It was so awfully, brutally final. She sat in the crook of the willow, pressing her face against its rough bark, and cried for her friend with no shame and no comfort.

At last, she roused herself. It wouldn't do to linger too long. Her mothers trusted her and would likely not seek her out, but it would only take one of them passing her room to notice she was not in it. She wandered back along the banks of the Estuary, ignoring the Western Bridge this time, though it was the more direct route home. Instead she crossed at Faesa's Bridge, the very one she and Sera had run across on the day of the choosing ceremony. It was risky, taking her past the temple, but the hedge should provide her cover and besides, the High Priestess was sequestered. She was nearly to Dendra's Bridge on the opposite side of the island, which would take her straight home, when she heard voices.

Afraid to be caught out of doors when she was meant to be praying, Leela dropped to the ground and froze.

". . . worked before." It was the High Priestess; Leela would know her voice anywhere. "No reason to think . . ." The rest of what she said was muffled.

"Things were different then, you said." Leela recognized the voice of the oldest acolyte, Acolyte Klymthe. "There was an agreement."

"It was more than that." The High Priestess sounded sad. "And I was stronger then."

"I could have—" Acolyte Klymthe began, but the High Priestess cut her off.

"No," she said sharply. "You could not." Leela felt her head spinning. She did not fully understand what they were talking about, and yet something about this conversation set the hairs on the back of her neck prickling. There was a rustle of movement, and when the High Priestess spoke again, her voice was gentle. "It is not so easy as that, my dear Klymthe. You do not get to choose."

"Yes, High Priestess." Acolyte Klymthe sounded resigned. "The novices have kept everyone inside."

"Good."

"Will we make another sacrifice?"

"Not yet," the High Priestess said. Acolyte Klymthe said something Leela couldn't hear, and the High Priestess replied, "No. Believe me. They would not understand. And another ceremony would look suspicious. Mother Sun does not make mistakes."

"But this was not the work of Mother—"

"I know," the High Priestess snapped. Leela felt as if she had grown roots as deep as the hedge, pinning her in place. She could not move even if she wanted to.

"Let us call the City to the temple," the High Priestess said. "We must keep them calm." What she said next was too low for Leela to hear.

"Of course, High Priestess."

There was a shuffling of feet and then silence fell. Leela could hear her heart beating in her own ears. If what she had just overheard was true, then Mother Sun had not chosen Sera to be sacrificed after all.

The High Priestess had.

Leela did not realize how long she stayed behind the hedge, her mind reeling, until the bell began to toll, calling the City to the temple as the High Priestess had instructed.

She shot up and started running, arriving home to panicked mothers.

"Where have you been?"

"You told us you were praying in your room!"

"Leela, you cannot disappear like that. We were out of our minds with worry."

"I am sorry, Mothers," Leela said, her eyes downcast, her pulse racing. Something in her resisted the urge to tell them what she'd heard, a warning to keep this information to herself, and she held her tongue. Her orange mother tsked and handed Leela her prayer robe.

"You are just as bad as Se—" But she cut herself off before saying Sera's name. Leela's heart spasmed in pain. Her purple mother shot her orange mother a stern look.

"We know this is especially difficult for you," her green mother said gently, smoothing back Leela's hair. "But it is a hard time for us all. The City needs every Cerulean to be united in faith. Do you understand?"

"Yes, Mother."

She leaned in and whispered in Leela's ear. "And I could not bear to lose you, my darling. My heart would not survive it."

She kissed the top of her head and released her. Leela slipped her robe on and followed her mothers out the door to join the throng of Cerulean headed to the temple.

They knelt on their cushions in their usual family spot. Sera's three mothers were in their place near the Altar of the Lost, but they looked incomplete without Sera in their midst. Sera's orange mother was stoic in her grief—her face was a hard mask, her shoulders rigid. Her green mother's eyes were red and watery and she seemed to wilt, like the weight of her prayer robe was too much to bear. But Sera's purple mother was empty, her face blank and expressionless, as if the soul that resided inside her had vanished over that dais with her daughter.

"Hood up," Leela's orange mother whispered, as the High Priestess made her way to the pulpit. She spread her arms wide, her warm, confident smile fixed in place.

Who are you, really? Leela thought as she raised her hood and the High Priestess began to speak.

"I have prayed long and hard, my children, and in the end, the answer has come to me, though I fear this time it brings me little comfort. Mother Sun has spoken. Sera Lighthaven was *unworthy.*"

There were gasps and murmurs of shock, and Leela felt as if her battered heart could not bear another blow. Unworthy? *Unworthy?*

The High Priestess seemed so sincerely distraught, Leela did not have to look around the temple to know the Cerulean would believe her. They always did. She herself always had. And besides, this was easy to believe, easier than thinking Sera was special or pious or noble or any of the things they had been saying about her.

"She was not true enough to aid this City in its quest for a new home," the High Priestess said, and some of the novices were nodding in agreement. "But take heart, my children! For Mother Sun, in her infinite wisdom, has forgiven us all for the sins of only one—there shall be another ceremony when she has chosen a pure and deserving Cerulean. Put your minds and hearts to rest, for our City is in her hands."

The relief at her words was palpable—the Cerulean smiled at each other, orange mothers uttering prayers of thanks.

"We thank you, Mother Sun," the High Priestess continued, raising her hands, the moonstone on her circlet glowing against her forehead, "for the gifts you bring us, for your light and warmth, for your healing power. We beg you to receive us into your heart as we receive you into ours, to guide us on our journeys and protect our City from harm. This we pray."

For the first time in her entire life, Leela did not join in when the congregation repeated, "This we pray."

24

THE VERY NEXT MORNING, THE NEWS SPREAD THROUGH-
out the City that a wedding season was about to begin.

It was just as Koreen had predicted days ago in the
cloudspinners' grove. To Leela that felt like another century, a time when Sera was still alive and the High Priestess
could be trusted implicitly. Now she could not help but be
suspicious. Just as the City was teetering on the brink of
uncertainty and confusion, a period of joy and celebration
had been announced. It all seemed a rather convenient distraction.

And it was working. Sera's failure had been explained
away, their leader had reassured the Cerulean all would

be well, and now a time of love and laughter would begin. Everyone was out and about, harvesting food for the upcoming feasts, spinning fabric in the cloudspinners' grove for wedding gowns, digging for stargems in the mines, or making garlands of flowers in the Day Gardens. There was a unity to the work and the Cerulean thrived under it.

"Are you not even a little excited?" her green mother said that afternoon as they milked seresheep in the meadow. "To see a wedding season at long last. I know it is something you have always wanted."

Leela shrugged and focused on filling her pail with milk. A wedding season had been something she and Sera were supposed to experience together. They would decorate their dresses and giggle through the ceremonies and eat until their bellies were stuffed. They would dance the Lunarbelle and stay up past the hour of the dark, whispering of their own futures. That was how the wedding season was supposed to be.

The seresheep she was milking let out a loud bleat and Leela patted its silvery fleece. Her pail was nearly full.

"I will take this to the creamery," she said. Her green mother reached out and placed a hand on Leela's arm.

"Talk to me," she said. "Please. Your mothers and I . . . we are fearful of this pall that has befallen you."

Leela did not know where to begin. For a moment she considered telling her mother of the conversation she had overheard, but something in her whispered *no*.

"Everything is changing so fast," she said instead. "It is as if everyone has simply . . . forgotten her."

"No, my darling," her green mother said. "No one has

forgotten. But Cerulean do not deal with uncertainty well. We are happier when there is work to focus on, and a unity of purpose. We have that now."

"Do you think she was unworthy?"

"I do not know. I speak the truth," her green mother insisted, because Leela was shaking her head. "Sera was always a good friend, a loving, kind girl. Yes, she was loud, and boisterous, and my goodness, she had more questions than Seetha knew what to do with. Do I think her unworthy? No, I do not. But I am not Mother Sun, my dear. I never read the heart of Sera Lighthaven."

I did, Leela thought fiercely.

"And she will live forever inside *you*," her green mother continued. "Your memories and your love will keep her flame burning bright as a candle on the Night of Song."

But Leela did not want to keep Sera alive in her memory. She wanted her here, now, and the anger that seemed to have become her constant companion over the last two days reared up again. But she did not wish to lash out at another one of her mothers, so she nodded, tight-lipped, and stood, gripping the pail harder than she needed to as she made her way through the grazing seresheep. She felt in a fog, as if her green mother's words had pulled all her memories of Sera out like dresses from a closet and laid them before her.

"Oh!" She had not been looking where she was going, and some milk slopped over her pail as she bumped into another Cerulean. "I am so—"

But her apology died on her lips. Sera's purple mother was standing before her with a basket full of feed for the seresheep. Except she was not feeding them. She was staring vacantly at a spot just above Leela's head. She was the youngest of Sera's mothers, but she looked older now. Her hair was lank and unkempt, and her silvery skin had a sallow tinge to it.

"Good afternoon, Purple Mother," Leela said, addressing her formally as all Cerulean children addressed mothers.

"Estelle?" she said, her eyes unfocused.

"No, it's—I'm Leela."

Sera's mother started and seemed to come back to herself.

"Oh," she said. "Good afternoon, Leela."

"Are you unwell?" she asked.

Sera's purple mother looked at the basket in her hands like she had forgotten she was holding it. "I . . ." She seemed at a loss for how to answer.

"May I escort you home?" Leela wondered if she should fetch her green mother to help, but Sera's purple mother was shaking her head, her face twisting in pain.

"No," she said. "I cannot go home. She is . . . she is . . . *everywhere*."

And without a word of goodbye, she wandered off through the meadows like a woman in a trance. The seresheep parted for her as if they knew this was not a person to nudge with a nose in search of treats. And Leela knew that whatever grief she felt was but a faint echo of the agony burning inside Sera's mother. She did not know who Estelle was, however—Sera had never mentioned anyone by that name.

Koreen, Daina, and Treena were leaving the creamery as Leela arrived.

". . . and then there will be a birthing season!" Koreen was saying. "Imagine all those darling little babies."

"I've always longed to see a baby," Treena said wistfully. "Attending to pregnant seresheep is all well and good, but imagine helping to foster in a new Cerulean generation! Ileen said I could begin to help prepare the birthing houses as soon as tomorrow."

"And I shall be in the orchards," Daina said. "And Koreen in the cloudspinners' grove. How exciting it is to grow up."

"Indeed!" Koreen exclaimed. "I shall be leaving my mothers' dwelling soon enough."

"So shall I," Treena said.

"Me too," said Daina. "We should all find a dwelling together!"

"Until we find our own triads," Koreen qualified. Then she sighed. "What a time to be alive."

The words left a trail of sharp stings over Leela's skin. She did not feel as if she understood anything anymore—the High Priestess was a liar, Sera's joyful purple mother had become a broken shadow of her former self, and her friends had moved on from death faster than you could say will-o-wisp.

"If only the ceremony had worked properly," Treena said. "We would have a wedding season *and* be on our way to a new home by now."

That did it.

"If Sera had died properly, you mean?" Leela said. The girls started. Daina, at least, had the decency to look ashamed.

"Good afternoon, Leela," Treena stammered. "I did not see you."

The anger was a comfort to her now, a friend that sharpened her vision and sparked her courage.

"She is dead, and you are speaking as though she did something *wrong*."

"We did not mean to be rude," Daina said.

"But Sera did not break the tether," Koreen said. "So something *did* go wrong, didn't it?"

"Yes, but that does not mean it was Sera's *fault*!" Leela was breathing fast. The three girls backed away from her like she was something dangerous. She did feel quite dangerous at the moment. The loneliness, the unfairness of losing her friend, of knowing something she shouldn't, something she didn't understand but felt was more important than anything she'd ever known in her life, it was all building up inside her and she wanted to scream.

"We know you were her best friend," Koreen said. "But that does not change what happened. She was not worthy. You must accept it, Leela. The High Priestess said so herself."

"She was a better Cerulean than most in this City," Leela shot back. "Far better than you will ever be, Koreen!"

Then she stormed past them and into the creamery before she could say anything else that might get her in trouble. She slammed her pail down on the table, where the cheesemongers could collect it, and found herself face-to-face with Elorin. She was carrying several cloth-covered wheels of cheese in a basket, and her expression left Leela with no doubt that she had overheard the heated conversation.

"Good afternoon," she said.

"Good afternoon," Leela replied tersely.

There was an awkward silence. Leela had never been particularly close with Elorin and was not sure what to say. She just wished to be alone.

"I am a novice now," Elorin said. "I will be settling into the dormitory tonight."

Leela did not want to think about all her friends moving on, finding their purposes in the City, leaving their mothers' dwellings. She wanted everything to go back to how it was.

"That is wonderful news," she forced herself to say. "You must be very happy."

Elorin nodded, then bit her lip. "I thought she was very brave," she said, leaning close so that only Leela could hear her. "Sera, I mean. I do not know if I would have had the grace and courage she did."

Tears once again sprang to Leela's eyes—she felt as if her body had become an unending reservoir that would never run dry.

"Thank you for saying that," she whispered.

Elorin touched her shoulder. "Come to the temple if you need solace," she said.

Leela's smile was a frail, feeble thing. She did not want solace from the temple. She wanted her friend back and she wanted the world to make sense again. Elorin left her with a halfhearted wave, and Leela took her leave of the creamery with its clattering of pails and sharp, tangy scent of cheese.

What would Sera do now were she in my place? she thought. *Had she heard what I heard, what course of action would she have taken?* She probably would have walked right up to the temple and asked to speak to the High Priestess.

Was Leela brave enough to do the same? It was not just a matter of being brave, either. A tendril of hope was creeping into her mind, more tentative than the sunburst but with just as much power. What if she was wrong? What if she had simply misunderstood? It made far more sense if she thought about it—that Leela's young and untrained mind had misinterpreted what she heard was much more likely than that the High Priestess was somehow responsible for Sera's death. Perhaps Leela could ask about the choosing ceremony and how it had come about. That seemed a reasonable enough query. Maybe she could put her own mind at ease. Maybe then she would stop snapping at everyone and the storm growing inside her might be soothed.

She set off for the temple, making her way through the meadows and passing the orchards, until she was crossing Aila's Bridge and facing the gleaming copper doors. The temple seemed larger than it ever had before, its tip pointing to the sky like an admonishing finger. Leela's legs trembled and her chest seized up—she could not do this; she was not the Cerulean Sera had been. She did not know how long she stood there, her courage faltering, her heart torn. She wished she felt more grown-up, more sure of herself.

She wished she were not so alone.

"Leela?"

Acolyte Klymthe was walking down the steps of the temple, a watering can in one hand.

"Good afternoon, Acolyte," Leela said. The time was now. She must be brave, like Sera. "I was hoping perhaps I might speak to the High Priestess."

Acolyte Klymthe's eyebrows rose high above her close-set eyes. "Why, what on earth for, my child?"

Leela felt she should have better prepared herself for this situation now that she was in it. "I thought I might . . . ask her about . . . the choosing ceremony."

Acolyte Klymthe's expression softened. "She is sequestered for a time. Her energies are very low, I'm afraid."

Leela saw an opportunity to play on the acolyte's sympathies. "As are mine," she said. "With Sera gone, the City feels like a stranger to me."

"I am sure it must. But remember that time heals all. There will come a day when the hurt will not be so grave."

"I cannot seem to understand," Leela said. "Why was Sera chosen at all?"

Acolyte Klymthe sighed, and it sounded sincere, but Leela could not be certain. She was not used to detecting falsehoods. Cerulean rarely lied.

"Grief breaks us in different ways," she said. "For some, the need to seek answers can be powerful. But there are no answers to give here. Only the pain of loss and the solace of prayer. But do not fear. Even those Mother Sun deems unworthy of sacrifice are still held in her everlasting embrace. Sera may not have been the right choice, but she will not be forgotten by our Mother."

Leela's anger rekindled at the word *unworthy*, a spark that gave her the nerve she needed. She looked right into Acolyte Klymthe's eyes and said, "But I thought Mother Sun did not make mistakes."

A flicker of shock passed across the acolyte's face, and

in that brief moment Leela knew she had not misheard or misunderstood. Whatever secret Leela had stumbled upon, Acolyte Klymthe knew and was part of it.

"She does not," Acolyte Klymthe said firmly. "But sometimes we cannot see the true shape of her plan at first. All will be revealed in time. Meanwhile, I must tend to the roses in the Moon Gardens. I will tell the High Priestess you called."

Leela was left with her head spinning and her heart in her throat. There was too much mystery, and she did not know where to begin. She needed help. But she could not share this with Koreen or Daina or even Elorin, kind as she had been earlier. She needed someone older, wiser, someone she was certain she could trust, someone who would *believe* her.

Inspiration struck in a flash, a meteorite lighting up the dark recesses of her mind. She was shocked she had not thought of it before.

The only person who might believe her was the only person who missed Sera as desperately as Leela did.

Sera's purple mother.

25

THE FIRST WEDDING TOOK PLACE THE NEXT DAY AT THE hour of the lamb.

Fireflies lit the canopy of trees above as the Cerulean watched Plenna, Heena, and Jaycin circle each other over and over, repeating oaths of fealty. The girls wore wreaths of white roses in their hair, and delicate garlands of baby moonflowers around their necks. Their waists were belted with fire lilies glowing red-gold like the sun. The High Priestess held the three ribbons—orange, purple, and green—on a small white pillow. When the girls stopped circling, she lifted the pillow above her head.

"Mother Sun, bless this union now and forever, so that this triad may live together in harmony until the day they return to your everlasting light. May they find peace in times of discord, comfort in times of sadness, and constancy in the face of chaos; for the union of three souls is sacred and not to be undertaken lightly. This we pray."

"This we pray," the Cerulean echoed. Leela only mouthed the words. She kept her eyes fixed on the High Priestess, searching for a suspicious look or gesture, but she was as serene and elegant as ever. If Leela could detect any change at all it was that she seemed a bit tired—there were thin lines around her eyes and mouth.

Plenna tied an orange ribbon around Heena's neck, then Heena tied a green ribbon around Jaycin's neck, and finally, Jaycin tied a purple ribbon around Plenna's neck. Sera had been certain Plenna would be a purple mother, Leela thought sadly. She could almost hear her whispering, *Told you so*, in her ear.

When the last ribbon was secured, the High Priestess proclaimed, "A new triad is formed! All praise them! Praise Mother Sun!"

"Praise her!" the Cerulean called back. Plenna began to cry, and Jaycin took her in her arms and kissed her while Heena stroked her hair. And then all the Cerulean were laughing and clapping because young love shone brighter than the brightest star—that was what Leela's green mother always said.

The ceremony was repeated as another triad was wed, then another. Four weddings that lasted until the hour of the owl, when finally it was time for the celebratory feast.

Minstrel flowers sang as tables were brought out and laden with food and drink. Pitchers of crystal-clear water and decanters of sweetnectar were placed among platters of crisp fried eggplant, freshly sliced tomatoes with basil and seresheep cheese, stuffed squash blossoms, salads of apples, plums, and nasturtiums, and of course, a traditional Cerulean wedding cake in the shape of a dome, light and spongy and frosted with silver icing, dotted with blue roses.

"Go run and help Freeda with the water," her purple mother said, and Leela hurried to carry one of the large earthen pitchers to a table that was wanting.

"Thank you," Freeda said. She towered over Leela, clutching the remaining pitcher against her large chest. "Be a dear and bring those forks along as well, will you?"

Leela grabbed the forks and put them beside the pitcher, but she did not go directly back to her mothers. She wandered through the crowds, searching . . . until at last she found Sera's purple mother. She was sitting at a table alone, twisting a napkin in her hands and staring at a platter of glazed carrots with unseeing eyes. She looked worse than before—thinner, fragile, her bones straining prominently underneath her skin.

Leela was not quite sure what to do. She took a hesitant step forward. Sera's purple mother looked up from the carrots, and when their eyes met, Leela stopped in her tracks.

It was as if a light had been turned off inside her. Cerulean eyes were bright with the magic of their blood—it was the place where their magic shone through most clearly. But the eyes Leela stared into were dark and flat. They frightened her. Sera's purple mother had always been full of joy and laughter. Leela did not know the woman sitting before her, and her heart sank.

She could not help Leela any more than Leela could help herself. She should not have thought to burden Sera's poor mother with more heartache when she was clearly too distraught with grief. The bench opposite was empty, and she sat across from Sera's mother, no longer thinking of her own plans, wishing only to comfort.

"I miss her, too," Leela said, not sure if Sera's mother was listening or if Leela herself just needed to talk to someone who understood. "I miss her more than anything. It's an ache in my chest that won't go away, a pain in my heart that throbs worse with every beat. I am angry all the time. I am angry at my mothers, at my friends. I do not even know who I am anymore. And I wished to . . . to speak with you about something, but now I think I would only make things worse." She looked down at her hands folded in her lap. "Perhaps I need to learn to deal with things on my own," she murmured.

"The Night Gardens," Sera's purple mother said. Her voice was faint and hollow, like it was coming from the bottom of a well.

"Yes," Leela said. "The Night Gardens. That's where she . . . where she was lost to us."

Sera's mother lurched forward, holding her head in her hands. "Leela . . ."

"I am here." Leela reached out and put a hand on her elbow. Sera's mother peered at her from between her fingers.

"I feel I am going insane," she whispered. "I remember things that can't be real. Ever since the Night Gardens."

"I have brought you some food, Kandra." Sera's green

mother appeared with a plate piled high. Leela sat up, putting her hands back under the table. "Oh, good evening, Leela."

"Good evening, Green Mother."

Sera's green mother smiled, but her smile was too tight and did not curve upward. "How have you been?" she asked. "We do miss hearing your laugh around our dwelling."

Sera's purple mother flinched.

"I have been . . ." Leela trailed off. She could not lie to Sera's mothers. "I have been very sad."

Sera's green mother swallowed. "Yes. It has been difficult for us all. But what a lovely celebration." She swept out her hand at the crowds eating and drinking and chattering happily. "It is sure to put all grief out of mind." But her voice cracked on the last word and a tear spilled down her cheek. Sera's purple mother closed a frail hand around her wrist.

"Stop it, Seetha," she said. "Stop pretending. Please."

Sera's green mother scrubbed the tear away, putting the plate on the table. "You must eat, Kandra. You *must*."

Leela opened her mouth, unsure of what to say but devastated at what was happening to Sera's family. At that moment someone shouted, "The Lunarbelle, the Lunarbelle!" A group of novices began to sing, the minstrel flowers joining them, and several Cerulean musicians took up their harps and lyres and frame drums. Everyone rushed to form circles to begin the dance.

"Leela!" Elorin was at her side, smiling, with a wreath of pink and yellow tulips in her hair. "Come, let us dance!"

Leela allowed herself to be pulled away from the grieving

women, joining Elorin as they formed a circle with Baarha, Crailin from the Aviary, and a few of the cheesemongers. They clasped hands and began the complex, intertwining dance, but when the Lunarbelle ended and everyone sat down to eat, Leela saw Sera's purple mother sitting in the same spot, her plate of food untouched, twisting the same napkin with a lifeless expression.

Later that night, Leela lay awake, her stomach in knots.

She wondered if she would ever have a night of unbroken rest again. But she could not ignore the niggling feeling in her chest that was telling her to go to the Night Gardens. Even though Sera's purple mother had seemed beyond the reach of reason, something told Leela that she would find her there. Some deeply buried instinct called to her to trust herself.

She threw off her covers and slipped out of the window, her orange mother's snores fading as she crept through the glass dwellings, past the Apiary, wading through the moonflower fields until she came to the Night Gardens. Silence enveloped her completely as she entered them. No birds sang or crickets chirped. The Night Gardens had always filled Leela with a sort of fearful wonder, but tonight all she could think of was the last time she had been here. Yet she was determined not to let the past frighten her.

She brushed aside a low-hanging cloud on the leaf of a nebula tree and made her way through the gardens, all the scarlets and purples and grays bleached white in the moonlight. A will-o-wisp floated past her, its eerie blue light casting strange shadows on the tree trunks. She knew where she was going without really knowing, her feet carrying her of their own accord, and when she reached the raised dais jutting out over the falling water of the Estuary, she stopped. The memories were painfully clear—she could almost see Sera standing there again, falling into nothingness. Into death.

Her heart in her stomach, she stepped up onto the dais, seeing the glittering blanket of stars as Sera had last seen them. The planet below was so dark she could not discern the shapes of Kaolin and Pelago. She reached out and felt the barrier, pliable beneath her fingertips.

"Sera?"

Leela whirled around, nearly losing her balance. Sera's purple mother stood before her, her face wild with a hope that faded as soon as she saw who it was.

"Good evening, Purple Mother," Leela said.

Sera's mother raised her eyes to the skies above, but they did not reflect the moonlight. "I am not a purple mother anymore," she said. "You should call me Kandra."

Leela stepped down off the dais. "You are still her mother," she said gently.

Kandra cringed. "We are the only two who dare return to this place. No one else will come here."

"What about Sera's green and orange mothers?"

"We deal with her loss in different ways," Kandra said. "Otess will not stop praying. She has become cold and hard as a stargem in her devotion. Seetha tries to be positive, to look to the future, to see a time when we will not be so enshrouded with pain. For me it is like . . . like she took a piece of me with her. And I cannot seem to figure out how to live without that piece."

Leela was relieved to hear Sera's mother speaking so clearly, so rationally.

"That is very much how I feel," she confessed. "I am glad to find you here."

"I am always here," Kandra murmured. "I am close to her here. I cannot . . . I cannot bear that dwelling. I can't set foot in her room. It still smells of her. Seetha wanted to pack her things away, but Otess and I would not allow it. Her hairbrush is right where she left it. I can see it from the hall. In the very same place she left it . . ."

She reached out as if seeing it now, as if she could touch its burnished silver handle.

"And since she has gone I've begun to see things, things that cannot possibly be . . ." Her voice trailed off, her gaze shifting out over the gardens.

"What sorts of things?" Leela asked. Kandra did not seem to hear her.

"I am so angry," she continued, and Leela had the sense that she was confiding something she had told no other soul. "I feel I am a terrible person for this but . . . I am *angry* with Mother Sun. My heart should be full of love and trust in her endless wisdom, but it is not. It has become jaded and unyielding, and I fear I am losing myself. It is unfair to Otess and Seetha, unfair to our City. But I cannot change it. I can't bring myself to be at peace with what has happened. And I remember things that cannot be, that *cannot* be. . . ." She covered her face with one hand. "I am so sorry. You are a child. You do not need to be burdened with my fears."

This was her chance. Leela took a deep breath and

pretended she was brave.

"I am angry too," she said. "And then I overheard something. Something bad. About . . . Sera."

"Yes, I have heard things as well," Kandra said, rubbing her eyes. "They blame her. Unworthy, they call her." Her breath caught in her throat. "There was never a girl more worthy of light and love than my daughter. *Never.*"

"I know," Leela said. "But what I meant was . . . I heard the High Priestess talking about Sera. In the Moon Gardens, not two days ago. She didn't know I was there."

Kandra looked up, shock etched across her face. "The High Priestess?"

"Yes."

"You are certain?"

"I am." Leela felt this was significant to Kandra in a way she could not yet comprehend.

"What did she say?"

"I . . . it's . . . I am not sure you will believe me," she said. "I have been scared to whisper a word of it to anyone."

There was a sudden flash of color in Kandra's eyes, a spark of blue that vanished almost as soon as it appeared. "You will tell me what you heard," she commanded, and Leela took a step backward. Kandra seemed to realize she was being frightening—she softened, her shoulders wilting. "I'm sorry," she said. "Please." She crossed the space between them and took Leela's hands gently in her own. "I swear to you on the light and grace of Mother Sun and her Moon Daughters, on my love for this City and the love I bore my own child. I will believe what you say and I will not repeat to a soul what you reveal to me here."

Leela took a deep, quavering breath and began to recount the conversation she had overheard between the High Priestess and Acolyte Klymthe. The story came slowly at first, but then the words began to spill out of her, and the relief that came with the sharing of this secret was a rich, heady thing. By the time she finished, Kandra was a different woman from the one Leela had seen at the wedding or in the meadow. The emptiness in her expression was gone, replaced with a fierce determination. Her eyes were still dark, but a fire seemed to glow in their depths.

"This was *her* doing," she said. "Not Mother Sun's. Not Mother Sun's . . ." She repeated the phrase as if it could alleviate some guilt, as if it could give her strength.

"But why?" Leela asked. "Why would the High Priestess choose Sera? Why didn't the ceremony work?"

Kandra was silent for so long Leela wondered if she had not heard her. "Estelle," she murmured at last.

"Who is—"

But Kandra cut her off. "It has always been a curious thing," she said, "the longevity of our High Priestess."

"Mother Sun imbues her with long life," Leela said. "Or so my orange mother told me."

"Indeed. But she is by far the longest-reigning High Priestess in our history, is she not?"

Leela considered this. To be honest, she did not know much about the High Priestesses who had come before, except Luille, who had died on the previous planet during the Great Sadness.

"I suppose."

"Nine hundred years. How much she has seen." Kandra knelt by a crimson dahlia and stroked its petals. "How many Cerulean have lived and died in this City, with never a new High Priestess chosen."

"That is for Mother Sun to decide, is it not?"

"It is," Kandra agreed. "But it is up to the High Priestess to read and determine the signs Mother Sun leaves for her. She must identify her own successor. My orange mother told me the signs would be written on the doors of the temple. Otess believes they will be large and bold like a sun flare, for all the City to see. I think they will be more subtle than that."

"It is not known for certain?"

"It was once, I believe. Or perhaps not—perhaps it has always been a private knowledge passed from one High Priestess to the next. Our current High Priestess was chosen only weeks before the Great Sadness took Luille. There is meant to be time to transfer the knowledge and secrets of the most important post in Cerulean society. But one thing is certain—once a new High Priestess is chosen, the old one will surely die. That is the way of it, the nature and cycle of life." A will-o-wisp floated past and hung above them, casting an eerie blue light on Kandra's face. "It is not meant to be a violent death, like Luille's. But death is part of life. Fear of death is fear of living."

"You seem to have thought long on this matter," Leela said. She wasn't quite sure how this all related to Sera, though.

Kandra sighed. "Not me. I had a friend once, curious,

like Sera. She was fascinated by our current High Priestess's long life."

"Estelle," Leela said.

Kandra started. "How do you know her name?"

"You said it the other day in the meadow and then again just now."

"Did I?" She frowned. "I have not thought about her in so long. I have not been *able* to. . . ." Her hand curved around the dahlia, and for a second Leela thought she would crush it in her fist. "She found it strange that no new High Priestess had been chosen in so many long years."

"It is because Mother Sun values her very much. That's what my orange mother said."

"Ah, but who tells us that?" Kandra said, looking at her gravely. "*She* does."

Leela sorted through her words, trying to piece the meaning together. If the High Priestess was in control of choosing her successor . . . "Do you believe that is why Sera was sacrificed? To prevent a new High Priestess from being chosen?"

"I think," Kandra said carefully, "that it may go deeper than that."

Leela gasped. "You think *Sera* was to be the next High Priestess?"

"I don't know. Perhaps." When she looked at Leela again, there was a hint of her old warmth in her expression. "She loved you very much. I hope you know that."

Leela found it hard to swallow. "I loved her, too."

Kandra cupped Leela's face in her hands and kissed her forehead. "Thank you," she whispered. "You have given me a greater gift than you know."

"What is that?"

"You have given me *purpose*. And you have shown me that I am not losing my mind, losing myself. No . . . no the memories are real, they are *real*. . . ." She stood. "You were wise not to share your thoughts with anyone. Meet me by the birthing houses tomorrow after the weddings. I must see . . . I must know, one way or the other. Do not tell anyone, not even your mothers. Can you do that?"

Leela nodded without hesitation. "I will be as silent as the night sky." Then she paused. "What is at the birthing houses?"

Kandra's eyes grew distant with some ancient memory. "The High Priestess has many secrets, it would seem," she said. "And I think I know one of them."

26

THERE WERE FOUR WEDDINGS THE NEXT DAY, THE LAST one for the City's oldest unmarried triad, who had found each other late in life.

They sat at the head table, all smiles and clasped hands, as the High Priestess stood, raised a glass of sweetnectar, and declared, "Love at any age is a blessing upon us, but love that has been forged through time and patience is a rare treasure. We look to you three as a beacon of hope in these trying times."

Leela felt a prickle creep up the back of her neck at those words, a sudden premonition that something was about to happen.

"Caana was gracious enough to allow me to be

storyteller for this wedding," the High Priestess continued. "If you all would permit it."

"Yes, High Priestess," the Cerulean called. "Tell us a tale!"

"A tale of love!"

"A tale of courage!"

"I will tell you the story," the High Priestess said dramatically, "of Wyllin Moonseer and the Forming of this Tether."

Quiet fell at her words, more complete than the Night Gardens at the hour of the dark. The High Priestess paused for a moment, allowing the silence to permeate the gathering, weaving together an air of expectation, wonder, and unease that filled the spaces between the tables.

"Yes, my children," she said. "It is a story I have never before told. Wyllin was a Cerulean of great heart and tremendous courage, yet her name has not been said in many, many years. I am at fault for this. She was from a time best not remembered. Who among us would choose to dwell on the Great Sadness and all the loss and pain that came from it? But our City has reached yet another crossroads, where loss and pain weigh on our hearts once more." The High Priestess's eyes lighted on Leela, and she felt a pang of unease, as if this story was being told just for her, but to what end she could not tell. "Comfort can be found in the sharing of things past, in the remembrance of the interdependent web of which we are all a part."

The High Priestess set down her glass and took several steps forward. A knot of fireflies swirled overhead, casting a glittering light over her.

"Wyllin Moonseer was only twenty-one years of age when the Great Sadness occurred, just a year younger than myself. We had been born in the same season and had been friends since childhood; we played along the banks of the Estuary, hunted for eggs in the Aviary, and did all the things that young Cerulean do to occupy their time. As we grew older, I began to spend many of my days in the temple, while she found her purpose in making music—she was exceptionally skilled at the lute. However, the Great Sadness changed her, as it changed so many others."

The High Priestess paused, and there was no doubt she was seeing into the past as she told this story, unfolding memories from long ago with painstaking care.

"She was not on the planet itself when tragedy struck—only five of us made it back to the City alive, myself among them. Five out of two hundred. Wyllin began coming to the temple more and more, or praying for the lost souls in the Night Gardens. She talked to those who had lost wives and daughters and friends, held them when they wept, and listened to them when they railed against the unfairness of the universe. Some even cursed Mother Sun herself."

There were several shocked gasps at that, and many Cerulean looked at each other as if they could not conceive of such a thing.

"In the second year of our journey through space, six months before we found this planet, I lost an acolyte—Acolyte Grenda had been aged long before I was ever chosen as High Priestess, and her time to leave her corporeal body and join Mother Sun had come. Shortly after her death I asked Wyllin to be my new acolyte. She accepted, and I found such comfort in her presence at the temple. She was a true friend and confidante, one who I felt could read my heart without need of the blood bond."

Leela shifted uncomfortably. What the High Priestess was describing sounded very much like her friendship with Sera.

"We talked together late into the evenings, we gathered herbs together from the Moon Gardens, and she would often play the lute for me after meals and I would pour my fears out into her open loving heart. For I was a very young High Priestess, and my ascension to the role had an abrupt and bloody history. I worried I was not worthy enough to lead this City, that I was making mistakes. I was terrified we would not find a new planet in time, before our fields withered and died and our Estuary dried up. Fear became my constant companion, and only Wyllin's calm reassurance and steadfast friendship kept the terror at bay.

"It was she who first spotted this planet, the shapes of Kaolin and Pelago so unfamiliar then. The bells rang out from the temple for a full day and night, and a choosing ceremony was held the next morning. And my sweet beloved Wyllin was chosen to create the tether."

The High Priestess paused to wipe a tear from her eye. She seemed so sincere in her grief, but Leela could not allow herself to trust it.

"I tried to tell myself that it was an honor for her to be chosen," the High Priestess said. "But in my heart I was angry. I did not wish to lose my friend. As for Wyllin, she did not think herself worthy. I wonder if any chosen one has ever felt worthy—we all think ourselves so ordinary.

But Mother Sun knows us, inside and out. And Wyllin had a courage unlike any Cerulean I have ever known." Something about the way she said it made Leela certain that this, at least, was true. The High Priestess's words rang with clarity and feeling that Leela did not think could be faked. The watching Cerulean were captivated, enraptured, transported back to a time before their mothers or their mothers' mothers.

"She stood on the dais in the Night Gardens, and I lifted the barrier so that she could fall. And I tell you my children, it was the hardest thing I have ever done in my life. Our City was still raw and grieving—my own heart had only recently been soothed, and Wyllin was a significant source of that comfort. I lost more than a friend that day. I lost a piece of myself."

Leela felt as if they were finally arriving at the point of this story—her spine stiffened and she leaned forward, hanging on to every word.

"But our City is more important than any one Cerulean, and Mother Sun's will more important than all. She chose Wyllin Moonseer for a purpose, as she chose Sera Lighthaven for a purpose." A murmur ran through the crowd at Sera's name. Leela clenched her hands into fists under the table. She dared not look at Kandra. "We may not see it now, for Mother Sun's plans do not always reveal themselves right away. But there was a reason for Sera's sacrifice and a reason for her failure. This I promise you, my children. I am not the young High Priestess I once was, tentative and afraid. I have no fear for the fate of our City, only confidence in Mother Sun. She will not lead us astray. There will be another choosing ceremony in time, and the City will move. We need not worry on that account. And I hope that Sera has found Wyllin in Mother Sun's everlasting light, and that they are happy together, as all who are chosen deserve to be. Let us raise a glass to Sera and Wyllin."

She took up her glass of sweetnectar and the Cerulean followed suit.

"Sera and Wyllin," she called. "Praise them!"

"Praise them!" the Cerulean called back. The High Priestess's eyes landed on Leela once more, and in that one glance Leela felt a pressure on her back and a heat on her neck. It was a look that seemed to say, *There. Your curiosity should be satisfied now.*

Except it wasn't. Far from it. Leela allowed herself a quick glance at Kandra, seated three tables away. Her eyes were chips of onyx, her mouth in a thin line. Sera's orange mother sat beside her, her head bent in prayer, gently rocking back and forth. Many of the Cerulean were crying, Leela noticed. It had been an impassioned story, and one they'd never heard before. Leela could see its effects working their way through her community, soothing any doubts that remained.

"My goodness," her own purple mother said, dabbing at her eyes with a napkin. "That was quite a tale, wasn't it?"

Yes, it was, Leela thought. Whether it was true or not was an entirely different matter.

As the hour of the dark approached, Leela realized she was growing more and more accustomed to wandering the City late at night.

The Forest of Dawn was quite far from her own dwelling—she crossed at the Eastern Bridge and made her way past the cloudspinners' grove and the stargem mines, and the journey took her longer than she had anticipated. The forest was filled with the sounds of nocturnal life, rodents scurrying and insects chirping and chattering. She passed a small pond where luminescent frogs croaked in harmony, their slippery bodies glowing in bright greens and blues. The trees gave off a variety of scents that mixed together to create a pleasing quilt of pine and magnolia and crabapple.

When she arrived at the birthing houses, they were all dark save one. The houses looked much like any Cerulean dwelling, round and made of sunglass, except they contained only one room. There were twelve of them, set in a circle around a wide patch of grass with an obelisk of moonstone in its center. It made her think of the stone in her star necklace that she had given to Sera. Rosebushes were planted around each birthing house, blooming in pale pink and golden petals. And every house had a copper door.

One of the doors was ajar and a light shone from inside it.

"Kandra?" Leela called softly as she approached. Kandra's face appeared, lit by the lantern in her hand.

"Come," she said, and beckoned Leela inside.

Leela had never been in a birthing house before, more for lack of interest or necessity than anything. When she and Sera would come to the forest, it would be to jump from tree to tree like squirrels, or to catch frogs, or hunt for starbeetles. Leela might not have found her purpose in the City yet, but she had always known it would never be as a purple mother or a midwife.

The house's interior looked very much like her mothers' bedroom—domed with a large circular bed in the center, piled high with pillows and laid with soft blankets. But some things were different. A bassinet off to one side. A pile of extra sheets and towels on a table. A basin and pitcher. There were no windows.

Kandra set the lantern down and stared at the bed with distant eyes, then moved to the bassinet.

"This is the room where Sera was born," she said.

Leela hovered by the door. The place felt sacred.

"Did your purple mother teach you about how you were conceived?" Kandra asked.

"Of course." Every Cerulean child learned about the process of conception in her twelfth year—it was the one official lesson that green mothers would give over to the province of purple mothers. "A birthing season was announced and the High Priestess chose my purple mother among others, and blessed her so that she might become fertile. Every day Orange Mother went to the temple to pray, and Green Mother cooked offerings for Aila and Dendra and Faesa." The three Moon Daughters, Aila in particular, must be honored if a birth was to be successful. "And Purple Mother came to the birthing house until she sensed her time was coming and her body was ready for a child. She told me that she carried within her womb an egg and that when the time was right, the egg split and created a new life; that was me. She told me Cerulean are not like the laurel doves in the Aviary, that we do not need one male and one female to make an offspring, but that we have that power within ourselves."

"We do." Kandra sat on the bed and brushed her fingertips across the blanket. Then she gripped it in her hand as if she wished to rip it off. "I remember the first time I felt her stir in me," she whispered. "It was a terrifying and wondrous moment. When the egg inside me split and formed Sera, I felt nothing. I did not believe the midwives at first when they told me I was pregnant. But she grew and grew, my belly swelling up with her." She relaxed her hold on the blanket. "I'm sorry. This is not the story I brought you here to tell."

"Then why are we here?"

"Because this is where I saw her."

"Saw who?" Leela asked, though she thought she already knew the answer.

"Estelle," Kandra whispered.

Leela waited as the minutes ticked by and the flame in the lantern flickered.

"She was my best friend," Kandra said at last. "Like you and Sera. Like Wyllin and the High Priestess, if her story is to be believed." Leela felt a wave of relief at not being the only one to doubt the story's validity. "We played together as children and shared our first heartaches as we grew older. She was curious, like I said before, but in a more subtle way than my Sera was. None of our other friends thought her strange. She whispered her questions late at night, convinced she would be able to speak to Mother Sun directly."

Leela's eyebrows shot up her forehead. "That was rather vain of her."

"I thought so too at the time, but was it? I am not sure I believe anything I was taught anymore. I feel as if I do not even trust the very air around me." Kandra stood and brought the lantern with her to the open door. "Estelle had a sharp mind, and her magic was strong. I could feel it when we blood bonded, a heartbeat that was more powerful than mine. Her heart spoke to me of the desire to know more, to be more. Sera was always looking to the planet for escape, but Estelle looked to the stars. She wanted more than just the knowledge of Mother Sun's existence. She wanted tangible proof; she wanted a voice in her ear or a hand on her shoulder. She felt there was something missing in this City and that she alone could discover the cause and fill the void. She began to frighten me a little. And then I fell in love with Seetha and Otess—I found my missing tokens, that's how I always put it to Sera. They completed me. My life changed, my purpose became clear, and Estelle and I drifted apart.

"And so I was not by her side when she died of the sleeping sickness."

Leela gasped, her hand flying to her mouth. The sleeping sickness was the only disease that could kill a Cerulean, the only virus resistant to the healing power in their blood because it fed on their very magic. It came on suddenly, leeching a Cerulean dry until she was nothing but an empty husk. There had been spells of it throughout the years, though none in Leela's lifetime. It would run through the City like a fever, usually taking several lives before running its course. There was no cure for it.

"The bodies of those with the sickness must be destroyed, so Estelle's body was not wrapped in a pale blue shroud and released from the Night Gardens to find a home among the stars. One day she was simply gone. Hers was the third and final death, the sickness receding as it always did. It has not come back since. Only a few days after she died, a birthing season was announced. Otess and Seetha and I had been married for two years and were eager to have a child, though I confess it felt wrong to have such joy come on the heels of such sorrow."

Kandra left the house and walked across the small field of grass. Leela scrambled to her feet to follow.

"I came here one afternoon, before any purple mother had been blessed, when these houses were still empty. I was scared and sad, and I hoped I might find comfort in the place where a new life would develop, where I would meet my daughter. I felt guilt at losing my friend, not just due to death but also neglect. Friendships must be tended if they are to flourish, and I realized I had been a poor gardener. I made a vow then and there that I would teach my daughter to value all her relationships in life and not take anyone for granted. I walked from house to house, wondering which would be mine, and I found myself speaking out loud, talking to Estelle as I once had, sharing my fears with her, and my shame at the fading of our bond. I recalled little things from times past, jokes we shared and games we played.

"I came to the last house and knew it was time to leave, that this place could not give me the comfort I yearned for. And as I turned, I saw her."

Kandra held the lantern up to the obelisk. Ribbons of colors shot across its surface. "She stood right here," she said, gesturing to the space beside the stone. "Her hair moved as if by a light breeze, though the air was still, and her cloudspun dress was threadbare and tattered, like it was disintegrating. She looked wan and pale but *alive*. Very much alive. 'Kandra,' she said to me. 'I heard you.'"

At this, Kandra fell to her knees, a sob ripping from her chest. Leela knelt beside her, afraid to touch her, afraid to say anything.

"I thought I had gone mad," she continued. "'You are dead,' I said to her. 'No,' she replied. Her eyes were so dark, like a night sky with no moon or stars. 'And yes,' she said. "'We are all dying. It cannot continue. She will not stop.'" Tears spilled down Kandra's cheeks. "Forgive me, Leela. I was so afraid. I ran away." She crumpled, her head falling onto Leela's shoulder. "I ran away," she whimpered. "She called my name, she called for me to come back, and I ran and ran."

"It's all right," Leela said, rubbing her back. She had never comforted a purple mother—or any mother, for that matter. It was usually the other way around. "You should feel no shame. You were frightened. You were seeing things."

"No," Kandra said, sitting up. "I was not. She was real. I know it in my bones, in the very magic that lives inside me. When I finally collected myself enough to speak, I went directly to the High Priestess. I told her what I had seen. I remember being startled at how quickly she seemed to take my account seriously—she bade me to stay in the temple and left. When she returned, she said she had searched high and low but there was no sign of Estelle anywhere in the Forest of Dawn. "Your mind is stretched to impossible limits," she said. "Estelle is dead, Kandra. Grief can be a powerful thing. But do not fear. I can take the pain away." And then she put her hands on either side of my head, and I felt a . . . a glow, a pulse, a gentle whisper inside my mind. Her hands were so hot, I remember thinking it was as if she was truly filled with Mother Sun's light.

"When I woke, it was daylight and I was in my own bed, with my wives. They told me I had been out late at the temple conversing with the High Priestess, hopeful that I would soon be blessed to bear a child. Otess warned of being too pushy, but Seetha thought me very brave. I smiled and pretended I remembered what they were talking about. In truth, I could not recall a thing after deciding to go to the forest. I assumed I must have changed my mind.

"The very next day I was chosen by the High Priestess along with several other purple mothers, and I went to the birthing houses. They held no special significance to me. I had no memory of the previous day spent there. The only thing that felt any different was that if ever I thought of Estelle, she would fade quickly, her face out of focus, my memories pale and distant, like echoes. Until I simply stopped thinking about her." Kandra pressed her forehead against the obelisk. "Until she vanished from my thoughts almost completely. Almost," she whispered.

"So what happened?" Leela asked in a hushed voice. "How did you come to recall this? Why now?"

Kandra gathered herself slowly, her hands clutching the folds of her dress, her face twisted in pain.

"When Sera died, something inside me broke. Whatever hold the High Priestess's magic had over me, whatever spell she may have cast, my grief for my daughter shattered it. I thought I was going mad when the memories came back, as clear as if they had just happened yesterday. I could not conceive of the High Priestess lying to me, or erasing my experiences. It simply did not make sense—she is our hope and our guide and she would never do such a thing, I told myself. I thought whatever these visions were had to be false. And they had happened nearly nineteen years ago, so how was I to even trust them? But it felt so *real*. And then you told me what you overheard in the Moon Gardens and I thought, 'I am not crazy. The High Priestess is not who she seems to be. And my daughter became ensnared in her web.'

"I kept hearing Estelle's voice, over and over, saying, 'She will not stop.'"

They both sat in silence. Leela reached out and touched the moonstone, surprised to find it cold—her own pendant had always been warm when she held it. "Do you think she is still here?" she asked. "That Estelle is in this forest somewhere?"

"I do not know. I think not. How could she escape detection all these years?"

"Perhaps the High Priestess has hidden her."

"But where? And for what purpose? What could she have possibly wanted with Estelle?"

Leela thought for a moment. "You said she was like Sera. What if Estelle was also chosen to be the High Priestess? What if the High Priestess has been keeping any potential successor away?"

Kandra wiped a stray tear from her cheek. "But why keep her alive at all then? If she was so willing to sacrifice my daughter, why not Estelle also?"

Leela did not have an answer to that. She could not help but think the two were related somehow. And the High Priestess's lies were at the very heart of the matter.

But why, and to what end, Leela could not see.

27

THE WEDDING SEASON LASTED ONLY ANOTHER SEVEN days, one of the shortest in recent history.

Even so, Leela felt relieved when it ended.

All the dancing and feasting and protestations of love were wearing on her. She saw her City in a new light, afflicted by a wrong so subtle that Leela herself could not put a finger on it. She watched helplessly at every wedding as the High Priestess blessed the happy triads, and tried to see beneath her mask, to find some clue as to the reason behind her lies, but it was impossible.

She and Kandra would meet every night in the Forest of Dawn, searching for a sign of Estelle or where she might have come from, talking themselves in circles, repeating their stories until they knew each other's tales by heart. They never found any hint of a Cerulean or a hiding place or a secret lair. Sometimes they would simply sit by one of the ponds in the light of the frogs and remember Sera—her big, bold laugh, her insatiable appetite for fried squash blossoms, her thirst for knowledge, her longing to see another planet. Other times Kandra would tell stories about Estelle, things she had forgotten that were rising to the surface of her mind now.

When the last wedding had come and gone, the City was quiet the next morning, a drowsy calm settling in the air, as if even the blades of grass were exhausted. Leela could hear her mothers still in bed, the murmurs of conversation interspersed with kisses. She wondered what they would think if she told them everything, about the High Priestess, about Sera and Estelle, and her late-night meetings with Kandra. They would listen, she thought, but they would not believe. They would likely pity her and attribute the stories to shared grief over Sera. Worst case, they would take the matter up with the High Priestess herself, and that was something Leela could not risk. Not when she still knew so little.

We are all dying. It cannot continue. She will not stop. Leela and Kandra had puzzled over this for hours. "She" was likely the High Priestess, but what was "it"? What was Estelle warning could not continue?

It was proof she needed, something concrete, and not just for herself. Even if the other Cerulean were not aware, Leela knew there was something wrong in the City Above the Sky, and while she would rather anyone else have been the one to have overheard what the High Priestess said, the fact was that it had fallen on her shoulders. She might only be Leela Starcatcher, but she was a Cerulean and her blood was magic and she was not going to be afraid anymore. Sera had died for some secret, possibly sordid reason, and Leela would know why and make sure it would never happen again.

At least she knew where the High Priestess would be now. During the wedding season she had not kept a strict schedule, and so Leela would come upon her in the orchards or the meadows or the mines with no warning. But life would return to normal, and the High Priestess would be where she usually was—the temple. That was where Leela must start. She got dressed and went into the kitchen, where her orange mother was making licorice root tea.

"Good morning, darling," she said as Leela took a seat at the round wooden table. "I must admit, I am glad the wedding season has ended, as brief as it was. It was a delight to witness but so tiring!"

"Indeed, Orange Mother. The City feels very quiet today."

"It does, doesn't it?" She sighed as she poured cups of tea for the two of them, filling the kitchen with the scent of anise. "You know, the season when your mothers and I got married lasted nearly a month. I thought I never wished to see another feast again as long as I lived."

Leela smiled. "I would like to have seen that," she said. "You and Mothers getting married."

Her orange mother sat at the table across from her and took a sip of tea. "I was so young then," she said wistfully. "If you can imagine." She winked. "Your purple mother loved to laze in bed in the morning as much as she does now. That hasn't changed. I don't believe she will come out of the bedroom today until the hour of the light."

"I can hear you, Lastra!" her purple mother called out, and Leela and her orange mother exchanged quiet laughter.

"And what are your plans for the day?" her orange mother asked. "Your next apprenticeship is the stargem mines, is it not? But I don't think anyone in the City is expected to jump right back into their routines."

"No," Leela agreed. And she had no interest in apprenticeships any longer. Most of her friends had found their calling and she had found hers—she simply could not tell anyone about it. So she would have to concoct a story, but with some truth to it. She could not bear to think of herself being as deceitful as the High Priestess.

"I thought I would go to the temple," she said. "It has been so long since I have prayed."

Her orange mother looked delighted. "What a fine idea! I can accompany you if you wish."

Leela bit her lip. "If it is all right with you, Orange Mother, I would like to go alone."

Her mother looked crestfallen for a second but recovered quickly. "Of course. You are grown now. Your silly old mother keeps forgetting. I suppose I want to keep you as my child for as long as I can."

"I will always be your child," Leela said, reaching across the table for her hand, "no matter where I live or how old I am or what I call you." Once a daughter left her mothers' house to live on her own, she no longer called them Mother, but their given names. It was strange to Leela to think of calling her orange mother Lastra. "Shall I stop by the Apiary and bring some honey home for our bread tonight?"

"That would be lovely." Her orange mother tucked a lock of hair behind Leela's ear. "I am very proud of the woman you have become, Leela. The loss you have suffered, especially for one so young . . . yet you have forged ahead with light and love in your heart. You are an inspiration. I hope you know that."

Leela felt her throat tighten. "Thank you, Orange Mother." She finished her tea in silence, then took her leave of the dwelling.

The temple was nearly empty when she arrived, mostly novices and a handful of tired-looking orange mothers. Heena was among them, leaving just as Leela entered.

"Good morning, Leela," she said warmly. "I did not know you were so devout. Most of the girls our age are still in bed."

"I wished to pray for Sera at the Altar of the Lost," Leela replied, astonished at how smoothly the lie slipped out. Was this how lying worked, becoming easier the more you did it?

Heena blinked and her lips twitched. "Oh. Yes, of course."

"And you?" Leela asked.

"I am praying for a birthing season to begin."

"Already?"

She laughed. "I know. But Plenna is eager to bear a child. Though I have reminded her over and over that it can be years between a wedding season and a birthing season." Heena smiled indulgently.

"Then I hope Mother Sun hears your prayers," Leela said.

"We have already been so lucky in that we did not have to wait long to be married, like some other triads. Plenna may have to learn some patience." She gave Leela a playful nudge. "Have any Cerulean caught your eye? You are such a caring and thoughtful girl."

"I . . ." Leela had so much on her mind, she had not thought about love or desire at all since Sera had died. Those feelings seemed foreign to her now, fragments of a life that no longer existed. "No, not as yet. But I thank you for the compliment. Excuse me, I must pray."

Heena watched her walk away with a mixture of confusion and pity on her face. But Leela's mind had already bent to more important matters. She knelt before the Altar of the Lost. The intertwining threads of sungold and moonsilver that formed the shape of a sun shone in the late morning light, the blue stargems representing each life lost in the Great Sadness sparkling at her as she waited. She would sit here and pretend to pray all day if she had to. The High Priestess would have to appear at some point. Wouldn't she? Leela wondered if she should feign interest in becoming a novice. That might bring her closer to the High Priestess physically, but it was no guarantee that she would learn anything of significance.

She ran her fingers across the altar's surface, the gems catching on her skin.

Mother Sun, she prayed. *Something is wrong here. The City is run by a liar and I do not know for what purpose, or how to expose her. I know that I am no one of any*

*importance, really, just one young Cerulean among a thou-
sand. But I fear this task has fallen to me, and I will find
the answers if I can. If you can hear my prayer . . . help me.
Please. Show me the way. Give me a sign.*

She waited, holding her breath, hoping her prayer had
been heard. But the minutes passed until they turned into an
hour and nothing happened. She shouldn't have expected it
to. She thought about what Kandra had told her of Estelle,
of how she had hoped to speak directly to Mother Sun. It
was hubris. Mother Sun spoke to the High Priestess. It made
Leela's head hurt to think of what that might mean. Was
Mother Sun aware of the lies?

Just then, a stargem caught her eye. It was all the way
on the far edge of the altar, and the color was leaching from
it, its facets dissolving and becoming smooth until it looked
like . . . a tear. An actual, salty, wet tear. The one beside it
shimmered and became clear, then the next, then the next,
until all the stargems were changing, paling, and Leela
stared at an altar filled with tears.

She reached out a trembling hand to touch them when
suddenly Elorin was at her side.

"I thought that was you, Leela! What a joy to see you
here."

Leela started, pulling her hand back, and the stargems
were as they had always been, dark blue and glittering. She
flexed her fingers, wishing the young novice had left her
alone for a just a few seconds longer.

"It is nice to see you too, Elorin," she said, getting to
her feet.

"Oh, I am sorry. I did not mean to interrupt you,"

Elorin said, her silver cheeks darkening. "A novice must never interrupt a Cerulean at prayer."

"It's all right, do not worry yourself. I was finished anyway." She glanced at the altar again. Perhaps the tears were just a trick of the light. Maybe she was trying to find signs that did not exist.

When she turned back, Elorin was looking at her strangely.

"I have not seen you here alone before."

"I wished to feel close to Mother Sun for a while, that is all."

Elorin turned her gaze to the ceiling. "Do you remember how Sera always said she felt closest to Mother Sun when she was at the top of the temple's spire?"

"I do," Leela said. "I am surprised *you* remember that."

"I think I was a little jealous of her," Elorin said shyly. "She did not seem to worry about saying whatever came into her head. She did not care what others thought about her."

"She did, sometimes," Leela said. "But never for very long."

Elorin allowed a small smile at that. "All the girls thought me quite pious and boring. But the truth is, I always knew I would be a novice. I like the temple; it feels like home here. I like sleeping in the dormitory with the other novices, and tending to the Moon Gardens, and singing to Mother Sun in the mornings. And if Sera felt at home at the top of the spire, why should she not climb it? We all have our quirks, I think. Even my mo—even Jandess and Kilia and Reinin." Elorin stumbled over her mothers' true names.

"Even the High Priestess," she added quickly, as if to gloss over her almost-mistake.

The skin on Leela's arms prickled. "Oh?" she said, trying to sound casual. "Does she climb to the top of the spire as well?"

Elorin laughed. "No, nothing like that. But there is a secret place in the temple she will go to when she sequesters herself, and she has been there much recently. Only the acolytes know it. Novice Belladon told me it is impossible to find. It is the place where she can refresh her mind and recommit to her faith." Her gaze drifted to the altar. "She has led us with such devotion, and for so long. We are very lucky to have her."

Leela clenched her jaw. But she saw an opportunity in Elorin, perhaps a way to visit parts of the temple she had never been to before. She must try to find this secret place Elorin spoke of.

"Would you show me the dormitory?" Leela asked. "I would very much like to see where you are living now."

Elorin looked delighted. "Why, of course!" She led Leela outside, taking her around to the back of the temple, to a plain wooden door with a brass handle. She opened it, revealing a set of sunglass steps leading down into a pale silver light.

The dormitory was a large circular room that Leela guessed was directly underneath the main sanctuary of the temple. Lanterns hung from the walls at even intervals, extinguished now in daytime. Neatly made beds filled the space, with little nightstands beside them littered with various personal belongings. Elorin led Leela to her own bed. A pretty golden comb, a vase with a single moonflower inside it, and a ring in the shape of the many-pointed star set with a large red stargem lay on her nightstand.

"I sleep between Novice Cresha and Novice Baalin," she was saying. "Cresha is very nice, but Baalin snores. Sometimes it is like sleeping beside a seresheep."

Elorin giggled at her own jest. How Leela envied her in this moment, the simplicity of her life, and steadiness of her purpose.

"And what of the acolytes?" she asked, because surely whatever secrets the High Priestess kept, they would not be found in the novice dormitory. "Where do they sleep?"

"Oh, they have rooms higher up in the temple," Elorin said. "We novices are not allowed inside them; they are private. Except for a few of the very old novices who are tasked with ensuring their cleanliness from time to time." She frowned. "Now that I think of it, I have never heard where the High Priestess sleeps. No one has ever spoken of it."

"Perhaps she sleeps in the secret spot you mentioned."

"No, I do not think so . . . but I suppose I do not rightfully know."

"Or maybe she does not sleep at all," Leela mused, thinking nothing would surprise her anymore.

Elorin grinned. "Now that would make her truly exceptional."

They left the dormitory and wandered through the Moon Gardens, passing some novices pruning rosebushes and an orange mother leaving an offering at the foot of Aila's statue. She nodded to them as she left.

"Many orange mothers have come to pray for a birthing

season to begin," Elorin whispered.

"Yes, I saw Heena earlier when I arrived," Leela said. Aila's moonstone statue gleamed iridescent white, shot through with tendrils of color that chased each other like minnows, vanishing and reappearing. Aila was frozen with her arms raised to the sky, a smile etched across her face, her long hair wild about her as if caught in a cheerful breeze. Already a small pile of offerings, garlands of flowers and plates of food, were gathering at her feet. And Leela knew with a heavy certainty that there *would* be a birthing season soon, but not because Mother Sun willed it so. It would be a continuing distraction, one designed to keep all Cerulean thoughts away from Sera and the failed ceremony.

"These statues require very special care. Only the acolytes tend to them. Acolyte Endaria told me there used to be much more moonstone in the City before the Great Sadness."

"Yes, my green mother told me that too," Leela said, only half listening.

"Acolyte Endaria says moonstone is like the beating heart of the City. Or it was. Now these statues are the only pieces left. Well, these and the obelisk at the birthing houses. And the stone in the High Priestess's circlet, of course. Acolyte Endaria said there used to be a fountain in the Night Gardens made of moonstone as well, but it was broken into pieces many centuries ago."

Leela had perked up at the mention of the obelisk. "I did not know that," she said. "Why?"

"It was during a time when the sleeping sickness came," Elorin said. "She said the Cerulean hoped the moonstone would protect them from the disease, and since there was no new moonstone appearing in the City anymore, they took the fountain apart. It didn't work, though."

"My green mother told me moonstone was rare because it was formed from the tears of the Moon Daughters themselves," Leela said.

"My green mother said it was once used by Cerulean to communicate on the planets, back in the days when we would visit them," Elorin said.

"Oh?" Leela had never heard that explanation before.

"To be honest, I think she was making that up. I do not think any of our green mothers really knew what it was for. It is beyond ancient."

Just like the High Priestess, Leela thought. *Perhaps they both hold secrets.*

Kandra could not explain why Estelle had appeared where she did, in the Forest of Dawn by the birthing houses. Maybe it was not the forest or the houses that were significant. Maybe it was the obelisk of moonstone.

Though she could not fully explain why, she felt a sudden rush of gratitude that she had given Sera her necklace.

"Leela?" Elorin's face was creased with concern. "Are you all right?"

"I . . . yes. Forgive me. I was thinking of Sera, that is all." She was happy that she didn't have to truly lie this time.

"Of course." Elorin gazed at Aila's joyful expression. "She does remind me a bit of Sera, if I think about it. Untamed, you know?"

Leela opened her mouth but could not find the words to

say all that she was feeling in this moment. Delicate chimes began to ring from inside the temple.

"I must go," Elorin said. "You will come back and visit me, won't you?"

"I will," Leela said, and she meant it. Elorin kissed her cheek, then scampered off to the temple. Leela gazed up at its golden spire and wondered where the High Priestess was now, and what she was planning. The gardens fell silent around her, and Leela lost all sense of time, her mind churning, until she realized the sun was close to setting. She raised herself and was about to leave when she heard a familiar sound, a laugh she would know anywhere. Sera's voice seemed to emanate from the statue of Aila herself, and it sounded to Leela like she was laughing and crying at the same time, as if she had experienced something joyful yet heartrending. Leela took a step forward, barely able to control the wild hope rising inside her.

"Sera?" she whispered. But the laugh was already fading away, vanishing into the rustle of the wind and the chirping of sparrows in the rosebushes.

Leela stood before Aila for a long while, waiting, watching, listening, until she finally had to accept that she had imagined it. Sera wasn't feeling joy or heartbreak, she wasn't laughing or crying or both. She wasn't anything anymore.

Another orange mother arrived with offerings, and Leela left the gardens and trudged back to her dwelling, feeling no closer to answers, but holding the sound of Sera's laughter close in her heart.

28

SERA'S LAUGH WAS STILL RINGING IN HER EARS WHEN SHE met Kandra by the birthing houses the next evening, at Leela's request. This time, Leela arrived first, carrying her own lantern, and waited by the obelisk.

"I am glad you asked to meet," Kandra said as she approached. "I have found something that may be connected to the mystery we seek to unravel."

"What is it?" Leela asked eagerly.

"I was speaking to Magdeena in the orchards this morning—she was my purple mother," Kandra explained. "I asked if she could remember another time the sleeping sickness fell upon the City, before the bout that took Estelle. She said there was one period right before I was born. She was pregnant with me, and my other mothers were fearful of losing both a wife and a daughter. I wonder if the sleeping sickness is somehow related to the birthing seasons."

"But how?"

"That I do not know." Kandra looked worried. "But I fear there will be another birthing season soon. If only to serve as another distraction."

"I was thinking the same," Leela said. "Though no one has fallen ill yet."

"Yet," Kandra murmured.

"I have news too," Leela said. "I saw my friend Elorin at the temple yesterday—she is a newly blessed novice, and she told me of a secret place that the High Priestess disappears to. But she does not know where it is—only the acolytes know, she said, and I do not think it would be wise to ask after it."

"A secret place?" Kandra raised an eyebrow. "No, that information is best kept to ourselves, I agree. It must be in the temple somewhere. . . ."

"She spoke of moonstone as well," Leela continued, "as we stood before Aila's statue. Did you know there was once a fountain made of moonstone in the Night Gardens?"

"I did not." Kandra frowned. "Who told her that?"

"Acolyte Endaria. She said the Cerulean broke it into pieces during a bout of sleeping sickness, centuries ago, thinking perhaps it could protect them from the disease. But it didn't."

"Moonstone is a very powerful material—it possesses its own magic, or so my green mother told me." Kandra gestured to the obelisk. "She thought it was related to the tether, somehow." Her face was half-shrouded in darkness, but Leela was happy to see her eyes glowing faintly blue, her strength coming back to her. "I've discovered over the years that not every green mother tells exactly the same tales. I'm sure you must have noticed this too—they learn from their own green mothers, as we all do, and so the stories shift subtly from telling to telling. Seetha tried hard with Sera, because she had so many questions, to be as specific as possible. She even asked the High Priestess for advice and answers on occasion." Kandra grimaced. "Now I cannot help but wonder if that was an influence on Sera being chosen. Had she asked the wrong question?"

Leela could not bear to think that Sera was somehow to blame for her own death.

"I was wondering . . . what if it is not the forest that holds the key to where Estelle is hidden," she said. "What if it is the moonstone?"

Kandra looked the obelisk up and down. "You think she is inside it?"

"I am not sure what to think. Only that we cannot answer why she appeared here when she was supposed to be dead, but we know moonstone is sacred and possesses *some* kind of magic. So the two could be related."

Kandra began to circle the obelisk, and Leela followed. She wasn't sure what she was expecting to find. It looked the same as it always had. Leela placed her lantern on the ground, thinking perhaps there was something that could not be seen but felt. As she brushed her fingertips across the base of the stone, she gasped—a faint breath of icy air was wafting up from the ground beneath it.

"Can you feel that?" she said, and Kandra reached out, her fingers skimming the grass.

"Where is that air coming from?"

"It's like it's coming up from the ground," Leela said. "But that can't be. . . ."

Kandra was already on her feet, pushing against the stone. "She might be underneath it," she said, "not inside. Leela, help me."

As soon as Leela placed her hands on the polished cold surface, she felt a crackle run through her fingers and up her wrists into her arms, her magic reacting in a way that she'd never felt before. Her knees buckled as a vision came upon her, an entirely unfamiliar place swimming before her eyes—it was a large, dark room, lit by flowers that glowed in purple and pink and orange. There was a tree with silvery white bark and turquoise leaves, and red curtains hung on either side of the flowers. She could not see the ceiling—above was only darkness. She pulled her hands away as if she'd been burned, and the vision faded.

"What is it?" Kandra asked. Leela did not know how to answer. She had no idea what or where that place was, but her magic was sizzling and pulsing as if begging for the vision to return. There was a faint blue glow in all ten of her fingers.

When she looked back up at the obelisk, markings had appeared in a narrow line down its trunk, markings that Leela could not read but felt she understood anyway—like a signpost, pointing the way to something.

Show me, she thought, or perhaps her magic thought it, for it spun and swirled around her heart.

With a faint groan, the obelisk slid to one side, and Kandra let out a shocked cry, her hands flying to her mouth. The next second she and Leela were peering down into a large square space carved into the earth, a chill emanating from its depths.

A set of sunglass stairs led down into the darkness. In the light of the lantern, Leela could see that the stairs had been sealed off four steps down, a smooth pane of sunglass blocking wherever they led to.

Kandra climbed down the steps and pressed her hands against the sunglass barrier. "Estelle?" she called softly. "Estelle, it's Kandra."

They waited for what felt like ages, but only the hum of insects and the scurrying of nocturnal creatures answered them.

"Where do you think it goes?" Leela whispered.

But Kandra had turned to stare at her with wonder in her pale blue eyes. "How did the obelisk move?"

"I . . . read the markings," Leela said. "I asked it to show me."

Kandra looked from Leela to the stone and back to Leela again. "What markings?"

Leela was about to point them out when she saw they had vanished. She sat back hard. "They were right there," she said, bemused. "I saw them. They were *right there*."

Kandra climbed back up the steps, shaking her head slowly. "Something is happening," she said. "A change. Can you feel it?"

Leela did not know what to say—she was feeling altogether too many things to pinpoint any one in particular. "I saw something," she said, and described the vision of that strange room to Kandra. "I don't know what it means. I have never seen any place like it."

Kandra looked at her in a way she had never been looked at before, and it took Leela a second to work out what the difference was. She was seeing Leela not as a child but as an equal.

"Can you put it back?" she asked.

"What?"

"The obelisk."

Can I? Leela thought, and it was as if her magic had been waiting for her to ask. Her palms began to glow, markings once again appearing on the smooth white surface of the stone.

No one must know you have opened, Leela thought, and the obelisk seemed only too happy to oblige her, sliding back into place, covering the stairs and wherever they led to.

"Mother Sun," Kandra murmured. She turned to Leela. "Did you see anything that time? Another vision?"

Leela shook her head.

Kandra stood and helped her to her feet. "Sera. The tether. Moonstone. These stairs. Estelle. There is still some connection we cannot see. But by the grace of Mother Sun, Leela," she said, taking her in her arms and holding her tightly, "I am so grateful we have each other."

The vision she'd had, plus moving the moonstone, were weighing so heavily on Leela's mind the next day, she realized she had not heard a word Elorin had been saying.

"I am so sorry," she said, as she followed Elorin out of

the temple. "I did not mean to be distracted. Tell me, what has gotten you so excited?"

For Elorin was flushed and smiling, practically bouncing as she and Leela entered the Moon Gardens. Leela could not help eyeing each of the statues as they passed, first Dendra with her solemn face bent in prayer, then Aila and her joyful smile, and finally Faesa, her cupped hands outstretched as if holding the wisdom of all green mothers in her palms. Leela kept waiting for symbols to appear on them, but as of yet, they remained the same as they had always been. She wondered if she would see that place with the flowers and the tree again, if she touched one of them. Her magic seemed to sparkle at the thought.

"My first Night of Song is fast approaching!" Elorin said. "I have been practicing the songs all day."

The Night of Song was a monthly tradition in which the novices roamed through the City for a full night, carrying candles and singing. It was an ancient ritual, one that stemmed from the days when the City had just been created, a time of darkness before the first tether was formed.

"That is very exciting indeed," Leela said.

"Novice Belladon has been helping me. She says I have a songbird's voice."

The temple bells began to ring out and both girls jumped.

"What has happened?" Leela asked.

"I don't know," Elorin said. "But come, we must go."

Cerulean were spilling into the temple, and Elorin joined the other novices to help distribute prayer cushions. Leela made her way to her family spot, her orange mother looking delighted to see her already there when she arrived.

Leela caught Kandra's eye as she entered with Sera's other mothers, and they exchanged a dark look.

Once the entire City had gathered, the High Priestess emerged and crossed the chancel to stand behind the pulpit.

"My children, a new blessing is upon us—Mother Sun has decreed it is time for a birthing season to begin!"

Cheers of joy and cries of "Praise her!" echoed throughout the temple.

Kandra had been right, Leela thought. But there was no sign of the sleeping sickness. Were they wrong on that count? Perhaps the sickness was a coincidence, unrelated to Estelle or the stairs or the High Priestess.

But Leela did not think she believed in coincidences anymore.

She saw Plenna weeping with happiness in Heena's arms. Even Leela's own purple mother seemed excited, though since Leela was still living at home, she would not be chosen to bear another child.

"It has been so long since the laughter of little ones has graced this City," she said to Leela as they left the temple. "I wonder how many new purple mothers will be showing up at our dwelling for tea and advice. The season you were born I felt we had at least two visitors a day!"

"Three," Leela's green mother interjected. "The house was overrun."

Her orange mother laughed. "Indeed it was." She sighed and put a hand to her heart. "My goodness, so much is happening so quickly. My head has not stopped spinning from the wedding season."

"Purple Mother, are you disappointed that I am still at

home?" Leela asked, suddenly fearful that she was disrupting her mothers' lives with her secret quest. "Would you like to have another daughter?"

"Oh, my sweet girl," she said, wrapping her arm around Leela's shoulders. "I only want you to do what is best for you, and if that means staying with us, then so be it. I am in no rush to bear another daughter—and Cerulean are not bound by restriction of age as human women are, so I have many more years of fertility ahead of me. You are not depriving me of anything."

Her green mother took her hand and her orange mother said, "We love you more than anything, and that is all that matters." Leela smiled and felt grateful that no matter what else was happening around her, there was one constant in her life, and that was the love between herself and her mothers. Regardless of the myriad ways her City was changing, that stayed the same.

The advent of the birthing season meant that the temple was crowded day and night. Orange mothers were constantly at prayer and green mothers would leave food in the Moon Gardens, at the feet of the statues of Aila, Dendra, and Faesa, in the hopes that the purple mothers of their triads would be chosen. It gave Leela no opportunity to inspect the moonstone in private, nor could she search for the secret place Elorin had mentioned. Not that she quite knew where to begin. Perhaps it was somehow connected to one of the acolytes' chambers. Acolyte Klymthe, maybe?

Plenna was the first to be blessed by the High Priestess and sent to the birthing houses. Two more were chosen the following day. So Leela should not have been surprised when she ran into Kandra in the Moon Gardens the next afternoon.

Elorin was chattering to her excitedly—tonight was the Night of Song.

"Novice Cresha says we are to take the route that leads through the Night Gardens," she was saying. "And to keep close by her side. I've been practicing the songs for two days. I hope I do not forget the words. Oh, look, it is Sera's purple mother!"

Leela turned away from the statue of Aila, where several green mothers were leaving offerings, and saw Kandra walking up to them.

"Good afternoon," Leela said politely.

"Good afternoon, Purple Mother," Elorin said, and Kandra could quite not hide her wince. "I have not seen you here outside of daily prayers."

"The High Priestess has asked to see me," she replied. Her jaw was set, her eyes flat, and Leela felt a sinking in her stomach.

"Kandra Sunkeeper." The High Priestess stood in the center of the gardens and beckoned Kandra to her with a warm and loving smile on her face. Leela felt her heart climb into her throat and hide there, pulsing against her neck.

Kandra went to her obediently. "Yes, High Priestess. You called for me."

"I did. I have wonderful tidings." The High Priestess placed her hands on Kandra's shoulders. "You have been blessed by Mother Sun to have another daughter. You may leave for the birthing houses as soon as you are ready. What a joyful day for our City!"

Elorin let out a tiny gasp. Leela could not see Kandra's face but her own head swam, the trees around her taking on a pale glow, the temple growing fuzzy. How could Kandra bear another child so soon after losing Sera? It was wrong. It was *cruel*. Kandra was rigid as the High Priestess kissed her forehead and then swept off to return to the temple. Leela watched helplessly as Kandra left the gardens in a daze without a backward glance, her shoulders hunched and her back bent.

"What a blessed day," Elorin said, but the words sounded forced, more manners than feeling. "She will bear a child again."

"Yes," Leela murmured. She could not quite feel her legs underneath her, and her fingers were numb.

"I—I must get back to practicing," Elorin said. "Excuse me."

Leela hardly noticed her go. She staggered through the juniper trees until she collapsed in the grass next to the statue of Faesa, landing on her backside with a heavy thump. A dragonfly lighted on her knee, its wings purple and blue and lined with green. Leela felt it was judging her with its beady eyes.

Do something, it seemed to say, but she did not know what to do. It fluttered away to land on Faesa's foot, then took flight and vanished.

But Leela was not watching it any longer. She gazed at the base of the statue of Faesa, reaching out a hand to feel the faintest trace of cold air on her skin. Leela was willing to bet all her worldly possessions that there was a set of stairs beneath this statue.

A pair of green mothers passed close by, talking excitedly with each other, and Leela pulled her hand away and stood.

I will return, she vowed, looking up into Faesa's wise eyes. *And I will find the secret that lies beneath you.*

PART FIVE

Old Port City, Kaolin

29

AGNES

AGNES SPENT THE MORNING AFTER HER FATHER'S SICKEN-
ing demonstration carefully forging a letter of permission
to the bank.

The fact that Sera's blood had healing power was beyond
incredible. Agnes had already added several paragraphs on
it to her essay for the Academy of Sciences. But the way the
blood had been taken against her will, the ease with which
Xavier had cut Leo's hand . . . it had all made Agnes sick.
Ebenezer Grange had looked disgusted. And the eagerness
on the watching men's faces made it even worse, the greed
and the possessiveness, as if Sera was something to be pur-
chased, something to be used.

She finished the letter—her seventh attempt to get her

father's signature perfect—and sat back to admire her work. It was pretty near exact, and it had to be. She needed more money than originally planned. Because she was not going to Pelago alone. She was taking Sera with her. If this tether was really in the ruins, then maybe it could help Sera get back to her city in the sky. It was a start, at least. Agnes could not allow her father to cart the girl around the country, selling off her blood.

The truth was, Agnes had never really had a friend. And though she hadn't known Sera long, she cared about her, and felt that Sera cared about her, too. They had seen into each other's minds, into each other's memories. Sera knew who Agnes truly was and accepted her without hesitation or question.

So she would purchase a berth on Vada's ship for Sera as well. And for that she would need more than six hundred fifty krogers. Plus, she'd need money for food and lodging and travel to Braxos itself. Two thousand should cover their passage on the schooner. Vada would not be able to refuse such a sum, or so Agnes hoped. She decided to take out three thousand krogers total—it was the most she felt she could withdraw without arousing suspicion. She wasn't quite sure of the exact figure her trust held, but it was sizable. Three thousand krogers would not make much of a dent.

And privately, she could not deny that she was eager to see Vada again; she could not get those dove-gray eyes out of her mind.

Leo knocked on her door for the third time that day, and she was jolted back to the present.

"Agnes," he said. "I really need to talk to you."

She ignored him, carefully folded the letter, and put it in her purse. Then she pinned a Solit brooch to the collar of her blouse, fixed a small golden hat to the bun on the crown of her head, and gave herself a final appraising look. Pious, conservative, professional.

She opened the door and found Leo with his hand poised to knock again.

"I'm going out," she said, pushing past him.

"I need to talk to you," he said again, following her down the stairs.

"I don't have time right now. I'll be back tonight. We can talk then."

She couldn't imagine what Leo would have to say that would be of any importance. Shouldn't he be happy Father was including him in this scheme? Though she did remember fleetingly the look of horror on his own face throughout the demonstration.

She decided to walk to the bank, so she would not have to concern herself with Swansea calling her a hansom cab. The last thing she needed was for her father to find out.

She made her way through the quiet streets of Upper Glen, and when she finally reached Jevet's Park, she found herself wishing she'd brought a parasol. September was almost here, but you wouldn't know it from the weather, which seemed determined to resist any shifting of seasons. The sun beat down on her as she strolled the tree-lined gravel paths, sweat trickling down her spine. A harried-looking servant with six dogs on leashes passed her, and a young couple canoodled on a bench in the shade.

She took one of the southern exits out of the park and entered the financial district, bustling with men in suits and bowler hats, carrying briefcases and walking about like pompous peacocks shaking their tail feathers. She got lots of nods and tips of hats and good days. There weren't very many women on the streets, and Agnes felt as if there was a spotlight on her.

When she saw her father's motorcar parked in front of the offices of Conway Rail, her knees locked and her heart dropped. Eneas sat in the driver's seat, reading the paper. Agnes kept her face down and walked quickly, not daring to look up, blink, or even breathe until she had reached the steps of the bank.

The interior of the Old Port branch of the Kaolin National Bank was all green marble, with onyx and gold decor. Great columns held up the arched ceiling, and a long table ran down the center, where men stood filling out deposit slips or writing checks. There were leather couches set around oak tables decked with glass ashtrays and neat assortments of newspapers. The headlines were still all about the ruins—the Seaport was filling up with fortune seekers, and the first Kaolin ships were getting ready to depart for Pelago. She wondered when the first Pelagan ships would reach the shores of Braxos—Pelagans had the shorter distance on their side, as well as more skill at sailing.

Several men stared at her as she got in line for the tellers, and she had to resist the urge to fidget. She could feel her mouth going dry, her confidence folding in on itself. The line felt interminable. By the time it was Agnes's turn, she was sweating more than she had been in Jevet's Park. She dabbed at her hairline with a silk handkerchief.

The teller who sat behind the golden bars was a young Kaolin man whose nameplate proclaimed him to be Mr. Wilder.

"Good afternoon," he said, his eyes automatically darting left and right, searching for a chaperone. "How may I help you?"

"Good afternoon," Agnes said. Her tongue felt swollen and clumsy. "I would, ah, like to withdraw some money from my account. Three thousand krogers. Please."

"Certainly. Is your husband with you today?"

"No, I am not married."

"Your father then?"

"I—I have a letter of permission." Why could she not stop stammering? She fumbled in her purse and produced the forged document, sliding it under the barrier.

When Mr. Wilder opened it, his eyes went wide. "You are Xavier McLellan's daughter?"

"I am," she said, jutting out her chin. It was something she'd seen Leo do before, but she didn't think she had the swagger to pull it off.

"And he was not able to accompany you today?"

"Unfortunately not."

"May I ask why?"

Agnes had not thought up an excuse. "My father is a very busy man." Oh god, what if he came into the bank while she was here? She should have scouted the exits.

Mr. Wilder studied the document for a full thirty seconds. "Excuse me for a moment," he said, and then left the window.

Agnes's pulse was pounding all over her body. Should she stay? Should she run? She spent so much time debating, her feet frozen to the pristine marble floor, that by the time Mr. Wilder returned with a man who looked to be his manager, her internal struggle was rendered moot.

"Miss McLellan?" he said, peering at her over his spectacles. He had a very bushy mustache with a single rhinestone stud on the left side, and his black hair was parted in the center and heavily waxed.

"Yes," she said.

"I'm afraid I will need to contact your father before you may withdraw money from your account."

"And why is that?" she asked.

"There is a notation in your file," he said. "It's standard procedure, you see."

"But you have his letter of permission."

"Unfortunately, your account does not accept letters of permission."

Agnes might not be a good liar, but she was sharp as a tack when it came to spotting inconsistencies. There was no reason for a letter of permission to be denied, unless . . . unless her father had explicitly stated it to be so.

"I see," she said with a poor attempt at nonchalance. "Do not bother my father. I will speak to him myself this evening."

"I'm afraid he will have to be informed, miss."

The room began to spin. Xavier could not, under any circumstances, know that she was here. As her brain whirred, trying to come up with an excuse, a familiar voice broke into her thoughts.

"Agnes?"

Ebenezer Grange was standing not five feet away. Agnes went from frightened to terrified in a heartbeat. Then, to her great surprise, Ebenezer came up beside her, took her hand, and linked it around his elbow.

"Are they giving you trouble, darling?"

She could only blink at him. *Darling?*

Ebenezer smiled at Mr. Wilder and the manager.

"We are hoping to take out a little extra money to plan our honeymoon. Agnes is my fiancée, you see."

Her head had the good sense to nod, she was pleased to note. Her brain was having a difficult time keeping up.

"We didn't tell him what the letter of permission was for—we wanted to keep a few things in our marriage our own. I thought he would have called ahead, as I was unsure whether I would be able to meet Agnes here today. I see Mr. McLellan was far too busy to make the arrangements. But then, he does have his hands full at the moment, doesn't he, Mr. Inklet?"

So Ebenezer knew the manager. Agnes was gripping his arm so hard she was probably cutting off his circulation, but she managed a smile and hoped it looked demure. Or, at the very least, natural.

"He does indeed. I did not realize you were engaged. I must have missed the announcement in the *Telegraph.*

Congratulations, Mr. Grange." Mr. Inklet looked down at the letter and back at Ebenezer. "There is a note on the account—"

"That prevents a fiancé from giving permission for his future wife?"

Mr. Inklet frowned. "Well, no, there are no exceptions for—"

"Excellent!" Ebenezer gestured to Agnes with the arm that wasn't currently being paralyzed. "Give her whatever she asked for."

"Of course, Mr. Grange. Right away."

Agnes stared up at Ebenezer's slightly smudged glasses and hoped she looked desperately in love instead of desperately overwhelmed.

When Mr. Wilder returned with the stack of krogers, Ebenezer's eyes widened for a brief second before he pulled himself together.

"Three thousand krogers, Miss McLellan. Shall I count it out for you?"

"No, thank you. I trust you."

He put the money in an envelope and handed it to her.

"That will make for quite a honeymoon," he said to Ebenezer with a sly wink.

"We can hardly wait," Ebenezer replied.

Agnes held her breath until they were outside the bank.

"I . . . don't know what to say." She wiped the back of her neck with her handkerchief. "I mean, thank you. Thank you very much, Ebenezer."

"I take it your father didn't actually sign that letter of permission?"

She could feel the guilt blossoming across her face.

"Don't worry, I won't say anything." He shrugged. "It's a stupid rule, in my opinion. It's your money, isn't it?"

"You're quite a progressive thinker for an Old Port society boy."

"I'm no society boy. We both know where my family stands on the social ladder, no matter how much my father would like to think otherwise."

"And you know I don't give a fig for social ladders. You're twice the man your father is."

Ebenezer grinned. "Why, was that a compliment, Miss McLellan?"

Agnes had to laugh. "They slip out sometimes. When deserved."

They walked down the steps of the bank together to the sidewalk. Xavier's motorcar was mercifully gone, Agnes noted.

"So what do you need all those krogers for?" Ebenezer asked.

She hesitated. "A rainy day."

"Right. Sorry, it's none of my business."

"No, I . . . I'm trying to help a friend. That's all."

"Well, that is one lucky friend."

They stood for a moment in the shade of the bank, men in suits swarming past them.

"You're quite a good actor, you know," Agnes said. "My father should hire you for one of his productions."

It was Ebenezer's turn to laugh. "I don't think my father would much approve of me taking up an actor's life. Besides, your father's interests lie elsewhere now." He took his glasses off and cleaned them on his shirtsleeve. "Would you like a ride home? I don't much fancy the idea of you walking around with all that money."

Agnes felt another rush of gratitude for this scrawny, bespectacled boy.

"I would love a ride," she said. "But I'm not going home. Could you take me to the Seaport?"

30

SERA

The tether.

It was still there. She had seen it with her own eyes in the picture of that stone temple, shooting straight into the sky from its highest point, a thin chain that glinted where the light hit it. And she had overheard Agnes's father say to all those males that it was on an island that hadn't been seen until now, which meant the picture was recent. The City Above the Sky was there. Her home. Her family. Sera's eyes pricked with tears. They had not left her.

They'd brought her back to her crate after that red-haired male took her blood again, and she squinted, welcoming the morning light as Francis cranked open the cover over the glass ceiling. He slid a bowl of soup and a glass of water through the opening in Sera's crate, and then, to her surprise, a blanket. "I figured you could use something to sleep on," he said. Then he blinked. "Wow. That's an awfully pretty dress they put you in."

Sera had forgotten about the dress. It *was* pretty, she had to admit—she especially liked the pink lacy part. Dresses in the City Above the Sky only came in shades of white and blue. The maid called Hattie had taken out the pins she had put in Sera's hair, and now it fell in big bouncing curls around her shoulders.

The blanket was soft and gray, and Sera wrapped it around her as if she could hide away in it.

"I hear they started calling you Azure," Francis said, standing up and brushing some dust off his knees. "That's nice, but not your real name. We don't know any of your real names, do we, Boris?" He moved to prune some of the young saplings, talking to them gently as he talked to all things. "No, we don't know anything," he murmured.

My name is Sera Lighthaven, she wanted to say. *I am a Cerulean and I am going home.*

Just how she could accomplish this was unclear. But as James and the other storytellers arrived to start the day's rehearsal, Sera refused to fall into despair again. For the first time since she had come to this planet, she felt a real, pure, true hope take root inside her, a seed that was strong and fast-growing. She knew the tether was still there and she knew where it was. That was more to hold on to than she had had yesterday morning. She wasn't sure where that temple itself was, or the island it was on, but she was confident Agnes would know. And now they could actually *speak* to each other.

She ignored the storytelling today, the voices of the performers fading into background noise as she mulled over her blood bonding with Agnes. It had worked—she had been right to try it, despite the thrill and terror that had come along with the unexpected intimacy of sharing memories. And then the sense of control she had, the way she had commanded her magic and it obeyed her. But now, just as she was beginning to truly understand it, she was threatened by men wishing to take it from her. She could not let that happen.

It was as if, in the time since she'd been on this planet, her magic had become stronger, declaring itself in ways that she was unused to. But she liked it. It was like connecting to a piece of herself she'd never truly known, the same way she had felt when she realized she was attracted to males. James caught her eye then, delivering an impassioned monologue about his determination to bring Errol and Boris back to Kaolin and defeat Gwendivere; she tried not to give in to the weightless, shivery feelings, the thought of running her fingers over the muscles of his arms, entwining his hands with hers, his lips pressing against her own. . . .

She shook her head and turned away from the stage. Focus, she had to focus. Her magic might be getting stronger, but it could not get her out of this crate, nor could it break the chains that had bound her wrists last night. She knew in her heart of hearts that Cerulean magic was not made for that sort of thing—it was healing, and loving, and communicative. It wasn't violent or aggressive. And even if she did get out, where would she go next? She needed help. She could not do this on her own.

The performers only practiced until early afternoon. Once they had gone and the theater was empty, Sera called out for Errol. It took some time, but he finally emerged, looking disgruntled.

"It is too bright, Sera Lighthaven. Light may be pleasant for Cerulean but not for mertags." He held up a clawed hand to block out the sun.

"Errol, I need to ask you something," she said, her fingertips flashing. "Do you know of a temple made of stone? It would be on an island somewhere, on a cliff overlooking the sea, with spires protruding from it, and a many-pointed star above its doors."

Errol let out his croaky laugh. *"She speaks of the temple of Braxos,"* he said. *"But no human has seen Braxos in many, many long years, by waves and whitefish. So how does a Cerulean know of it?"*

"I saw a picture," Sera said. "In the place they took me yesterday. The humans *have* seen it, Errol."

All the laughter vanished from Errol's face, and his huge eyes bulged even bigger. *"That is not possible,"* he said, his filaments lighting up in serious blues and grays. *"Humans cannot find Braxos. Only mertags know which waters lead to it."*

"How do mertags know where it is?"

Errol puffed out his smooth green chest. *"The first mertag came from Braxos. It is known by all of us. It is in our scales, in our fins, in our bones.*"

"Is it close?" she asked. "How do I get there?"

"*Not close, Sera Lighthaven. Oh no, in Pelago is where it lies, across the Adronic Ocean and far, far to the north, in islands hidden by rock and fog and other dangers.*" He shuddered.

"But you could find it? If you had the chance?"

"*Of course I could.*" He swept out a hand at the space around them. "*But neither you nor I will be sailing across the sea to Braxos any time in the future.*" Then he cringed, hissed at the light shining down from the ceiling, and wriggled back into his pond with a plop.

A thought occurred to her then. If Errol was right—and she believed he was—then *he* was the surest way to find this island. She must bring him with her. And she felt a private relief at not having to leave him behind. But now there were two who had to escape instead of only one. She chewed on her bottom lip, wondering if she was creating more problems for herself than she could solve.

Suddenly Errol's head popped back up over the mossy banks. "*Ask Tree,*" he said. "*She will know Braxos too.*" Then he vanished.

Boris looking to be sleeping. It was hard to tell with her three-eyed tree face—it wasn't expressive like a human's, or even a mertag's. Her branches drooped and her saplings seemed to lean toward her as if wishing to rest their heads against her trunk. More flowers had grown around her since Sera's arrival, cheery yellow chrysanthemums, big blue hydrangeas, and slender red tulips. And right beside Boris's trunk there were tiny silver flowers that Sera could swear were moonflowers, except that moonflowers were Cerulean and should not grow on planets. It was a jubilant explosion of color that was at odds with the prison they were all trapped in.

She sighed and brushed a curl out of her eyes. She didn't know how to speak to Boris. Errol's lights had come naturally and blood bonding with Agnes had made sense, but how exactly did one talk to a tree?

"There must be a way," Sera said. "If I can hear *her*, I can make her hear *me*."

The High Priestess would probably know the answer— she had been around at the time when the Cerulean would visit planets. She must know how this facet of their magic worked. But hadn't Sera just been feeling a sense of control over this part of herself? Hadn't she been feeling stronger all on her own? She looked down at her hands, and they began to glow.

Show me what to do, she commanded. *Show me how to speak with her.*

Her chest started to tingle, lightly at first, but then the sensation traveled down her arms, tickling her as if a hundred flower petals were drifting over her skin, and tiny spots of light appeared on her palms like stars. Sera watched in awe as the first star rose up out of her hand, her magic slipping out of her skin as seamlessly and precisely as a thread through a needle. But the lights were not stars—they looked like dandelion seeds, tiny bulbs with stems attached to a halo of delicate silvery hairs. As soon as the first one emerged, others begin to rise, until a dozen or more of them were floating in her cupped hands. And once she saw them, she somehow knew what she was supposed to do. Very carefully, she lifted her hands and blew the seeds of magic toward the sleeping Arboreal.

They were captivating to watch, almost ghostly in their movements. The first one reached Boris and landed lightly on a blue-green leaf; the others seemed to take its command and followed suit. Soon her leaves were dotted with tiny shimmering lights, the seedlings' feathery hairs pulsing in the air. And then they began to melt, leaving a farewell flash of silver before vanishing.

Boris made a noise that sounded to Sera like a person being awoken abruptly from a dream, if that person was a tree—a shocked creaking groan, like a large branch bending before snapping.

"*Seeds of life,*" Boris said. "*Seeds of love in my leaves, in my roots, in my trunk. How I missed you.*"

"H-hello," Sera stammered. Her voice once again had a slightly different timbre in her ears, but instead of a higher pitch, it was low and rustling. "My name is Sera Lighthaven, and I—can you hear me? Can you understand my words?"

Boris looked at her with her three wise eyes and she felt like a little girl again, because despite Boris's small stature, Sera had the overwhelming feeling she was looking into the eyes of something as ancient as the High Priestess.

"*She speaks the wind,*" Boris gasped.

"I—yes, I speak the wind." Sera was delighted. "Do you

know of the island of Braxos? And the temple on it?"

"*I know you,*" Boris said, the same refrain Sera had heard her say before. "*And you know me.*"

"Yes," she said. "I know you and you know me. But the mertag who lives in the pond says you know the island with the stone temple on it."

Boris turned her leaves back and forth as a woman might when examining a new ring on her finger. "*The first seeds came from the island. Seeds of life and love. Seeds to grow hope and replenish. I have not seen a seed in many, many years and I am old, older than the men in this false forest, older than the fish in that false pond. The Arboreals have become small and few. The island fades from our minds and hearts. I fear this world is not as it once was.*"

"But what is it?" Sera asked, her patience straining. "Have you seen the tether? Is that where the seeds came from?"

It seemed to her that the tree frowned. "*The island lives in all of us, as it lived in our Mother. We are all connected. Even the fish. Even Sera Lighthaven.*"

Sera pressed her forehead against the crate slats. Boris could not help her; she could only tell Sera what she had already guessed. She stared down at her palms and wished her magic could make her fly. Then she could get to Pelago or anywhere else.

"Mother Sun," she whispered, her breath catching in her throat. "What am I supposed to do? Please. Help me."

"*Hush now, little sapling,*" Boris said, and her words were like a song. "*Hush now, don't cry. All will be well.*"

But Sera could not see how. Errol and Boris might know the island, but neither of them could get her there.

Boris began to hum then, a gentle melody like a child's song, and it reminded Sera of the tune her purple mother used to play on the harp in the morning, a call for the dwelling to wake.

A light appeared at the base of Boris's trunk, not silver like the dandelion seeds, but golden yellow. Sera couldn't tell what it was, exactly, except that it was small and thin, no bigger than her littlest finger. Then it began to move, scuttling across the wooden platform toward her like an insect, and when it reached the crate, it crawled through the slats and hopped up to perch on her knee.

It was an odd-looking creature; a golden blade of grass with arms and legs and a tiny crown on its head. It gazed at her with wide yellow eyes, then did a little dance on her kneecap, finishing with a sweeping bow and doffing its crown. Sera could not help herself—she smiled and applauded. It felt like what was being asked of her. The creature beamed and put its crown back on.

"*She knows you,*" Boris whispered, and she sounded so tired. "*And you know her. But she will not stay for long.*"

Even as the tree spoke, the little grass creature began to fade, pieces of it disintegrating until nothing but golden dust remained.

"Boris, I—I'm so sorry," Sera cried. "I don't know . . . I didn't mean to . . ."

"*Do not be sad, sapling. My sprites are not born to live forever. She had her time. Others have had longer. Do not mourn them. They come from the earth and they return to the earth. The humans tried to take them, to steal them, but they are too quick and too clever.*" The slash of the Arboreal's mouth quirked like she was trying to smile. "*I must sleep now. My roots are old and they have been through much. But a great gift you have given me, Sera Lighthaven. Seeds of light and love. The greatest of gifts.*"

Silence wrapped around the space, as soft as the blanket around her shoulders, and Sera felt herself growing tired, as if Boris's words had cast a spell upon her. She curled up in a ball, yawning. And as she began to drift off, she could not shake the feeling that Boris had seen a Cerulean before. But Sera could not see how that would be possible.

She awoke at dusk, the sky in the glass circle above turning a velvety blue limned in pale orange. Francis must have forgotten to close the cover, and Sera drank in the colors of the evening. She stretched, her fingers curling through the slats, and as she sat up a prickle ran down the length of her spine, a warning that told her she was being watched. She turned and saw a shadowy figure walking down the aisle.

"Agnes?" she called hopefully.

Then he stepped into the light, and Sera's heart sank.

"No," Leo said. "Not Agnes."

It took Sera half a second to comprehend what he said.

"You . . . you can understand me?" she gasped.

He walked up the steps to the platform. She was struck by his expression, so different from the one she was used to, the one she first saw after he had declared her to be *his*, caught up in a net and terrified. He looked older, she thought, or maybe *worn* was a better word. *Defeated*, perhaps.

"I . . ." Leo looked down at his hands as if they could give him the words he needed to say. "Sera, I need to talk to you."

31

LEO

HE'D HAD TO LIE HIS WAY PAST THE PEMBERTONS GUARD-
ing the Maribelle to get in.

The theater was dim, the only light coming in from the
glass ceiling, the sunset tinged with orange. The crate was
onstage, and Leo could see Sera's form reclining within. A
thick curl of blue hair had fallen through the slats. She was
still in the pink lace dress he had chosen for her, a blanket
draped loosely over her slender frame, and the curve of her
back moved softly with each slow breath.

Did she dream? he wondered. Did she see her home
behind her closed lids? Did she miss her parents, her
friends . . . maybe she had a sibling too, someone she fought
with or teased. Leo knew absolutely nothing about her, yet

he had taken her anyway, without a care, without a thought. All his life he had wanted to be just like his father, and with a start, he realized that he was.

He also realized he was standing watching her sleep, and that was a bit creepy. He took a step forward and she stirred. Her body stretched, her fingertips peeking through the slats, the curl vanishing as she sat up. She shivered, turned around, and saw him.

"Agnes?" she called hopefully.

Leo walked forward until he was at the edge of the pond. "No," he said quietly. "Not Agnes."

She stared at him, shocked, as he walked up the steps to the stage.

"You . . . you can understand me?" she gasped.

He'd forgotten that he was the only one who knew that information—he hadn't even gotten to tell Agnes. He felt bent as he approached the crate, beaten down by the knowledge of what he'd done. He wished he could unlock the chain and let her out, but he didn't have the key.

"I . . ." He looked down at his hands. "Sera, I need to talk to you."

One of the saplings rustled, but otherwise the stage was silent. When Leo finally forced himself to look at her again, she was watching him with an expression he felt was usually reserved for spiders or unwanted vermin.

"How do you know my name? How can you understand me?" she demanded.

"I don't know." He stumbled over the words and cleared his throat. "Agnes told me your name. She didn't mean to, it just slipped out. And I . . . I thought maybe you would *know*, you know, how I can understand you now when I couldn't before."

It was deeply uncomfortable for Leo to realize *she* might have understood *him* this whole time. What other awful things had he said? He vaguely remembered bragging about her at the inn they'd stopped at in the Knottle Plains.

"And why would I tell you?" she snarled. "I am a Cerulean and my blood is—oh." Her lips parted and a light shone in her eyes. "My blood is magic," she whispered, running her hand over the crook of her elbow where Kiernan had stuck her.

"I beg your pardon?" Leo supposed he shouldn't be surprised by this revelation, and yet somehow he was.

"My blood mixed with yours," she murmured, almost like she was talking to herself. "You have my magic inside you now, like Agnes does. Except I chose to give it to her. I would guess that's why you can understand me."

"You would *guess*?" He rubbed his palm where his father had cut it.

She glared at him. "What are you doing here? What do you want?"

"I just wanted to tell you that . . . I'm sorry." The words came out on their own with no warning. "I'm sorry for what I've done."

"Is that all?"

Leo bristled. "What else can I do?"

"You can let me out of here."

"I don't have the key," he insisted.

"You got me into this place and you have no power to get

me out?" she said. "Why should I believe that? Humans lie."

"I'm telling the truth," Leo said desperately. "I mean, can't your magic sense if I'm lying or something?"

"Cerulean magic is not a parlor trick. It is not a catch-all."

"Isn't there something it can do? It's magic, for god's sake." He wasn't sure how he was supposed to prove to her that he was being sincere.

Sera folded her arms across her chest. "You are not very good at apologizing. Is this how you always go about it?"

"I—" He opened his mouth, then closed it. He felt his face go red. "Honestly, I can't remember the last time I apologized," he admitted. "For anything."

"This does not surprise me."

"I heard what you said to Agnes, about those ruins, about a tether." She froze, and Leo knew he had touched a nerve, that whatever this tether was, it was significant. "It sounded like it was important, and I was hoping . . ." He trailed off.

"Hoping what?" Sera asked vehemently. "That I would reveal to you the secrets of my people? You let them hit me. You are the reason I am in this crate. You are helping them steal my blood!"

"I didn't want to," he protested. "I didn't know my father would do that, I swear."

"And yet you stood by and did nothing when it was taken from me," she said.

The lump of shame in Leo's throat was swelling with every word she spoke.

"You don't understand," he said. "My father . . . he's a powerful man. I can't speak against him. I just can't."

Sera was sitting up, her face pressed against the slats, and the ferocity in her gaze took Leo's breath away. "Your father did not take me from that pit," she hissed. "*You* stole me. I was scared and alone and you took me against my will and declared I was *yours*. I am no one's! I am Sera Lighthaven and my blood is magic, and you will not take another drop of it from me!"

Her eyes glowed like blue flames and a sudden crackle of light ran over her skin, across her cheeks, down her neck, over her arms . . . it was a light that Leo felt in his own veins, a sizzling, spitting heat that snaked its way through his body and exploded in his heart like fireworks. In the span of one pulse, he gasped and fell to his knees as the theater vanished and memories swarmed around him.

It was his fourteenth birthday, and his grandmother had bought him his first shaving kit. All the other boys his age were beginning to grow their beards, but no matter what Leo did, his face remained stubbornly smooth. "Too much of the whore in him," his grandmother said to his father. Xavier didn't look at him or speak to him for the rest of the day.

He was sitting in an utterly fantastic garden, watching three girls playing some sort of game. They all looked like Sera and they had flowers in their hair. One girl kissed another. Leo knew he would never have what they had, and the loneliness was a secret agony.

He was a little boy. It was winter, and Robert's mother was teaching them how to make snow angels in Robert's back garden. Leo burned with jealousy when she clapped and hugged Robert, telling him what a beautiful angel he'd made.

He was standing in a bedroom in front of a mirror, three women with different-colored ribbons around their necks beside him. They looked at him with such love in their eyes, he thought his heart would burst. There was a girl his age there as well, and she said, "I have a gift for you too. But I . . . I would like to give it to you privately." When the three women left, the girl handed Leo the necklace with the star pendant.

He was in the dining room at home, sitting next to Agnes, declaring that he would accompany his father's men to the Knottle Plains. Xavier McLellan smirked at him. "Perhaps you've got more of me than your mother in you after all," he said.

He was standing on a glass dais, staring out at the vast and endless stars dotting the impossibly black space before him. He raised his arms, blood streaming from two cuts on his elbows, and fell.

Leo screamed, his body jerking, and he came back to the present, startled to find himself kneeling on the floor of the stage. Sera had her head in her hands, and her palms were glowing blue. "What . . . was . . . that?" he panted.

He could still feel the sensation of falling, and the mix of emotions from all those memories, both old and unfamiliar. His grandmother's gravelly voice, the envy of Robert's mother, the yearning to be what his father wanted . . . they were all mixed up in a longing he didn't understand, and a friendship he missed but had never had, and a fear that had shaken him to his very core, along with a courage he'd never known he possessed.

"We couldn't have blood bonded," Sera was murmuring to herself. "We *couldn't* have. I didn't touch him, I didn't . . ."

"Did you . . . did you see everything I saw?" Leo asked, mortified.

"Of course," she said, rubbing her temples like she could erase the memories.

He sat back hard. "Those were private."

"I know," she snapped, looking up. "You saw my memories, too. You think I wanted to share those with you? To share anything with you?"

He deflated. "No," he admitted. He was still trying to catch his breath. "Who was that girl, the one who gave you the necklace?"

Sera pursed her lips, and Leo knew he would have to offer more.

"It's just that . . . I have it. The necklace, I mean. It fell out of Kiernan's bag when you tried to run, and I picked it up and kept it. It didn't feel right, giving it to my father. It's yours, isn't it? It's yours." Leo felt like he was talking in a dream.

"You have Leela's necklace?" she gasped.

He nodded. "I should have brought it. I'm sorry. I wasn't . . . thinking." He pressed the heels of his hands against his eyes. The images from those memories were so sharp, so vivid. "I haven't thought about my grandmother in a long time. She died the year after she gave me that kit. I forgot how much she hated me."

There was a long pause.

"Why did she hate you?" Sera asked.

Leo sighed. "Because I look like my mother, and she hated my mother."

She pursed her lips, considering. "What is a grand-mother?"

The question caught him off guard. "A grandmother is, well, she was my father's mother."

"Oh."

"You don't have grandparents?"

"No."

"What about those three women I saw?" he asked.

"Those are my mothers," Sera said.

"You have *three* of them?"

"Yes."

He didn't get a chance to ask exactly how three women could make a child together because Sera was turning the topic back to him.

"Your father is cold," she said. "Compassionless. But I did not see your mother. Where is she?"

"She died," Leo said, and for the first time, it seemed to him a sad thing. Sera's face softened.

"I am sorry," she said reluctantly.

He shrugged. "I never knew her. I forgot how jealous I used to be of Robert's mother. I've been jealous of Robert for so many things, I guess I lost count."

"Your memories are all filled with shame and envy and hurt," Sera said.

"You took the measure of my father," he pointed out. "Cold and compassionless. That was the house I was raised in."

"How awful," she said.

Four days ago, Leo would have scoffed at this girl. *I am a McLellan,* he would have said. *I don't need anyone's pity. My father is rich and revered, my family name one of the greatest in Old Port. I can have anything I want with just a snap of my fingers. I have a closet full of the finest clothes and servants who are at my beck and call and friends with wealth and connections. I don't need anyone's pity.*

But now he saw how worthless that all really was.

"I wanted to impress him," he confessed. "That's why I took you. You saw the way he looks at me, the way he's always looked at me, all my life. Like he wishes I'd never been born." The lump in his throat was making it hard to breathe. The truth of those words was a brutal blow. "When I found you, all I could think was I'd finally done something to make him proud. That maybe . . . maybe now he would love me." It sounded so pathetic when he said it out loud.

"You should not have to take away someone's freedom to earn love," Sera said.

"No," he agreed. "I shouldn't." Stripping away the idolization of his father was alarming—it was making Leo see his whole life in a new light. "I thought if I could be just like him, my life would be perfect. He told me once that I had to decide which kind of man I wanted to be. And now I think I chose wrong."

He looked up into a pair of startling blue eyes, not fire any longer but calm and deep as the Adronic Ocean.

"You are alive," Sera said. "You are here. You have free will. There is nothing that is keeping you from choosing to be the right kind of person."

Leo swallowed and the lump in his throat dissolved. "You're right," he said.

She leaned back against the crate and they sat together in silence. Her face was in shadow, but he could see the length of her collarbone curving delicately out from beneath the lace dress. A thick blue curl rested on her shoulder. He thought back to what James had said, that she was beautiful in a unique way. Looking at her now, Leo thought she was so much more than beautiful. She was more than any girl he had ever known. There was more heart and courage inside her than could possibly be contained in so slight a frame.

"You fell," he said. "In space."

His stomach swooped, remembering the feel of his feet leaving the dais, of emptiness rushing up to meet him.

She nodded.

"You fell without being pushed or forced, like . . . like you chose it. Why?" Leo could not imagine what would inspire such bravery or foolishness, depending.

Sera stared at him for so long, he felt ashamed for asking.

"I'm sorry," he said. "You don't have to tell me. I don't really deserve to know anyway."

"Mother Sun chose me to break the tether," she said softly, her face still hidden in shadow. "But I failed."

Leo let that sink in. He did not understand it, not at all, but he was certain that the tether was the same one she claimed to have seen in the photograph of the ruins.

"So you need to get back to this tether so you can break it?"

"I need to get back to the tether so I can go *home*," she said, and the image of those incredible gardens swelled up behind his eyes. From the little he'd seen, Sera's home was beautiful and peaceful and full of love. And now she was locked in a wooden crate. All because of him.

There is nothing that is keeping you from choosing to be the right kind of person.

There wasn't, if he was brave enough to do something about it. And if this girl was brave enough to jump off a balcony into space, he should be brave enough to do the right thing, even if it meant going against his father. Especially then.

Leo stood. "I've been here too long," he said, suddenly worried one of the Pembertons would come in to check on him. "I've got to go. But I'm going to help you, Sera. I promise. You don't have to say anything. You don't even have to believe me. But I'm going to make this right." He hurried down the steps, pausing halfway and turning back to her. "And next time I come, I'll bring the necklace."

As he left the theater, he felt like a different person from the one who had entered it. A change was beginning, but what sort of change he couldn't say. All he knew was that the life he had imagined for himself was slowly disintegrating, and he found he wasn't missing it one bit.

32

AGNES

AGNES COULD NOT STOP CHECKING HER PURSE EVERY FEW minutes as she and Ebenezer made their way to the Seaport.

The Granges didn't have a chauffeur, so he drove them himself, taking a route through Ellsbury Park to avoid the traffic in Central Square and then cutting across the garment district, affectionately nicknamed Vestville.

"It's not going to run away, you know," Ebenezer said after the fifth time she opened her purse. "Krogers don't have legs."

Agnes gave him a halfhearted smile. "No, I know, I just . . . well, I've never carried this much money before."

"Me neither. Not that I'm carrying it, I mean—I've never helped anyone take out that much money before."

"No? You don't go from bank to bank helping devious young ladies try to withdraw money from their own accounts regularly? You should, you're very good at it."

Ebenezer laughed. "Well, like I said, it's your money. It's not as if we stole it."

"No," she said, fingering the golden bills. "It's my mother's money, technically, since all his money stems from hers. Which makes it even more irritating that I need my father's permission to take it out."

"She was, um, Pelagan, wasn't she?"

Agnes rolled her eyes. "Ebenezer, everyone in Old Port knows my mother was Pelagan. It's not exactly a secret, though Leo and my father both wish it could be. They sweep her under the rug like she's an embarrassment."

"Is that why your father is so obsessed with Pelago?"

"What do you mean, obsessed?"

He glanced at her sideways. "Well, the anti-Talman plays and now that Pelagan tree and fish that he was showing off last night. It's like he wants to take revenge on Pelago or something."

"He's a spiteful man who was forced to let a woman save him from bankruptcy," Agnes said. "You can bet he wants revenge for that. And she's dead, so he can't take it out on her."

"You don't think he cared about her?" Ebenezer asked. "Not even a little?"

She gave him a pitying look. "No," she said. "Not even a little." She stared out the window at the textile factories flashing past. "And he won't let us love her either. Well, Leo doesn't care, like I said, but . . . I wish I could know who she was, what she was like. If there's anything of her in me." Her neck went hot and her eyes felt wet. "Sorry," she said, snapping her purse shut. "This isn't something I usually talk about."

"It's all right," Ebenezer said, keeping his focus on the road. "And . . . I'm sorry. That doesn't seem fair at all."

"Well, life isn't fair," Agnes said. "Especially if you're a woman in Kaolin."

They crossed into the East Village, which served as Old Port's artist colony. The buildings were painted in bright colors, pinks and yellows and blues, and the residents dressed in outlandish clothes, revealing necklines, and feathers and high-heeled boots. Cafés spilled out onto the sidewalks, tables filled with bohemian types drinking wine or espresso, smoking cigarettes and discussing the latest book or philosophy or song. Agnes loved driving through the East Village but had never dared to walk its streets; she felt so apart from it, like an unwelcome guest. Her high-collared blouse, fine skirt, and Solit brooch would make her stand out here more than she did as a woman in the financial district.

"Why do you think she married him?" Ebenezer asked.

"Sorry?"

"Your mother. I mean, I get that your father needed her money, but if they didn't love each other, why did *she* agree to the marriage?"

Agnes thought for a moment. "I have no idea."

"Maybe he was quite the handsome catch back then," Ebenezer mused.

"Ew," she said, cringing. "I don't want to think about that."

He chuckled. "Fair enough."

He made a good point, though, she had to admit. Why *had* her mother married her father? Why leave Pelago and come to Old Port, where she was seen as a freak, an oddity, a perversion of what a proper woman should be? She looked so strong and carefree in the photograph Agnes had. It was hard to reconcile that woman choosing to be with someone like her father.

But then, as she had pointed out to herself many times, she did not really know anything about her mother.

They turned left onto Anchor Avenue, and soon the first sails were in sight, masts peeking up over the huddled taverns and brothels and shops that lined the docks.

"This friend you're helping, is she on a ship?" he asked.

"No." Agnes paused. "How do you know it's a she?"

He gave her a look. "I don't think you'd be going through all this trouble to help some Old Port boy."

"You're awfully perceptive."

"Perceptive enough to know when to stop asking questions," he said with a sigh. "Let me know where to drop you."

"The Wolfshead Tavern," she said.

The streets were packed with cars and horse-drawn carts, and every space between was crammed with people.

"They're all in search of that island?" he said in awe.

"Wealth is a powerful motivating factor," Agnes said.

"Do you think your father is right, that those ruins can let you see the future or speak to the dead?"

"No," she murmured. "But there is something special in them, of that I have no doubt."

Ebenezer pulled the car over when they reached the tavern and let it idle. The building had stained-glass windows and a carved wolf's head over the open front door. Music and raucous laughter could be heard from inside. Agnes felt a thrill of fear that had nothing to do with the tavern's appearance or clientele. Vada was in there. She suddenly wished she'd dressed a bit less conservatively.

"Agnes, are you sure about this?" Ebenezer asked.

"I am," she said. Then she surprised both of them and leaned forward to peck him on the cheek. "Thank you, Ebenezer. You're the best man I've ever met in Old Port."

"Another compliment," he said, looking bemused, his face pink, his glasses slightly askew.

She laughed. "Don't let it go to your head." Then she stepped out of the car, gathered her skirts and her courage, and walked into the tavern.

The interior was lit by an enormous chandelier crafted out of antlers hanging from one of the rafters on the ceiling. There was a long bar curving around half the room, chipped wooden tables with men playing cards, and booths tucked away where prostitutes were dandled on the laps of sailors. Agnes felt even more out of place here than she would have on the streets of the East Village. Men at a few of the tables closest to her turned to stare, one old sailor licking his lips; she stiffened, kept her gaze ahead, and marched up to the bar.

"Good afternoon," she said to the bartender, a portly man with thick glasses and a dirty rag tucked into his apron.

"Drink?" he asked gruffly.

"Er, no thank you. Actually, I'm looking for someone. She's a Pelagan sailor, about my age, named Vada. She frequents this establishment and I was, um, wondering if you'd seen her today by any chance?"

The bartender spit on the ground. "Drink?" he asked again, and Agnes realized she was going to have to purchase something if she wanted information.

"All right, I'll have an orange juice, please."

He stared at her like she had stopped speaking Kaolish. She was beginning to think she should have just gone to the ship first to see if Vada was there, but the docks were so crowded and she didn't want to risk running into someone who might tell her father she was here.

"Agnes?"

She turned and saw Vada's head sticking out of one of the booths, a prostitute in a flimsy purple dress sitting on her lap. All the blood rushed to Agnes's face, prickling as its heat traveled across her scalp and down her spine.

"Oh, there you are! Hello!" The words came out stilted and overly cheerful, and Agnes wanted to crawl under one of the tables and hide. She'd managed to sound somewhat normal the first time she'd met Vada. What was wrong with her now?

She suspected it had to do with the prostitute's breasts pressing against Vada's shoulder. The girl giggled when she saw Agnes looking and fluttered her fingers.

"Care to join us?" she asked.

Vada hoisted the girl off her and stood up. "Sorry, May, got business to attend to," she said, giving her a kiss on the cheek. May pouted and left to find a new client. Vada sauntered over to the bar; her walk reminded Agnes of a panther, fluid and predatory. The shark fang dangled from her neck and her vest was open, her shirt partially unbuttoned, offering a teasing glimpse of her freckled chest.

"Good afternoon, Kaolin lady," she said. "I see you are keeping your word."

"You thought I wouldn't?" Agnes asked.

Vada shrugged. "It is not in my nature to trust the Kaolin people." Her lips twitched. "For you I may have to be making an exception."

Agnes flushed with pleasure. "I have the money," she said, opening her purse. "But I need—"

"Do not be hasty," Vada said, putting a hand on hers and snapping the purse closed. "Let us have a drink first. It is not wise to be showing our business off so publicly."

Agnes noticed that several eyes were darting in their direction, and she saw two sailors whispering to each other, smirks on their faces. At that moment, the bartender slammed the orange juice down on the bar.

"Yes," she agreed. "All right. A drink."

Vada looked confused. "What in Saifa's holy name is that?"

"Juice," she said meekly.

"Are you in nursery school?" Vada cackled at her own joke. "Gregory, two ales." She slapped a five-kroger bill on the bar and the bartender began to pour the drinks from one of the copper-headed taps. "We do not seal a deal with juice," she said, picking up the pints and carrying them to the nook where she had been entertaining May before. Agnes took a seat across from her, grateful that the booth provided them a measure of privacy from the tavern's prying eyes.

Vada raised her glass. "You might have thought to wear something a little less"—she paused, searching for the right word—"rich."

Agnes tugged at the collar of her blouse. "I don't own anything less rich."

"Somehow this does not surprise me." She took a drink of ale, her catlike eyes trained on Agnes's face. They were the gray of the sky before a storm today, and Agnes thought she could lose herself in them for hours. "We agreed on six and fifty, did we not?"

"We did, but I was hoping I could make an amendment to the arrangement."

One eyebrow arched. "Amendment?"

"Not in terms of price," she said quickly. "I need to purchase another berth."

Vada threw her head back and laughed again. It was the wild laugh of someone who did not care who heard her. It sounded to Agnes like freedom.

"Kaolin lady, you are either very brave or very stupid. You are lucky I am agreeing to take one Kaolin passenger. Now you want two?"

"She isn't Kaolin," Agnes said.

"You have another Pelagan friend? Why, I am burning up with the jealousy."

"She's not Pelagan either."

"You are speaking in riddles," Vada said, growing irritated. "Perhaps our deal should be called off."

"I can pay you two thousand krogers, up front." Agnes

took most of the bills out of her purse and slid them across the table.

Vada stared at the money, dumbfounded. "That is no small sum." She took it quickly and counted it under the table. When she'd finished, she whistled. "Two thousand krogers," she murmured. She flashed Agnes a wicked grin. "Well, my mama will not be happy with me, but then, she is rarely happy with me. All right, Agnes." She raised her glass again and gave a pointed look at Agnes's own ale. It was the color of wheat with thick white foam on top. "*Slansin!*" she said, clinking their glasses together.

"*Slansin*," Agnes said, taking a delicate sip. The ale was strong, earthy with a bitter tang. She coughed and Vada chuckled.

"I am going to have to teach you how to drink, Kaolin lady."

"I'm used to champagne, that's all."

"Of course you are."

Agnes jutted out her chin defiantly and downed half her ale in three large gulps. Wiping her mouth with the back of her hand, she slammed the glass on the table and prayed she wouldn't belch and ruin the effect.

Vada tilted her head, fingering the fang around her neck. "It's a start," she said. She finished her own drink in one long draught and got up to get another round before Agnes could protest.

"So tell me," she said as she set a full pint next to Agnes's half-finished one, "how is it that the daughter of a Byrne has to purchase a berth on such a bastard ship as the *Maiden's Wail*?"

"Well," Agnes said, taking another drink and considering her response carefully, "like you said, I don't look like a Byrne. I'm so very . . . Kaolin."

"This is true," Vada agreed.

"Pelagan ships aren't taking on Kaolin passengers. And I can't get passage on a Kaolin ship without my father's permission, as you so aptly pointed out last time we spoke."

"Still," Vada said. "I cannot believe Ambrosine Byrne would not send word to some ship or other that her granddaughter needed passage to Pelago."

Agnes shrugged and hid her face in her beer until she finished it. But when she put her glass down, Vada was watching her with narrowed eyes.

"She does not know you are coming to Pelago," she said flatly.

Agnes swallowed. "She does not."

"You lied to me."

"I did."

"I do not appreciate liars, especially not Kaolin ones." Vada sat back and folded her arms across her chest.

"I wasn't lying about being a Byrne," Agnes insisted. She almost wished she had the photograph of her mother with her to prove it. "My father has never let me write to, much less meet, my mother's family. He acts like she never existed—we aren't allowed to talk about her at all. I've spent eighteen years wondering what she was like, what sort of woman she was. Eighteen years grieving over a stranger. Or maybe not grieving, but . . . missing? Is it possible to miss someone you've never met?" Her head felt light, and her mouth seemed to be moving of its own accord, her brain having a hard time keeping up. She stared into the depths of her empty glass as she spoke. "Leo looks just like her, Eneas always says, but not me. I don't know if there's anything of her in me. I don't know anything of Pelago except what I've read here and there, and of course it's all covered up in Kaolin propaganda. There's a whole part of me that's a mystery, an entire side of my family I've never known. And if I stay here, I'll be strangled by rules and etiquette. I'll drown in expectation."

Vada was looking at her with some mixture of intrigue and sympathy. "I never knew my father," she said. "My mother has been with many men. Many women, too. Myself, I prefer women. Men are such big babies, needing this, demanding that." Agnes felt a jolt run up her spine, and a high-pitched laugh escaped her lips. Vada grinned and continued. "But if I wished to know him, she would tell me. We have no secrets. I am sorry you do not know anything about Alethea Byrne. For myself, I have heard that she was very beautiful and very headstrong. It is well known in Ithilia that your grandmother did not approve of the marriage. Alethea broke with Pelagan traditions when she married your father—she did not have permission from the family matriarch."

"Really?" Agnes leaned forward, greedy for more information.

"Really. And now her daughter sits before me, breaking the traditions of her own country. So there *is* something of her inside you. You are both headstrong." The storm in Vada's eyes roiled. "And you are both beautiful."

Agnes's throat swelled up. She picked up her second

ale and took a sip. "You're just being nice," she said. "You haven't seen my mother. She was stunning."

"I have seen you," Vada said with a shrug, as if that settled it. She drank her beer and looked around the bar, and Agnes tried to collect herself.

"Ambrosine Byrne has a reputation," Vada said. "You should be aware of that. She has much power in Pelago—some even call her the fourth pillar of the Triumvirate, though never to her face. She is deeply influential and not one to be crossed. I do not recommend showing up at her door unannounced."

"She's not the only reason I'm going to Pelago," Agnes said.

"Oh?" Vada tapped the corner of her mouth with one finger, like she was trying not to smile. "Aren't you just full of surprises. And what other purpose would a Kaolin lady have in my country?"

"I've passed the first round of admissions to the University of Ithilia's Academy of Sciences," she said in a rush, her fingers clenching around her glass. "I want to be a scientist. I want the chance to be more than what I could ever be here. That was why I wanted to leave initially, when I first approached you. But it's gotten more dire, more important than just my own life. I have to help a friend, someone in desperate need, and I . . . I've never had a friend before and she's trapped just like me, only worse, much worse. She's got to get to Braxos and I have to help her get there. As impossible as that sounds, I have to try at least. She's got no one else on this entire planet to help her but me."

Vada took a long drink, considering Agnes's words.

Agnes could hear her heart pounding in her ears, a muffled *thump thump thump* that made her feel frightened and alive at the same time. Vada leaned forward, her hand reaching out to cross the space between them, casually confident like all her movements were. Agnes ached to be so sure of herself—she kept her hands tight around her glass as Vada's fingers brushed softly over her knuckles. Her touch sent electric sparks up the bones in Agnes's hand, a heat like Sera's magic filling her up.

"I was wrong," Vada said with a tender smile that stole Agnes's breath from her lungs. "You are no mouse. You are a lion."

Agnes let out a hysterical giggle and Vada's smile turned playful. She sat back and Agnes almost reached out to keep her close, but stopped herself.

"Come," Vada said, nodding at her barely touched beer. "Let's get you drunk. Of all the folk in this bar, you need it the most."

33

LEO

IT WAS AFTER MIDNIGHT AND AGNES STILL WASN'T BACK.

He'd lied to Swansea and told him she had already come home and gone straight to bed. His father returned around ten thirty, went to his study for half an hour, then climbed the stairs to retire to his room. The house grew quiet until no one was awake but Leo.

He sat on his bed, turning the star necklace over and over in his hands. It was so light, the stone unlike anything he'd seen before—white and round like an opal but shot through with wisps of color that would appear and vanish as quickly as he saw them. He thought about Sera's friend who had given it to her, how special that moment between them had been. Leo didn't have any friends like that. When he really thought about it, it seemed as if Robert liked being his friend because he had so much Leo did not.

The minutes ticked by and he began to worry. Maybe he shouldn't have lied for Agnes. Maybe she was actually in trouble, or in danger, and people should be out looking for her. He was just considering waking up Janderson and sending him to the police station when he heard a noise, like someone had fallen up the steps to the brownstone. Then there was muffled laughter. Then the sound of a key fumbling in the lock.

Leo was out of his room and down the stairs as quickly and quietly as possible. He opened the door and found Agnes and another girl, tall with a thick auburn braid, dressed in pants and a leather vest. Agnes was leaning on her and giggling. Leo had never seen his sister giggle before.

"Leo," she said with a lopsided grin. Then she hiccuped. "See, Vada, this is my brother and he's a Byrne face, a face . . ." She frowned. "A face of a Byrne."

"Agnes, are you drunk?" he hissed.

"She only had four ales," the other girl said with a thick Pelagan accent. "She is a lightweight, your sister. But it is cute. Like me when I was twelve." She studied him, her eyes narrowing. "You *do* have the face of a Byrne. All right, little lion," she said to Agnes, patting her head. "I believe you."

His sister smiled triumphantly, then burped.

"Come on," Leo said. "Let's get you inside before Father or Swansea wake up and ship you off to Larker Asylum."

"He's not usually this serious," Agnes said in a mock whisper. "He's the fun one. I'm the serious one."

The girl smiled and passed her off to Leo. She slumped

against his shoulder, then quickly righted herself.

"I can stand," she insisted. "I'm fine."

"Good night, little lion," the Pelagan girl said. "Good night, face of a Byrne."

Then she sauntered down the steps, whistling as if perfectly at ease, seemingly unaware that everything from her braid to her boots to her accent made her unwelcome on Creekwater Row.

"Did you have a nice day?" Agnes asked. "I had a very nice day. She's nice, Vada is. Well, not *nice* nice, but she's funny. Well, not funny but . . ." She lost the thread of her thoughts and her voice trailed off.

"Yeah, she's definitely something." How Agnes came to get drunk with a Pelagan girl who whistled and smelled like the Seaport was a whole other story, but not one that he felt should be told on the front steps. "Come on, quiet now, okay? Let's get you to bed."

She stumbled twice going up the stairs, but he managed to get her into her room without waking the house. She fell back onto her bed and stared up at the ceiling. Leo had to acknowledge the incredible role reversal that was going on this evening—he'd been sneaking around trying to do good and help Sera, while his sister was the one out getting drunk.

"You know I'm not going to let you live this down for, oh, at least a year," he said as he knelt to unlace her shoes.

"That's okay." Agnes let out a little sigh. "It was worth it."

"Who was that Pelagan girl?"

"Vada. Her name is Vada." She said it softly, like it was

precious. "She's a sailor. She's going to help me get Sera to Pelago."

Leo dropped her shoe and stood up. "Sera?" he said. "To Pelago?"

Agnes clapped a hand over her mouth. "I didn't say that. You didn't hear that. I didn't—"

"Are you going to get her to that . . . that tether? The one she saw in the photograph of the ruins?" He sat on the edge of the bed.

"How do you know about that?"

"I can understand her now. I saw her tonight—talked to her. Father's keeping her locked up in a crate in the Maribelle."

"What . . ." Agnes rubbed her eyes. "How did she . . . did you two . . ." She tapped her index fingers together. "The thing with the glowing and the magic . . ."

"What?" Leo wondered if the Pelagan had miscounted the number of drinks Agnes had had. "No, I think it was when her blood healed me. Is that how it happened with you? Did she heal you too?"

Agnes pressed her index fingers together again. "No, no, it was the *thing*," she said again, insistently. "Blood bond, that's what she called it. And I saw . . ."

"You saw her memories, didn't you," he said.

She sucked in a breath. "Yes."

"She saw mine too. Did she see—"

"Yes," she said again.

They sat in silence, lost in thought.

"What did you see?" Agnes asked.

"Grandmother McLellan being her usual charming

self," Leo said wryly. "Making snow angels with Robert
and his mother. I saw her friend who gave her the star necklace and her three mothers. That's weird, isn't it? Three
mothers."

"I saw them too," she said. "And her city made of
glass."

"How do they even make babies? I mean, there didn't
seem to be any men."

"I know. It's wonderful, isn't it?" She lay down again.
"A city with no men."

"Thanks," Leo said.

"Parthenogenesis," Agnes said, sitting back up abruptly.

"Um . . . bless you?"

She frowned at him. It took her eyes a second to focus.
"Parthenogenesis," she said. "It's the process by which an
embryo can develop from an unfertilized egg. I think Sera's
people, the Cerulean, must procreate using some form of
parthenogenesis. I've only ever heard of it happening in bees
and lizards and sometimes birds. But they are magic, I suppose. . . ." She cocked her head. "What were you doing there
anyway? Why did you go see her?"

"Because I wanted some answers. I tried to talk to you,
didn't I? But you had more important things to do, like get
drunk with Pelagan sailors."

Agnes giggled again. "I had *very* important things to
do," she clarified.

"I can see that." Leo scratched the back of his neck.
"And I wanted to apologize to her. For, you know, the net
and . . . everything else."

She stared at him, then threw back her head and laughed.

"Shh!" he hissed. "You'll wake the whole house!"

Agnes pressed her face into her pillow, her body shaking with laughter. "I'm sorry," she gasped, coming up for air. "You went to apologize? Oh, I wish I could have seen that. Have you ever apologized before? For anything? What did you even say?"

There is nothing that is keeping you from choosing to be the right kind of person.

Leo hesitated. It was different confessing to Agnes than it had been to Sera. She might have seen a few of his memories, but he had known Agnes his whole life, and he had spent much of that life obsequiously following his father and trying to make her miserable. He wasn't sure she would believe what he told her now. But he supposed he had to start somewhere. He picked a piece of lint off his trousers and stared at his knee when he spoke.

"I don't want to be like Father anymore. Whatever this new business is, this . . . selling of Pelagan creatures, of Sera and her blood, I don't like it. I wish I'd never gotten involved in it. I wish I'd never brought her to him. And when all those memories came back, it was like seeing my life clearly. I don't think he's ever cared about me at all. I think he would rather I'd never been born."

Agnes was quiet for so long Leo thought she might have fallen asleep.

"He doesn't love me either, you know," she said. "He told me to my face he wished I had been born a boy. Yet I still wish he would show me some . . . some modicum of affection. It's pathetic. But he's our father. He's the only parent we have." She hesitated, then leaned over the edge of her bed. For a second Leo worried she was going to get sick, but then she was back with an old, worn photograph in her hands.

"Here," she said. "I know you always say you don't care about her, or don't want to talk about her, but she existed, Leo. She was real. And I have to believe she would have loved us no matter what."

Leo stared down at the picture of a woman with his face. All the times Eneas had told him he was her spitting image came back to him in a rush, all the times he'd rolled his eyes and reassured himself that he couldn't look *that* much like her.

But he'd been wrong. The woman in the photograph had a nose just like his, and the same-shaped eyes, and an identical chin. His curls were caught up, windswept, around her face. His smile curved on her lips. She had a bicycle and was wearing pants and a thick sweater. His own mother, wearing pants. And she looked so happy. On the rare occasion that he'd thought about her at all, he pictured her on her deathbed after giving birth. He'd imagined her sweaty and exhausted, with circles under her eyes. He'd imagined someone weak, someone who refused to stay alive for her children, who didn't care enough.

It hit Leo then that he blamed his mother for dying.

A tear fell onto the photograph, blurring her face. He wiped it away and held the picture out to Agnes, embarrassed.

"Look at the back," she said. He turned it over and saw, in delicate cursive, the words: *Taken by X, March 12. Runcible Cottage, the Edge of the World.*

"*He* took this?" Leo could not imagine a scenario in which Xavier would be in the same company as a woman wearing this sort of outfit, much less making said woman laugh the way his mother was laughing.

"I know," Agnes said.

"What's Runcible Cottage?"

She shrugged. "Beats me. And I'm not about to ask."

They both stared down at their mother.

"You won't tell him I have it, right?" she said.

"No. Never. He'd probably make you burn it." He handed the photograph back to her. "Will you tell me what this tether is?"

She leaned against her pillows and yawned. "I'm not sure I entirely understand it. It's part of her city, a city in space. The tether attaches the city to our planet, and she thinks if she can get to the tether, she can get back home."

Leo took his time processing her words. In the end he decided that a city of only women that floated around in space was no crazier to believe than magical healing blood.

"I've got to help her, Leo," Agnes said, her eyes fluttering closed. "She can't . . . Father is stealing her . . . it's all wrong. She shouldn't be here and we did that, me and you together. I was there, I was responsible too. I should have let her go, could have, but I was scared and I don't want to be scared anymore. And I *don't* want to live in Old Port and I *don't* want to marry Ebenezer Grange." Her head sank deeper into her pillow. "He's nice, though," she added sleepily. "Very nice. Very helpful. But not for me. No, not for me."

"I'm going to help her too," Leo said. "I promised I

would, and I'm going to keep that promise." He smiled. "What do you know, we're on the same team for the first time since . . . well, ever."

But Agnes was already drifting off, her breathing slow and steady. He went to the bathroom and filled a glass with water, took two aspirin out of the medicine cabinet, and crept back to her room.

"Agnes," he said, shaking her gently. "Sit up and take these."

She took the aspirin obediently, then lay back again.

"You're being very nice," she murmured. "It's suspicious."

"Get used to it, little sister."

She growled with all the ferocity of a kitten. "Three minutes, Leo. Three lousy minutes."

"And I get to lord it over you until the end of our days."

She let out a drowsy laugh. He put the glass down on her nightstand as his sister slipped into unconsciousness, then unpinned the silly hat from her bun and left it on her dresser. The photograph of their mother was still clutched in her hand, and he placed it next to the glass of water. Alethea Byrne looked so *alive*. Leo had always been irritated by Agnes's curiosity about her, but now he was beginning to understand. There was a whole side to the two of them that they knew nothing about. Maybe if Leo had cared more about his mother, he wouldn't have been so desperate to be like his father.

He turned off the light and went to his room, pulling on pajamas and getting into bed. That night he dreamed he was a little boy again, just learning to ride a bicycle, and a woman with red curls and a marvelous laugh was cheering him on. Then the dream shifted and he was grown, staring into a pair of brilliant blue eyes as a warm, silvery hand slipped into his own.

Leo woke with his mother on his mind.

There was something he was missing, some connection his brain couldn't quite make. He thought back to the conversation he had overheard between Kiernan and his father, the night after that first dinner when everything changed.

You're lucky I got you out of Pelago when I did. Ambrosine Byrne could snuff out this operation before you can say "mertag."

It had sounded as if Kiernan had some relationship with Leo's grandmother, and more surprisingly, that his father knew her too. Xavier had been worried about Ambrosine assembling ships to search for the ruins of Braxos like some feud existed between them, and that couldn't possibly be. What would they have to feud over? Their only connection died eighteen years ago. And when Xavier mentioned never setting foot in Pelago *again*, as if he'd been there before— now that was something Leo was certain he would know, had it happened.

Of course, it was more than likely Xavier kept many things from his children. But there was something about Braxos . . . his father wanted it, his grandmother apparently too, and so did Sera. Leo sipped his coffee and stared out his bedroom window overlooking their back garden, considering his options. Agnes had booked passage on a ship to Pelago, which was impressive in and of itself. But she would need to get Sera out of the theater, and Leo knew she would not be allowed in until the night of the show.

But *he* could get in.

"Sir?" Janderson's voice cut through his thoughts.

"Sorry, what?"

"Your father wishes to see you, sir. In his study."

Does he know? Leo thought, panicked, though about what he couldn't decide.

But he didn't let his fears show. "All right," he said, putting his coffee down. "Thanks, Janderson."

He left his room and headed downstairs. The study door was closed and Leo knocked, trying to slow his heart.

"Come," his father said.

He was signing some papers and did not look up until he was finished. Leo took a seat in one of the uncomfortable hardback chairs and waited.

"Leo," Xavier said finally, shuffling the papers and putting them in a drawer. "The event the other evening was a smashing success. That girl you brought me is a gold mine. Hubert Conway was practically begging to invest. And he's going to build me a train unlike any that has ever been seen before, at a fraction of what it will cost, so long as I let him in on ten percent of the profits. I talked him down to seven percent, naturally, but his name adds an extra layer of credibility. These Pelagan creatures will be most difficult to transport. I am fortunate he already has several empty train cars that are perfect for the modifications I will need."

"That's wonderful news, Father," Leo said, but Xavier continued as if he hadn't spoken.

"The first stop will be Alacomb. I already have some

buyers lined up there, to lease Boris to enrich the soil on their farms. Good thing that tree is small enough to be moved fairly easily, he'll need to be replanted quite a bit. From there you'll head to the Gulf of Windsor, where Errol can be rented out to replenish the waters around the coast. The girl's blood can be sold anywhere along the way, but we'll need to be careful with the pricing. You'll leave soon after the final production. Hubert has assured me my train will be ready as quickly as possible. I'll expect daily reports once you are on the road. You will make yourself available to Kiernan over the coming days; he'll teach you about each creature and what it needs in terms of care, and what it is capable of. You will attend him both in his laboratory and at the theater. The Arboreal should be easy as long as he doesn't throw any more punches."

Leo was overwhelmed by all this information, but his father didn't seem to notice.

"The mertag can be difficult," he continued. "He has a certain sort of defense mechanism that left one of my other men with third-degree burns and the loss of three fingers on his left hand." Leo hadn't realized Errol was dangerous. "And we already know the girl likes to try and run. I'm making sure Kiernan is well stocked with anesthetic of the strongest grade. That blood of hers burns it off like it's nothing."

He leaned back in his chair, drumming his fingers on the desk. "You'll have to perform the same demonstration as you did at the party, of course—her blood must be seen to be believed. You may cut yourself or have James Roth do it, it doesn't matter to me. I'm sending him along as my auctioneer of sorts. His handsome face and celebrity status should do nicely. The blood must be priced high enough so as to be exclusive. We don't want to drain her dry. Janderson will pack for you—you may take him with you, if you wish. I know how you enjoy the trappings my money provides." He checked his pocket watch. "That will be all."

Leo tried not to show how dazed he felt. His father was sending *him* across Kaolin—that had never been the plan, had it? Or maybe it had and Xavier was only just now deigning to tell him.

"What?" Xavier asked, and Leo realized his shock was showing. "You've always wanted to be a part of the business, haven't you? Now you are. Don't disappoint me."

"Yes, Father. I am eager to start this journey." Leo had to do better. He had to leave this meeting with more information that he currently had. But he couldn't just come out and say, *Oh, by the way, whatever happened between you and my grandmother?*

"What about Braxos?" he asked.

"What about it?"

"You are sending ships there. I only wondered why you would not send me on that voyage, when you have Kiernan and James Roth here taking care of the creatures."

Xavier's thick eyebrows rose a full inch up his forehead. "Send *you*? To Pelago? My god, Leo, you sound like your sister."

Too much, Leo thought. *You've gone too far. Roll it back.*

He laughed heartily. "My apologies, Father. I suppose

all the talk of riches and women and fountains of youth got me excited. But you are right, this new venture is more important."

Xavier stroked the place where his beard was shaved to a point. "It is," he agreed. "I'm afraid you'll miss Agnes's wedding. Though I assume that won't be an issue for either of you."

He chuckled and Leo followed suit, as he always had before. "No," he said. "I won't be heartbroken to miss that."

"I should think not."

It occurred to Leo then that his father might actually enjoy the hostility between him and his sister.

Xavier took out another stack of papers and began to read through them. When he saw Leo was still there, he frowned. "That will be all. Kiernan is expecting you in his lab this afternoon at three."

Once Leo was out of the study, he climbed the stairs back to his bedroom and sat down heavily in the chair at his vanity. His father had planned to send him away, to be cut up over and over, to sell Sera's blood bit by bit. To rid himself once and for all of his Pelagan son. It made perfect sense, now that he saw things clearly. The island was where Xavier's real passion lay. Leo could read it in his father's face as plainly as reading the headline of the *Old Port Telegraph*.

Leo looked at his reflection in the vanity. Determination gleamed in his turquoise eyes. His mother's eyes. He ran a hand through his curls, his mother's curls, and smiled his mother's smile.

"Well, Father," he said aloud. "It seems Agnes and I have something in common after all."

Then he stood and headed to his sister's room, to let her know she would not be helping Sera escape alone.

34

SERA

THINGS CHANGED IN THE THEATER OVER THE NEXT SEV-
eral days.

In addition to James and the other performers, suddenly
there were males painting big pieces of wood or sawing
away at things, hanging lights and polishing surfaces, running strange-looking machines over the floors and seats.
Several of them seemed to be working on what looked like
a giant swing, a platform attached between two chains.
Women came in with rolls of bright-colored fabrics, cutting and sewing and chatting with each other. They often
cast Sera curious looks, though she and her crate had been
moved to a spot behind Boris and her garden, so she wasn't
as visible as she had been before.

The garden had flourished since Boris had shown Sera her sprites, and the man with the two-pronged face hair named Martin was extremely excited by all the new flowers. There were ones with red and gold stripes that would bite you if you came too close to them, ones that sparkled when the sun began to set, and some that changed colors from day to day. He and a few other males kept talking about Sera, and she got the impression they expected her to have a role in the story of James versus the evil Pelagan woman. Leo hadn't returned with Leela's moonstone, nor had Agnes come, and the seed of hope she'd planted in her heart was beginning to wilt.

The fifth day after her evening talk with Leo, she discovered her role in the play.

"So, what's the verdict, Martin?" James asked. "To what use are we putting our special silver friend?"

"I heard she's a witch," Gwendivere whispered to the man with the hairy lip named Grayson.

"I heard she's a sort of healer," he replied.

The woman scoffed, "Not likely! No, I heard she can cut men just by looking at them. I heard she cut Xavier's own son."

"Attention, please!" Martin clapped his hands. "As you all know, some adjustments have been made to the last scene. My darling Gwendivere, in the final confrontation between you and James, you will stab him with a poisoned blade. James, you will fall to your knees, cursing the Pelagan goddesses and such. William has written some very nice lines for you, and then we will bring, um, um . . . what are we calling her?"

"Azure," James said.

"Yes, then we bring Azure down from the ceiling, lights will flash, and James will be healed and declare it a miracle from the One True God. Then the show will end as it always has. Gwendivere is defeated, James brings Errol and Boris—and now Azure as well—back to Kaolin, the famines and droughts are ended, and all is well." Martin beamed around the room. "Satisfactory? Everyone on the same page? Excellent, we will practice this new ending without Azure for now. They are still working on her setup."

Sera wondered how she was meant to be brought down from the ceiling. But the answer came later in the day, when Francis arrived to take her out of her crate.

Sera did not try to run—there were too many people around; she would not get far if she did. She had to believe that Agnes would help her, and Leo too, as strange as that felt. She had seen into his memories, and what she'd seen had only inspired pity. She found she could not hate him, now that she understood him.

She could hate his father, though.

James sauntered up as Francis was letting her out; he smiled and offered her a hand that she took only because she had longed to know what his skin felt like. Warm and rough, as it turned out. His hands were large, his fingers strong, and they inspired a flood of other sensations all over her body. Mother Sun, being attracted to someone could be quite befuddling and downright irritating when you were trying to focus your mind on other matters. Sera wondered how her mothers were not distracted by each other all the time.

It felt good to be free of the crate. She stood and stretched as the swing was slowly lowered from the ceiling. There were circles of iron on the chains and Sera quickly learned that they were for her, to keep her attached. Francis helped her onto the wooden platform, locking the iron around her wrists. He looked miserable, and when their eyes met, he muttered, "I'm sorry."

He stepped back and the swing began to move. The initial lurch was frightening, but then she was rising up and up, away from all the staring faces, away from the horrid crate, and she felt a whoosh of freedom, like she was back at the top of the temple. The glass ceiling came closer, but she was lifted higher until she was behind the curtain that ran along the top of the stage, and the red seats disappeared.

She looked around—perhaps there was some window or vent up here she could crawl through. But the scaffold she was attached to was sunk into flat wall on either side. There were no windows or doors or other visible means of escape. And she couldn't get out of these irons anyway.

"She seems awfully calm up there," Martin said.

"Guess her kind isn't afraid of heights," James replied.

Afraid of heights? Sera wanted to laugh. She wondered how long they would keep her up here—she certainly preferred it to the crate and all the staring.

As it turned out, they kept her there the whole afternoon. The performers repeated the same part of the story over and over, and Sera would be lowered down so that she hovered at a level with Boris's topmost branches, then raised back up again.

It was maddeningly repetitive. Sera could not help but

feel that every second that passed was a second she was not on her way to the tether, and though she knew it was not an easy task to accomplish, she still wished she could have the sense that *something* was happening. Surely Agnes or Leo had to come to this place sometime. Unless they had been found out, or sent away. Sera had not considered that possibility, and it stunned her into stone as she was brought back down to the stage and shuttled to her crate.

"Excellent work, everyone, excellent work today," Martin said, clapping his hands. "It's all coming together. I'm confident we'll be ready to go by opening night. And in the nick of time too, it's only days away!"

The performers began putting on hats or shawls and leaving the theater in twos and threes. When only Martin and James were left, the theater doors opened and the red-haired man called Kiernan entered, followed by Leo. Sera's heart leaped with hope, an odd reaction to seeing the person she had so recently despised. She watched them through a break between two of Boris's saplings.

"Good evening, Mr. Jenkins," Kiernan said, shaking Martin's hand. "Mr. Roth," he said with a nod to James. "How did it go today?"

"Very well," Martin replied. "You may tell Xavier she fits in perfectly. The height doesn't seem to bother her at all. And as you can see, something has definitely been having an effect on Boris. I don't know what Francis is watering him with, but these flowers are just . . ."

"Magnificent," Kiernan agreed. "Leo, we'll take some cuttings of the new ones; I don't recognize all of them. Boris could be gifting us with new species. How exciting!"

Sera kept her eyes trained on Leo, waiting for a moment when she could speak to him, swallowing down all the questions she had.

"I hear you refused Xavier's offer to travel with young Mr. McLellan and myself around Kaolin," Kiernan said to James.

Leo's scissors froze in the act of cutting a flower, and Sera listened closely.

"I'm no salesman," James said, flashing Kiernan a charming grin. "The stage is the place for me, and if Xavier is no longer in the theater business, well then, I think our work together is at an end."

Kiernan gave him a pitying look. "My dear boy, your work with Xavier will be at an end when he says it is at an end. Surely you have taken the measure of him by now. He is not one to be trifled with or refused." Kiernan's normally cheerful face grew somber. "Trust me on this."

James shifted from foot to foot. "I've been in worse scrapes with worse men."

"No," Kiernan said, and something about his tone made Sera shiver. "You have not."

James smoothed back his hair, a casual movement that she thought was an attempt to hide his unease. "Well, I've got an appointment with the owner of the Lugsworth The-ater. See you later."

"So James isn't going on the train, then?" Leo said after he left.

"He is. He just does not realize it yet." Kiernan sighed. "A shame. He is so young and talented, but I fear he did not know what he was getting into when he signed on to work with your father."

"Not many people do," Leo said.

Kiernan smiled at that. "He is an expert businessman. Makes it a point to know everything about everyone."

"What does he have on *you*?" Leo asked, and Kiernan's smile faded.

"He helped me out of a spot of family trouble, that's all."

Leo let the subject drop, but Sera got the sense he did not quite believe the man. The two of them moved over to Errol's pond, and from what Sera could hear it sounded like Kiernan was giving advice or instructions on how to re-create the pond somewhere else, detailing the type of moss and the temperature of the water and such.

"And we must never touch Errol with our bare hands," he was saying, "or with anything metal. He's got quite a strong voltage. We use wooden hooks and nets."

She waited impatiently as Kiernan ran through more instructions, hoping Leo would not leave without speaking to her. The chance came at last when Kiernan was packing up his things, putting jars of flower cuttings into his square black bag.

"Excuse me just a moment, dear boy, nature is calling," he said. "I must use the facilities before we leave."

"No problem, Mr. Kiernan," Leo said. "I can finish putting these away."

He knelt by the bag, carefully placing each jar inside, until Kiernan was gone. Then he hurried over to the crate.

"I have the necklace," he said, fumbling in his pocket.

"Agnes and I are working together to get you out. She's got passage for you on a ship, if you can believe it. But we still need to get you out of *here*. I thought I'd be coming around the theater more, since I'm working with Kiernan now, but you wouldn't believe the way that man can go on and on about a leaf or a water sample. I've been stuck in his lab for almost a week."

At last, he produced the necklace, and Sera let out a wild sound, half sob, half laugh, as she reached through the slats and took the moonstone in her hand. Such a small thing yet of unnameable value—a piece of her home, a connection to her friend.

"I would give it back to you now, but if anyone found it, they'd take it away," Leo said.

Sera could not take her eyes off it, blurred as they were with tears. "I understand," she said. "This is enough. For now." She stroked the moonstone gently. Holding it in her hands made her miss her City more than ever.

"The problem is the Pembertons," Leo said, almost to himself, and Sera got the feeling this wasn't the first time he'd mulled over this issue. "There are so many of them, day and night, guarding all the exits. Even if I could distract a few of them, it wouldn't be enough." He sighed. "Besides the fact that I still don't have the key to this damn chain."

"There are no windows in this place?" she asked. "No . . . no spaces I could crawl through?"

"That's the only window," he said, pointing up to the glass ceiling. "So unless you can fly across the rooftops of Old Port, I don't think—"

"Yes," Sera said, ashamed she had not thought of it

before. The glass ceiling, the one place where she could see the sky. Mother Sun had been calling her from there all along. "That is how I get out."

"I don't think that will work," Leo said. "First you've got to get up there, then you've got to break the glass, then you've got to get to the Seaport. And like I said, unless you can fly—"

"These rooftops," she said. "They have spires? They are like dwellings?"

"Um, yeah, I guess there are spires, and apartment buildings and churches and factories—"

"And are they close together or far apart?"

"Close together," he said. "Most buildings in this city are right on top of each other."

Sera smiled triumphantly. "Then I can fly," she said. The moonstone glowed, as if applauding her words.

Leo looked about to protest, then stopped himself. "That still doesn't get you out of the crate."

"They put me in the story as a performer," she mused. "I am brought down from the ceiling on a swing."

She studied the theater. If she could get some momentum, she should be able to jump to the top balcony. And the walls were covered in painted wood carved into various shapes, providing excellent hand- and footholds. The ceiling itself was separated into panes by thick lengths of iron, a lip of iron ringing the entire circle.

She sighed. "But the swing has metal bracelets for my wrists. I do not know how to get out of them."

"Plus, you'd still have to break through that glass," Leo said.

Sera bit her lip.

"I think we need to find another way," he said. "Besides, you'll only be on the swing for the . . . for the . . ." He sat back hard and slapped his hand to his forehead. "For the show. The show. My god, could it be that easy? Well, not easy, no, not in the slightest, Agnes will have a heart attack when I tell her, but . . ."

"Leo, you aren't making any sense."

"What if you broke out *during* the play?" he said. "There will be so many people . . . a distraction could work then. There's no way Father would be able to control the situation. It will be dangerous, and certainly the timing would have to be . . . but this whole thing is dangerous, isn't it? Now, what sort of distraction, that's the question. . . ."

"Well," Sera said, thinking it was high time she took some control over her predicament. Mother Sun had been watching her, trying to guide her, to show her the way out, and all this time she'd been sitting around feeling hopeless. "We have a Cerulean, an Arboreal, and a mertag in this theater. I'm sure Boris and Errol and I can come up with something."

"You and . . . Boris . . . and Errol," Leo repeated. He glanced at the tree, then the pond. "You can talk to them too?"

"Of course," she said.

"But what about the shackles? Can they help you get out of those as well?"

"No," said a small voice from offstage. "But I can."

Leo jumped as Francis emerged from the darkness.

"What . . . you . . . were you listening in this whole time?" Leo demanded. But Francis only had eyes for Sera.

"You *can* understand us, can't you?" he said to her. "I knew it. I could tell by your eyes. And I've been wanting to help you, to help all of you, Boris and Errol too. None of you should be here. It isn't right." Leo and Sera were both staring at the small, pale young man, dumbstruck. "I would let you out now if I could, but they don't let me keep the keys. People don't understand, you know? They think they're so smart and anything that isn't human is just a dumb brute. But I worked with animals my whole life before coming to Old Port, and they're just as intelligent and sensitive and deserving of respect as . . . as James Roth or Xavier McLellan himself." He looked Leo in the eye as if daring him to contradict. "I hate this place. I hate what your father is doing."

Leo was blinking very fast. "Sorry . . . who are you? You're the one who feeds them, right?"

"Francis has always been kind," Sera said, gripping the blanket he'd given her with one hand. "I believe we can trust him."

"If you want to get her out of the shackles, I can do that. It's my job to put her in them, so . . . I just won't lock them." Francis shrugged, his face turning red, as if embarrassed that was all he had to offer. "If you think that will help."

"Yes," Sera whispered, wishing he could understand her. "Oh, thank you, Francis. Thank you."

"She says thank you," Leo said. "And . . . yeah, I mean . . . thank you."

Francis smiled at her shyly.

The door to the theater opened with a loud *boom*, and Francis vanished backstage as Leo turned and grabbed the star pendant, stuffing it into his pocket. Sera felt an ache in her fingers at the loss.

I'm coming back, Leela, she vowed.

"All set then, Mr. Kiernan?" Leo was saying, closing the bag.

"Yes, yes, thank you for your patience. I'm afraid my stomach is still adjusting to the Kaolin diet. Come, let's retire to my lab. I must store these samples properly."

Leo half turned in Sera's direction as if to say goodbye; then the two men left the theater. The lights switched off and the flowers around the pond began to glow. Sera stared up at the glass circle.

I hear you now, Mother Sun, she thought. *I see you. Thank you for Agnes and Leo, for Errol and Boris, for Francis, and for the hope you have given me. But how am I to get through that glass?*

A light on the ground caught Sera's eye as a tiny crowned sprite scampered up from the earth around Boris's roots and into her crate. She held out her hand and it climbed up into her palm. This one was slightly thicker and taller than the last one—Sera waited for her to dance, but instead she twirled around and lifted herself right off Sera's palm, floating and twisting in the air, little sparks shooting out from her tiny hands and feet like embers that were hot where they touched Sera's skin. Another sprite darted out from beneath a silvery white root and propelled itself, floating and sparking, toward her sister. They whirled around each other joyfully before floating back to the ground and disappearing underneath Boris.

She didn't realize Errol had been watching until his filaments flashed. *"Tree sprites,"* he said in awe. *"I have not seen tree sprites in many years. Sparkle and swim, they do. Fly and dance. Tricksy, like minnows. Tasty like minnows too. But must be careful. They burn and bite."*

He crawled over and began rooting around in the earth.

"Errol, stop, don't eat them," she cried.

"Why not, Sera Lighthaven?" he asked, looking up, his face crusted with dirt. But Sera had a sudden inspiration.

"A distraction," she murmured. "Boris, are you awake?"

The Arboreal roused herself with a rustle of branches. *"Who speaks to me?"*

"It's Sera." Boris was always forgetting her name. "Tell me, how many sprites do you have beneath your roots?"

"Many hundreds, and more, ever since you sent me seeds of love and light," Boris said. *"In times past so few, so few, without a Mother to guide them. Their home was lost, across the sea, across the years. But now they keep me warm. They sing in their sleep."*

Many hundreds. That should be enough, shouldn't it? "And just what exactly can they do?"

"Why," Boris crooned, *"they can do anything the Mother asks them to."*

"All right. Good." Sera collected her thoughts, deciding where she should start. "I need your help with something, if you are willing. You too, Errol."

Errol cocked his head, a daisy dangling from the corner

of his mouth. He swallowed it and looked at her with a plaintive expression.

"*Whatever you need, Sera Lighthaven.*"

Sera raised her eyes to the sky once more.

"I need to find a way to break that glass."

35

AGNES

"ABSOLUTELY NOT," AGNES DECLARED WHEN LEO HAD finished detailing his conversation with Sera from the night before. They were combing through the racks of dresses at Elvira Chester's Fine Gowns and Ladies' Wear. "That's insane."

"This whole thing is insane," Leo pointed out.

"And you trust this boy, this Francis?"

"Sera does," he said. "He's been taking care of all of them while they're stuck in the theater. He seemed sincere in his desire to help, I'll say that. Didn't think much of Father. And let's face it, we need him."

"But how is Sera supposed to break a glass ceiling?"

"She seemed to think she could figure something out," he said.

Agnes let out an exasperated growl, and one of the salesgirls shot her disdainful look.

Xavier had insisted that Leo choose something for her to wear to *The Fabled Fate of Olverin Waters and His Triumph Over the Mistress of the Islands*. That was the title for this final production, and Agnes thought it quite the mouthful. But she supposed it got the point across. Xavier had never been one for subtlety when it came to his plays.

When Leo had told their father there was nothing suitable in Agnes's wardrobe, he sent the two of them out with Eneas to Elvira Chester's, a store Agnes had spent her entire life avoiding. Everything was lace and frills and chiffon, pink was the favored color, but the worst part was the clientele. Snobby old women with upturned noses complained loudly about how they didn't make dresses like they used to, and giggling girls chattered about the latest fashion or who had just gotten engaged or which Old Port boy was the most eligible bachelor (it was always, *always*, Robert Conway).

But it did afford her and Leo time to talk privately without their father becoming suspicious. Agnes realized on the drive to the store that the change was noticeable—the sulking silence that usually hung between them was replaced with muted conversation. She'd caught Eneas watching her in the rearview and quickly turned to stare out the window for the rest of the ride.

Eneas had mailed her essay to the University of Ithilia yesterday. Agnes had felt an exhilarating sense of accomplishment that was fading now in the face of what they were about to attempt. But she had tried, at least. Whether they accepted her or not, she had tried.

Leo leaned forward and lowered his voice. "She is *magic*, you know," he said. "Maybe she has some secret glass-breaking power we don't know about."

"I don't think that's how her magic works."

"How would you know?"

"I just don't think it's aggressive in any way. Otherwise why not break out of the crate? If she had some kind of superstrength, don't you think she would have used it from the very first, when you trapped her in that net?"

Leo shifted, looking guilty. "I thought we agreed that that was both of our faults."

"Please." Agnes rolled her eyes. "*You* actually caught her. *I* merely did not act quickly enough to set her free."

"You always have to be right, don't you," he grumbled.

"Miss McLellan, we have some options for you." The salesgirl in charge of her was a twentysomething blonde named Gertrude who kept giving Leo doe-eyed looks. Agnes felt it was a testament to her brother's newfound personality change that he didn't seem to notice.

She had pulled a rack of dresses out, each one pinker and frillier than the last. Agnes folded her arms across her chest. "No," she said.

Gertrude looked confused. "But you haven't tried them on yet."

Agnes met her eyes with a steely gaze. "No," she said again.

"How about something in blue or green?" Leo suggested. "Pink isn't really her color."

"Of course, sir." The rack was wheeled away.

"Here's the thing," Leo said, leaning forward again. He'd been saying that over and over for the past several days. Agnes hadn't realized that teaming up with her brother would result in a million questions she didn't have answers to. She hadn't thought him a curious person, but now she was discovering a whole new side she had never seen before. Maybe it had always been there, hiding beneath the veneer of vanity and excess and self-congratulation, tucked away in the same place he'd hidden his conscience.

Or maybe it was just the release of their father's grip on him—on both of them. They were a team for the first time in their lives.

As much as she hated to admit it, it was sort of nice.

"What's the thing?" she said.

"Well, you've got the ship all sorted out, and Sera is working on getting out of the theater, but how are *we* going to get to the Seaport?"

"What do you mean 'we'?" Agnes asked.

"I'm going to Pelago with you."

"No, you're not," she said.

Leo looked stunned. "Yes, I am."

"But I haven't negotiated your berth with Vada."

"So negotiate."

"Ugh, Leo." Despite his sudden change of heart, he still saw things from an infuriatingly male perspective. "I don't have enough money to buy passage for you."

The thousand krogers she'd kept would have to go to food and more travel and other, unforeseen expenses.

"Ugh, Agnes." Leo imitated her tone perfectly. "I don't

need your money. I have my own."

He was right, and the fact that Leo could walk into the bank and take out however much he wanted without needing a letter or a chaperone stung.

"Fine," she said. "But I can't go to the Seaport again. If the papers can be believed, it's getting dangerous down there, and besides, what if one of Father's men recognizes me? His ships are leaving for Pelago any day now."

"I'll go myself then. I know what she looks like."

"She won't deal with you, you're a man," Agnes said. "And a Kaolin one at that."

She felt she was being horribly petty. Her brother was trying to help. In fact, he was the only line of communication between her and Sera at the moment, something she should be grateful for. And she was.

But she couldn't help being just a little jealous too. *She* wanted to be the one talking to Sera. This was her plan. She had started it all.

But Leo appeared undaunted. He turned so he was in profile. "I've got the face of a Byrne, don't I? That's got to mean something to Pelagans. Every damn one I've ever met has mentioned it. Eneas, Kiernan, even Vada said so. It's about time I got some mileage out of it."

That could be true, Agnes thought. She herself had used their grandmother's name to convince Vada initially. But she remembered the warning Vada had given her about Ambrosine and worried that perhaps the currency of Leo's face would come at a greater cost than she could foresee.

"How much did you pay her already?" Leo asked.

She pursed her lips. "Two thousand krogers."

He inhaled sharply. "Two—are you insane? Is she insane? That's . . . that's . . . extortion!"

A couple of giggling girls paused their conversation and gave Leo curious looks.

"Keep your voice down," Agnes hissed. "It isn't extortion if it was paid willingly. No Pelagan ship would take Kaolin passengers, and no Kaolin ship would take a woman without a chaperone. I did what I had to do. I wouldn't be surprised if she charged you two thousand for your passage alone, being a Kaolin man and all."

She saw this sink in, Leo recognizing the hurdles she had to jump that were simply never an obstacle for him.

"Okay," he said. "Two thousand krogers. No problem."

"No, I suppose it isn't for you," she said.

"But that still doesn't—" Leo was interrupted by Gertrude returning with three new gowns.

"No pink this time," she said, her cheeks flushed. "Shall I take them to the dressing room?"

"Yes, please," he said. Agnes didn't even bother looking at the selection. As she closed the curtain behind her, she heard Leo say, "I'll let you know if we need any further assistance, thank you."

"Very well, sir."

Agnes began to unbutton her blouse. "You're right, though," she said through the curtain. "I haven't got a plan to get to the Seaport. I guess I figured a hansom would be easiest."

"You think we'll be able to just hail a cab? Agnes, we are trying to cause a *distraction*. A ceiling is going to be broken, glass will be falling, people will hopefully be running and screaming. I think we're going to have to get out *before* all that happens."

He was right and it irked her. She undid her skirt and it pooled around her feet. The first gown was dark teal silk with a black lace bodice and bell sleeves. Black tassels hung from the hem of the skirt. She laced the back up as best she could and opened the curtain.

"No," Leo said immediately.

"You don't think—"

"You look like a middle-aged widow. Next."

She closed the curtain and shimmied out of the dress. The second gown was purple with a massive amount of petticoats that Agnes had to fight her way into. The sleeves were short and puffed, the skirt dotted with purple and white bows.

"Sera said she gets lowered on the swing in one of the final scenes," Leo continued, "so we should leave before that. Maybe at intermission? But Father would notice our absence if we both disappeared. . . ."

She opened the curtain and Leo's eyes widened for a half second before he burst out laughing.

"Dear god, how did that woman get a job here?" he exclaimed.

Agnes had to laugh too. "Okay, last one," she said, hoping the final gown would work. She was already tired of this store and couldn't stomach the idea of staying here all afternoon. "What if you made some sort of excuse at intermission?" she said, closing the curtain and struggling out of the endless layers of skirts.

"What kind of excuse?"

"I don't know, you're working with Kiernan. Maybe you can pretend something is wrong with Boris or Sera and you need to check it out."

There was a pause from the other side of the curtain. "That could work. But what about you?"

The last gown was incredibly simple, red satin, off the shoulder, fitted at the waist, with a train that spilled out behind her. Agnes slipped it on—it was lightweight and remarkably comfortable.

"Wow," Leo said when she pulled back the curtain.

"I like it."

"Yeah, that's definitely the one. And bloodred is in this season. It's perfect."

Bloodred. An idea came to Agnes in a flash, and a slow smile spread across her face. It would be uncomfortable but worth it, she knew.

"What?" Leo asked.

"I know how to get out of the theater in the middle of the show without Father asking any questions."

When they arrived back at the brownstone on Creekwater Row, Agnes took the package up to her room and hung the dress in her wardrobe.

Two more days. That was all the time that was left until the show, and then the ship would set sail the next morning, hopefully with all of them aboard. Two thousand krogers had to be enough to obligate Vada to let them spend the night on the schooner. She wondered if Leo would be able to buy his way onto the ship. She briefly considered returning to the Seaport to find Vada and ask her, but she hadn't been exaggerating when she told Leo the Seaport was becoming too dangerous. More and more travelers, fortune seekers, and adventurers were pouring into Old Port every day, eager to join the search for the ruins and claim its riches for their own. There were constant reports of fighting and brawls, resulting in an increased police presence. The other day she'd read that a man had been stabbed over a berth on a ship. As much as she would like to see Vada again—with less ale this time, certainly—she felt the risk was too great.

Agnes shivered thinking about so much time on a boat alone with Vada. Perhaps that was part of her hesitation to bring Leo along as well, if she was honest. How could she be herself, her true self, when her brother was there reminding her of who she used to have to pretend to be? She couldn't imagine how Leo might react if he knew. He was changing, sure, but she wasn't certain it was possible for him to change *that* much.

But it was no good worrying over the future when the present was quite enough of a problem. Had Sera found a way to break the ceiling? Could she really get all the way up to it in the first place? How would she find the Seaport? What sort of distraction could be caused that would be enough? According to Leo, Sera could talk to the others, the mertag and the Arboreal, but Agnes could not bring herself to have faith in them. She was a scientist, after all. She needed to see things with her own eyes.

It was so frustrating not to be able to just sit down with Sera and hash all this out. She heard voices downstairs and paused. Her father, she could tell, and possibly Kiernan. She crept to her bedroom door and listened.

". . . not suitable for this sort of interview," Xavier was saying. "It's all about optics. Leo will be fine. You've taught him well, haven't you?"

"Of course I have. I have always done as you've asked. It's just that I am responsible for them. I brought them here, I took care of them—"

"Leo brought me the girl, and she is the most crucial piece." Xavier's voice was so frosty, Agnes felt its chill whisper across her skin.

There was a sullen silence; then her father called, "Leo!"

She heard footsteps down the hall, and her brother said, "Yes, sir?"

"I am bringing a reporter from the *Old Port Telegraph* to the theater tomorrow to get a sneak peek at my new venture. You will accompany me. Bring a syringe for the girl's blood. We will leave at two o'clock sharp."

"Yes, sir."

"Good. If you will excuse me, Kiernan, I have some letters to attend to. Go to the Seaport and check on the status of my ships. And pay Roth a visit—I know he has been talking to Wilson Everett at the Lugsworth. Remind him where his focus needs to lie."

"Very good," Kiernan said, but he sounded weary. Agnes heard the door open and close, and then Leo was trudging up the stairs.

"Did you hear that?" he whispered.

"Look on the bright side," she said. "This may be our last chance to know if she's come up with a solution to the ceiling problem. You've got to find some way to speak to her alone."

"I know," Leo said.

Dinner that night was a quiet affair, each of the three McLellans lost in their own thoughts. Xavier excused himself early and Leo went to bed soon after, still fretting over his day tomorrow. Agnes would have given anything to be able to take his place. She hated this sense of powerlessness.

She was about to go upstairs herself when she heard the sound of a hoot owl. It hooted twice, paused, then hooted again.

Eneas.

She rushed to the dining room window, and he was there by the motorcar waving at her to come out. She went out through the kitchen and met him behind a large rhododendron bush.

"I received a notice from the post office," he said. For one shocking second Agnes thought the university was responding to her essay, before she remembered it had only just been mailed. Eneas's hands trembled as he held out a thin silver envelope stamped with wax. The seal had a flowering tree with a snake slithering at its roots. "The crest of the Byrnes," he said, and his voice shook as much as his hands.

"What?" Agnes ran her fingers over the dark red wax.

"Take it inside, quickly. Don't let anyone see. Go!"

She tucked it into her pocket, whirled, and ran back into the kitchen, startling Hattie as she was washing the dishes. Once she was safely in her room, she took the letter out. Her name was written in a very handsome script in black ink. There was no return address.

She broke the wax and slid the letter out.

My dearest Agnes,

I hope this letter reaches you. I have friends at the University of Ithilia and received surprising (and welcome) news. Come find me when you arrive. I will say no more here except that I have longed to meet you.

Your loving grandmother,
Ambrosine Byrne

Agnes read the letter three times and by the fourth, tears were obscuring her vision. She sat down at her desk and smoothed the paper out, running her fingers over the words, each one as precious as if they had been spoken aloud.

Her grandmother knew she was coming. Her grandmother wanted to meet her.

36

SERA

AFTER LEO LEFT HER, SERA HAD EXPLAINED THE SITUA-
tion to Errol and Boris and they had talked late into the
night. They'd had to stop when day came and the performers returned, but picked up their planning again when the
next night fell. By the following morning, she felt they had
come up with a solid plan.

Errol would serve as a navigator, not only to direct
the ship to Braxos but also to get Sera to the Seaport—she
would not know where she was going once she got to the
roof. Errol did not relish the thought of leading humans to
his sacred island.

"They will take and take from it," he muttered. *"They
will steal its beauty and its riches."*

"Not these humans, Errol," she had said. "They aren't like that."

He had snorted. *"All humans are the same, Sera Lighthaven. Lusting for land, greedy for power, no thought for any creatures but themselves."*

She felt awful leaving Boris behind, but there was simply no way to take the Arboreal with them. The tree was only too happy to help and insisted in her windy voice that her sprites would perform however she instructed them, and that the humans would not be able to look away from the glory of their light.

"Do not be sad for me, little sapling," she had crooned. *"I have lived a long life, a good life. And you have given me the greatest gift of all. You have given me seeds of light and love."*

They'd worked out a solution to break the ceiling—Errol had a defense mechanism hidden in his scales and skin. His lights were not just for show or for communication.

"We mertags have lightning in us," he told her proudly when she had presented the problem of the glass. *"If we are attacked, we run a current over our skin. Shocks the enemy, it does. Burns them. Very nasty, very effective."*

"Then how did the humans catch you?" Sera asked. "Why did you not use this power against them?"

Errol had frowned at her. *"I did. Lightning cannot be used more than once at a time. It must be replenished."* Then he croaked out a laugh. *"But I got one, oh yes I got one good. He won't be touching a mertag again anytime soon. Now they only touch Errol with wood or nets, never skin or metal."*

"And you think if you touch the glass and run the lightning over your skin, it will break?"

"*I am sure of it. But be warned—I will be clinging to your back at the time. I will burn you, my friend. By cockles and clams, I will burn you.*"

Sera smiled. "It's all right, Errol. I heal quickly. And I have faced worse dangers."

Errol had looked dubious, but Sera was confident she could withstand anything she put her mind to at this point. Pain no longer frightened her. She had suffered the agony of losing her home, her best friend, her mothers. And she had survived. She would do anything to get back to the tether. No fate frightened her except one: failure.

The hardest part would be the timing. Sera would be lowered down on the swing, the shackles unlocked. Boris would push her out over the pond, and Errol had to jump at just the right moment to catch hold of her and climb onto her back. Sera would then have to make it to the balcony, and she didn't know how heavy he would be. There was simply no way to test this beforehand. Getting to the ceiling didn't worry her at all; in fact, she was eager to be climbing again. She wanted to feel like herself, to remember who she was. She was Sera Lighthaven and she was not meant to be chained.

But for now she had to wait, and she had already been waiting for a full day and night since she last saw Leo. She hoped he would return before the performance tomorrow. Time was running out.

At least Francis had been around during rehearsal, with a reassuring smile and whispered words of encouragement, reminding her there were others on her side. She wished she could thank him properly. He was the first person besides Agnes who had shown her kindness on this planet.

The boom of the door closing startled her out of her thoughts. Her heart leaped as she caught a glimpse of Leo's face, but he was not alone; his father was with him. Cold fury curled in Sera's stomach like a fist. There were two others as well, a man in a fedora and tweed jacket with a pen and notebook in hand and another, lumpier man carrying a box with a lens on it.

"In the name of the One True God," the fedora man said, gazing around in awe. "What have you done to the place, Xavier?"

"I told you this would be a once-in-a-lifetime experience," Leo's father said. "The Arboreal has been producing at a rate that has shocked even my Pelagan scientist. He claims there are several new species of flower up there. Tell him, Leo."

Leo seemed startled at being addressed. "Er, yes, well, that one will bite you if you get too close—Dragon's Tooth, that's what Kiernan calls it. And those change color depending on the time of day. We call those Sunrise Sunset."

The man didn't seem interested in flowers. "It's been said you're working very closely with this Pelagan . . . ah . . ." He searched through his notes. "Ezra Kiernan. Been quite a while since you attached yourself to a Pelagan, hasn't it, Xavier?"

"He is necessary to the needs of my new venture, Rudolph. I am not *attached* to anyone." Every word Leo's father spoke was dripping with disdain. "But in order to procure these creatures, I needed men on the ground, men who knew the country and what to look for. Ezra was sufficient for those purposes."

"There's a rumor that he's from Culin—"

"Next question," Xavier said, and his tone left no room for debate.

Sera did not think she had ever seen someone so rigid and unyielding. The man with the fedora moved to a new subject as they approached the pond.

"This is where we keep the mertag," Xavier said. "He will clean our lakes and rivers, replenish the Gulf of Windsor, and make our waters rich again. With his help we will not have to rely so heavily on Pelagan imports."

The man paused in his writing to peer into the water. "I don't see anything."

"He's shy," Xavier said dryly. "Leo, if you will."

Leo did not seem happy as he walked up the steps to the stage. He went behind the curtain, but before he disappeared he shot Sera an apologetic look.

There was a creaking sound, like when Francis would unveil the glass ceiling, and a net came down, splitting open like a mouth and dropping into the pond. Seconds later, the net came up with Errol caught in its jaws. Colors flashed over his skin and across his fins and tail, brilliant zips of scarlet and teal and gold.

"Release me!" he cried.

"Let him go!" Sera shouted, forgetting for a moment that she should not speak, that it would only draw attention to herself. They could not understand her and would not heed her even if they could.

"Was that the girl?" the man in the fedora asked eagerly, trying to make her out through the garden. The man with the box had set it up on a tripod and the lens was trained on Errol. There was a flash and a puff of smoke.

"Put him back, Leo," Xavier called, and Errol was slowly lowered back into the pond. The three men climbed the steps to the stage, and the man with the box focused it on Boris and her flowers. There were more flashes and puffs of smoke.

"The Arboreal may not look like much," Leo's father was saying. "But when he was first planted here only a little over a month ago, this was all bare earth. And now look at him."

Leo skulked back onto the stage to join them as Xavier explained how he was planning to exploit the poor tree.

"And now," he said, once the fedora man had finished jotting down notes on Boris, "the grand finale."

They skirted around the garden to where Sera was crouched in the crate.

"Leo," his father said, with an almost lazy nod toward her. Leo was taking something out of his pocket, his other hand clenched into a fist. His jaw was so tight Sera thought he might break his teeth. He crouched by her and whispered, "I'm so sorry. But please give me your arm."

This is the last time I will let anyone take my blood from me, she thought as she reached her arm out through the slats. Xavier could not be allowed to suspect anything. Leo was not as gifted at using the needle as Kiernan had been, and she winced as it pierced her skin. He did not take very much, but it still made her feel woozy afterward. When he stood, Xavier once more had a knife in his hand.

"Now," he said to the men, "watch carefully and get the camera ready."

He ran the knife easily across Leo's hand. It seemed to Sera that he derived pleasure from this demonstration, his eyes glowing with a feverish light. Leo himself made no sound or movement. When his father applied a few drops of Sera's blood to the wound, his skin healed over and the red line across his palm disappeared. The man's box was clicking and puffing away. The fedora man gaped as if incapable of shutting his mouth.

"What . . . how . . . my god, Xavier. My god. It's incredible. A medical miracle."

"Yes, she is certainly the jewel of this whole endeavor," he agreed. "And she is *not* Pelagan," he added, as if that was the most important distinction. "She was found right here in Kaolin, by my son."

"It's impossible," the man said, reaching out to touch Leo's hand. She saw him twitch as if wanting to jerk away, but he stopped himself.

"It is not," Xavier said, "as you have just witnessed with your own eyes." He clapped his hands together. "That should do it, I think. Come, I'll show you the paintings I had commissioned for the foyer on our way out. Graham Willowby originals."

"I thought Willowby retired," the fedora man said.

"I was very persuasive."

The man with the box chortled. Leo hung back.

"I'm just going to water Boris a bit, Father. Some of these flowers are looking like they might wilt." He was a convincing liar, Sera had to admit.

His father frowned. "Very well. Meet us in the lobby."

"Yes, sir. I'll only be a minute."

He made a show of going off to fetch the watering can, and by the time he had returned with it, the other three men had left the theater.

"I'm sorry," he said again, dropping the can and kneeling by the crate. "I didn't want to, but I had to. If my father suspected—"

"I understand," Sera said.

"We only have a minute—"

"I know." She proceeded to tell him the idea she and Boris and Errol had come up with. Leo's eyes grew wider and wider until she could see the whites all around them. When she finished speaking, he sat back, expelling his breath in a huff.

"You're saying there are hundreds of sprites . . . under there?" he asked, pointing to the Arboreal's roots.

Sera nodded. "Boris, could you show this human male one of your sprites, please?"

Leo looked even more surprised at what must have been a whooshing, wind-like sound coming from deep in Sera's chest. A tiny, glowing, blade-thin sprite popped up from the earth, sparks shooting out from her crown as she rose a few feet in the air and performed several twirls for Leo's benefit.

"Gah!" He scrambled backward and Sera laughed.

"She won't hurt you," she said.

"Right." He looked a little embarrassed at his own reaction, but Sera felt a surge of hope that the sprites would indeed be a successful distraction. If Leo was reacting like this to only one of them, imagine what hundreds could be capable of.

"They're quite friendly, actually. Very sweet. They like to dance."

The sprite floated her way over to Leo, spinning and twirling. She landed on his knee and gave a deep bow. Then she hopped down and scampered back to Boris, blowing some sparks Sera's way in farewell before vanishing into the dirt.

"Wow," Leo said. "Yes, I think they should be fairly diverting."

"Leo!" his father called, and he jumped to his feet like he'd been electrocuted.

"Coming, Father," he called back. He turned to Sera. "I'll see you tomorrow night."

"Tomorrow night," she said. He looked about to say something else, then reconsidered and hurried off the stage and up the aisle, leaving her alone with her friends. She gazed at the circle of glass overhead, the sky as blue as the forget-me-nots she and Leela used to weave into flower crowns.

I'm coming, mothers, she vowed. *I'm coming, Leela.*

PART SIX

The City Above the Sky

and

Old Port City, Kaolin

37

LEELA

LEELA HAD TO WAIT UNTIL THE NEXT EVENING BEFORE she could return to the Moon Gardens, because she could not sneak around during the Night of Song.

The voices of the novices carried over the entire City in rippling waves, their candle flames reflecting off the sunglass-paved paths as they walked, singing all through the night. Leela had always loved the Night of Song, but this year it grated on her nerves. She felt raw and impatient. She needed to see what lay beneath that statue—she felt certain the answers she was seeking were close at hand. She turned the vision she'd had when she touched the moonstone over in her mind, the strange place with the pretty tree and purple-pink flowers. And Sera's laugh, which had seemed to come from the statue of Aila itself. And the markings she had seen on the cold, smooth obelisk.

Sera. The tether. Moonstone. These stairs. Estelle. Kandra had said that these things were all related somehow. Leela repeated them over and over, as if the connection might suddenly become clear. But she was still puzzling when dawn's light crept in through her window and the singing faded away. The novices would be sleeping tonight, the temple silent. It was her best chance. She could not afford to wait any longer anyway.

Sera. The tether. Moonstone. These stairs. Estelle.

Sera. The tether. Moonstone . . .

She sat up in bed, her heart pounding. Moonstone was clearly magical, though no one could seem to agree on what exactly its magic was. And no one besides Leela knew that Sera had carried a piece of it with her when she fell. But now the few pieces of moonstone left in the City were sending Leela visions, and laughter, and markings, and revealing secret underground stairs. And the tether *had not broken.* What if Sera was alive out there somewhere? What if she was trying to communicate to Leela through the moonstone?

She threw back her covers and slipped into a cloudspun dress. She had to speak to Kandra. She had to tell her about the necklace.

"Breakfast, darling?" her orange mother said, stirring a pot on the stove and yawning. The smell of potatoes and rosemary made Leela's stomach growl, but she had no time for food.

"I'm just going to wash up in the Estuary, Orange

Mother," she lied. "Save some for me. It smells delicious."

"I make no promises, your green mother is famished," she said with a wink. Leela forced a laugh and kissed her on the cheek. She left her dwelling and took a less-traveled route that led her past the Aviary and some of the communal gardens on the outskirts of the City.

She didn't dare believe her own conclusion, not yet. She couldn't bear it if she was wrong—it would be like losing Sera all over again. But there was *something* about moonstone that was beyond what she had been taught, beyond what was remembered in Cerulean society.

When she arrived at Sera's dwelling, she found it silent. There were no murmurs of conversation, no scent of cooking breakfast, nothing to indicate that anyone was living here. The path to the front door felt impossibly long, but suddenly she was peering into Sera's sitting room, the familiar couch with its blue upholstery, the framed pressed flowers hanging on the walls. It was as if Sera would come running in from her room at any moment, skid to a stop, and admonish Leela for being late.

"Leela?" Sera's green mother stood in the hall, a silver hairbrush clutched in her hands. It was Sera's brush, the one Kandra could not bear to touch.

"Hello," she said. "I was wondering if I might speak to Kandra for a moment."

Sera's green mother started, and Leela realized she had never used Kandra's true name around her before. No one even knew they were friends.

"She left for the birthing houses at dawn," the green mother said, her grip tightening around the brush.

"Yes, I . . . I heard she was blessed to have another child." The words felt wrong as she said them.

"She was." Her smile was painful to look at, stretching across her face in a thin line. "We are so grateful to the High Priestess for choosing our family. Sera would be . . ."

But her voice trailed off. The silence between them grew thick with sadness, until Leela could take it no longer.

"Forgive me for intruding on your morning," she said, backing out the door and hurrying down the path. She knew where she must go next, but she would have to find some way to get to Kandra unseen. She would be in serious trouble if she was caught—once a birthing season began, the houses were sacred and only midwives and purple mothers were allowed near them. She crossed the Estuary at the Western Bridge, and the Forest of Dawn loomed up over the nearby dwellings, leaves in every shade of green reaching toward the stars. She picked her way through the trees, grateful that her late-night visits had made these woods as familiar as the paths around her own dwelling.

She stopped when she saw the first house, ducking behind an old oak. Since none of the houses had windows, it was impossible to distinguish who was in which one, or which were empty. She could not see the obelisk from this vantage point. She crept from tree to tree, listening to see if maybe she could hear Kandra's voice. The obelisk came into view, and a ripple ran through the magic in Leela's veins, like the moonstone remembered her and was calling out in welcome. She caught sight of Plenna, entering a house at the far end of the semicircle, a pile of blankets in her arms, and quickly hid behind another tree.

"Leela?"

She jumped and whirled around. Kandra was standing there with a bucket of water in her hands.

"What are you doing here?" she hissed, moving to join Leela in her hiding spot.

"I had to see you," she said. "I had to tell you—"

"Tell me what? Oh, Leela, if you are caught here—the High Priestess was visiting only an hour ago!"

"There is something I never told you," Leela said. "Something I never told anyone." She paused and took a breath. "Almost a year ago, Sera and I were digging in the banks of the Estuary and I . . . I found a piece of moonstone."

Kandra gasped. "What?"

"I don't know where it came from or why it was there. We kept it a secret, me and Sera. We did not want to share it with anyone." Leela's face burned with shame.

"There has not been any new moonstone in this City for centuries," Kandra said, dazed.

"I know. Maybe it was wrong, but Sera and I wanted to keep it as something just between ourselves. We did not think it would hurt anyone. We did not believe moonstone had any special use at all. I made a pendant out of it, set in the many-pointed star. I put it on a necklace and gave it to Sera before she . . ."

Kandra's eyes lit up with memory. "The gift you needed to give her privately. I remember. The chain about her neck. She never showed it to us, and there were so many other things to . . ."

Leela swallowed. "Yes. But now, I think they are connected—the moonstone and Sera. The vision I had, and the markings on the obelisk, and . . . and I heard Sera's voice. Through Aila's statue. She was laughing. Or crying. Or both. I'm not sure. But I *know* it was Sera."

Kandra's face turned mournful. "I know what you wish to believe, but—"

"There is cold air beneath the statue of Faesa," Leela said fiercely. "And I bet beneath Aila and Dendra as well. I'm going to the Moon Gardens tonight, and I'm going to find out what's underneath them. They are all connected, I just can't see how."

"No, you mustn't. It is too dangerous."

"Kandra?" one of the midwives called. "Where are you?"

"I have to go." Kandra kissed Leela's forehead. "Please. Don't do anything foolish."

Then she stepped out from behind the tree and called back to the midwife, joining the other purple mothers at the birthing houses.

Leela's heart was pounding. She waited for several long moments before turning to head back home. But Kandra's pleas had not dampened her determination one bit—she was going to find out what was below that statue, and she was going to find out tonight.

Every minute felt like an hour, every hour like a day.

Dinner was a cheerful affair for her mothers—one purple mother stopped by while they were having their tea and asked so many questions of Leela's purple mother that Leela had to excuse herself. She couldn't stand any more questions when she had enough of her own.

At last the house fell silent and Leela slipped out of her window and hurried to the temple. It was dark, the novices exhausted from the Night of Song as Leela knew they would be. She crept through the Moon Gardens until she reached the statue of Faesa, drenched in moonlight. She knelt and felt the cold air emanating from its base. Then she stood and looked the statue in the eye, wondering if more markings would appear. Nothing happened. She stood there, counting her heartbeats and waiting. A butterfly landed in Faesa's cupped hands, flashing its magenta wings at her twice. Leela reached out and it flew away, her fingers curling around the smooth stone instead.

As soon as her skin touched the moonstone, her magic ignited and another vision swam before her eyes. It was a different room this time, smaller, with a large copper basin in one corner and a desk and chair in another. And there was someone in the room, someone with pale skin, turquoise eyes, and thick black curls. It was a person unlike any she had ever seen, and there was something off about her, besides her coloring, that Leela could not put her finger on. As if echoing up from the bottom of a dark well, she heard Sera's voice.

"Leela," she whispered. Leela's heart spasmed and the vision dissolved in a burst of blue sparks. When she looked at the statue again, markings had appeared, running down the length of Faesa's robe.

Show me, she spoke to the stone silently, as she had with the obelisk, but her heart was not as tentative this time, and she felt a force of will building inside her. *Show me the secret that lies beneath you.*

Leela stepped back as the statue of Faesa slid to the side. She peered down at a set of winding sunglass stairs, vanishing into the darkness. She had never been more frightened in her life, her pulse racing, every hair on her scalp standing on end.

"Is Sera down there?" she asked aloud, but Faesa was just a statue and could not answer her. Leela felt as if her bones had been replaced with air, a disorienting lightness filling her up.

She sent up a prayer to Mother Sun and began to descend the stairs.

38

AGNES

THE MARIBELLE THEATER WAS SWARMED.

Agnes could not control her wildly beating heart as Eneas pulled up to the theater. She had spent the ride squeezed in between her father and her brother, trying to fidget as little as possible. In her beaded clutch were the thousand krogers, the letter from Ambrosine, and the photograph of her mother. It was terrifying having such illicit material so close to her father, but it was all she would be taking with her. She wondered if Leo had anything stashed away in his tuxedo jacket, something he could not bear to leave behind in Old Port.

She hadn't told Leo about the letter yet—there were more important things to focus on at the moment, and the letter wouldn't matter if they didn't make it to the Seaport. He'd relayed what Sera had told him, about Errol and Boris and the sprites. It all seemed unreal to her. So much could go wrong, so much was out of her control. If this plan failed . . . she didn't want to think about that.

The article about Sera and the others, about Xavier's newest venture, had been published in the *Telegraph* that morning, which was probably why throngs of people crowded the streets leading to the theater. There were groups of Solit protesters proclaiming these creatures to be heretical, enemies of the One True God that should be burned at the stake, and clusters of Old Port's poorest citizens begging for Sera to heal them. If Xavier took any notice of them at all, Agnes could not tell. Her father seemed lost in thought the entire ride, staring out the window with unseeing eyes, as if his mind was on other things. It seemed odd—this was the night he had been anticipating for months, perhaps longer.

He roused himself as the car pulled to a stop. A reporter recognized them and there was a shout of "Mr. McLellan!" Suddenly, they were surrounded. Eneas pushed through the reporters to open the back door.

"Smile, Agnes," Xavier said without looking at her. She hated that her lips automatically pulled up in response. He was the first out of the car—Agnes and Leo exchanged a glance before Agnes slid across the seat and took Eneas's offered hand. Leo followed after her and the two of them flanked their father, Leo right by his side, Agnes a little behind him—this routine was familiar to them both, after so many premieres.

This is the last time, Agnes realized. *No matter what, I'll never have to go through this awful charade again.*

Bulbs flashed behind the red ropes that kept the press at bay. Questions were shouted and everything felt too loud and too bright. Whenever her picture appeared in the paper, Agnes looked like she was staring directly into the sun—eyes squinting, cheeks scrunched up. The questions pelted her like pebbles, pinging between her ears.

"How does it feel to be engaged?"

"Give us a smile, Miss McLellan!"

"Agnes, who are you wearing?"

They never asked Leo who he was wearing, and he was the one who picked out this damn dress. Agnes smiled as hard as she could and said nothing.

"Xavier, what made you decide to leave the theater business and start up this Pelagan venture?"

"*Pelagan* venture?" Xavier stared down at the reporter with an expression of utter contempt. "My only aim is to right the wrong that has been done to this country. My goal is to return Kaolin to its former glory, and I will use any methods at my disposal. I am a patriot, sir. All I do, I do under the eye of the One True God, and he knows what is in my heart. These creatures I have discovered will make our land and seas healthy again. Where they were found has no bearing on what they can do."

"They'll make you a pretty penny, though, won't they?" another one shouted, and Agnes recognized him vaguely as one friendly to her father.

Xavier's eyes glinted in the flash of the bulbs. "Why, my dear Rudolph, they already have."

Then it was more fake smiling, their father between them, his hands on their shoulders, the picture of a perfect Kaolin family man.

If only he knew what his children were really up to.

That thought made Agnes smile for real.

Finally, they were ushered into the huge marble foyer. Bars were set up at either end, bottles of champagne chilling in silver buckets, crystal flutes standing neatly side by side. Waiters carrying platters of hors d'oeuvres glided through the crowd, offering smoked salmon pinwheels and caviar on toast. A string quartet played softly in the corner by the stairs to the mezzanine.

Xavier McLellan spared no expense when it came to self-promotion.

There were photographs set on large tripods, the same ones from the house along with one of Sera in the pink lace gown, her hair done up like a Kaolin girl. She looked frightened. Men were lined up to make bids, mostly men who owned cattle ranches or large farms in the west for Boris, shipping and fishing industrialists from the Gulf of Windsor for Errol, but Sera's line was the longest. A drop of blood that could cure all? People were going nuts over it. The prices were sky-high, simply because there was so little to be sold. There was a small photograph of the vial Kiernan had taken from her at the party, which seemed to be all that was for sale at the moment. Xavier was not foolish enough to bleed his golden goose dry.

Agnes stared at the picture of the vial with hatred in her heart. That was all her father was going to get from Sera. He wasn't going to take a single drop more.

"Leo." Xavier didn't even need to raise his voice and his children's heads swiveled in his direction. He was standing with the mayor and two city council members. "Come, they wish to hear the story of the capture of our Azure."

"Ugh," Leo muttered. "I'll be back."

"Play the part," Agnes reminded him.

"Of course, darling sister," he said, putting on his most debonair smile and striding over to the four men. The mayor shook his hand and Agnes watched, fascinated, as Leo began to tell the tale of Sera's capture with great gusto, as if he really was his old self.

"Your brother seems to be enjoying himself." Ebenezer Grange appeared at her elbow, two champagne flutes in hand. He offered one to Agnes.

"Yes, he's never happier than when rich old men are showering him with attention," she said.

He laughed. "So how did it go at the Wolfshead?"

Her face went hot. "Oh, it was fine, just fine."

"No one tried to steal your virtue, I hope?"

Agnes choked on her champagne. "No, no. Thank you again for the ride."

"Anytime." He clinked his glass with hers and gazed at the photographs. "It feels just as unpleasant now as it did back at your house," he said. "Seeing everyone clamor for pieces of them."

"It does," she agreed.

"Have you seen any of the show?"

"No, Father would never allow it. Leo used to get to see some dress rehearsals of his other shows, but not me. It wouldn't be appropriate, he always said. Though I don't think even Leo has seen any of this production."

"Strange that it's only one night," Ebenezer mused.

"Well, he's got the whole country of Kaolin to save," Agnes said dryly. "He can't waste time with theatrics."

They exchanged a grin as the lights flickered in the foyer, indicating that the audience should begin taking their seats.

"See you after the show," Ebenezer said.

Agnes was surprised by the knot that rose in her throat. She wanted to tell him that she was leaving, that she was sorry, and that if she *had* to marry a man from Kaolin, she was happy it would have been him. But she couldn't say any of that, so she smiled and nodded, passing her glass off to a circulating waiter. Leo entered the theater first, and she was about to join him when her father pulled her aside.

"Don't think I don't know what you've been doing," he said quietly. Agnes's heart dropped to her stomach like a stone. "I know you've been poking around the Seaport. How many times must I tell you, Agnes—you are *never* going to Pelago. If any one of my men sees you there again, I will call off this wedding and have you locked up somewhere dark and silent where you can never hurt this family or its reputation again. Do I make myself clear?"

It took every ounce of will she had to jerk her chin down in a quick nod. She felt light-headed, her fingertips numb, as her father strode away and she followed weakly behind him.

He knew about the Seaport. But he did not know about her true plans—if he did, she would surely have been thrown into Larker Asylum already. She took her seat, avoiding Leo's eyes, unwilling to reveal anything else to her father.

Her resolve began to harden as her pulse slowly returned to normal.

This plan would work. It had to.

And Xavier McLellan had no idea what was in store for him.

The lights dimmed and the crowd hushed as Martin Jenkins emerged in front of the curtains to thunderous applause.

"Welcome, ladies and gentlemen, to the very exclusive, one-night-only premiere of *The Fabled Fate of Olverin Waters and His Triumph Over the Mistress of the Islands*!" There was more clapping. "Most of you have likely seen the day's paper, so you know this production features some very *unique* performers as well as Kaolin's most seasoned actress, the Lady Gwendivere, and its rising star, the one and only Mr. James Roth!" Cheers and whistles drowned out his voice for a moment. "Of course, it is a tragedy that we are losing such a pillar of the community in our noble patron Mr. Xavier McLellan, but we wish him the best of luck with his new venture, one that will surely strengthen Kaolin's land and seas and, most importantly, its people. Thank you, Xavier, for all you have done for theater in Old Port. And now, without further ado, I invite you to sit back, relax, and enjoy the show!"

39

LEO

THE PLAY WAS A VERY HIGH-QUALITY PRODUCTION, LEO had to admit.

Boris's lush gardens gave more life and color to the stage than any set or scrim ever could. The flowers around Errol's pond glowed faintly and the pond itself seemed to lend a certain magic, as if the audience was really peering into a faraway forest. The glass ceiling, while of course highly unusual for a theater, actually added to the ambiance, creating the sense that the viewer was outside with stars twinkling overhead. James Roth was spectacular, Grayson Riggs was as hilarious as he always was, and Lady Gwendivere played the part of the evil Pelagan to absolute perfection.

Errol made his debut about halfway through the first

act, when the net was lowered from the ceiling and he was scooped up inside it. His scales flashed jade, copper, scarlet, peach, as he wriggled and struggled, while the audience oohed and aahed at the colors, and Leo's entire opinion of the play soured. He caught sight of Agnes, seated on their father's other side, a half-horrified, half-awed expression on her face, and he remembered she had never actually seen Errol, only that murky photograph.

As Lady Gwendivere cackled and explained to the audience how she planned to keep the mertag all for herself so that the pond by her house would never run dry and she would never go hungry, Leo found his attention wandering to Sera. Was she still in that awful crate, or had they moved her somewhere else to make space backstage? He wondered if she was as nervous as he was right now.

He pressed his palm against the pocket of his tuxedo pants for the millionth time that evening, feeling the comforting prick of the star pendant through the fabric. He and Agnes had agreed to bring only what was absolutely necessary, and even then only what they could carry without alerting their father. Leo was willing to bet the four thousand krogers he had stashed away in various places—the inner pockets of his tuxedo jacket, the toes of his shoes, tucked beneath the waistband of his underwear—that Agnes was bringing the photograph of their mother. Leo didn't own anything of sentimental value, but he had promised to return the necklace to Sera and he would be damned if he broke that promise.

He had left his favorite pair of cuff links on the vanity in his room for Janderson. With them was a note that simply read, *Thanks for putting up with me.* He felt the man had earned them.

The first act ended with James setting sail for Pelago to free Errol and Boris from the clutches of Lady Gwendivere and bring them back to Kaolin to save his farm and end the famine destroying the country. The curtain closed and the audience erupted in applause. Xavier stroked the point of his beard and did not clap. He never clapped for his own productions. Leo used to think it a sign of strength and power. Now he just thought it made his father look like an asshole.

The lights came up and Agnes seemed pale and sweaty, like she might throw up. She had to keep up appearances better, Leo thought. If Xavier began to suspect anything, they were screwed. Fortunately, their father didn't even glance at her as the mayor and his wife, sitting in the booth behind them, had leaned forward to offer congratulations.

"My god, that fish creature was something else, Xavier. I thought Arabella was going to faint."

"But that tree is absolutely lovely. And the garden—I've never seen flowers like those before!"

"I beg your pardon, Father," Leo said. "But Kiernan told me to check on the creatures at intermission, just to be sure everything was going smoothly."

Xavier's eyes glossed over Leo, and began moving toward the throngs below waiting to congratulate him. "Yes, of course," he said with a dismissive wave of his hand. Leo shot Agnes a hard look and she stood.

"I'm going to get a refreshment," she said in a stilted voice. Their father gave no sign that he had heard her—he had already turned back to the mayor. She and Leo made it down to the lobby and he gripped her elbow.

"Get it together," he hissed. "You look like you're going to faint."

"Father knows I've been to the Seaport," she said.

"*What?*"

"He told me before the show started. Threatened me, really." She tugged at her dress. "Guess he's going to be disappointed on that score."

"Does he know about us working together?"

She shook her head. "He thinks I'm trying to flee my engagement and run off to Pelago." Her face turned sad. "Poor Errol," she murmured. "In that net . . . and Boris is so lovely. They're real, Leo. They're marvelous and real and . . . god, he's such a monster, keeping them like this."

"Yes, yes, we've established that. But we've got our own jobs to do. We've got to trust Sera now. She'll get them out."

"Not Boris," Agnes said. Leo thought she might cry, but instead she took a deep, fortifying breath. "I know. You're right. It's just all so overwhelming, now that it's happening." She let out a disgruntled huff. "I should've known one of his spies would have seen me at the docks."

"At least he doesn't know what you're really up to," Leo muttered, glancing around at the attendees milling about, gossiping over the first act in between sips of champagne and bites of caviar. He had to get backstage. He wanted to see Sera one last time before this whole plot began—or ended. One way or another. "I'll get us a cab and have it waiting at the corner by the backstage door. You leave when—"

"Right as James Roth and Grayson Riggs start to sword fight. I know." Agnes pressed her clutch to her chest and gazed up at him, her cinnamon eyes full of anxiety. "We can do this, right?"

"We can do this," Leo said.

She flashed him a wobbly smile.

Leo wove his way through the crowds and platters of canapés back to the theater, where he pretended to check on the moss in Errol's pond just in case his father happened to be looking.

"Get ready, Errol, you're almost up," he muttered. Then he climbed the steps to the stage and slipped behind the curtain. Crew members were clearing props and rolling on set pieces for the beginning of the second act. Sera's crate was nowhere to be found.

"She's in dressing room three," Francis said softly, and Leo whirled around. "The one with all the Pembertons by the door."

"Thanks."

"I won't let her down," he promised.

"I know," Leo said, and he found he truly believed it. Whoever this slight young man was, he had a big heart and his every word rang with sincerity. Leo wondered how someone like him had ever come to work for Xavier McLellan.

He wanted to say more but didn't have the words, and even if he did, they would be too dangerous. So he held out a hand.

Francis grinned and shook it. "Good luck," he said. "Take care of her."

Leo nodded, a lump growing in his throat. He found the

dressing room easily enough, and the men stepped aside at the mention of his father. The room was small and warm, a copper basin in one corner and a desk in another. Sera was sitting in a stout leather armchair, and she stood as he entered.

"Leo," she said, a smile breaking across her face. A smile. For him. Leo felt a sudden wave of light-headedness. They had bathed her and done up her hair in a pile of soft blue curls. She wore a stupid crown in the shape of the sun on her head, but her dress was magnificent—champagne satin that clung to her body in a way that suddenly had him feeling very distracted. He buttoned his tuxedo jacket and cleared his throat.

"It's almost time," he said. "I'm off to get a cab to take me and Agnes to the Seaport. Agnes says our ship is small and at the very northern edge of the docks. It's called the *Maiden's Wail.*"

"Got it," Sera said with a nod. "Errol says he can find any ship, day or night. He's very confident."

"That makes one of us."

Sera took a step toward him. Leo could feel the heat from her body, the floral-starlight scent of her surrounding him.

"I misjudged you," she said.

He swallowed, trapped by her sapphire gaze.

"No," he said. "You didn't. But you changed me. And I . . . I'm grateful for that."

Then he bowed low, as he would to a Kaolin woman of high birth. But Sera was so much worthier than that. He felt his face go red and he straightened, feeling like a bit of an idiot. But she looked pleased.

"Is that the way Kaolin people say goodbye?" she asked.

"Er, no. It's the way they show respect," he explained.

"Ah." He could see her filing it away in her sharp mind. Then she bowed to him.

"Did I do it right?" she asked.

"You did," he said, unable to suppress his grin. "Oh!" He reached into his pocket. "I brought it back like I said I would. It will be yours again once we're all safely on our way to Pelago."

The pale stone gleamed in his palm as he held the necklace out. Sera took it, tears filling her eyes.

"Leela," she whispered, cupping the pendant in her hands.

"Five minutes to places, folks!" a voice called from the other side of the door. "Five minutes!"

"I've got to go," Leo said. She handed the necklace back to him. "I'll see you at the Seaport."

She nodded. "The Seaport."

"Good luck, Sera."

She shot him a rueful look. "I do not need luck. I have Mother Sun watching over me."

"See if she can look out for me and Agnes, too, while she's at it," Leo said. He would take all the help he could get at this point.

Sera's smile shone brighter than her sun crown. "She will."

40

AGNES

"Where's your brother?" Xavier asked as they took their seats for the second act.

"He came to tell me the girl was having a bit of a fit," Agnes said, repeating the line they had practiced the night before. "He's staying back there to keep her calm."

"Let's hope he is capable of that," Xavier muttered. Agnes felt it best to keep her mouth shut. She was not the liar Leo was.

The lights dimmed and the curtain opened. She barely heard the lines being spoken onstage. Was Sera up there behind the top curtain right now? She hoped they could really trust this Francis person to leave her unchained on the swing. And besides that, would Errol actually be capable of breaking the glass ceiling?

Agnes would not be around to see any of these questions answered. She waited and waited, fighting the urge to fidget, her hands clenched so tightly around her clutch that her fingers were starting to go numb.

At long last, Grayson Riggs appeared onstage, unsheathed his sword, and challenged James to a duel.

"Father," Agnes whispered. He waved her off. "Father," she said again more insistently.

"What?" Xavier snapped.

"I've got to use the restroom."

"You can wait until the show is over."

"No, I must go now. It's . . ." Agnes steeled herself. "It's my monthly cycle, Father."

All the color drained from Xavier's face. She might as well have just confessed to murdering someone.

"Go," he said without looking at her. She hurried out of their box and rushed down the stairs to the foyer, wishing she could throw her arms up in triumph. How easy Kaolin men could be manipulated by a simple mention of "ladies' matters." When she'd relayed her idea to Leo, the look on his face was proof enough that it would work.

The foyer was deserted except for the waiters cleaning up glasses and dirty plates and crumpled napkins. Agnes pushed through the doors and hurried past the hulking Pembertons, fanning her face as if to indicate she only needed some air. The dress did not allow for much movement, and she teetered in the stupid high heels Leo had made her wear until finally she reached the corner and turned.

Her brother was nowhere to be found. He was supposed

to be at the end of the block, but the block was empty. And not just of Leo, but of anyone. There were no people—but more importantly, there were no cars. She looked behind her and realized the block in front of the Maribelle was the same. She lifted her skirt and walked as quickly as her shoes would allow, passing two Pemberton guards beside the stage door and keeping her face averted.

"All right, miss?" one of them asked.

"Yes, I'm fine, thank you." Her voice was high and breathy, and she did not stop walking until she reached the corner. The block behind the theater was empty too, but to her left she saw that it was because the police had cordoned off the area. There were crowds filling the surrounding streets. Her father must have someone in his pocket at the police department. There was no other way to explain the presence of so many officers.

But that didn't give her any clue as to where Leo was. She crossed the back of the theater, but there was no sign of him. What should she do? She didn't believe he had simply left her—once she might have assumed it, but not anymore. He was as invested in this plan as she was.

She walked down Fifty-First Street back toward Loxman Avenue and the main entrance to the theater. Perhaps she should try and find a car herself. She'd nearly reached the corner when Leo came running down Loxman from the north.

"There you are," she said. "Where have you—"

"No cabs," Leo gasped, panting as he leaned forward and put his hands on his knees. "Some streets are filled with people, some with cars." He gestured to the theater. "Fancy cars. Police. It's a nightmare. We have to get to Oxbridge or maybe even Wellfleet Avenue. There's no way a hansom can get through all those cops."

"But that would take us too much time, wouldn't it?" And the police might recognize them. And the crowds might be too dense to get through. And . . . and . . . and . . .

"Won't Vada keep Sera safe until we get there?" Leo asked.

"She doesn't know who Sera is," Agnes said miserably. "Oh, Leo, what do we do, what do we *do*?"

She wrung her hands, cursing herself for not seeing this coming, for not being more prepared for any situation.

"I don't know," Leo said. "But we've got to move. We can't stay here or Father will—"

"Can I help you two?" A Pemberton with broad shoulders and a nose that looked to have been broken more than once had approached them from the theater.

Leo came to the rescue with a perfect lie. "I'm just looking for our car," he said pompously. "The play was a bit too much for my sister. I think that horrid fish man frightened her. Frightened me too, if I'm honest. Have you seen that thing?"

"No," the Pemberton said.

"Well, I don't recommend it. Old Xavier's off his rocker if you ask me."

Agnes was wondering how long Leo could keep this up when a green motorcar pulled up to the curb. Eneas hopped out and circled around to open the back door for them.

She stared at him in shock. Thankfully, Leo's reactions were quicker than hers.

"Where have you been?" he demanded. "We've been waiting a full five minutes."

"Apologies, sir," Eneas said, bowing as Leo gripped Agnes's arm and steered her into the back seat.

"Well, take us home at once," he said. "Good evening to you, sir," he added to the Pemberton, who was watching them with far too suspicious an expression for Agnes's liking.

Eneas pulled away from the theater and waved at a police officer, who seemed to know him and allowed him past the barricade on Fiftieth Street. No one spoke until they had left Central Square and were driving through the smaller, residential streets of Graham Hill. Eneas headed straight to Seaview Drive, which wound along the shoreline and would take them directly to the Seaport.

"How did you know?" Agnes asked. "That we needed help?"

"I saw your brother running through the streets like the dickens and figured that whatever you two have been up to over the past week, it wasn't working out the way you planned." He gave her a wry look in the rearview—Agnes could feel her mouth hanging open.

"You *knew*?" Leo asked, also looking astonished.

Eneas chuckled. "I've known you two since the day you were born, and not in all that time have I ever seen you be anything but combative with each other. And then all of a sudden you talk together politely with no fights and no snapping?" He shook his head. "You are lucky your father hates to look at you," he said to Leo. "Or he might have noticed as well."

The line of tension in Leo's jaw stood out in sharp relief in the light of the gas lamps that lined the road.

"And you," Eneas continued, turning his attention to Agnes. "I heard there was a wealthy Kaolin girl at the Wolfshead talking to a Pelagan sailor. The Wolfshead, Agnes, of all places? Do you know how dangerous that was?"

Shame crept into her belly, and embarrassment—she'd thought she was being clever, but really she stood out like a sore thumb.

"I know," she said. "One of Father's men saw me."

"I'm not surprised. Thank the goddesses he did not lock you up immediately," Eneas said. He eased the car past a slow-moving horse and cart. "I assume you booked passage to Pelago? Or did Ambrosine send a ship? You never told me what was in her letter."

"What let—" Leo began, but Agnes held up a hand to silence him.

"She didn't, but she wants to meet me. Someone at the university told her I had applied. She knew I was coming."

"What univer—"

"In a second, Leo," she said. "Eneas, we're trying to get Sera—the girl Leo and I found in the plains—we've got to get her to Pelago. And Errol too, the mertag. They don't deserve the fate Father has in store for them. And I want to help Sera get back to her home if I can, and we think the ruins are connected to her city somehow."

Eneas kept his eyes on the road, and she could tell he was debating what to say next.

"And he is part of this?" he asked, glancing at Leo. "*He* is going against that man?"

"I am," Leo said, jutting out his chin.

Eneas studied him in the mirror; then his face broke into a beaming smile. "Well," he said, "perhaps you've got more of your mother in you after all."

At last they reached the Seaport, and Eneas pulled up to the docks.

"What about you?" Agnes asked. "What if he finds out you helped us? Won't you be in trouble?"

He turned and set his warm brown eyes on her. "My dear, I made your mother a promise. I would watch over her children and make sure they were cared for, that they were loved. No matter what, she said. I have not always been able to honor that promise. But my oath is to you, not to him. I will not be staying in this hateful city. Do not worry about me." He looked from Leo to Agnes, and when he spoke again, his voice was strained. "She would have been very proud of you both," he said. "Very proud." He cleared his throat. "Now off you go. Good luck. If you stop at Arbaz, drop my name at the market there. My sister can give you help if you need it. Her name is Phebe Ofairn."

"Thank you," Agnes said. *"Feados na thaeias dul leatsou."*

He smiled. "May the goddesses go with you, too."

Leo opened the door, and they were about to get out when Eneas said, "One more thing." He hesitated. "Be careful around your grandmother. I know you are eager to meet her, Agnes, but . . . try to see things as they are, not how you wish them to be. Now go!"

They hurried out and shut the door. Eneas threw the car into drive and they watched the taillights vanish. The

Seaport was not quite as busy as it was during the day, but there were far more people than normal for this time of night. Music and laughter could be heard from a nearby tavern. A drunk man stumbled past them, whistling. Agnes was suddenly very aware of her expensive gown and the money in her clutch. She tucked it under her arm and turned to Leo, who was staring up at the stars.

"Look," he said, pointing. "Aetheus's Harem."

She smiled weakly. "The Knottle Plains feels like a lifetime ago, doesn't it?"

He nodded, still gazing at the constellation, and Agnes got the sense he was thinking of something else, something private.

"She's coming, right?" he said. "She'll make it out. She'll get here."

"Yes," Agnes said, touching his arm and wondering if there was more to her brother's devotion to this trip than a sudden burst of conscience. "She's coming. Let's get to the ship."

41

SERA

Sera waited on the swing as the play continued beneath her.

She could still feel Leela's moonstone in her hand, as if it'd left an imprint on her skin. It had always been warm, but this time when she touched it, it was hot, like the High Priestess's hands. True to his word, Francis had helped her onto the swing and closed the iron bracelets but not locked them, so once she had been hoisted above the stage, it had been a simple matter of wriggling her wrists until she was able to slip free.

Free. She clutched the chains tight—not because she was fearful of falling, but as a way to channel her nerves. Freedom was so close, but there was still much to be done.

Her magic was like fire inside her, popping and crackling, as if it knew how crucial this moment was, that a time was approaching when she would be on her way to the tether.

She peered beneath her as James and the man named Grayson pretended to fight with swords. She wondered what her life would be like in the City, if she were able to make it back, knowing now how she felt about males. She supposed it was better than thinking she was incapable of love. She would simply resign herself to a life without that sort of desire, those sorts of wants. But she would have her mothers back, and Leela, too. That would have to be enough.

For some reason, Leo's face popped into her head. The way he had bent his body toward her as a sign of respect. And he had brought the necklace back like he said he would. Not all males were terrible, she thought, even ones that had been at first. People could change, it seemed.

The fight ended and Gwendivere came onstage. She and James had their argument and then she pretended to stab him.

Here we go, Sera thought as her platform was lowered. *Mother Sun, give me strength.*

There were shrieks and cries as she appeared, followed by thunderous applause. Sera didn't understand what they were clapping for—she hadn't done anything. Not yet at least. She felt one of Boris's leaves caress her bare foot.

I can do this.

"Go, *little sapling,*" Boris whispered, and her branches bent back, then slammed into the swing, pushing Sera out over the pond. The people watching gasped, but then

Sera was swinging back over Boris, and suddenly, the air was filled with sprites. They spilled out of the earth like golden bees, sparking and twirling, darting this way and that, forming and re-forming, and the crowd went wild, getting to their feet to clap and stomp and whoop. James and Gwendivere stood by, stunned. Sera swung back through a cloud of shimmering sprites and yelled, "Now, Errol!"

The mertag burst out of the pond, his skin a green glow, his arms raised toward her. She almost missed him but managed to grab one of his wrists as she fell back through the sprites and over Boris.

Once more, she thought as Errol swung himself onto her back. She released his wrist and he clung to her tightly, his clawed fingers digging into her skin. He was a little heavier than she had expected. She leaned back to gain momentum and suddenly a cloud of sprites was behind her, pushing her forward with more speed. She kept her eyes focused on the upper balcony, a private box where only four people were seated.

She sent up a final prayer, held her mothers' faces close to her heart, and jumped. For five or six endless seconds, she was airborne and the freedom was exhilarating. She pointed her lithe body toward the balcony, her arms outstretched, and when her fingers closed around the polished wooden banister, she wanted to cry with joy. But there was no time for tears. Her body slammed into the front of the balcony, knocking the air from her lungs. She held on, determined, as all the sound around her dulled and sparks exploded in front of her eyes.

Her breath returned in a sudden, painful gasp, and it

was as if someone had turned up the volume louder than it had been before. People were crying out with uncertainty, shouting or cheering, as if unsure whether this was part of the show.

"Go, Sera Lighthaven!" Errol cried. *"The ceiling, the ceiling!"*

Sera gritted her teeth and pulled herself up. The people in the box were hysterical, one woman shrieking, "Get it away, get it away!"

She shimmied to the wall, her hands sliding over the banister, until she reached the wooden carvings that adorned this part of the theater, making perfect handholds and footholds. She climbed up as easily as if she were back on the temple's spire, and when she reached the ceiling, she turned and looked back.

The sprites were still swarming about the stage— Gwendivere had fled, James was swatting at them frantically, and the front rows of the audience were beginning to realize something was amiss. She looked up and saw Leo and Agnes's father in another box across from her and he was gesturing to her, a man in a suit beside him with something long and metal pointed at her. There was a whizzing sound by her ear and a dart with a little feather sticking out of it sank into the wood near her right wrist.

"Now, Errol, *now!*" she cried. A webbed hand reached over her shoulder and splayed across one pane of glass.

"Forgive me, my friend," Errol said, and as the lightning flashed over his scales in a brutal surge of energy, Sera felt an agony unlike anything she had ever known, a pulse

of unbearable heat shooting through her body, burning in her veins and scalding her heart. She might have screamed, she couldn't be sure, but the next second every pane of glass had shattered and the entire ceiling exploded in a deafening crash that rained down shards like razors of crystal upon the audience. The confusion turned to shrieks as people began to run toward the exits.

The pain in Sera's body dulled and she managed to pull herself up onto the roof of the theater, Errol still clinging to her back. She could feel the glass cutting into her skin where it was left jagged and poking out of its iron casing. The roof of the theater was warm on the soles of her feet, and she looked down to see chaos below. Sprites chased theatergoers this way and that, women shrieked and cried, men tried to bat them away in vain, and on the stage, Boris swayed gently. Sera could hear her humming.

"Thank you," she whispered, and her voice came out like the wind.

The Arboreal turned her three eyes upward. "Go," she said, and then the hum turned to a whistle, almost like a call. The sprites flocked to her, billowing around her as the whistle grew ever more shrill and urgent, and they began to burst, one by one, like fireworks, and where their sparks settled on the Arboreal, fire flared up.

"Boris!" Sera cried. "No!"

But the tree was already alight, her topmost leaves crowned in flames that quickly snaked down her branches, charring her beautiful silvery bark, turning her blue-green leaves to ash. She made no sound or cry as she burned, but from somewhere in the theater, Sera heard the sound of Xavier McLellan screaming, "Put it out, you goddamn fools!"

"*Tree was very brave*," Errol said sadly. "*But we must run now, Sera Lighthaven.*"

Tears streamed down Sera's cheeks, but she knew he was right. There was no time to mourn for Boris. They had to get to the ship. She stood and steadied herself, adjusting to his weight now that she was on her feet. Quickly she tied the skirt of her dress up so that it sat around her thighs, leaving her legs free.

"Which way, Errol?"

He sniffed, then pointed. "*That way.*"

The world was so different up here—peaks and plateaus, shadowy towers and glowing windows. If her life weren't in danger, Sera would marvel at the strangeness of these human dwellings, each one unique, made of unfamiliar materials.

As it was, she slid down to the lip of the roof, where a wide gutter ran, pelted to the end of the building, and jumped.

Errol's terrified wail was sucked away by the wind. Sera landed on the opposite roof, which was a bit lower than the theater and mercifully flat. She sent up a prayer of thanks to Mother Sun and kept running. The next roof was shaped like a triangle, with strange flakes of wood decorating its surface. They made for easy hand- and footholds until she jumped to the next roof.

Shiny tile.

Bare concrete.

One even had a golden spire like on the temple.

Sera felt the weight of the theater, of the crate, of all that time locked up melting away. She ripped the crown out of her hair and tossed it aside, reveling in the feel of the wind against her cheeks, humid as the air was. Errol was miserable, judging by his moans, and after one particularly plummeting leap, she heard a retching sound and felt something slimy on her shoulder. But Sera did not mind. She was *free*. She was out under the sky again. Somehow, impossibly, their plan had worked. She heard wailing sounds in the distance that seemed to be growing closer but paid them no mind.

At some point, a sharp scent hit her nose, and Errol's limp form went rigid with excitement.

"The sea, the sea!" he cried. *"Can you smell it, Sera Lighthaven?"*

"Yes," she gasped. It was salty and tangy and reminded her of the taste of tears. She moved faster now and at last took a great leap onto the roof of a very noisy establishment with lots of music and laughter spilling from its windows. She found herself gazing at a vast expanse of blackness. The smell was stronger here, with a fishy undertone. The roof overlooked a broad thoroughfare, which was mostly empty at the moment. On the opposite side were vessels the likes of which Sera had never dreamed of—hulking monsters with huge pieces of fabric hanging off them, draped in thick ropes, wooden poles as tall as trees.

No sign of Leo or Agnes.

She jumped to the next roof, and the next, and the next, her sharp eyes piercing the darkness, searching . . .

"Do you see the ship, Errol?" she asked. When he gave no reply, she began to worry, but suddenly he cackled.

"*There,*" he said.

Sera had run out of roofs. She dropped to the ground, sending a jolt up her spine, and ran like lightning toward the wooden beast Errol had pointed out—it was smaller than the others, which was maybe why Sera thought it looked friendlier.

And then she saw them, her two friends, waiting for her on the dock.

42

LEO

"YOU ARE NOT MEANT TO BE HERE UNTIL TOMORROW," Vada said. "And you told me passage was for a girl, not a boy." She pointed at Leo. "He is a boy."

"I know. The other girl is coming," Agnes explained. "And . . . he needs to come too."

Vada took a long drag of her cigarette. "No, Agnes," she said. "You ask too much."

"I have money," Leo said. "Four thousand krogers. Please."

Sirens began to wail in the distance, and both he and his sister jumped.

Vada frowned. "Is that about you?" she asked.

"Um, yes, I think maybe it could be," Agnes said. She needed to get better at lying.

"We're trying to do a good thing here," Leo said. "We're trying to help someone."

"That is no matter to me." Vada walked down the gangplank and turned to speak only to Agnes. "My mother is back, with the rest of the crew. She was displeased with me already, and now you ask that I bring along three passengers chased by policemen? I think not." She reached into her vest and handed Agnes a thick wad of krogers. "I spent some already, but take the rest. It is yours. I cannot help you."

"You must, please," Agnes said. "You promised. She . . . she needs us."

"You still have not told me who this 'she' is. You say she is not Pelagan." Agnes shook her head. "Nor Kaolin." Another shake. Vada threw up her hands, exasperated.

"Vada?" A voice came from within the schooner.

"Shit," she muttered, putting out her cigarette on her boot. A woman appeared on the deck, flanked by several other sailors, women with weathered faces and grim expressions.

"Who are you talking to?" the woman demanded, before catching sight of Agnes and Leo. "Ah. Is this the Kaolin girl who tricked you into allowing not one but two berths?"

"I didn't trick anyone," Agnes insisted. "I paid fair and square."

The woman strode down the gangplank, the sailors trailing behind. They were all lean and muscular, Leo noted, with scuffed boots and worn leather vests.

"And we have more," he added. He reached into his jacket and pulled out a fistful of krogers. The sirens grew louder.

"Did you bring Kaolin lawmen down on us, girl?" the woman hissed.

"Mama, she is wealthy and well dressed. How was I to know she would bring the police?"

"It is your job to protect this ship while I am away, not sell it to the highest Kaolin bidder."

"But they are Byrnes, Mama."

Vada's mother scoffed, "Her? A Byrne?"

Leo had never been so grateful to have his mother's face. "We are," he said, stepping into the light so the woman could see him. "I am Leo McLellan and this is my sister, Agnes. Our mother was Alethea Byrne."

The woman's eyes widened. "By the grace of the goddesses," she murmured. "You are indeed a Byrne. I would know those eyes anywhere." She frowned. "She can come. You stay. We don't take Kaolin men on this ship."

"But—"

"Please," Agnes begged. "Our father will kill him if we leave him behind."

For the first time that sentence did not seem like an exaggeration to Leo.

"Agnes!" a voice called, dancing across the wind. "Leo! I'm here, I'm coming!"

"Sera," he gasped, his knees melting with relief. He whirled around as one of the sailors muttered something in Pelagan.

Sera raced up to them like a silver-gold blur and stopped

short, panting. "I'm here," she said. "We made it."

Her dress was torn and dirty, the pile of curls on her head coming undone, and she had tied her skirt up, leaving her long legs bare. Leo had never seen a woman look so wild and untamed. The sirens grew closer.

Errol slid off her back, his filaments flashing as he crawled to the edge of the dock. Several of the sailors cried out at the sight of him, and he slipped into the water with a loud plop.

"He is happy to be back in the sea," Sera said. Then tears filled her eyes. "Boris is gone, though. Her sprites turned to fire. She asked them to, I think. She burned herself to give us time to escape."

Leo did not quite understand the tightness in his throat, the ache in his chest. He had never thought of the Arboreal as anything but a tree. Or maybe he had. Maybe his feelings toward Sera had radiated out, to Errol, to Boris. Maybe he was seeing everything differently now.

Agnes seemed to know what to do better than he did.

"Oh, Sera," she murmured. "I'm so sorry." She wrapped her arms around the girl, and Sera's shoulders trembled for a moment before she pulled herself together.

"So this is a ship," she said, staring at the schooner in wonder.

Leo turned back to Vada and her mother. All the enmity in the sailors' eyes was gone, replaced with expressions of reverence. But not for him or for Agnes. It was Sera they were staring at.

"This is her," Agnes said boldly. "This is the friend I

told you about. She's special, and she needs our help. So you must—"

To Leo's immense surprise, Vada's mother dropped to her knees, Vada and the other sailors quickly following suit, falling to the ground like dominoes.

"*Thaeia*," Vada's mother whispered, touching her forehead with two fingers.

"*Thaeia*," the others repeated, making the same gesture.

"What are they saying?" Leo whispered to his sister, knowing she spoke some Pelagan. But it was Sera who answered. He should have figured. She could talk to everything.

"They are calling me goddess," she said.

Agnes gasped. Leo shook his head slowly back and forth. "What?" he said dumbly.

Vada's mother stood. "*Thaeia*," she said, "I am Violetta Murchadha, of the island of Feinlin. I have sailed the seas between Kaolin and Pelago since I was only a child before her first bleeding. I have weathered tempests that would make grown women weep. I would be honored to bring you to Pelago. The *Maiden's Wail* does not look like much, but she is as sturdy a ship as any you will find, even by Pelagan standards."

"My goodness," Sera said. "That is very kind of you."

The sailors looked at each other, confused, and Leo remembered they would only hear gibberish.

"She said that's very kind of you," he explained.

"How is it that a Kaolin man can understand the words

of a Pelagan goddess?" Violetta said, aghast.

"I think that's a story best saved for when we are far away from Old Port," Agnes said.

One of the sailors said something in Pelagan, and Vada snapped back at her. Then Violetta began barking out orders, also in Pelagan, and the sailors darted up the gangplank.

"What's happening?" Leo asked.

"That one said it is bad luck to start a voyage at night," Sera said. "And then the younger girl said, do not be an idiot, Saifa will protect us. And then Violetta told them to ready the sails and some other things I didn't quite understand."

Errol's head popped up from the water, his filaments flashing red and gold.

"Errol is ready to leave," Sera announced.

Vada appeared on the deck, her arms folded across her chest. "Well?" she called down to them, and Leo got the sense that she was teasing his sister and it made him feel protective of Agnes in a way he couldn't quite explain. "Are you coming, little lion?"

Agnes's lips twitched and she looped her arm through Sera's. "Ready for a sea voyage?" she asked as they walked up the gangplank.

Leo felt a small sting of jealousy until Sera turned back to him. "Come on, Leo," she said, holding out her hand. He hurried forward, then stopped, reaching into his pocket and taking out the star necklace.

"Here," he said. "It's time you had this back for good."

Her eyes sparkled as she took the chain and slipped it

around her neck. She tucked the pendant beneath the satiny folds of her dress.

"Thank you," she whispered.

Then she curled her fingers around his and they boarded the ship together.

The Pelagan sailors were expert and quick. Not ten minutes later, they had hoisted anchor and cast off, the lights of the Old Port docks slowly fading in the distance, the wail of the sirens swallowed up by the sea.

Leo watched the only home he'd ever known disappear into the darkness, and he felt ready to embrace this new life he'd chosen, no matter what fate had in store for him.

43

LEELA

THE STAIRS WERE COLDER THAN ANYTHING LEELA HAD ever felt before. It was a cold that burned.

They were steep and spiraled, so that she had to grip the walls with her hands to make sure she did not fall.

Mother Sun, she prayed. *Where are you taking me?*

She could not suppress her wildest hope—that Sera was down here, wherever here was. After all, Estelle had come back after Kandra thought she was dead. And Leela had heard Sera's voice twice now. She had *not* been imagining it. Plus, those visions, and the way the moonstone was reacting to her . . .

Colored lights began to shine at her feet as she descended, and when she finally reached the bottom of the stairs, she gazed around in wonder. Great columns rose up, glowing blue from the inside. There were paths that wove through them, emitting pale green light, snaking around pools of crystal-clear water that studded the floor; through them Leela could see straight down to the planet below. There was no sound of birds or hum of insects. There was no life at all. What was this place?

Then she looked up.

It was as if she was upside down. A forest sprawled across the ceiling, lush trees and wildflowers and brambly bushes growing toward her. It was disorienting, like standing in the sky. Leela followed one of the green paths. As she moved out away from where she imagined the temple must be above her, the trees grew shorter and stunted, the wildflowers withered, and the bushes became thorny and brittle. Whatever this sky forest was, it was dying.

The silence around her was unnerving, as was the crumbling foliage above. The farther out she traveled, the worse it became, until the ceiling was nothing but ash and mold.

Swish, plop. Swish, plop.

The sound was so faint, she could hardly hear it over her pounding heart. But then it came again.

Swish, plop.

It sounded like it was coming from near the stairs. She hurried back along the path, avoiding the clear pools—something told her they were dangerous, that they were not to be touched. Had Sera somehow fallen into this vast underbelly she'd never known existed? Was Estelle here, too?

She had passed the staircase, the swishing and plopping growing louder, when she heard a voice that made her blood run cold and her knees lock.

"Eat up, my beauties," the High Priestess said. "I need you to be strong for me now."

It took all of Leela's willpower to find the courage to move. She crept forward, trying to keep out of sight behind the glowing blue columns without stepping off the path into one of the pools. She came to a wide, circular space, and it seemed like it was the exact size and shape of the temple. They must be right beneath it. The pools vanished, replaced by icy circles with markings carved onto them. Instead of dead trees and bushes, frost-covered vines hung in great boughs, heavy with a strange fruit Leela had never seen before—round, plump orbs of pure gold. She peered around one of the columns, wondering where the High Priestess was among these vines, when she had to clap her hands over her mouth to keep from crying out at what she saw.

The tether was slicing up through the open space, glowing brighter than the columns around her. It burst through the largest pool of water Leela had seen in this place and was planted firmly in a cone of moonstone protruding from the tangle of ice-white vines above. There was a red-orange light in the moonstone's center, and it pulsed like a heartbeat. The High Priestess was circling the pool, muttering to herself. Then she stopped, crouched down, and passed her hand over something on the floor Leela could not see. *Swish.* She held out her other hand and one of the golden fruits fell into her palm. She dropped it into whatever she was crouching over. *Plop.* Then she passed her hand over the ground again.

She repeated this pattern several more times, crouching

in various places that made no rhyme or reason to Leela, dropping fruit and then making the same gesture.

"That should do for now," she said, standing and rubbing her hands together. Then she sighed. "For now."

She shook her head and her posture shifted; for a moment she looked old and bent, showing her years in a way Leela had never seen before. "This was not how I meant it to be," she whispered, like she was explaining herself to the floor. "But it is up to me and me alone. As it has been for so many long years. I am doing the best I can."

She held out her hands toward the tether like she was warming her palms over a fire. Leela watched in horror as pure white light began to glow from beneath her, from the circles where she had dropped the fruit. The ground started to shake and the High Priestess's face contorted in agony, yet she made no sound or cry of pain. The tether shone brighter and brighter and Leela was reminded of the light in the clay bowl, the one that had been used to choose Sera for the sacrifice. It grew so bright it was painful to look at, and Leela squeezed her eyes shut and pressed herself against the column's cold surface.

Then the light was gone and the ground went still, and she heard the High Priestess's footsteps. She passed within a few feet of where Leela was hiding, and Leela held her breath so as not to make a single sound.

She counted to one hundred before she allowed herself to move. Her knees were stiff as she walked toward the tether. It was more beautiful than she could have imagined, sometimes blue, sometimes gold, its interlocking links so fine and fragile that no Cerulean jeweler would ever be able to replicate it. She could see the magic running across its surface, tiny bursts of sparkling light. She stopped at the edge of the pool. Some instinct told her this place was sacred but forgotten, and she felt as if she stood before a giant beast with a stick, steeling herself to prod it and wake it up.

There was a circle of ice at her feet and Leela crouched down to inspect it. What had the High Priestess been doing? The markings carved into its surface were not the same as the ones on the obelisk or the statue, though they vaguely reminded Leela of the ones on the temple doors. But as she stared at them, they seemed to form a word—a word Leela could *read*.

Estelle.

She gasped. Tiny shavings of ice were scattered about the name and she brushed her palm over the letters to wipe them away. Instantly, the ice turned from opaque to as clear as one of the pools. Leela cried aloud and fell, landing sharply on her backside.

There was a *Cerulean* inside the ice.

Estelle was naked, her body curled into the fetal position, her face tormented, as if trapped in a terrible dream. But her chest rose and fell. She appeared to be inside a stalactite—Leela could see the edges and point of its cone below Estelle's curled feet. She reached out to touch her, to wake her, to ask her how she came to be here, to bring her back to the City above, but the ice was cold and unyielding. Her hand could not penetrate it.

Then something to the left caught her eye.

Another stalactite.

Quickly, she stood and moved to the next circle. Another

name: *Inora*. Brushing her hand across its surface, she saw a different Cerulean, slighter than Estelle, in the same fetal position, bearing the same tormented expression. Leela pressed her face so close to the ice that her nose grew tight and numb. She looked left. Then she looked right.

Stalactites stretched out in both directions, surrounding the tether and beyond, sticking out from the underbelly of her City like icy candles.

And inside each one was a Cerulean.

Leela went from circle to circle, reading every name, gazing down at woman after woman curled in silent agony. But none of them was Sera.

Exhausted and overwhelmed, she sat back on her heels. The moonstone's red-hot heart glowed at her, but she found no comfort in its beat. This strange place contained more questions than answers.

"I don't know what you want from me," she whispered to it, tears filling her eyes. "I don't know what I'm supposed to do. I don't know how to help these Cerulean or what the High Priestess is doing with them. I just . . . I wanted my friend back."

She wiped her nose with the back of her hand. She had been wrong. Sera wasn't here—she probably wasn't even alive. It was a fool's hope, and Leela felt her body sag as she stood to leave. It would be unwise to linger, lest the High Priestess return.

She walked past the large pool and the tether began to sing, a single beautiful strain more delicate than a violin. The music stopped her in her tracks as if compelling her, and her eyes were drawn to the pool's clear depths, to the shapes of Kaolin and Pelago far below. Then the water rippled and another vision surfaced, stronger and clearer than any of the others, swallowing her up. She could feel her feet on the cold ground, and yet it was as if she had been transported to an entirely unfamiliar place.

She was on a ship, thick masts with sails hanging from them, billowing in the wind—Leela did not know how she knew this, never having seen a ship before, but she did, as certainly as she knew her green mother's laugh or the colors of a minstrel flower. She stood on its prow, wind whipping through her hair, as waves crashed against the hull, sending up salty sprays and a bitter tang. Above her, the stars were nothing more than tiny pinpricks of light, so much farther away than she was used to.

Suddenly, another heart began to beat inside her chest, a pulse she was so very, very familiar with because it was the only one she had ever felt besides her mothers'. It was a pulse she would have known anywhere.

It was Sera's heart.

For a half second that seemed to last an eternity, she caught a glimpse of her friend, her hair done up strangely, her eyes lifted toward the night sky. Sera's face was filled with hope, her irises brighter than Leela had ever seen them, and as she gazed at the stars she whispered, "I'm coming."

Then the vision vanished, the pool becoming clear again, and Leela fell to her hands and knees, gasping for breath. All the pieces felt like they were falling into place. Those strange rooms and people these visions had shown her . . . they were from the *planet*.

Leela felt dizzy and pressed her forehead to the cold

ground. If what she had just seen was true—and she was far past the point of doubting herself in the face of such overwhelming power—then Sera *was* alive. But she would not be found in this cold underbelly of her City, or floating in the wide expanse of space.

She was on the planet. Somehow, some way, she had survived the fall.

Shaking, Leela rose to her feet, her heart pounding forcefully as if it had absorbed Sera's beat into its own rhythm. The fiery orb inside the moonstone pulsed along with her two heartbeats, connecting Leela with the very roots of the City that she loved so dearly. She felt a determination set in, a conviction as cold and strong as the columns surrounding her.

Whatever the High Priestess's schemes, she had not managed to kill Sera.

And Leela was going to find a way to bring her home.

Acknowledgments

This book challenged me in ways I could never have begun to guess when I started writing it. It broke me down and built me back up again, and I am beyond proud of what it became over that process. But, of course, books are not written in vacuums, and this one would never have been what it is without the help and support of some truly incredible people.

Karen Chaplin, editor extraordinaire, thank you for guiding me through yet another book and for suggesting the idea of restructuring, even though it made my brain want to explode. You always know exactly how to steer my stories so that they are the best they can possibly be, and I'm eternally grateful for that. Rosemary Brosnan, thank you for believing in yet another one of my weird, wild fantasy tales, and for being so wonderfully supportive. Bria Ragin, your insights and keen eye for trimming the fat on this book were invaluable. To my copyeditor, Valerie Shea, and production editor, Alexandra Rakaczki, you guys were so thorough and amazing. I could not have asked for a better team to keep an eye on every detail, especially the timelines, which I am just the worst at. David Curtis and Craig Shields, I have no words to adequately express how in love I am with this cover. I am in awe of your talent, and thank you for wrapping my words in a package more stunning than I could have ever imagined. Huge thanks to the entire sales team, especially Andrea Pappenheimer; to the amazing marketing duo of Bess Braswell and Sabrina Abballe; and for the fabulous publicity skills of Olivia Russo.

Charlie Olsen, you are the best agent an author could ever hope for, and I'm endlessly grateful for everything you do. I raise a mug of the Green Dragon's finest ale to you, sir. Thanks and hugs to Lyndsey Blessing for handling all things international.

I would not be able to complete a draft, much less revise and revise and revise, without the help of my incredible friends and beta readers. Caela Carter, thank you for handling my panic attacks with such patience and for reminding me that no, it is not actually possible to write one million words in two days. Alyson Gerber and Corey Ann Haydu, thank you for your wisdom and support and for always answering my frantic texts with calm reminders that everything is okay. Jess Verdi, I don't know how I would ever write a book without you. Thank you for your endless insights, your shoulder to cry on, and your unflinching belief that I can actually do this. Compel.

To my author friends who kept me sane during this process: Heather Demetrios, Donna Freitas, Jill Santopolo, Lindsay Ribar, Alison Cherry, and Mindy Raf. Thank you all for putting up with me and sharing your time and your hearts. Erica Henegen, thank you for loving me just the way I am and for cheering me on even when I didn't think I deserved it. Matt Kelly and Jared Wilder, there's no one else I would rather drink wine and binge *Parks and Rec* with. Ali Imperato and Melissa Kavonic, I am so grateful for all your enthusiasm and unwavering love. Linda Hu, a million thanks for helping me design Agnes's lab and answering all my science-related questions.

There are a couple of local spots in my neighborhood that I love to write at, so I have to thank Cherry and Derek at Mess Hall and Ryan at Vinatería for helping me cope with the writing of so many drafts of this book.

To my family—both Ewing and McLellan—I can't thank you all enough for the support and encouragement you've given me throughout the years. Extra hugs and thanks to Ben, Leah, Otto, and Bea. And, of course, to my parents, who have believed in me since I was five years old and announced I was going to be an actress when I grew up. It didn't quite work out that way, but you've supported every creative endeavor I undertook without a word of discouragement or warning (except maybe "please get health insurance"). I love you guys so much.

And to Faetra, my Moon Daughter of wisdom. I miss you every day.